J.E. REED

RISE
OF THE
WOLVES

THE CHRONOPOINT CHRONICLES

Edited by Catherine Jones Payne
of Quill Pen Editorial

Cover Design: Kirk Douponce, Dog Eared Design.

RISE OF THE WOLVES
Copyright © 2019 J.E. REED

ISBN: 978-0-578-57279-6

Visit the author at jereedbooks.com

Facebook: J.E.Reed.author
Twitter: J_E_Reed_author
Instagram: jereed_kiuno

Also available in ebook

To Milo and all the adventures we shared.

T. E. Reed

RISE
OF THE
WOLVES

ELITE

REALM: 5

DAY: 227

Elite walked amongst the broken bodies strewn across the field. Bodies from yesterday's battle. Bodies left in his wife's wake.

Scorpios had filled him in on her magic and how she'd rushed in, knowing Elite's forces were outnumbered and unprepared. He wasn't sure whether to be thankful or furious at the wretched world that had drawn his wife in so deeply.

She was what others were calling 'the lightning user' and judging from the carnage left behind by her magic, she had an important role to come. His jaw ticked as he remembered the way she'd fallen into his arms. The exhaustion and red marks that ran along her body… Kiuno was the last person he'd ever expect to take a human life.

Elite's gaze fell back to the cold, hollow eyes staring towards the heavens. He clenched his fists. He should have been there to protect her. He should have prevented her from having to make such a choice.

His gaze darted to the wagon as it lurched forward. A year, close enough anyway. It was a long time, and he knew the woman he'd fallen for had shifted.

Kiuno carried scars far deeper than those that ran along her skin. The way she'd reacted upon waking told him as much. Fear. Too much fear.

Elite rested one hand on the hilt of his sword and swept his gaze over the bodies again. He lingered on a familiar face, and his gut twisted.

They had to leave their dead behind. The enemy could close in on them again at any moment and with all the injured...

His eyes trailed back to the wagon. Maltack's hands hovered over the red lines that marred Kiuno's body. Another, Liam if he remembered right, sat with her. Worry lines etched his young face. She'd found allies in his absence and thrived in a world hell bent on their destruction.

He smiled despite the circumstances. She was safe and if he could prevent it, he'd ensure she never suffered again.

Elite's boot crunched the seared grass, and his eyes traced the zig-zagged pattern of her magic.

He cringed as memories of another invaded his thoughts. A woman who carried herself like his wife. The wind had tugged at her long, brown hair, obscuring her face from his view.

He'd run. Her magic flared, but it was too late. Her comrades fell and the monsters tore her apart before his eyes.

Elite had dropped to his knees at her side, calling Kiuno's name as he tried to stop the flow of blood. But when he turned her over, his heart thawed.

He shouldn't have felt relief, but Elite couldn't help it. That girl wasn't Kiuno. Even so, he'd buried her and the search for his wife continued.

Silver, her cousin, insisted Kiuno was more than capable of caring for herself.

He knew that. But he also knew about her stubborn tendencies. Her rash actions and an impulsiveness this world might not forgive.

The wagon creaked as the horses started uphill. Elite trailed behind and the mocking, dead smile of a hollow caught his attention. It stared at him as if promising a gruesome return.

Elite kicked it in the face and trotted back toward the cart, his heart urging him to stay close.

She was alive. No matter what evils she might have faced to get here, she had come, and he'd make sure they'd never be separated again.

TRAITOR

REALM: 5
DAY: 229

Fire crackled in the stone hearth as he sat upon a nearby stool. Not the most comfortable, but at least he could get a few moments alone with Kiuno. If only she weren't comatose.

Palindrome kept Kiuno sedated, claiming the rest would aid in recovery. He disagreed and argued she should be up and moving to promote circulation to her limbs. Too much rest made a person weak.

He clasped his hands in delight as he remembered the immense scars she'd carved upon the earth.

That strength. It awed him beyond words. Perhaps he even feared it.

His smile vanished as he gazed at the woman lying in the bed before him. Great power came with consequences and left her vulnerable.

Kiuno's companions watched her in shifts, though for what reason he couldn't be sure. She wasn't in danger and no one would dare enter these quarters with sinister ambition.

He stood. At least no one they'd suspect.

He hovered at her bedside and observed the rhythmic rise and fall of her chest. Deep red marks spread down her arms in a beautiful design.

He traced one with his finger. It was as if the lightning had painted her skin with the finest of details.

He caressed her cheek and pushed a strand of hair from her face.

Such a gentle woman. Yet a terrifying soul lay just beneath the surface, waiting for the chance to break free.

He smiled, longing to test it. Perhaps he'd see the depth of that soul when she realized the truth.

He couldn't wait for their reactions.

No one knew or suspected.

Her eyes fluttered and she winced. He gave her hand a reassuring squeeze. She returned it.

"Water."

His heart fluttered at her raspy voice and he filled a cup from the bedside table.

With the care one might show their child, he lifted Kiuno to a seated position and tucked himself at her side for support. Her fingers shook as she clasped them around the cup, but he held it steady.

Long shadows danced along the walls as he waited for her to finish.

"How are you feeling?" he asked.

"My head is pounding." Her eyes roamed across the marks on her wrist, but if they bothered her, she didn't say.

"Where is everyone?"

He helped her lower back to a lying position. "Here and there."

"Is she awake?" Palindrome entered and his annoyance flared as she all but shooed him from Kiuno's bedside. He bit his tongue and used the dim lighting to hide his displeasure.

A faint glow emitted from Palindrome's palm. Kiuno claimed it offered some relief, but it never lasted.

The red, interwoven designs remained untouched as if defiant against the healer's intervention.

Interesting.

Palindrome pulled a vial from her pocket, but Kiuno shook her head. "I don't want to sleep anymore."

"Then how about a bath?"

Kiuno's eyes traveled to her blood-stained clothes and she nodded. Palindrome gave him a dismissive look, and he did his best to smile. She'd think it stemmed from understanding and sympathy.

What a fool.

3

REECE

REALM: 5
DAY: 229

Reece slumped on a log and sat back only to sit forward again. His eyes roamed between hundreds of faces and then to the towering walls. He hated being here but after seeing Kiuno hurt he couldn't leave until he saw her conscious and well.

Another drunken soldier sloshed his drink on Reece's boot as he passed by. Reece cursed, shook the liquid from his foot then continued to bounce his leg.

The urge to hunt Kiuno down grew by the second. He should have known she'd get herself into trouble, but this? Taking on an entire army with no chance of winning?

He clicked his tongue. She really was reckless.

Reece's mind drifted back to the cliff. She'd have died without him and he'd still let her go to this castle alone. Reece had convinced himself she could handle it—yet she'd returned barely conscious.

If he'd accompanied her, then Kiuno might not be suffering now. He could have stopped her and made her see reason.

Reece chuckled to himself. Then again, maybe not.

Reece recalled the charred ground when he'd arrived on the battle-field. Some whispered of the lightning user, but he'd seen Kiuno's magic.

He furrowed his brow. And he'd also seen her lose control.

Reece stood and ran his hand through his hair as he weighed the possibilities. If *he* could figure out her secret, how long would it take others to do the same? How much danger was she in from this point forward?

"You look like you could use a drink." Nsane, his best friend, held out a mug. Reece took it and drained the contents without question.

Nsane had seen her magic too. He knew, yet both kept their mouths shut for fear of being overheard. Spies ran within the castle walls.

Scorpios claimed Kiuno knew the leader here, but how well and would he use her power for personal gain?

Reece sighed and sat down again. He'd worried for Kiuno from the start, but he hadn't expected the pull he felt now.

"She's with one of their commanders. If you're curious."

Reece eyed his empty mug. "Is that supposed to make me feel better?"

Nsane motioned for another companion to get them refills. "Her husband is with her. He'll keep her safe."

Husband. The word tasted like stale liquor on his tongue. His feelings were irrelevant. Kiuno possessed a rare loyalty for those close to her heart and that loyalty extended tenfold for the man she loved.

Reece wanted to convince her staying in the castle was a bad idea. But it wasn't his place and judging from the way her husband hovered like a protective guardian, it never would be.

REUNION

REALM: 5
DAY: 229

Kiuno sank her arms into the warm water and flinched. She traced the floral-like marks stretching from her fingertips to shoulders and down her torso. All of them burned as through molten fire had run through her veins.

Palindrome fiddled with Kiuno's knotted hair and huffed. "How long has it been since you washed this?"

Kiuno shrugged. "It wasn't important at the time." Elite had been the only thing on her mind for months. Not to mention the countless situations she'd encountered along the way.

Palindrome ran her fingers through matted hair. "You've been around men too long."

Kiuno's mouth curved into a smile, but she couldn't argue. This was the first time she'd had the chance to sit down with another woman. Palindrome had all but pried her from Elite's grasp.

Elite. Kiuno clutched her wrist. She'd endured more psychological pain than she ever thought herself capable. All to find him. Now most of that pain seemed like a distant memory.

Palindrome shifted and Kiuno glanced back at the magnificent woman's golden hair. It fanned in the water and despite the pain, Kiuno tried to sink herself deeper.

"You don't have to be so shy, we're both women."

"Says the Greek goddess behind me."

Palindrome's face fell. "I'm not perfect." She let her arms slip into the water and Kiuno turned to look at the crestfallen woman.

Palindrome clenched her jaw. "I left him."

Admittance.

Kiuno looked away. Six months before this world swallowed them, Palindrome disappeared without a trace. Kiuno tried to help K.J. in his search and both spent countless nights scouring the Internet for clues.

Nothing turned up and the pain of her disappearance haunted K.J. day and night. Kiuno supposed it happened sometimes with long distance relationships, yet the two stood together now. Perhaps even stronger than before.

"I know." It was all Kiuno could offer.

Silence settled over them like a thick blanket before Palindrome went to work again. Her fingers caressed Kiuno's scalp and struggled to sort through the last tangle.

"He wasn't even angry," she whispered.

"Did you expect him to be?"

"I expected... something, but he just kissed me. Said he'd wanted to do that from the beginning and wouldn't miss his chance now."

Kiuno smiled. "Yeah, sounds like him."

"I regret it you know, every moment, but if I try to apologize, he tells me to shush." Palindrome shook her head. "I wanted to come back, but when weeks turned into months, I guess I convinced myself he'd moved on." She sighed. "I just wish he'd give me a little of what I deserve."

"You and I both know that isn't K.J."

She didn't respond.

"He has you now, that's all that matters."

"You're right." Palindrome ran her fingers through Kiuno's scalp several times. "Done."

Despite the pain, Kiuno ducked beneath the surface for a final rinse, then Palindrome helped her out of the water.

Without something to obscure her form, every mark sat visible. Kiuno's body had acted like a rod and pulled powerful lightning through the unseen magical networks beneath her skin. It felt as though an entire storm had torn through her.

The last few moments of battle were a blur. Someone had taken her to Elite. K.J., if her memory served.

Kiuno thought she'd pushed too far. She thought those moments were her last and it'd terrified her to no end.

She glanced at her palm. If this is what she'd suffer then she never wanted to use that magic again.

Palindrome tousled her hair and Kiuno's gaze wandered to the bracelets around her wrist. She traced the first letter of the jade stone and memories of wind and fire threatened to surface.

"Arms up."

Kiuno obeyed and Palindrome slipped a sleeveless shirt over her head before tying a familiar looking cloth around the blue stone. Her fingers lingered. "I wasn't sure if it was important."

Kiuno couldn't meet her gaze. Blood and dirt covered the once white material. Evidence of the trials she'd endured, but she shook off the memories and focused her thoughts on a singular target. Elite.

Exhausted but refreshed, Kiuno followed Palindrome into the night air where the soft breeze kissed her burning skin.

Barefoot, the women walked along a grassy path. The castle loomed before them and silence radiated within its shadow.

The two passed a short line of wash areas, but all sat empty. Most hovered near the fires ahead and the echo of their voices disrupted the silent night.

Kiuno paused and glanced up into the starry sky. The towering walls offered protection from the outside world. She took a breath. But it wasn't the structure that eased her fears. Somewhere in this crowd Elite waited.

Palindrome took her hand and the two continued through the damp grass. So much time had passed. Would he be the same man she'd fallen in love with or would she find someone this world had corrupted?

The voices grew louder. Too loud for her aching head. Several unfamiliar faces greeted Palindrome, and many stared at the marks running along Kiuno's skin.

Kiuno tried to ignore them.

A fire popped and her heart jumped with it. Sweat caked her palms, Kiuno's breathing sped up, and her legs rooted themselves to the ground.

Sounds blended and her throat constricted. It's fine, she told herself. Everything is fine. She tried to breathe, but her body wouldn't obey.

Slender fingers cupped Kiuno's face. "Focus on me."

Kiuno stared into Palindrome's eyes, but her body still trembled.

"Breathe."

Kiuno tried, but it caught in her chest.

"No one is going to hurt you."

Kiuno closed her eyes. She knew that, but still. Something in her gut told her to run. It screamed for her to flee beyond the walls and seek refuge on the open plains.

Palindrome placed a light arm around Kiuno's shoulders. "Come on. We're almost there."

Kiuno took a step. Then another. She focused on her shaking legs and forced her mind to ignore everything else.

What was she afraid of?

Palindrome stopped and pointed. "There."

Kiuno's heart jolted at the sight of him. It felt like meeting him for the first time. Like high school all over again.

Silver, her cousin, sat on a log and Elite stood with his arms crossed before the fire. Kiuno used the moment to study him. She'd known him through high school, yet he appeared so different now.

Lean muscle. Facial hair. Weapons at his side. She prayed the atrocities of this world hadn't killed his free spirit.

"Do you want to go to him?" Palindrome asked.

Her body answered, carrying her forward before she even knew she'd moved. Palindrome didn't follow, or if she did, Kiuno no longer noticed.

Elite's head turned, their eyes met, and her stomach fluttered.

In seconds, Elite's strong arms enveloped her body. Kiuno hissed at the contact and sharp pain radiated along the marks of her shoulders. Elite cupped her face with a gentle caress and pulled her into an aching kiss that sent butterflies soaring through her chest. Whistles sounded from those watching but neither cared as he twisted one hand through her wet hair and clutched it like a lifeline.

Ages had passed. Had it really been less than a year?

The two pulled away, both breathless.

Elite pressed his forehead to hers. "I've missed you."

Kiuno couldn't form words. Instead, she pressed her lips to his again and all her fears dissipated to nothing.

Elite pulled back and examined her body. "How are you feeling?"

"Good. I think."

Somehow, she felt both awkward and satisfied, as if she didn't know how to act in his presence yet relished in it.

Elite searched her face as he traced a mark that stopped just beneath her chin. "I searched everywhere for you."

They stood in silence and his thumb followed her jawline in a slow back and forth motion. Elite's gaze seemed to drift, and a haze covered his vision. His jaw clenched and she wondered if he were reliving the constant fear of death that had haunted her in their time apart.

Elite guided her to the fire and Kiuno smiled when Silver stood. He wrapped his burly arms around her body and gave a tight squeeze. She winced again.

"Good to have you back cuz."

"Good to be here. I see you didn't waste time with forming your own army."

"Couldn't afford to. You've seen what's out there. I'm just happy to find you. Might have some peace and quiet for a change." Silver glanced at Elite.

She gave Silver a playful smile. "Don't pretend you weren't worried about me too."

"I wasn't. I knew you'd be fine." The seriousness of his words struck her. So many had faith in her when she didn't have faith in herself.

Elite pulled her to the log and the two sat down. His hand never left hers.

Silver threw another log into the fire. "Scorpios filled us in on the trouble you've been causing."

"I haven't done anything out of the ordinary."

Silver raised a brow. "Running headfirst into a horde of monsters is ordinary?"

"Well no—" She paused as a memory of Kikyo, Elliott, and slaves flashed through her mind. She'd been stupid back then. Overconfident. She gave them a sheepish smile.

"You could have been killed." Elite gripped her hand tighter.

"I could say the same to you."

The two men exchanged glances and Silver nodded to her arms. "What caused those?"

Kiuno lowered her voice. "You've heard about the Fire from the Sky?"

Silver nodded. "Scorpios told us about the stone, but I didn't think it'd cause that."

"How many know?" Elite asked.

"Our friends. And I imagine K.J.'s figured it out. Palindrome saw the stone in the bathhouse."

Elite ran a hand over his face. "Great. Now he'll want to use you. That's all I need."

"K.J. isn't like that. You ought to put some faith in him. He did just save your lives."

"And I'm sure we'll pay for it in full."

Kiuno wondered what their journey had led them through. If her experiences were anything to go by then pleasant people were few and far between.

Elite shifted and the motion caused Kiuno to cringe.

"Can't the healers do anything about those?" he asked.

"Palindrome and Maltack tried."

His face fell and he traced his thumb over her palm. "That magic is dangerous."

"I know."

A comfortable silence settled over the trio as they watched the fire. Her thoughts floated back to the battle. To the pain. She had so much to tell Elite, yet she found herself devoid of words.

Kiuno's gaze shifted to the crowd of people. Some danced, others drank, but it seemed all forgot about the dangerous world outside the walls.

She glanced to the silhouettes standing guard at the top. With something so sturdy, what did they have to worry about?

Kiuno sighed and leaned her head against Elite's arm.

"They gave us a room if you're tired."

Tired didn't even begin to describe it.

She nodded, and Elite turned to Silver. "We're turning in."

Her cousin lifted his cup. "Don't let me stop you."

Elite helped Kiuno to her feet and she gave Silver a light hug before following her husband through the crowd.

Noise assaulted her again, but she gripped Elite's hand and focused on her steps. He cradled her shoulder with one hand and led her through the space with the other.

Kiuno relaxed as the sounds faded and Elite guided her through the castle entrance. Fires lit their way and they passed the occasional person who seemed to wander through the halls.

The shadows twisted and tugged at her fears, but Elite never loosened his grip. He looked straight ahead and guided her through the darkness unafraid.

Elite pushed open a wooden door and the creaking hinges shattered the stillness of the hall. He lit a candle, then set himself to the task of lighting the fire.

Kiuno stood inside the doorway and glanced over the room. A small chest sat at the end of the bed with fresh folded clothes on top. The walls were bare, though she didn't imagine decorations were on most peoples' minds.

The bed drew her attention with soft furs promising a night of rest.

The fire cracked and smoked and Elite stood. Kiuno shivered.

He closed their door, slid the lock in place, and stepped behind her.

His warmth pressed into her back and she leaned against him, relishing in his touch.

Elite kissed the side of her neck and traced his fingertips down her arms.

Another shiver ran down her spine.

Kiuno turned and pressed her lips to his in a blaze of passion.

The fire cracked again, their clothes hit the floor, and his touch erased the stresses of the outside world.

COMRADES

REALM: 5

DAY: 230

The early sun shining through their small window woke Kiuno from her blissful sleep. She kept still and relished in Elite's arms as he clutched her to his side.

Kiuno glanced at their door then to the tiny lock keeping the outside world at bay. She'd like to keep it there and never return to the promised chaos waiting on the other side.

Warm furs engulfed their bodies, but Kiuno couldn't help running her fingers down Elite's forearm, tracing the foreign muscles. She smiled and Elite turned sleepy eyes to her in question.

"Good morning," she said.

He traced his fingers over her face and tucked a strand of hair behind one ear. Kiuno tried to turn over, but her stiff muscles protested, and she settled back.

She huffed. So much for a lover's reunion.

"You're in pain," he said.

"Not much I can do about it."

Elite propped himself up and placed a tender kiss on her lips. Sparks of need shot through Kiuno's body and she wrapped one hand behind his head. His fingers twisted through her hair and their tongues met. Her heart sped, but when Elite's hand gripped her side, pain radiated across her skin. She broke their heated embrace with a hiss of pain.

Elite pressed his forehead against hers and the two took a few moments to calm their racing hearts. "There'll be time," he said.

"As if being without you wasn't torture enough."

He kissed her forehead then stood.

Kiuno furrowed her brow. "Somewhere to go?"

"I have to see Silver and get a few things situated."

She glanced toward the faint light shining through their window. "Is he up this early?"

"Usually earlier."

Kiuno recalled late Saturday afternoons when her cousin slept in. She and Elite would laugh endlessly taking bets on who could wake him first. She sighed. "I guess we've all changed."

Elite's gaze ran up and down her form. "Not all changes are bad."

She tilted her head and watched muscles ripple when he pulled a shirt over his body. "No, not all."

Natural light guided their way to a familiar set of stairs. The pair descended and entered the main hall, then veered toward the left entryway. She noted the three grates hanging overhead and her skin crawled as she imagined the spiked ends slamming down on an invading enemy.

Last night, the cobblestone path had been empty, but with morning people lined the streets. The fresh stench of animal manure permeated the air and a distant ringing had Kiuno wondering if she were ready to face the sunrise.

Elite guided her through the inner gatehouse and to the field from last night. In place of bonfires and drunken comrades stood several dozen parties taking part in rigorous training.

She'd been unconscious when entering and riddled with anxiety last night, but with the sun Kiuno finally observed the area.

Two thick walls guarded the inner castle and armed patrols paced the top of both. The buildings stood along the inner wall, leaving the outer space open.

Kiuno examined the men stationed at the outer gate and a familiar face drew her attention. She held up a finger to Elite then darted toward her friend.

"Leaving without a goodbye?" Kiuno placed her hands on her hips.

Reece turned, a smile on his face, but it faded as his gaze dropped to her arms. He recovered and the smile returned. "Goodbye? Aren't you coming with me?"

She hesitated, and his expression faltered. Leave? After everything she'd done to get here?

"I—"

Reece shifted the box in his arms and placed it on the wagon. "Don't worry about it, as long as you promise to visit."

"You aren't upset?"

"I figured you might stay." He wiped sweat from his brow then nodded toward her arms. "So, what happened?"

Elite joined them and Kiuno glanced at the prying eyes in the surrounding area. "I overdid it with the magic."

Reece followed her gaze and seemed to understand. "If I'd known you were running headfirst into a fight, I never would have let you leave. Why are you so reckless?"

"You're one to talk, cliff jumping and all."

"Cliff jumping?" Elite raised his brow.

Reece held out his hand. "I assume you're Elite?"

"I am." Elite grasped Reece's palm.

Reece tilted his head toward Kiuno. "Keep an eye on this one and call us if she gets into any more trouble."

Reece grabbed another box and slid it beside the previous one.

"Do you have to go?" Kiuno asked. Her heart sped at the thought of matted, feral dogs and monsters lurking in the shadows.

"I'm not one to be tied down. If you were leading, I might reconsider, but as it stands I can't let my people follow a leader I don't know."

Kiuno averted her gaze and Reece gave her a playful shove. "You act like we'll never see each other again."

"There's just so many bad things out there. People. Monsters."

"Cliffs," he added.

"What if you get hurt?"

"We aren't a group of defenseless boys." He coiled a rope around his arm. "I'll see you after our next hunt."

Kiuno tried to smile. "All right. Be careful."

He waved, hit the back end of the wagon twice, and jumped in. Several others swung into their saddles and rode ahead.

Kiuno lingered, watching them disappear through the gate with his people at his side.

Elite kissed the side of her head. "Do you worry this much over everyone?"

"Only the people that matter."

Elite guided her back to the outer yard, and they spotted Silver through the crowd of trainees. Her cousin squared off with a young man and a semi-circle of others watched the exchange.

It hardly seemed fair. Her cousin towered over his pupil with battle ax in hand. The young man charged, but Silver parried the blow and flipped his opponent onto his back.

Silver took a few breaths and extended his hand to help the individual to his feet. "Never leave yourself open after an attack, keep your footing and be ready for a counter strike."

"A teacher struggling to catch his breath?" Kiuno called.

Silver gave Kiuno a lopsided grin and his students snickered. "They keep me in shape."

Silver pointed to two others and the pair entered the space to face off.

"Remember, keep your footing."

"Maybe I should bring Liam out here to train with you."

Silver tugged his gaze from the boys. "Who's that?"

"Someone I picked up along the way. He's only about twelve though."

Silver huffed. "Don't let age fool you. We have a few young ones who've brought down guys bigger than me."

He took a drink from his waterskin and glanced at the two on the field. "I'm surprised to see you out of bed. Thought you two would hide from the world for a few days."

"I wish."

Silver tilted his head toward Elite. "I convinced the higher ups to let us function as our own unit. The man in charge said our numbers were perfect."

"What's our positioning?"

"Second line. After the first falls back to recover."

The two prattled on about strategy and Kiuno let her gaze roam across the field. The scene reminded her of a military graduation she'd witnessed years ago.

Men and women alike jogged the inner wall's perimeter while their peers spared one another in practiced combat. The scene took her back to Elliott's first month of grueling sessions.

"Earth to Kiuno." Silver waved a hand in front of her face.

She blinked. "Yeah?"

"K.J. said he wanted to see you."

"When?"

Silver clicked his tongue. "Where did you go just now?"

Kiuno gave him a sheepish smile. "Sorry, guess I spaced."

"I said he stopped by earlier and wanted to see you sometime today."

"What for?" Elite asked.

Silver shrugged. "I didn't ask."

Kiuno chewed her lip. She needed to meet with K.J., especially after the battle, but she didn't want to leave—

She startled when Elite cupped her face and drew her into a gentle kiss. "Go on ahead. I'll stay here."

Kiuno wrapped her hands around his. "Promise?"

"Promise."

Kiuno turned back Silver. "Did he say where he'd be?"

"Your guess is as good as mine."

Kiuno hovered and watched as Elite joined Silver in their training session. She marveled at how the men responded to her husband and wondered how long they'd traveled together.

It wasn't until Elite's attention shifted to a young man that Kiuno headed back to the castle. Something tugged in her gut, but she fought against the rising fear. It was silly. Elite would be the last person to ever break his word.

Kiuno's legs burned with each step, but she remembered the way to what she'd deemed K.J.'s office. Only a few met her on the stairs in passing and no one stood guard outside the room.

She peeked inside the crack of the double doors and found K.J. seated at his desk. His pen scratched across a parchment's surface. It paused at her knock.

"Are you busy?"

"Not at all, come in." K.J. stood, gestured her to a chair, and sat when she did. "How are you feeling?"

"Like I've been baked in an oven."

He grimaced. "Sorry to hear it."

His eyes roamed down her arm. "Palin will be around to see you again. It's doubtful she'll give you much peace. It irks her when she can't fix something."

"Sounds like someone else I know." She ran her fingers along the smooth surface of the chair. "Silver said you wanted to see me?"

He folded his hands. "About what happened on the field. I have my suspicions, but I'd rather hear things from you."

Kiuno leaned back and untied the cloth from around her wrist, and the light from the window reflected off the blue surface.

"Just as I thought." K.J. leaned back and pinched the bridge of his nose. "Of all people, it had to be you. Scorpios was right. You are trouble."

"You already knew that."

He smirked. "I suppose I did."

She tied the knot and silence filled the space. "I didn't ask for this and honestly, I'd give it up if I could."

"With those consequences," he indicated her arms, "I can't imagine anyone would want it, but at least in your hands it won't be abused."

He leaned forward again, taking on a serious tone. "Before we discuss anything else, I need to ask a question. I offered your friend Reece the chance to stay with us, but he's declined. I still plan to move forward with our original agreement in hopes that he'll join in the future. Unless you tell me otherwise."

"He's a good man, just likes his own rules I guess. What exactly is your question?"

"Are you staying?"

She furrowed her brow. "Shouldn't that be obvious?"

"I assumed, just needed to be sure."

"I've found everyone I was searching for and if Reece is close by then there's no reason for me to leave. At least here I can be of some help."

"You'll be a lot of help. You always have been, but I can't let you do much until Palindrome gives you the clear. I'm not fond of being scolded."

Kiuno laughed as she imagined Palindrome barging in and screaming at her friend while others stood off to one side, helpless in his defense.

"I'm not sure what I'll be able to do. In just seven months there's been more progress than I ever imagined possible. I can't believe the organization you already have let alone the fact that we're in the fifth realm."

"Seven?" he asked.

Kiuno bit her lip as she thought back. "It might have been eight."

"Kiuno, how long have you been here?"

Her heart quickened as she recalled the difference in seasons when she'd arrived in the first realm. "No more than eight months."

"Strange. Most of us, including myself have been here at least fifteen. It makes me wonder. Do you remember hearing about strange disappearances?"

Kiuno shook her head. "Nothing. In fact, I remember messaging you that weekend. There's no way you were here, I would have noticed eight months of not talking to you."

K.J. stood and walked to the window. "I wonder if whoever brought us here had a way to hold people before transporting them to this reality."

"You think we have other memories wiped along with our names?"

"It's possible."

"But what's the point?"

"What do you do when you set up a game? You put your important pieces where they'll be protected. If it's strategy based, then some players might save their ace in the hole for last." He looked pointedly at her. "And it seems you were the last to arrive."

"How do you know there isn't anyone new?"

He glanced back out the window. "I've sent my scouts to the first realm to check. Those staying behind have formed their own communities, but there haven't been any newcomers."

"Why me?"

"That's the question isn't it?"

Kiuno dropped her head in her hands.

"There's a meeting next week between the five leaders in this realm. I was hoping you'd come."

"Making me one of your officers again?"

K.J. laughed. "If you want to call it that. I need you to be a new face. Make them curious."

"Throwing me to the wolves. You should be ashamed."

K.J. smirked. "I might be if I didn't believe you enjoyed the game."

6

RELICS

REALM: 5

DAY: 230

Kiuno limped from the room and down the stairs. Voices floated up from the main dining hall and upon rounding the corner it seemed as though hundreds of faces sat waiting to bombard her.

Most had seated themselves at the wooden tables while others stood in small clusters having their own conversations. Her head spun with the hum in the air.

Kiuno scanned the sea of faces for Elite. Her eyes flicked from one human to the next and her breathing sped up with each passing second.

Kiuno took a step back in retreat. She couldn't do this. Not—

Her heart skipped when someone grabbed her hand, but Kiuno turned to find Liam's smiling face.

"Joining us?"

His hopeful expression calmed her racing nerves. She nodded.

He all but skipped his way through the crowd while dragging her along. She watched everyone the way a cat might when threatened, but her gaze returned to her young friend.

With the mud and fear wiped from his face, Liam looked like a normal twelve-year-old. She tried to think back, but the events of her time with him the last few months were a blur.

The cabin and a cold winter. The creatures. Finding Scorpios. Reece. Then the battle to save Elite. It wasn't as though he'd had much time to be a kid.

A man bumped into her and Kiuno's body tightened like a coil. She took a step back and prepared for an attack, but he turned with a smile on his face, laughing, and apologized.

Liam squeezed her hand and she forced a smile of her own. He continued to pull her through the throng. Her heart pounded, but two familiar faces melted all the stress from her shoulders.

"There she is." Blue rose and wrapped her in a light hug. Despite his careful grip, she still yelped. "Guess those tattoos aren't all they're cracked up to be."

"You've no idea."

He glanced her over. "Well, at least you're intact."

Kiuno might have laughed if not for the recollection of severed limbs.

"So, what have you been up to?" Blue asked. "I haven't seen you since they hid you away in that recovery room."

"Nothing much yet. Feels like I've been thrown into an alternate universe."

"Literally," Blue said.

"And you guys?"

"K.J. has me running around the castle delivering sensitive information and orders."

"Sounds fancy."

"I enjoy working with people and Liam helps me keep things in check. We tried to put Liam in the kitchens, but he didn't care for it much." Blue playfully elbowed him and Liam swatted his arm away.

"Because it's full of girls and they don't leave me alone."

Blue laughed. "I've never heard that complaint from a young man before."

Liam's cheeks heated. "Not like that. They're annoying."

Kiuno smiled. "He's too mature for the young ones."

Blue chuckled and Maltack shifted, catching her attention. Her eyes darted to the floral design snaking from the back of his hands to the center of his forearms. He tried to slip them from her view.

"I hurt you?"

He sighed and placed his marked arms back on the table. "You needed K.J.'s help and I had to shield him."

"But, how did that hurt *you*?"

Blue wrapped one arm around Maltack's shoulder. "Because this boy has enough determination to make us all feel lazy."

Maltack gave an uncomfortable smile. "I couldn't let him die. You'd never forgive yourself."

Kiuno glanced at the marks that ran heavy along her arms. A twisted reminder of the hell she'd unleashed. "Thank you."

Blue waved his arms. "Don't get all heavy on us. It's been bad enough with all of them hovering over you. Where's the fun?"

"All right, all right. Does Palindrome have you on lockdown too?" Kiuno asked.

Maltack shook his head. "Not as much as she wants. I helped with the injured after the fight, so she has me working with the healers. She's also teaching me how to manipulate deeper tissues, but I think organs are a specialty only she can master."

The kitchen doors flew open and a buzz of excitement spread through the hall. The smell of cooked meat floated through the air and her stomach growled in anticipation as plates rushed past. They dug in without prompting.

Meat, bread, potatoes. Her mouth salivated as she looked at more food than she'd ever seen in one place. Kiuno grabbed a roll and relished in the flavor that burst across her palate.

After gorging herself on everything she could reach, Kiuno sat back and placed a hand on her stomach.

Blue stood first. "Well, I guess this is where we part ways." He nodded toward her. "Where will you be?"

She picked at the last bit of food on her plate. "I haven't been assigned anything yet, but K.J. is taking me to a meeting with the other leads next week."

"Ah, a big shot now," Blue teased.

"Yeah, yeah." She waved him off.

"Come on kid."

Liam stood and gave Kiuno a playful wave before bounding behind Blue.

"I have something to show you," Maltack said. He stood and she followed, leaving the clattering, crowded hall behind. She searched the faces once again as they exited the castle and strode along a dirt path.

Maltack opened a wooden door and gestured her inside. The smell of dusty pages met her senses as she scanned the room. Leather-bound books sat crammed upon shelves that stretched to the low ceiling.

Maltack grabbed two candles, lit them with his fingertip and handed her one before he headed down a narrow set of spiral stairs. She followed, still scanning the shelves. It seemed so odd to have a library in a place like this.

Maltack paused at a desk where a small journal sat upon the surface.

"Palindrome showed me this place after the battle. She said I might learn something from the medical texts, but then I found this." He pointed to the journal.

Kiuno joined him in an adjacent chair and he continued. "The books from the first realms didn't give us much detail, but this one lists everything we've seen and more." He flipped a few pages and turned the book toward her. "And there's a detailed map of the first four realms as well."

"I bet that made it easy to find stragglers."

"Most, but it's been difficult to convince them beyond the third realm. They're afraid."

"And rightfully so." She shivered, thinking of the chirping creatures from the fourth realm. "They'll come, eventually."

She glanced back to the book and flipped through a few pages. "What have you learned?"

"The magic isn't as intricate a system as I feared. It's like a muscle in the body. Some people have it and some don't. When we flex that muscle, the elements answer.

"This book also details more monsters than I can count, including Nikita's kind." He flipped toward the back and pointed to a large winged lion with the caption 'Felinian' at the top.

"Each species has a name?"

He nodded and Kiuno scanned the page. "Thirty-foot wingspan?"

"According to Jim, she's not even a year old. She's grown a lot in the short time we've been with them. Who knows how big she'll be come winter?"

Maltack flipped all the way to the back. "But, right now, I think we should concern ourselves with these."

Kiuno followed his finger to five objects sketched on the page. "Relics?"

Maltack nodded. "And none sound good." His finger hovered over the first. A sphere depicted in the palm of a hand. "It says this one suppresses magic of all kinds within a ten-foot radius. Even yours."

Kiuno chewed on her lip. "Not sure I like that one." How many times had her magic saved them from a dire situation?

"I don't either. After the fight there's been talk of the lightning user among us and it won't be long before everyone figures it out."

Maltack pointed to the second. A diamond-shaped jewel depicted within a user's wrist. "This one is far more sinister. It attaches to your body and embeds itself in the user's system causing them to act upon their darkest desires."

"Why would anyone want that?"

"It gives them control over the monsters."

Kiuno grimaced. "Giving up your morals for power? Wouldn't a person's reason distort?"

"It would, along with slowly killing you. The longer one uses it, the harder the jewel is to extract."

"All right, noted. Find this relic and bury it as far underground as we can."

Maltack pointed to a third. A lightning bolt hanging on a necklace. "This one allows the user to use lightning, just like you and I'm sure it'll be the most sought-after relic."

"So, the people who saw the magic on the field might not know whether I'm the lightning user or have the relic."

"Correct, which means they'll want to find out."

"And the last two?"

"The Transference Crystal and the Memory Stone."

"And those are?"

"The crystal allows one to jump to any realm and the stone places memories inside a body."

"Like a dead body?"

"It doesn't specify."

"Great. Are all these objects in this realm?" she asked.

"I assume so." He flipped to the final page. "And this is all we know about the coming realms."

Venture on as carefully as you can,

for the other levels are nothing but brutal land.

The jungles will test you,

the monsters will crawl.

Dreams will caress you,

and paradise will be your downfall.

Barren terrain will be your next test,

one frozen with ice, the other surely hexed.

Fight till the end and do not disappoint,

for there's nothing you've faced quite like Chronopoint.

"That's not cryptic or anything." Kiuno leaned back in her chair.

"It's all we have." Maltack closed the book and stood. "Palindrome wanted to see me after lunch, so I guess we can speculate later."

"Don't push yourself too hard."

"Not any harder than you." He smiled then headed up the stairs, leaving her alone in the vast library.

She sat in the chair for several moments, staring at the little book before standing. The events of the day had already left her drained. Both mentally and physically.

Her legs ached as she climbed the tiny staircase and exited to the warm sun hitting her face. People still ran from place to place but all ignored her in their passing.

Anxiety crawled like a viper in the pit of her stomach. How long was that going to last?

Kiuno followed the path toward the outer training yard in search of Elite. Several groups still worked with one another, but where Silver had been a smaller group had taken his place. They used sparring swords to face off against their opponents.

When the metal clashed, her mind jolted and she pivoted to the outer gate house.

The crowds thinned and when she walked through the gate a fresh breeze ruffled her hair in greeting. No one stood out here except the guards at the gate. She headed toward the only tree in the immediate area.

It wasn't overly tall but provided a nice bit of shade from the hot sun. Pink blooms lined the ground and branches. It gave off a gentle fragrance that lured her to settle against the trunk and fade away.

KIUNO JOLTED when a guard shook her. "Sorry, didn't mean to startle you, but I didn't think you'd want to be locked out." He pointed to the gate and the last of those walking through it. Dusk had settled. Kiuno rubbed her eyes. She must have been more tired than she thought.

Kiuno followed him through the gate and the heavy doors swung shut. Metal scraped against stone as four portcullises dropped into place. People still lined the area, but now they sat around campfires, relaxing as the world turned to night.

With sore legs, Kiuno ascended the stairs to their room, expecting to find Elite waiting, but it was empty. She walked back down the stairs to search the dining hall, but none of the faces were the one she sought.

Despite her rest, exhaustion still hit her hard. She tried to calm her racing heart. Elite was with Silver and everyone knew how much her cousin loved to chat. He was fine. She chewed on her lip. He was fine.

Instead of pacing—which she really couldn't do—Kiuno asked directions to the roof hoping to quiet her racing thoughts.

Once again, she climbed the stairs and it felt like a thousand years melted from her shoulders when the cool night breeze hit her face. The stagnant air in the castle suffocated her and their small window did little to relieve the feeling. For months she'd slept beneath the open sky with the stars as her light.

She sighed, leaning against the stone tower. The sun sank in a streaked display of purple and orange and stars dotted the sky one by one. Out here the moonlight was her fireplace and her friends the wall. If only they didn't have so much to worry about beyond the real one.

Their happiness brought Kiuno joy, but she'd miss their constant companionship. In the castle, they'd be separated, just like they'd been back home.

What were each of them doing and what would her own contribution add? It seemed K.J. planned to use her in diplomacy, but did she possess the skills to help?

Kiuno took a long breath and rested her chin on her hands as she scanned the area. Long months of worry and suffering had led her to this moment, but the fight was far from over. Now, something entirely new was about to unfold in a world she knew nothing about.

This was the front line.

"Couldn't sleep?" She jumped and turned to find K.J. in the doorway.

"Elite isn't back yet, so I came out for some air."

He moved to stand beside her, leaning against the cool stone. "You'll get used to sleeping under a roof again."

Would she? She looked out at the various fires and the men standing along the wall. Memories of flashing fire and burnt flesh flickered through her mind's eye.

"Did I really kill all those people?"

He didn't turn, instead focusing his gaze over the grounds as he looked between posts. "Do you regret saving Elite?"

"Of course not."

"Then don't regret what you had to do. You came, despite me telling you not to and in doing so minimized casualties on our side." His voice softened. "When we get home, I'll help you through it. But for now, it's better not to think about it."

Silence surrounded them as she tried to absorb his words. He'd experienced war. Is this how they handled it?

"You don't know what the hollows are, do you?"

"The what?"

"I thought not. The things you killed were creatures we call hollows. They look like people, move like people, but they're no different from the monsters you've encountered. Though it troubles me this group was so organized."

"Not people?" she whispered.

"You didn't slaughter hundreds of people Kiuno. I won't say you didn't kill any, but I can promise at least half were created for the purpose of this game."

Her heart lightened. "How are they different?"

"Think of them as an Artificial Intelligence. They don't talk, at least not that I've heard, and they don't feel pain, which makes them formidable, but their bodies will die if a mortal wound is inflicted."

"You said they were organized?"

"I've not seen them work with people before."

"So, what does that mean?"

He gazed into the darkness for several moments. "It means we're getting close and the person who set this in motion doesn't want us moving this fast anymore."

"The creator you mean?"

He nodded.

"But how could someone convince people to stay in a place like this?"

"Isn't the better question, how are we going to convince them to leave? Think about it. This is a perfect world. A fresh start. People don't have to work at dead-end jobs and aren't forced to pay bills. They are literally free in every sense of the word."

"What about their family?"

"Who says they're not here? Everyone has their own reasons for wanting to leave. Some have family, others are afraid, and some want home simply because it's home. But if you look at the bigger picture, if you were guaranteed safety and all your friends and family were here, what reason would you have to leave?"

He had a point; one she couldn't argue. If someone could guarantee her safety, would she stay? If she'd never lost Kikyo...

"What about you?" she asked. She needed to know. From the look of things, he could lead a fulfilling life right here.

"I've been challenged to beat a game."

She laughed. "I guess that's good enough."

"Kiuno?" The two turned to find Elite in the doorway, his gaze shifting between her and K.J. He took in short breaths as if he'd been running.

She glanced at the darkened sky. "Sorry, I guess I lost track of time."

K.J. extended his hand. "We haven't had a chance to talk. I'm K.J., it's nice to finally meet you." Elite hesitated before taking his hand and she recalled the mild jealousy Elite carried toward her friend.

"Elite." Silence echoed and she turned to stare out over the open area again.

"I was just about to turn in." K.J. said. "We'll talk later Kiuno. Just worry about healing for now."

"I'll try to keep myself occupied."

"I don't think that comforts anyone."

She laughed again. "Good night." He waved and vanished down the stairs. Elite wrapped his arms around her from behind, and she leaned her head against his chest.

"Everything all right?"

"Yeah." She still couldn't block the images of people dying from her thoughts. The flashing of steel. The blood and screams. It didn't matter that they weren't real, it still felt real.

"Do you know about the hollows?"

Elite ran his hand up and down her arm. "Yes, didn't you?"

She shook her head. "No, I thought—" She couldn't voice her fears, but knew Elite understood. His hand traced down to the two bracelets and she fought against flinching when he turned the green one over. It occurred to her that no one had mentioned them until now.

"All that time we spent apart, I tried to imagine you safe and be-lieved I would walk into an inn to find you serving drinks."

A sad smile tugged at her lips. "You should have known better."

His arms tightened around her and a burning sensation shot through her shoulders.

"I know, but still. The image of you fighting, being out there with-out someone to protect you and then seeing you on the battlefield barely able to stand."

"I'm more than capable of protecting myself."

"But you shouldn't have to."

"None of us should."

His fingers turned over the gray stone and what she presumed to be an impending argument faded. "Who were they?"

"People I failed." She choked on the words and a familiar pain crept to the surface. Everything was happening so fast and no matter how much she wanted it to slow down, there didn't appear to be time.

Elite turned her around and tucked a stray strand of hair behind one ear. "You didn't fail anyone. You can't control what happens in this world."

An old conversation with Scorpios floated back to her. *You dishonor them.*

"I just," her voice shook, "wish I could have done more."

"We all do." Elite pulled her to his chest, and she wrapped her arms around his back. He kissed the top of her head. "Tell me about them."

REST

REALM: 5

DAY: 231

Kiuno's eyes fluttered open, her body warm with Elite's arm wrapped around her middle. Light shone through their small window and she sighed, moving his arm to sit up.

"You used to enjoy sleeping in," Elite said as he shifted to one side.

"Yeah, I guess I did." Silence filled the air as Kiuno stared at the cold fireplace. What else had she enjoyed before survival had taken precedence? Painting. At one time the feel of a brush had sparked creativity, but now a sword had taken its place.

Elite interrupted her thoughts. "Did K.J. give you anything to do?"

She shook her head.

"Do you want to go find Scorpios then?"

She turned. "You know where he is?"

"If he's in the same spot as yesterday then yeah."

Kiuno jumped out of bed and dressed before Elite could say another word.

The two walked down the stairs, past the main hall, and out into the crisp morning air. Kiuno took in a lungful, letting it drown the suffocating smell of the castle. Perhaps Reece was onto something by preferring the outside.

A clear blue sky shown overhead, and dew clung to blades of grass as they padded toward the outer training grounds.

She paused upon rounding the wall. Magic flew in every direction. There were thousands, each gliding with their weapons as they manipulated the elements at their disposal.

She continued to follow Elite as they walked along the outskirts of the display. Earth users grew vines to both attack and defend by throwing and catching their opponents. Entire trees shot from the ground and the branches sprung up to wrap their comrades in a powerful bind.

Those using water were equally fascinating. They seemed to pull the particles from thin air, twisting and weaving it to their mind's creation. Shards of ice solidified in midair then struck into wooden boards with deadly force.

Kiuno studied them, wondering what Scorpios might be capable of.

"There."

Kiuno followed Elite's finger to a man in the far corner. She watched as Scorpios twirled the staff around his body, pulling water along the same path. His students tried to mimic the action and several fumbled. Most were dripping with water. It didn't take long for him to notice the two approaching.

Scorpios whispered to his students and they continued with similar exercises in his absence.

"Glad to see you up and moving." He gave her a light hug. "Are you still in pain?"

"It's bearable."

His eyes roamed down her arms and he sighed. "Why do you cause so much trouble?"

"Not sure it's in my nature to stay out of it."

He let out a hearty chuckle. "That's the truest statement I've ever heard."

Scorpios turned to Elite and the two clasped one another on the back. "How is Silver faring?"

"He's glad to have a bed."

"Ah, yes. The comforts of home."

"So, what are you doing out here?" She gestured toward the group still spraying themselves with water.

"Training. Palindrome thought I'd be a good fit. Maybe you'll be able to help me. Speaking of," he held up a hand, jogged to the group, and returned holding her metal staff. "I believe this is yours."

She took the weapon and ran her hands down the familiar smooth surface.

"Once you're feeling better, we'll show Elite what you can do with it."

A grin spread across Kiuno's face. "I'm sure he'll love that."

8

TRAITOR

REALM: 5

DAY: 235

He watched day after day as Palindrome continued to assess her wounds and heal what little she could.

It still puzzled him how the marks reacted as if they had a barrier of their own. Anything could be healed, down to a lung being stitched back together, but for some reason the marks across her skin refused to react to the healer's magic.

He stood in the grass, watching, taking in everything that was Kiuno. He'd said it before, but that fire was something he admired. He grinned. The lightning suited her too.

Kiuno fought against her friends' advice. Even his. She wanted to move, but then, that was how she processed. It was like a meditation ritual with her. The physical pain kept the mental at bay.

Despite her exercise, none would spar with her. He might have, if not for everyone glaring at him when he suggested such a thing.

Disappointment flooded him when Palindrome insisted Kiuno

didn't use her magic for a time. It would put a hold on his plans, but he'd rather her be at full strength anyway.

He remembered the glow on the field. The burst of electricity as it hummed around her like something alive. His skin crawled in anticipation.

Soon. He told himself. Soon.

9

ALLIANCES

REALM: 5

DAY: 237

A group of twenty-five set out across the grassy plains. Kiuno sat atop her horse, tugging at the tight leather that hugged her figure before fanning out at the waist. Despite the cool breeze, sweat dampened her undershirt and the raw marks itched beyond belief.

She sighed. Perhaps she should have stayed home.

Her gaze drifted to Elite and Maltack. They rode on either side of her and kept close. Their eyes scanned the distant horizon. She knew what Elite watched for, but Maltack appeared more curious than apprehensive.

Despite her discomfort Kiuno smiled. She should take some delight in everything they'd accomplished. Her friends were safe. They had walls to protect them from the dangers in the realm and for once she wasn't rushing somewhere with the shadow of death following.

Small birds flocked together overhead and landed from place to place as their troupe marched through the grass. She wasn't sure what to expect out here, but if the animals weren't spooked then she saw no reason to fret either.

Kiuno tilted her head back to absorb the sun. A few days separated them from the next castle. She wondered what the leader would be like and what K.J. expected of her when they arrived. Manipulative diplomacy wasn't her strong suit. It was his.

"You're quiet," Elite said.

She tilted her head toward him. "And you worry too much."

He chuckled and she went back to absorbing the sun's rays and lost herself in the meditative sway of the horse's gait.

With evening, the group staked the horses' leads in the ground and Maltack started the fire.

Kiuno settled down beside Elite and watched the stars dot the open sky.

Elite wrapped his arm around her shoulders. "I guess I'm to deal with men fawning over you?"

"Only until we're out of there. We shouldn't be there long."

He pressed his lips to her hair. "If one of them touches you—"

She pressed a finger to his lips. "You've no idea what I've done to men who've tried."

"I guess that's a story you have yet to tell." His breath tickled her ear and she giggled. He pressed his lips to hers and she drank him in as if she'd never get enough.

WHEN THEY approached the walls Kiuno jumped from her saddle and took a few moments to stretch her cramped back and legs. She rubbed at tender skin where she'd started to chafe in unpleasant places.

Perhaps she should have done more riding than walking on her journey to this realm.

A stagnant moat wrapped itself around the castle and emitted a foul stench sure to keep the scariest of monsters away.

A curtain wall sat behind it with a thick drawbridge already down and awaiting their arrival. The group filed in.

The castle didn't have an inner curtain wall like K.J.'s, but that didn't mean it was any less organized. Buildings lined the castle itself and soldiers stood at attention along the wall.

K.J. exchanged words with the guards, then gestured them to follow. Kiuno scanned the inside of the castle and searched for any signs that might warrant caution, but it appeared they weren't the first group to arrive.

After ascending two flights of stairs and taking more turns than she could count, the guards left them at a large room with more than enough cots lining the walls. Blankets sat in neat piles on each.

She paused at the doorway. "When will the meeting start?"

K.J. unbuckled his sword. "Within the hour. Leave your weapons here."

She pulled the daggers from her belt and shoe. "Will it take long?"

He shrugged. "Hard to say. Depends on how long it takes all parties to come to an agreement. Some last a few hours, others go on for days. We'll stay a night regardless to let the horses rest."

K.J. removed a small knife from his boot, sat on his cot, then looked toward Elite. "He'll have to stay here with the others. You and I will go into the room. There'll be another behind us, but you won't see much of him."

Kiuno unbuckled her sword as she walked toward Elite. He'd seated himself on the adjacent cot and watched as she placed her weapons down.

"Let me guess," he said. "I'm staying here."

She gave him a halfhearted smile. "I won't be far."

"But you'll be weaponless." He nodded toward K.J. "As will he."

"I have other weapons I can use if it comes to that. Trust me when I say you'd know something is wrong."

Elite wrapped his arms around her waist and pulled her toward him. He buried his face in her stomach, then met her gaze. "Try to play nice."

A smile tugged at her lips. "No promises."

After several minutes Kiuno followed K.J. and their guide down a dark corridor. The castle carried the same stagnant smell as the one she'd come from.

After rounding two corners, they entered a large meeting room with a high ceiling and long wooden table in the center. A fire roared in the hearth, giving unpleasant warmth to the room. She wished she could have worn something less stuffy, but she had marks to hide.

Kiuno followed K.J. to the far side of the table and the two seated themselves to watch the door. The third man stood against the wall, but she didn't have time to examine him as another entered the room.

Two guards accompanied an older man with peppered hair and a warm smile. A smile lifted Kiuno's lips when she examined the guards. Perhaps they saw her as K.J.'s guard.

"Grayson," K.J. whispered.

She nodded and tried to keep herself from fidgeting. K.J. sat like a statue with his hands folded beneath his chin and eyes locked on the door.

Kiuno chewed her lip, then stilled herself. She should have asked more questions and become familiar with the alliances' inner workings.

A young Asian woman walked in next, followed by three men. The woman's sharp eyes glanced over the room and Kiuno half expected her to glare at them, but she tilted her head and gave them a curious smile.

Kiuno's racing heart slowed a fraction. She gave K.J. a sideways glance, but he didn't whisper a name this time.

Another man entered the room only moments after. Middle Eastern if she could place him right.

He glanced around the room, held her gaze longer than she thought necessary, then seated himself beside the woman.

Four out of five. Kiuno's gaze darted between the stranger's faces, but it seemed they wanted to study her as well. After two counts of uncomfortable eye contact, she kept her gaze on the table. The way K.J. remained still made her feel like an antsy kid who'd been trapped in a car for hours.

Minute after minute crawled by, but the entire group sat in silence. She wondered which of them had threatened Reece's group, but before she could think too much on it another male entered the room.

Repulsion shot through her core. He strutted; chest stuck out as if he were to be waited upon without complaint. He gave the woman a smug smile, then shifted his gaze to her. Kiuno sat straighter and held his stare, almost as if in challenge. He smirked and sat in the remaining seat. No guard accompanied him.

Grayson, the older gentleman, broke the silence with a deep voice. "Since I'm the one who called this meeting, I'll begin. Unfortunately, we haven't found the portal, but I'd like to discuss plans for heading to the northern forest."

His eyes traveled around the room before continuing. "My scouts haven't been able to find safe passage around the forest and I fear the portal might be on the other side of those wicked trees."

Kiuno stayed silent, unsure about anything related to such.

"Are people still disappearing inside?" K.J. asked.

Grayson nodded. "None have returned."

Silence settled over the room and despite Kiuno's too warm attire, a shiver ran up her spine.

"We've tightened security and erected barriers, but without help I fear we'll have to pull back."

"Numbers will increase our strength." K.J. sat back. "I assume the mountainside is impassible?"

The Asian woman answered. "We've tried many ways but haven't found a safe route."

The detestable man made a sound of disapproval.

"Something to add?" Grayson asked. His brows rose and Kiuno glanced between the two.

A smug expression met her gaze again, then he nodded toward K.J. "There's no reason for all of us to go. K.J. has twice the manpower, let him send his men for a change."

K.J. rested his hands on the table. "For the sake of knowledge and the union of our alliances, I think it's best if everyone works together. Wouldn't you agree, Atilla?"

Kiuno swore he said the name for her sake.

Atilla's expression darkened. "Since it seems you have no intention of bringing it up, I suppose I'll be the one to break the ice. Who's the lightning user?"

Kiuno's heart jolted and she froze as every eye turned toward them. She forced her lungs to take slow breaths, afraid any shift would give her away. She hadn't planned for the possibility of them knowing and prayed they couldn't see the fear in her eyes.

Kiuno stared at a swirl in the wood as they awaited K.J.'s reply.

"Well?" Grayson pressed. Atilla wasn't the only one eager for K.J.'s answer.

"I regret to say I don't know who it is."

"Lies," Attila spat.

"We received information that one of our scouting teams encountered some difficulties. Naturally, I responded with aid and when we arrived the lightning user was already at work. I'm still not sure if that individual is within our ranks or out running through the woods as we speak."

Attila scoffed. "Are you saying you don't check those who come into your walls?"

"Clearly not, otherwise your spies wouldn't have any knowledge of that event." At that, they all stiffened. "I think we can skip the denial. We all know full well each of us takes precautions against the others."

Grayson cleared his throat. "Aren't you curious who it could be?"

"Of course, I'm curious." K.J. said. "But I'm not in the habit of forcing people to work for me. When this individual feels comfortable, they'll come forward and if they're within my walls, then at least we'll know they're safe."

Kiuno let out a slow breath, but when she glanced up, the Asian woman's curious eyes were fixated on the mark beneath her chin. She gave Kiuno a knowing smile, then slid her gaze back to Grayson. Kiuno chewed her lower lip.

Atilla clicked his tongue. "Your beliefs are irrelevant for this situation. If that person is among you, each of us has a right to know."

"You'll have a right to know when you're willing to fight with the rest of us," Kiuno said. "You want K.J. to send his men to the forest, yet you demand to know who his men are. Seems that only benefits you."

The Asian woman smirked and Attila's face shifted from red to purple. "Seems you brought a mouthy one. Again."

Grayson cleared his throat before anyone could respond. "I think a short break is in order. We'll meet back in about an hour."

None moved. Grayson sighed and slid his chair across the wooden floor. The woman followed and soon everyone filed out.

Once out of earshot, K.J. chuckled. "Did you enjoy that?"

"Not any more than you."

"Attila is a man of power. It irks him when someone else could pose a threat. And compared to his army, we already outnumber him three to one. I'll be interested to see what he does now."

"I think the woman knows."

"Leena? I saw her staring. Let her have her suspicions."

"You're not worried?"

"If she thinks you're the lightning user, it just means she'll be more likely to help in the future. I don't foresee her sharing sensitive information with the other leaders."

Kiuno didn't feel near as confident. The thought of being used as a weapon and fought over wasn't appealing in the slightest.

"So how far out is this forest?" she asked.

"A day and a half from our place, depending where we set up."

"I can't believe how big this realm is."

"I fear they'll only get bigger. If all parties agree to go, I'll send one of my generals to oversee the troops before I get there."

"You're heading there yourself?"

"Of course."

"Who's going to watch the place while you're gone?"

"I have plenty who can handle it. Palindrome won't let me go anywhere too dangerous without her. The only threat that concerned me was Reece, but your assurance has eliminated that."

"Glad I could help."

"His worry for you is what convinced me. He didn't take it well when you returned unconscious, and I think if not for Elite, he would have been by your side day and night."

"I imagine I'll be joining you in this expedition?"

"If you'd like. You seem to like the open air."

"The castle is a bit stuffy."

The two went back to their room and K.J. discussed his decision with a few men she didn't know. Kiuno listened, then followed him back to the meeting room. They were the last to arrive this time.

Grayson clasped his hands together. "Now that we've had a few minutes to cool down, have you decided?"

The woman, Leena, spoke first. "I'll be going."

"As will I," K.J. said.

"The same." She met the Middle Eastern man's gaze but hadn't heard him speak until now.

All eyes turned to Attila, who heaved a sigh. "I guess I'll be going." His gaze drifted to hers and lingered a moment. "I apologize for my behavior earlier. I wasn't thinking clearly."

Kiuno's mouth parted, sure she'd misheard, but the surrounding surprised faces told her otherwise. "It's fine," she said and smiled awkwardly. He offered a smile in return.

Thereafter they discussed layout, provisions, and how many it would take to hold such a fort. Each agreed to be separate, but close enough in case of an incident. Kiuno tried to keep up and commit K.J.'s plans to memory. She'd ask him for more details later.

When the meeting ended, Kiuno all but ran from the room and headed straight for the balcony. Sweat poured down her back and her tunic clung to her wet skin. The sooner they left, the sooner she could get this thing off.

"A bit hot for that attire, isn't it?"

Kiuno shifted as Atilla leaned on the balcony at her side. His gaze ran up and down her form and amusement glinted in his expression.

"I guess I could have chosen better." She laid her hands flat on the stone and tried to focus on the landscape, but her gaze flickered to the hallway.

Where are you K.J.?

"Are you new to his group?"

"I've been there a few weeks."

"I like your brazen attitude. You'd make a great leader." He took a step closer, glancing over his shoulder as if he were about to tell her a secret. "I wonder if you'd help me in that regard?"

She chewed her lip and fought against the instinct to step back. She refused to be intimidated. "That's kind of sudden, don't you think?"

He laughed, stepped back, and followed her gaze to the people below. "These days we can't afford subtlety. Better to state what you want."

"I suppose."

"But?"

"Well," She looked over her shoulder, trying to appear torn, "I'm already in that position."

He didn't look surprised or disappointed. "He picks good ones, I'll give him that. If you ever tire of his company, you know where to find me." He smiled and her skin crawled in response.

"Sure." He made a small bow before striding down the hall without looking back. K.J. appeared a few moments later with a disgruntled Elite close behind.

"Offering you the world?"

She grinned. "And then some."
"He'll try to manipulate you with the allurement of power."
Kiuno laughed. "I wish him luck."

QUARREL

REALM: 5
DAY: 246

Kiuno stood before Maltack's students and waited for him to finish lining them up.

"Are you sure this is a good idea?"

Maltack waved off her concern. "It'll be fine. I'm here. We need to see what you're capable of anyway."

Those who struggled with their fire magic ranged from a teenage girl to a few men in their forties. Their eyes trailed down her arms and Kiuno resisted the urge to cover them as she awaited Maltack's instructions.

"This will be a simple exercise. Kiuno," he pointed to her, "will hit us with her magic and you're going to shield. Don't worry if you mess up. I'll be taking the brunt of the force."

Several murmured amongst themselves but Maltack gave her a reassuring smile.

Kiuno closed her eyes and searched for the spark that flowed from her body's center. In a place she imagined her soul to reside.

To her surprise it met her with the eagerness of a child and flowed through the currents beneath her skin like water on a familiar track.

Kiuno tested the pathways and waited for the pain. A tingling sensation ran across her marks, but the area didn't burn as she'd expected. Another moment passed and she allowed the flames to burst forth and fanned them around her body, testing and pulling as one might an injured limb.

"How does it feel?" Maltack asked.

She looked at him and then to Elite, whose features carried a mixture of anxiety and awe. "Never better."

Maltack shifted his feet. "Whenever you're ready."

Kiuno glanced at his hands. Slender scars ran from his fingertips and stopped just past his wrist. If he could block and withstand the pain of her lightning, then what was a little fire?

Kiuno gripped the flames and burst them forward. Several students shrieked and fell back before the fire spread over an unseen force and stretched in a semi-circle around the group. Her magic hid their faces from view, so she turned to Elite for guidance. He nodded, indicating all was well.

"There's no reason to be afraid," Maltack called to those beside him.

Kiuno watched their feet. Those who'd fallen rose one by one and the force of the barrier strengthened. She kept a steady flow and took note when different areas along the barrier's surface hardened. Without Maltack, she could have easily broken through. The students were nothing compared to the impenetrable wall his magic created.

After several minutes Elite indicated her to stop and the flames wisped away with the wind. Three faces displayed their triumph while others hung their heads in disappointment.

"You all did well. Practice a while longer then take a break," Maltack said.

He joined her and smiled. "Your control is improving."

"You think so?"

"There were a few strays I had to catch, but most of the flames went exactly where you directed them."

She beamed. Control had always been an issue where her magic was concerned. Perhaps now they'd have time to solidify the hold on her abilities. The flames at least.

Kiuno's gaze drifted across the field. "Have you seen Scorpios?"

Maltack tilted his head in thought. "He mentioned training, but I imagine he's just about finished by now. Follow me."

Kiuno and Elite followed Maltack through the lines of those training. Occasionally Maltack would raise his hands to prevent stray magic from colliding with them as they circled toward the back side of the castle.

Kiuno grabbed Maltack's arm upon spotting Scorpios in a crouch.

"Something wrong?"

"You think I'm going to miss out on the opportunity to see him spar?"

Maltack chuckled. "Enjoy the show."

Scorpios circled his opponent. Iggy, if she remembered right. Both held a staff, and she wondered if they'd use their magic or stick to combatives. Out here, either went.

The pair lunged, both mimicking the other's movement like an elegant dance. Her heart raced as she waited for one to slip, but the two collided time and time again with flawless efficiency.

Both used the same magic. Both used the same techniques. Kiuno had half a mind to ask if they'd trained together in the real world.

After several minutes, Scorpios and Iggy bowed and turned to greet their new arrivals. Neither man claimed victory.

"You caught me," Scorpios said.

"I didn't know you were hiding."

"Can't have too many learning my weaknesses, now can I?"

She glanced at Iggy. "I think he's learned a lot."

Scorpios followed her gaze. "We all need an adequate sparring partner."

"Adequate?"

He cringed at her tone. "I mean someone I don't have to hold back with." His shoulders slumped when he realized his statement wouldn't sting any less.

Kiuno turned to Maltack. "I think Scorpios just insulted me."

Maltack tried to cover the smirk on his face. "I guess there's only one way to fix that."

"You're still healing." Scorpios reminded her.

"That's what I told her," Elite said.

"So, you guys are allowed to fool around, but I'm not?" Kiuno glanced at Elite then back to Scorpios. "You aren't the only one who needs an adequate sparring partner."

Scorpios looked between her and Elite and then to Maltack.

Their young friend shrugged. "I can make sure neither of you gets hurt."

Scorpios raised a brow in question, but Kiuno answered. "It's true, I might not be able to beat you in physical combat, but we both have other weapons at our disposal."

Scorpios frowned. "I don't think that's a good idea."

"Scared?"

He chuckled and those surrounding them backed away.

Iggy tossed his staff to Kiuno and stood beside Maltack. "I can help shield as well."

Kiuno ran her fingers over the soft wood. She'd been so accustomed to using the steel staff, she'd forgotten how light a wooden one could be. She'd need speed if she hoped to match Scorpios.

The two positioned themselves before one another and Scorpios sighed. "Just remember, you asked for this."

Elite whispered to Maltack, but she couldn't hear. He worried for her and she didn't doubt him questioning Maltack on how their session would go. She'd make sure he knew how strong she really was.

Watch me.

Kiuno tugged at her magic and ran at Scorpios. He dodged her first swing, no surprise there, so she fanned her fire to ensure he couldn't counter. Scorpios's tactic revolved around conservation. She'd have to force him into using his magic.

She shot a ball of fire at him and he dodged to the right where her staff was already in midswing. He met the weapon with his own and twisted it around, but not before she burst flames around her body again. A wall of water met fire, covering the area in steam.

He didn't pause, instead he brought his weapon up to collide with her side. Kiuno winced and pulled at the flames as they met in another wall of steam. She met him strike for strike, but as she spun Kiuno pulled her attack and he smirked, sending a wave of water to crash her against the ground.

"There's no reason to hold back."

She spluttered and water dripped from her hair and clothes. She glanced at Maltack and Iggy. They sat in perfect concentration.

Scorpios waited; the water coiled tight around his body like a waiting serpent. "Is it Maltack's abilities you doubt or mine?"

"I'm not doubting anyone."

"Yourself then?"

She remained silent.

"You won't hurt me if that's what you're worried about."

Kiuno gripped the staff. He was right as usual. Her instinct to protect prevented her from unleashing her potential.

She took a breath. If she didn't learn the limits of her power now, it might prove detrimental later. She pulled at the hot core and Scorpios switched his stance.

She launched forward again, this time unconcerned with Maltack and the gathered crowd.

Their staves cracked together in a blinding flash. Searing pain shot through her arm and the force knocked her and Scorpios to the ground.

Water rained down and Kiuno clutched her burning arm.

Despite the pain, panic shot through her body and she sat up in search of Scorpios. Maltack pulled him to his feet and both ran toward her.

Scorpios crouched down. "I'm all right, though I can't say the same for the staff." He looked at Maltack who held up two pieces, the center blackened on both sides.

Kiuno let out a slow breath. "I'm sorry."

Scorpios held out a hand and pulled her up. "No harm done."

"That was unexpected."

Kiuno turned to K.J.'s voice and found more than a few new faces surrounding them. She prayed no one figured out what happened. Elite took her arm to examine the area and she followed his gaze. A raw mark covered her skin, but it followed the path of a previous one.

"I can't believe you can do that," Elite said.

"Oh, she's capable of far more," K.J. said. Elite glared at him, but K.J. didn't seem to take notice. "We're about to discuss terms for travel."

Kiuno nodded toward the castle. "Lead the way."

Their small group followed K.J. back to his office where several faces, including Silver and Palindrome, sat waiting. A map was rolled out on the table with the corners held down by small weights.

"Have a seat. Before we talk about our upcoming journey, there's something we want to run by you concerning the battle arrangements." K.J. sat beside Palindrome. "We've agreed Maltack and Scorpios are best suited to be your backup and once your job is finished, they'll fall back to their preassigned ranks."

"Back up for what?" Kiuno asked.

K.J. sat forward. "Utilizing your unique talent is in everyone's best interest. I had several take assessments of the damage you inflicted on the battlefield and the results were staggering. Once Palindrome and Maltack figure a way to harness that power I'm sure it'll only get stronger. Your job will be to scatter the enemy and disorganize their forces."

"That means…"

K.J. nodded. "You'll be the first to confront the enemy."

Elite stood. "That's absurd. Didn't you see what happened a few minutes ago?"

K.J. remained calm. "I did, but once we learn to control it—"

"Controlling it requires practice. The fire is one thing, but the lightning almost killed her."

Palindrome folded her hands. "Technically, the exertion almost killed her and the fact that Kiuno pulled from the storm's lightning. We only want her out there for a few minutes, just to throw the enemy off balance."

K.J. continued, "I don't foresee any immediate issues. We have the forest to deal with for now. In the meantime, I'll have you with Palindrome's main force. The rest—"

"You're putting her at the front anyway?" Elite curled his fists.

"We station all those with magic at the front. They take out what they can before the ground forces close in."

"But you lose them."

"As is with any battle."

"I won't have it."

"Elite." Kiuno placed a hand on his arm, but he pulled away.

"I won't see you on the front lines, you've done enough fighting."

"If I can help, I want to. Maltack will be with me."

"Absolutely not. I won't see my wife dead on the battlefield. There are plenty of other things you can do."

The entire group fell silent.

Kiuno stood to be level with him. "I'm not a weak little girl that needs protection."

"Have you forgotten that you were half dead when I dragged you off that field?"

Her anger flared. "And have you forgotten that if it weren't for me, you wouldn't even be here?"

"You're not going."

She scoffed. "Is that so, just who do you think you are?"

"Your husband and if you respect me at all, you'll do as I ask."

"Respect? You're going to talk about respect while trying to command me to do something?"

"You could die out there," he shouted.

"So, could any of them," she shouted back.

His face hardened. "I don't give a damn about them."

"Well I do." She turned to K.J. and lowered her voice. "When the time comes, I'll be there." She glared at Elite who looked ready to burst. "I'm not a child and if I can protect someone, then I will and there's nothing, *nothing* you can do about it."

11

ELITE

REALM: 5

DAY: 246

Elite's boots pounded against the grass as he flew through the outer gate. His eyes darted across the open field in the dimming light. He paused outside to catch his breath and collapsed against the wall. He'd searched everywhere. The training grounds, their room, the main hall…

He cursed and slammed his fist against the wall then jogged back toward the castle. *Why does she think it's okay to put herself in danger?*

Their room was still empty, so he ran back down the stairs toward the main hall and looked out over the sea of faces. When she'd stormed out, he'd remained in the room, but no one commented on their argument. *Am I in the wrong? Shouldn't I have the right to protect my wife?*

He sighed and walked up the stairs again toward the tower he'd found her at the other night. He'd looked twice already, but he didn't doubt her moving around to avoid him. She never enjoyed confrontation.

Why hadn't he grabbed her and prevented her from leaving his sight? They'd been apart for so long. He'd spent night after night wondering if she lay bundled in an inn or scared and cold outside, a victim of the elements.

As Elite opened the tower door, he saw the one person he wanted to avoid.

K.J. stood with his arms draped over the stone railing and turned when the hinges creaked.

Elite glared at him and bit his tongue. K.J. would get an earful later, right now he needed to find Kiuno.

"You can't keep her from fighting," K.J. called.

Elite stopped, his fists clenching and unclenching. "So, placing her at the center of battle is your solution?"

"It is."

Anger pulsed through him. "You're going to get her killed."

Silence.

"Tell me. Did you ever question why she was there that day?"

"I assumed she was with you."

"Across the field? Away from my forces when I knew nothing of her abilities?"

Elite remained silent.

"I told her to stay behind." K.J. turned to face Elite. "I had her escorted to a room. I had people keeping an eye on her, but it didn't matter. She followed me. She fought where I couldn't protect her. So, let me ask you. Is it safer to include her in the battle plans or hope we get to her when she rushes in on her own?"

"I prefer to keep her away from it altogether."

K.J. clicked his tongue. "And how do you propose we do that? Tie her up? Lock her away? Do you want her to hate you? Here's a lesson on strong-willed women—they'll do as they please. It's our job to ensure they're safe in the process."

Elite's mind floated back to past arguments. Her stubbornness went unmatched. She did what she wanted or convinced him otherwise.

When she'd trained with Scorpios earlier in the day, their friend hadn't tried to hold her back. Instead, he'd encouraged her. All Elite had done was worry.

"Want my advice?"

"Not really."

K.J. smirked. "Talk with her. Calmly. That woman loves you more than anything in this world. She was willing to give up her life for you. Never forget that because she'll do it again."

Elite clenched his jaw. "Do you know where she is?"

K.J. pointed to a tower on the outer curtain wall. "She's at the tower I gave to the felinian."

NEVER FORGET

DAY: 246

REALM: 5

Kiuno wrapped her arms around her knees and rocked back and forth with tears falling down her face. She hated this. Hated this world, and hated fighting with Elite. He had to understand. None of them had the luxury of sitting on the sidelines.

"Hiding out?"

Kiuno turned to Jim's voice as he walked through the doorway. Nikita kicked up the wind as she flew in from the side and landed with catlike grace.

Kiuno wiped her tears. "I'm trying."

Jim ruffled Nikita's fur, and the animal lifted her chin for him to scratch beneath. She stood almost to Jim's waist now. Her shoulders had widened, and her wingspan doubled. Curiosity replaced the usual suspicion in those emerald eyes.

Nikita tucked her wings in and crept toward Kiuno. She sniffed the air, then nuzzled the top of Kiuno's head. Kiuno couldn't help but smile

71

and reached up to scratch behind one ear. The animal gave a deep purr in response.

"I suppose I'm accepted now?"

"She can sense you're upset. Why are you out here alone?"

Kiuno bit the inside of her cheek. "I had a fight with Elite."

Jim chuckled. "A lover's quarrel."

"I don't see how that's funny."

Jim leaned against the stone balcony that surrounded the tower. "You'll run headfirst into battle to save him, yet when an argument arises, you run and hide. Ironic, isn't it?"

She looked away, watching the rise and fall of Nikita's side as she laced her fingers through the soft fur. "I guess it is kind of silly."

"What's this argument about?"

"He doesn't want me fighting."

Jim chuckled. "Does he know who he's talking to?"

A smile fought through her tears.

"Don't worry too much. You have decent instincts. Elite will come to terms with it. He just wants to protect you the way you want to protect the innocent."

Her heart clenched. "I don't like hurting him."

"We have a funny way of hurting those we're closest to."

Nikita raised her head and the two turned to see a breathless Elite at the top of the stairs.

Jim stood from the wall. "This is where I take my leave." He nodded to Elite in passing.

Nikita stood and peered over the edge of the balcony. Her tail flicked from side to side as she waited for Jim to exit below. Kiuno watched the felinian spread her feathered wings, jump from the edge, and soar into the night.

Elite took Jim's place and leaned against the cold stone. Deafening silence filled the space between them. She looked to the sky, noticing even the stars hid themselves from view on this dreary night.

"When we first met, I thought you were quiet because you were shy." Elite smirked. "But I quickly learned it was because you listened. You listen to the people around you and create ripples when you speak. Most aren't likely to challenge you because you weigh the pros and cons before acting. I understand this makes you leadership material, but you're still my wife." He shifted. "How am I supposed to stand by and watch knowing the worst could happen?"

Kiuno's heart thundered as she searched for words that would convey her feelings. "What would you do if someone asked you not to protect me?"

"You already know the answer."

"Then you can't expect the same of me. I refuse to sit idle when I know I can make a difference."

Elite's eyes softened and he averted his gaze. "And if you get hurt?"

"Then it's a consequence I'll have to face."

"It's one I'll also face."

Kiuno fell silent and Elite approached and held out one hand. She looked up into his face and took it, wanting nothing more than the arms that enveloped her. Elite sighed and buried his face in her hair.

"I wouldn't know what to do if I lost you. I thought I did once." His grip tightened, crushing her body against his. "I thought you fell, and my entire world fell with you."

Kiuno pulled back to look in his saddened eyes. "I won't fall."

Elite's hand traced her cheek and his warm fingertips left a trail on her skin. "How long has it been since you smiled?"

Her breath hitched while he searched her gaze.

"I see pain written all over you, consuming you." His hand threaded through her hair. "Smile for me," he whispered.

He pressed his lips against hers and she returned it with tears slipping down her cheeks.

Elite took one hand and held it out, then placed his other on her waist. "Have you forgotten how to dance too?" He took a step and she mirrored it as the familiar movements fell into place. His warm body pressed against hers in a rhythm only the two of them knew. A song beneath the stars. A promise of two hearts sworn together.

Kiuno laid her head on his shoulder and moved with his steps, allowing the memories of their home life to wash over her. The days they'd learned. The nights that spoke of dreams and promises of their future.

She pulled back and smiled and Elite cupped her face again. "There it is. Never forget how to dance." He pressed another kiss to her lips. "I know you want to save the world, but you are my world and losing you would be the same as dying."

Another tear rolled down her cheek. "I won't forget."

THE FOREST

REALM: 5

DAY: 248

The wagon rolled across the grassy path left by those who traveled ahead and jostled Kiuno from side to side. She glanced at Maltack, her young friend struggling to scribble in a journal. Kiuno wasn't sure she wanted to remember this place once they returned home.

Commotion from the front sent Kiuno's heart racing. She jumped from the wagon and stared at a forest that stretched an impossibly long distance in either direction. The trees stood three times taller than those from other forests of this world. The wind passed through the branches and Kiuno shivered. It appeared as though they hadn't been disturbed for millennia and harbored ancient secrets within their knotted branches.

The meadow stopped a few feet before the trees as if even it were hesitant to cross that threshold.

Twenty yards from the forest edge sat a wall of barriers, each manned by at least three guards. A ditch filled with murky water sat behind it.

The horses stopped, and those in charge set them loose to graze in the field. She joined Scorpios and Maltack to unpack their supplies. K.J. and Palindrome headed to his general's tent for updates on their progress.

As she lifted box after box and carried them to a designated tent, Kiuno's mind wandered to Reece. She'd promised to visit him within a few weeks but found she hadn't had the time. She made a mental note to stop by as soon as they returned.

Work occupied the better part of their afternoon until K.J. called them in for an update. "A few men have gone missing already. Because of this, everyone will stay in pairs. No one is to go out on their own." His eyes locked with Kiuno when he dismissed everyone else.

"I need you to stay with Palindrome, if you don't mind."

"Elite will be with Maltack then?"

K.J. nodded and Maltack agreed.

Elite followed her from the tent before she could run to find her charge. "Don't be gone too long."

She gave him a quick kiss. "I won't."

He caught her arm. "Don't leave her side."

"I won't. I'll be in the camp, nothing will happen."

Elite's hand lingered until she pried herself away.

Kiuno wandered around those setting up tents and others sharpening their weapons. Her gaze floated toward a stack of wood and she found Palindrome setting her load beneath a tent.

The woman took a moment to rest when she saw Kiuno approaching. "Do you need something?"

"K.J. assigned me to you."

She tried to stifle a laugh. "Of course, he did. Who is with Elite?"

"Maltack." Kiuno glanced at the stack of wood. "What are you doing?"

"Connecting with the people. Doing whatever needs to be done. I'm sure you understand the importance." She turned to a pile of freshly chopped wood. The smell of cedar floated through the air. "Right now, I'm getting these in that tent. It looks like it might rain tonight."

Kiuno looked at the clouds in the sky, sure it wouldn't rain, but she helped Palindrome anyway. Dusk fell fast, and she wanted to be in before nightfall.

With their task of stacking wood finished, Palindrome directed her to another area and then another. Palindrome mingled with person after person, each delighting in her presence. Many tried to refuse her help, but she wouldn't listen. She made herself loved, thus strengthening their alliance.

Night fell around the camp and the pair shifted another pile of wood. Kiuno imagined Elite pacing their tent, but she couldn't leave until Palindrome finished what she'd set her mind to.

Fires popped up around the camp, many on the outskirts to aid the guards watching for anything sinister crawling through the night.

Kiuno dropped the logs beside an unlit fire and stood to wipe her brow. Palindrome went back for another armful and Kiuno turned her gaze toward the sky. She stretched the ache in her backside.

She liked the hard work and understood Palindrome's draw to being productive. Perhaps Kiuno could help others with similar tasks once they returned home. Provided she had free time.

Kiuno tilted her head toward the ominous trees that loomed ahead. Everything about them made her skin tingle and crawl. She usually found the forest a welcome sight, but here it seemed like the branches watched, waiting to consume her with their shadowy grip.

Kiuno entered the tent and paused when Palindrome wasn't there. She turned back toward the unlit fire and ignited it with her magic.

"Palindrome," she called.

No one answered.

Kiuno's hair stood on end as she called the woman's name again. Nothing.

Her heart jolted and she dashed around the pile of wood. Her legs pounded the ground in time to her heart and she burst through K.J.'s tent to find him leaning over a map. Her eyes scanned the area, but Palindrome wasn't here either.

"Palindrome is gone."

K.J. stood straight. "What do you mean?"

"She went back to the tent for wood and then was just gone."

"Where was she last seen?"

Kiuno pointed and took off with K.J. and his companion following. The three of them alerted everyone in the vicinity and K.J.'s companion directed a small group of messengers to each alliance.

Kiuno followed K.J. back to his tent, and he kicked a chair across the area. It crashed into a desk and splintered across the floor. He ran his fingers through dark hair before turning to head out.

"What do you want me to do?" she asked.

He paused but didn't turn. "You've done enough." He exited, leaving her in the cold aftermath of his words.

Kiuno fell into another chair and tried to slow her racing heart. To her knowledge they hadn't found the missing people yet.

She glanced at the bottle of ink on his desk. She knew she'd face repercussions later, but Kiuno couldn't do nothing. She scribbled a few words, took two daggers from the rack at the entrance, and disappeared into the night.

K.J.

REALM: 5
DAY: 248

An hour passed and for the first time in years K.J. felt hopelessness settle in his gut like a nasty case of the flu. They'd scanned the perimeter twice and informed the alliances of her disappearance, but to them she was just another missing case.

He slammed his fist against the table and fell into a chair, staring at the broken one he'd kicked earlier. Four hours stood between them and sunrise. He rested his head in his hands. The likelihood of her lasting that long…

K.J. rubbed at tired eyes then glanced to a scribbled note on the table. His heart leapt.

I'll bring her back.

K.J. crumpled the tiny note and ground his teeth. He couldn't go after them in the dark, but morning might prove too late. He knew it and so did Kiuno.

ELITE

REALM: 5

DAY: 248

E lite ran past Maltack. *Missing?* He'd refused to listen to anything else until he confronted K.J. Rain beat against him and the trees loomed as a dark silhouette in the distance. They sent a chill through his bones and an uneasy feeling settled in his stomach.

Elite burst through the tent. "What happened?" The very man he disliked and for some reason his wife seemed to idolize sat with his head in his hands as if he'd been there for hours.

K.J. sat back and pushed a small note toward the edge of the table. "Palindrome went missing and Kiuno went after her."

That word again. Missing.

"What do you mean went after her?"

K.J. stood. "Kiuno informed me of Palindrome's disappearance and before we could escort her to you, she took off."

"What did you say to her?"

Anger flashed across K.J.'s face. "You assume a lot, don't you?"

Elite clenched his fists. "I know she's reckless, but she isn't suicidal. There's no way she'd run in there," he pointed toward the forest, "without being provoked. What did you do?"

Guilt washed over K.J.'s features. "She wanted to help. I told her she'd done enough."

His blood raged and Elite slammed his fist into K.J.'s face. K.J. crashed to the floor and blood dropped from the corner of his lip.

"You put this in her head."

K.J. wiped his mouth and stood. "I did nothing of the sort."

Elite marched forward and grabbed K.J.'s collar. "You told her to be the first line of attack and that's exactly what she's done."

"You better check yourself."

Vines wrapped around their bodies in a gentle yet firm hold and Maltack pulled them apart. "Guys, this isn't helping."

Elite glared at K.J. then exited the tent.

The rain dripped from his hair as he gazed toward the massive trees. He couldn't begin to fathom what might be hiding in those shadows. Elite checked his weapons and tightened his belt.

He recalled Kiuno's fear of the dark. She'd cling to him back home but despite that fear, she'd run into a wretched place where the monsters were real.

Elite made to run, but two sets of strong arms grabbed him from behind. He struggled against both, but they tackled him to the muddy ground.

"You can't run in there," K.J. said.

Elite gritted his teeth. "Why not?"

"Because you'll die. Think of how much she'd be hurt then. You have no magic. No backup. What do you expect to accomplish?"

"So what, we just wait?"

"We plan."

Thunder cracked overhead and Elite stood. "You have an army, get them ready."

"It's not that simple."

"Not that simple? That's my wife in there!"

"Don't you think I know that?"

The desperation in K.J.'s face eased his anger a fraction. Palindrome was in there too. They both had someone they loved in danger.

Elite took a breath. "What do you suggest we do?"

16

BEHEMOTH

REALM: 5

DAY: 248

Kiuno slipped through the shadows and around the guards with ease. Between the pouring rain and their dwindling fires it was no wonder people had gone missing.

Whoever took Palindrome had enough intellect to knock her unconscious. That meant a formidable enemy. Most creatures of this world were nothing more than monsters. Easy targets. But if they could subdue someone like Palindrome with such ease—Kiuno bit back her rising nervousness and crept forward.

Without tracks to follow, Kiuno entered the forest uncertain. The depths were black as pitch, but she didn't dare give light to the area, afraid any disturbance would be a beacon for her death.

Rain dripped from the canopy above as she fumbled through, dragging her feet across the ground. She used her hands to keep balance.

Kiuno squinted as her eyes slowly adjusted and crept along the mist-covered floor. Large knotted roots jutted from the ground like crooked rows of teeth. Kiuno used them to maneuver as she crawled from one hiding place to the next.

Her skin prickled. No movement. No life.

A crack echoed through the stillness and Kiuno dove beneath a root for cover. She pressed her back to the ground, stayed low, and fought to keep her breath even. Slimy water that reeked of days-old sewage pooled to her right.

Another crack.

Then a growl.

The silhouette of a monstrous creature rose toward the sky and blocked what little light shone through. Kiuno's heart raced faster as its low snorts and growls inched closer to her.

A web of roots broke beneath its weight and she used the noise to plunge herself into the muddy water.

Another crash of broken branches and its hot breath wafted only a few feet above. Kiuno gritted her teeth when the stench of rotted meat hit her full in the face.

She clenched her eyes and remained still. Smaller creatures wriggled beneath her fingertips, but Kiuno resisted the urge to recoil.

For the longest moment of her life, the behemoth lingered above her body, sniffing the ground and area around it before turning back from whence it came.

It dug at the earth a bit, sniffed the air, and stalked through the trees.

Kiuno let out a breath and fought against gagging as the filthy stench from the water invaded her senses. It'd also saved her life.

She turned herself over and crawled through the shallow muck.

With distance between her and the beast, Kiuno stood from the water and shook the creeping things from her body. She left the slime in her hair, hoping its disgusting scent would mask her own.

Droplets hit the water's surface as Kiuno continued to follow its path. Hopefully whatever or whoever lived here would keep near to the source, no matter how disgusting.

She crouched, ducking from place to place on the swampy terrain. Kiuno glanced at pits full of water and her stomach clenched with what might be lurking beneath the surface.

An eternity seemed to pass before the water ended at a muddy pit. She climbed a slippery bank to avoid the deeper part, but when she descended something crunched beneath her feet.

A smell fouler than the water assaulted her and Kiuno recoiled, covering her mouth in at attempt not to retch.

She shouldn't have looked.

Bones. Hundreds of them with rotted flesh still hanging from the ends. A caved-in skull rested beneath her boot. Flies buzzed the area and she swatted one who tried to land on her arm.

Kiuno darted from the trench.

They were eating them. Kiuno's mind conjured an image of Palindrome's mangled form, but she quickly averted her thoughts. She couldn't think that way yet.

Kiuno climbed out of the pit and paused at the top.

Iron cages stood in a straight line heading away from her and mounds of dirt lay on either side. The trees had been cleared, opening the canopy to the storm's downpour.

Kiuno crept closer.

Each mound had a hole large enough for two people to drop in. She counted ten, but shadows hid the rest from view.

Smaller trees and bushes grew through the tops, telling her they'd been there a while. Perhaps since the game's creation.

She crept forward a few more paces and closed the distance to the first cage.

Nothing moved.

An old iron door dangled from the edge of a rust-covered hinge and the rock serving as its platform had cracked down the center.

The remaining cages appeared newer; each door held closed by a heavy chain. A rock, the size of a large tire, hung from one end to keep the latch in place. It didn't offer Kiuno any comfort.

Kiuno glanced at the holes on either side of her. She crouched and peered around the corner before crawling toward the next.

A thin, bony creature quivered behind the bars of the second cage, but if it noticed her movement, it didn't respond.

At the next enclosure, the creature whined and the high-pitched noise echoed across the expanse. Kiuno sloshed through the mud and ducked between a rock and the stone base. She counted the seconds with droplets falling from her hair.

Nothing.

Kiuno took a breath and lifted herself onto the third cage's platform. The creature inside scurried to the far side and looked at her with wide, wild eyes. It shivered and tucked a furless tail between long hind legs. Her heart ached for its battered, bloody limbs.

Kiuno squinted in the dark. Three cages down sat a figure small enough to be human.

With heart racing, she jumped from the platform and ran the re-maining distance. She paused with her back pressed against the stone and glanced at the surrounding holes again.

Still silence.

Kiuno pulled herself onto the platform and her heart soared.

Palindrome sat with her head in her knees and to Kiuno's relief ap-peared largely unharmed. Kiuno tripped and a hushed curse escaped her lips. Palindrome's head shot up.

"Are you okay?" Kiuno whispered.

Palindrome glanced to her right, then crawled toward the cage door. Kiuno winced at her swollen eye.

"What are you doing here?"

"Saving you, what does it look like?" Kiuno's eyes scanned the area again before moving to examine the chain holding the latch. "Are you hurt?"

"I can heal myself, but if they find you, we'll both be in this cage.

Did you come alone?"

"Yes."

Palindrome gave her an appalled look, but Kiuno tugged at the fire in her veins and began heating a link on the chain.

"Why?" Palindrome hissed. "You have to be the most reckless—"

Rustling drew their attention and panic covered Palindrome's face. "Hide!"

Kiuno jumped from the platform and pressed her back against it as something slinked through the shadows on the other side. Palindrome shuffled away from the creature, pressing her back against the cage. Mud squished, and claws clicked against the stone.

A pinging pierced the air as the creature ran clawed fingers along the bars in a taunting fashion. Clicking followed and then a hiss. Kiuno slowed her breathing, praying it wouldn't look on this side of the platform. It lingered, sniffed, then squished back through the mud.

Kiuno counted to three before peaking over the platform in time to see a scaly tail disappear through a hole. She waited several moments before hoisting herself back onto the platform and continued her work on the link.

Palindrome crawled back to her, keeping one eye on the hole. "It'll hear when the chain drops."

Kiuno followed her gaze. "Be ready to run. Go straight ahead and follow the muddy water."

The link sweated and droplets of silver glided down the chain until the weight pulled it apart and the rock crashed to the ground.

A loud creak split the air as Kiuno shoved the latch from its crevice and Palindrome leapt from the cage. A roar echoed behind, but neither looked back.

The two scaled the muddy bank and neither paused when bones crunched beneath their feet. A spear flew over Palindrome's head. Two more plunged into the ground soon after, but then something wrapped Kiuno's ankle like a vice and yanked. Her chin smacked against a solid root.

Kiuno pulled a dagger and stabbed the dark figure, but her blade only sank into muddy soil. It dragged her along the ground and she cried out and grabbed a sturdy root.

Kiuno tugged at her magic and let the flames spin off into the darkness. The light reflected from the damp scales of lizard-like creatures. They growled and hissed then hid themselves in shadow.

Palindrome pulled Kiuno to her feet and the pair sprinted through the darkness.

The two ducked behind a tree and paused to catch their breath. Kiuno peeked around the trunk, trying to distinguish which shadows were natural and which were predators. "Did we lose them?"

Palindrome took a breath and peered around the other side before leaning her head against the tree again. "How far in are we?"

"I don't know. Not too far."

Kiuno's blood ran cold as a tree fell to their right followed by an earth-shattering roar. Her adrenaline kicked into overdrive when four eyes and a nasty snarl towered above.

She shoved Palindrome into the muddy water, then rolled beneath the nearest root structure.

The beast's strong jaw snapped it in half. She skidded to the other side then dove to another root system trying to keep anything between her and the teeth chasing her through the trees.

Its clawed paw dropped on the next set of roots and Kiuno rolled out and clamored to her feet.

She looked left. Right. Then sprinted toward the advancing beast and let the flames spiral down her arm. Fire blasted it in the face, and it roared.

Kiuno hid behind another tree.

Palindrome tried to sneak around a large trunk, but long claws slashed through it and Palindrome screamed as she ducked and covered her head.

"Run," Kiuno yelled.

Kiuno jumped from her hiding place and launched another assault of flames toward the creature. It turned and lunged. Kiuno stepped back and tripped. Her backside collided with the ground and she rolled just in time to avoid its massive paw.

She shifted to her feet and ran beneath the creature's legs. Kiuno drew her sword, but she miscalculated and the breath left her body when its paw slammed into her chest.

Kiuno skidded across the ground. Her arm twisted beneath her and a loud crack followed. Lightning-like pain lanced through her limb.

She screamed, gripped her elbow, then screamed again. The beast stalked forward, its fangs seeming to smile as it closed in on its prey.

Fear shot through Kiuno's bones and she tugged at the hottest part of her core.

Fire crackled around her body then burst forward in a flash of lightning that struck the beast in the mouth. Its claw ripped through her leg as it lashed out and backpedaled.

Kiuno tried to clutch both limbs, but Palindrome grabbed her collar and dragged her back.

The beast clawed at its face and dragged it across the ground.

Kiuno clenched her teeth and fought for breath through the unrelenting pain. Palindrome rested one hand on Kiuno's bloody leg and the other on her arm.

"Both are broken, but the leg is worse."

Kiuno writhed at her touch. "The leg, so we can run."

Palindrome placed both hands on Kiuno's leg and the faint glow made them both squint.

Skin and muscles squirmed beneath Palindrome's touch. Kiuno's stomach twisted as the area burned and itched all at once.

A resounding roar lifted the hair on the back of Kiuno's neck. Palindrome pulled Kiuno's good arm over her shoulder and hoisted her up.

Blood still rolled down Kiuno's calf and she winced as the two hobbled through the forest.

A tree fell, followed by a gurgled roar.

"I think we pissed it off." Kiuno's injured leg caught on a log and she moved the broken arm to catch herself only to hear the bones grind together. She couldn't stop the scream that escaped her lips again.

Palindrome uttered an apology and pulled her arm back across her shoulder.

Rays of morning light flickered through the trees ahead. Kiuno squinted in the lighting. Her breath came in panicked gasps as she fought to stay conscious. *How long have I been in here?*

The beast crashed through the forest floor behind and Kiuno's heart surged. "Hurry Palin."

The woman gripped her tighter and dragged her through the brush. Kiuno tried not to look behind. Thorns and branches scraped her arms and legs and tore at their clothes. Kiuno thought she could feel the hot breath closing in on them. She clenched her eyes, then the two women burst through the trees.

A line of men with weapons stood ready. Their hands were all over Kiuno before she could process they were no longer within the trees.

"Back away," Palindrome screamed.

The men shifted without hesitation. Palindrome, never having released her hold, gripped Kiuno's arm tighter and limped them behind the first line.

The beast broke through the trees and Palindrome let Kiuno collapse to the ground. Both watched as vines sprang from the ground to capture its feet and fire engulfed its massive form before it could flee.

The creature struggled, but once shards of icy glass buried themselves in its core, the world fell silent.

A shadow towered over her face and Kiuno glanced up to K.J.'s grimace.

"You look wrecked."

Kiuno closed her eyes in response.

"I need her in my medical tent." Palindrome turned to another. "Find Maltack. Tell him Palindrome needs him and it's an emergency."

K.J. scooped his arms beneath Kiuno's knees and torso. Every movement felt like a thousand shards of glass shooting through her body.

"She's lost too much blood," Palindrome said.

Kiuno's vision blurred and her eyes grew heavy. K.J. shifted her again and the jostling ceased.

"Anything I can do?" K.J. asked

"Get blankets."

"I'm here." Maltack burst through the tent flap, but Kiuno couldn't bring herself to look at him. "How bad is it?"

"I feel like I'm going to pass out," Kiuno said.

Muscles pulled in her leg and she cried out again when a bone shifted into place. She cracked an eye open to see K.J. return and set a pile of blankets on the nearby table.

Kiuno took a few breaths. "I brought her back."

"You're an idiot, you know that?"

Another shift in her arm and the lingering shadow engulfed her consciousness.

17

BURN

REALM: 5

DAY: 249

Kiuno woke, her body heavy and arms burning once again. She glanced down to find Elite's hand wrapped around her wrist and his head against the cot.

She ran her fingers through his chestnut hair and he stirred. Sleepy, concerned eyes met hers.

Silence echoed in the small tent. Elite brushed his thumb over her knuckles. He brought his lips down and pressed them against her hand then clutched it between his own.

"You're awake." The two turned to the tent flap as Palindrome entered. Palindrome glanced between them then started poking and prodding at Kiuno's body. "How's the arm?"

Kiuno flexed her fingers and circled her wrist. "Sore."

Palindrome moved to the leg and a searing pain shot through it the moment she flexed. Palindrome's fingers emitted their faint glow, and something slithered beneath her skin. Nausea bubbled in Kiuno's gut and she resisted the urge to grab the limb.

When Palindrome finished, Kiuno flexed her leg again, this time without pain.

"Is it dead?"

"I wouldn't be here if it wasn't, but that's the least of our worries. The creatures who captured me are still pouring in from the forest. They don't seem happy about my escape."

Kiuno tried to speak, but Palindrome stopped her. "We're taking care of it. You're in no condition to help."

Kiuno leaned back into her furs and Palindrome exited the tent.

Elite gripped her hand tighter. "Why did you do that?"

The pain in his voice gripped her heart like a vise. "It was my fault. What else could I have done?"

"Gotten help, I would have gone with you. Maltack would have gone with you."

Stopped her more like. Then Palindrome would be dead.

She touched his face, and guilt washed over her as he leaned into her palm. "I'm sorry."

"Promise me you won't do anything like that again."

"I promise." It was a lie and judging from his sigh Elite knew it too.

KIUNO DIDN'T remember falling asleep, but she woke when the late morning sun poured through the slit in her tent. She lay there for a few minutes then sat up. Her head spun, but she swung her legs over the edge of the bed. If there was one thing she hated, it was being alone.

Before she'd fallen asleep, Elite had wiped the blood from her body and helped her into new clothes. Slime and muck still caked her hair, but it was something that could be tended to later.

Kiuno limped to the tent's exit and moved the flap. Several people ran from one place to another, no longer attending to minuscule tasks.

The line of men who stood guard now held their weapons at the ready while magic sparked and faded at the forest's edge. She hobbled toward the chaos for a closer look.

After the behemoth beast and the flesh eaters Kiuno didn't want to fathom what else might be lurking within those foreboding trees.

"Palindrome won't be happy when she catches you up." K.J. said.

Kiuno shrugged and nodded toward the trees. "What are we going to do about that?"

He didn't answer, but worry lines stretched across his forehead when he wrinkled his brow. She noted the black circling his eyes and his worn expression.

"When was the last time you slept?"

A guilty smile spread across his face. "Probably too long, but if you don't tell Palin, I won't."

"Fine by me. Have you seen Elite?"

"Palindrome has him busy with Maltack. I can't imagine you enjoy his constant worrying."

"It's not good for him."

"He won't be happy you're up either."

"He's not happy with anything I do lately."

They both laughed and K.J. said, "It seems I'm not on his nice list either."

Kiuno noted his swollen lip. "What happened?"

"Nothing you need concern yourself with."

"But—"

"The scouts haven't returned, but with the challenges we're facing I'm willing to bet the portal is inside those trees. Getting the civilians through will be difficult."

She wanted to press him about Elite but decided now wasn't the time. "At least it's not something you have to worry about yet."

He crossed his arms. "Honestly, I've considered not moving them until we reach the final realm."

Shouting and sparks echoed from the forest's edge again.

"How long has this been going on?" she asked.

"All day. They're persistent creatures."

"Aren't you worried about burning the forest down?"

He opened his mouth and paused, then looked at her with a new spark in his eyes. "No, no I'm not."

She tilted her head and a smile broke across his face. "You're brilliant."

"Thank you?"

He strode toward the forest and she struggled to keep pace.

K.J. found Palindrome, but the woman looked at both with a scowl. "Always out of bed when you shouldn't be." She placed one hand on her hip, but something in K.J.'s expression drew her attention. "Something wrong?"

"No, everything's perfect. Gather the magic users and line them up along the forest."

"How many?"

"All of them."

Palindrome glanced at their line up then back to him. "I hardly think that's necessary." He made to move, but Palindrome caught his hand. "What's going on?"

"We're burning down the forest."

PROPOSAL

REALM: 5

DAY: 250

News of their escape from the forest spread through the camp like wildfire. Many shed tears at Palindrome's safe return and others hadn't even realized she was missing.

Several people thanked Kiuno for her daring adventure, but she could feel Elite's glaring eyes burning holes through her backside. She tucked herself in a wagon to hide from the masses and Elite walked alongside it.

Kiuno watched as magic users lined up along the forest edge. Those not staying packed their bags and headed back toward the castle. The forest would burn for a long while and they needed to replenish their supplies and rest.

Billowing clouds of smoke rose in the sky as the flames licked their way up the trunks. Those able to manipulate wind fanned the fire and smoke away from those packing.

Black clouds rising against a clear blue sky.

The scene was almost more ominous than the trees.

AFTER SPENDING the night tangled in Elite's embrace, Kiuno opted to ride again. Queasiness still gripped her stomach, but any more time looking back on the forest of death would drive her mad. She wanted to see the wide-open plains and the freedom they promised.

Kiuno tried to urge her horse forward to speak with K.J., but Elite thwarted her movement again. Her horse pawed the ground and she huffed but he pretended not to notice.

"What happened?" she demanded.

Elite gave her an innocent glance. "With what?"

"Between you and K.J."

His brow furrowed. "Did he say something?"

"He didn't have to."

"It's nothing to worry about."

Kiuno pursed her lips. "That's not fair."

"Neither is you running to your death. Again."

Kiuno sighed, but she didn't have the energy to argue. Instead, Kiuno turned her gaze to the stone walls in the distance. Familiarity. A haven that would protect them from the chaos of this created world. At least for now.

KIUNO MARCHED straight to their room, stripped from her dirty clothes and fell into bed. Her body was spent, and her muscles ached beyond words.

"You don't want to shower?" Elite asked.

Of course she did. She reeked. But she was so tired.

"Later," she murmured.

Despite her obvious need for sanitation, Kiuno still woke with Elite's body wrapped around her like a vise. If he'd been protective before she imagined it would be even worse now.

ELITE STIRRED when a knock sounded at their door. She was tempted to ignore it, but when it sounded again, Elite tugged on his dirty pants and opened it.

Blue stood on the other side and he quickly put a hand over Liam's eyes upon seeing Kiuno wrapped in nothing but a blanket.

"Um, K.J. wanted me to get her."

Elite grunted. "Of course he did."

Kiuno gave Blue a sleepy smile. "Tell him I'll be there soon."

He nodded, gave Elite a curious glance, and padded down the hall with Liam in tow.

"I suppose you hate him now?"

Elite leaned against the wall and folded his arms. "Now? Remind me what's changed."

She shook her head and slid back into yesterday's pants. Kiuno pulled the shirt over her head, but Elite grabbed her wrist before she could reach for her blades.

He tucked a stray strand of hair behind her ear and placed a kiss on her forehead. "I'll always dislike the thought of you in danger."

"That doesn't mean you have to hit my friends."

"Maybe I went a little overboard, but he had it coming."

She playfully poked his chest. "Self-restraint, or I'll keep you away from future meetings."

He smirked. "I'd like to see you try."

Kiuno tucked her knives into her boot then she and Elite trudged up the stairs to hear the latest news.

They entered the double doors and sat in the two empty chairs before his desk.

K.J. glanced at Elite and then to her. "The alliances aren't happy with my decision."

"To burn the forest, you mean? It's not like you didn't expect that."

"No, but I thought some of them might have agreed. They've requested I consult with them before taking any more drastic measures." K.J. crumpled the note and threw it into the fire.

"I'll be sure to remind you of that when the time comes." Kiuno glanced at an empty chair. "Where's Palindrome?"

K.J. rubbed his temple. "Planning a celebration. The civilians want in on the latest details and the magic users left behind were spotted on the horizon earlier."

Kiuno sighed. "Doesn't she ever get tired?"

IF KIUNO thought the last celebration was extraordinary it was nothing compared to this one. She'd bathed, finally washing the muck and grime from her hair before Elite guided her to their table.

Music, laughter, and dance echoed throughout the hall as friends and family celebrated their victory over another obstacle. Only a hundred more to go.

They hadn't found the portal, but everyone seemed sure it would be inside the forest. Better to look through the ashes she supposed than risk all their lives dodging behemoths and lizards.

Kiuno took a sip of the bitter liquid and leaned against the back of her chair. Elite sat to her right and Scorpios to her left. K.J. was across from them and had already drank his fair share of the booze. His ability to still form coherent sentences surprised her.

She smiled. Their other friends were expressing their drunken states by providing free entertainment. Silver, Blue, and Liam had taken control of the dance floor and become the laughingstock of the entire hall.

She clapped as another song ended, then Blue stumbled over to their table.

He knocked Elite's cup over, spilling the contents onto the floor, apologized, then reached for her arm. "You goin' to sit heres all night?" Mischief and playfulness danced in his gaze.

"Aren't there plenty of other pretty girls for you to dance with?"

He glanced around. "Why would I bother with anys of them when a queen sits before me?"

Kiuno laughed then glanced at Elite.

Elite held up his hands. "Don't look to me for help."

She feigned insult but allowed Blue to tug her to the floor. He twirled her once, then settled on a moderate tempo. It didn't take long for her to realize he needed more help standing than dancing, but his laughter became contagious and she indulged his merriment.

Kiuno didn't recognize the melodies, but the drums pulsed in her chest and the sound of woodwinds filled the hall in a rhythm she couldn't help but move to. Kiuno spun, passed from person to person to person.

She drank, sang, and before she knew what had happened became another part of Blue's and Silver's entertainment for the crowd.

Silver ran back to the table and pulled an intoxicated Elite to the floor. He stumbled once, but she caught him and the two let the music feed their souls.

The room smelled of beer, musky sweat, and forgotten dreams.

Kiuno sauntered back to their table and took another drink of the vile liquid Blue kept pouring down her throat.

Then she spotted Palindrome.

Palindrome sat a drink on a nearby table and smiled at the men seated there. The three of them looked at her as if she was the only woman in the room.

"She never stops working, does she?"

Sometime during the dancing, K.J.'s friend, Blade, had joined him and the two turned their heads to look at Palindrome.

"She claims it lets her bond with them," K.J. said over the roar of people.

"Seems they love her already."

He nodded. "She's worked hard to earn their trust."

The trio glanced at her again and watched a handsome young man stand. He delicately took Palindrome's hand and kissed her knuckles before twirling her toward the dance floor. Fire flashed through K.J.'s eyes.

"Here we go again," K.J.'s friend sighed. He pinched the bridge of his dark nose and she gave him a curious look.

"Occasionally they love her a little too much and well…" He tipped his cup toward K.J.

Kiuno's mouth gaped. "You mean after all this time K.J. hasn't staked his claim?"

K.J. spun to face forward and took a long drink from his cup. "It's not like we've had time."

She eyed him, but he kept his gaze on his mug. K.J.'s fingers gripped the handle so hard his knuckles turned white.

Kiuno tilted her head toward Palindrome and rested one hand on her cheek. "She sure looks lovely tonight."

K.J.'s face ticked.

Kiuno took another drink, sure it was the liquor making her so bold. "Too bad she's in the arms of another man."

K.J.'s eyes flashed. "Are you trying to make a point?"

"Just trying to figure out what you're afraid of."

He sat straighter.

A wicked smile spread across Kiuno's face. "Easier to get angry at those who would woo her than to declare your love publicly, huh?"

K.J. clicked his tongue, slammed his mug on the table, and slid his chair back. She took a drink and watched him march toward the dance floor.

K.J. pulled Palindrome from the young man and stood between

them. Tension filled the space for only a moment then the wooing stranger held his arms out in surrender.

Palindrome tilted her head at him and for several moments no one moved. Silence fell and the music paused as the entire hall seemed to hold its breath.

K.J. eased down to one knee and heat colored Palindrome's cheeks.

He held her hand and gave her a crooked smile. "I had planned to wait until we got home. Marry me?"

Kiuno clutched her hands together and Palindrome tilted her head with a shy smile.

"Took you long enough."

Cheers erupted, mugs hit the table, and new music blared around them as K.J. stood and Palindrome wrapped her arms around his neck. He dipped her into a deep, passionate kiss and the masses erupted again.

"How did you know that would work?" K.J.'s friend asked.

Kiuno smirked. "His drunken self just needed a little nudge."

UNION

REALM: 5

DAY: 257

Palindrome tilted her head to examine the dress hugging her body. Somehow, she made beautiful look fierce. "I heard you were the one who pushed him into this."

Kiuno folded her arms and failed to hide her smug expression. "I just gave him a gentle nudge."

"Nudge? You know he's a possessive man."

"I'm fully aware."

Palindrome adjusted her dress again and another woman—her name lost to Kiuno's memory—added a few more flowers to the top of Palindrome's braid.

"You think he'll cry?" Kiuno asked.

Palindrome scoffed. "He's not that sentimental."

An older woman with a raspy voice poked her head into the dressing room. "Everything's ready."

Palindrome took a breath.

"You ready for this?" Kiuno asked.

Her smile lit up the room. "Ready as I'll ever be."

KIUNO PADDED down the long aisle. Benches sat on either side of the walkway and lavender flowers lined everything from the archway at the front to the benches in the back. Many of the women even wore them in their hair to help celebrate the special occasion.

The entire castle had gathered upon hearing the news and Kiuno had never seen something so extravagant put together so fast. Food, flowers, the gown. It seemed like a fairy tale where a celestial being had waved their magic wand and commanded everything to be perfect.

Kiuno filed past row after row of people lined up to watch the procession. With the area filled to the brim, many stood on the outskirts and the sea of smiling faces made Kiuno's head swim.

In the third row Elite's smiling face greeted her and Kiuno's rising anxiety settled back to the pit of her stomach. She gripped his hand.

"Everything okay?" he asked.

"Everything's perfect."

A cool breeze swept through the area and ruffled Kiuno's long dress. The sleeves were cut at the elbow and her neckline squared with her shoulders, but the green material stunned her. She couldn't believe what people could create in this world.

A whistle sounded and the crowd turned to watch K.J. stride up the aisle with his friend, Blade, at his side. K.J.'s smile spread from ear to ear as Blade whispered something in his ear.

Her gaze swept across the people gathered. For once it was in celebration rather than mourning. Sure, they had their little parties, but this was something different. It wasn't just another excuse to dance and drink. This was a union. A memory that promised there was an after from this wretched world.

K.J. once told her he'd never marry. Life had convinced him he'd never find an adequate partner in life, but judging from the spark in his eyes, life had proved him wrong.

He stood with his hands clasped in front of him and for once he appeared well-rested. His trousers were neatly tucked into their boots and there wasn't a trace of dirt on his shirt.

A soft horn sounded across the crowd and everyone fell silent. All eyes turned toward the aisle. The back line stood and Kiuno took Elite's hand and did the same. They exchanged a smile and sweet memories flowed between them.

She recalled the nervousness and the butterflies in her stomach at her own wedding. But she'd had months to prepare. Palindrome had done it in days.

Palindrome walked down the aisle with Iggy at her side. She was all smiles, sweet and tender as whispers of awe followed her down the walkway. Palindrome's hair was braided back into a crown of lavender flowers with one tucked between each strand of waterfall curls.

The gown was elegant and flowing. It spoke of a strength within Palindrome's beauty and accentuated every positive quality of the people's beloved leader. Long sleeves hung loose at the elbow and pastel flowers wrapped around her bodice, tied at her waist, and trailed behind.

Soft music played all around them, but the performers were hidden from Kiuno's view.

Palindrome and her escort paused before K.J. and the clergyman— or whatever he was. The man ushered Palindrome forward then lowered his hands as a sign for the crowd to sit.

K.J. gave Palindrome his crooked smile and Palindrome sweetened hers. The pair stared into one another's eyes, the world and its troubles forgotten. They repeated vows, promising to uphold them no matter the trials to come.

The officiant produced a long red string from his pocket and placed K.J.'s hand over Palindrome's.

"The red thread carries a legend that speaks of two people fated to come together." He glanced between them.

"We're here, each of us, under impossible circumstances, yet the red thread of fate has shown through. The legend states when we're born, we're fated to a person and though the thread may tangle or stretch, it will never break regardless of place, time, or circumstances."

The older man lifted Palindrome's little finger and tied one end of the string to it. "Palindrome has been a friend to us all. She's faced impossible danger on our behalf, the latest threatening no chance of survival, yet here she stands, the fates bringing her back to the man her soul is bound to."

He wound the string around their wrists and hands before tying the other end to K.J.'s smallest finger.

"K.J. has led us through trials beyond imagination, always pushing us forward with the promise of a better future. I think I speak for everyone when I say the two of you were meant to spend your lives together."

He turned the couple toward the crowd. "You may kiss your bride."

Palindrome interlaced her fingers with K.J.'s and K.J. wrapped his other hand around the back of her neck and pulled her into a deep kiss. Kiuno clapped and cheered with the others then took Elite's hand and wrapped her fingers in his. They put tomorrow's worries aside and celebrated the union of two souls.

TRAITOR

REALM: 5

DAY: 257

A celebration. How utterly ridiculous. He stood at the back in the shadow of a building and folded his arms across his chest.

His eyes followed their smiling faces, the sea of people whispering of the perfect union. If it weren't for him, none of this would have even been possible.

He sighed. Yet here he was, left in the dark. Forgotten. Cast aside. Again. Perhaps he should have planned his disguise better, as it was, there wasn't much he could do yet. Unless he wanted to show all his cards at once.

But that would ruin the game.

And take away his fun far too soon.

He pushed up from the wall as the clapping ceased and marched back to the castle.

He needed to be patient.

Things were about to get interesting.

21

FELINIANS

REALM: 5

DAY: 270

Kiuno darted down the castle steps, sprinted through the gates, and all but threw herself into Reece's open arms. He twirled her around once and placed her feet back on the ground.

"I thought I told you not to be a stranger."

She shrugged, but her smile didn't disappear. "Well, you know, things come up."

He folded his arms. "Heard you got in a bit of trouble. Why wasn't I invited?"

"It wasn't anything Palindrome couldn't pull me out of. Besides, you're here now."

"You know, one of these days we won't be there to save you."

Her expression faltered.

"Forgetting something?" Elite called. He handed her the reins to her horse.

Elite and Reece clasped hands and Reece asked, "You excited to see the next realm?"

Elite scoffed. "Not excited for the long ride there."

Reece tilted his head toward her. "Not much for travel, is he?"

"I've always been the adventurous one."

Elite swung into his saddle. "If I let her take every wild adventure that ever crossed her mind I'd never sleep."

"Sleep is for the dead anyway," Reece said.

K.J. emerged from the castle and strolled down the stone steps. It'd been two weeks since the wedding and the two lovebirds had all but disappeared from the world.

Kiuno smiled. It was good for them. They needed time for themselves. She'd not wasted a minute of it and Kiuno felt her training with Maltack and Scorpios had finally made progress. Especially with Maltack. He'd all but mastered bending her magic to his will.

Kiuno mounted her horse and the rest of the men took their positions.

Palindrome had chosen to stay behind. She claimed there were neglected duties that called for her immediate attention. Kiuno's heart ached for the lovers' separation. She'd hate to do the same with Elite, but when one claimed a leadership position responsibility came first.

It wasn't the first time Kiuno silently thanked her lucky stars to not be a leader in this world.

A gentle breeze shifted through the plains and Kiuno tilted her head back to enjoy the open air.

Elite pulled his mare up beside hers. "Excited?"

She nodded. "I'm tired of being trapped behind these walls."

Reece fastened a bag to his saddle and swung up, adjusting the reins. "You're always welcome to join us Ki, no walls in sight."

"You'd like that wouldn't you?"

"Of course, I'd have someone to pawn Nsane's wife on."

"So that's why you're late," Kiuno giggled. "Did she pack you a lunch too?"

"Only the best."

Kiuno's horse pawed the ground and surged forward when the line moved. Nikita soared overhead, roaring into the breeze and Jim chased behind. The wind pulled at tendrils of Kiuno's hair, releasing them from her braid as freedom washed over her in an intoxicating rush.

Kiuno gave the horse a kick and they took off, leaving the others behind.

Freedom. How often did she let herself relish in the feel of it? Unbridled. Uncaged.

The animal eventually slowed and Kiuno allowed those at the front of the line to take their rightful place. She fell back with Elite and Reece and rode the rest of the day at their sides.

With evening, Kiuno helped light their fires then plopped on the ground beside K.J.

"So, where are we headed exactly?" she asked. Elite sat on her other side.

"Toward the mountain. It's a longer journey, but the scouts haven't found anything in the open so we're assuming the portal is hidden within the mountainside."

"Aren't the other alliances closer?" Elite asked.

K.J. smirked. "They are, but since I took it upon myself to burn the forest down, the leaders have given me *permission* to see things through."

She snorted. "Seems like you do everything."

"Only the stuff worthwhile."

The next four days passed without incident. Their group maintained a steady pace and the sun kept them company on their journey.

Upon seeing the mountain in the distance, Kiuno half expected the looming trees to have survived the flames, but their ominous shadows didn't greet them.

Instead, a blackened expanse of ash-covered land stretched as far as her eyes could see. Trees that once stood menacing and tall were nothing more than skeletal remnants of their former glory. They stood in patches as if defiant against the flame until the last trace of life had leached from their wooden veins.

The horses whined and pulled back from the charred landscape.

Eerie silence coated the air like a blanket as the horses took hesitant steps forward. There were no bugs in the air, no birds overhead, no lingering creatures to scurry beneath their feet. Everything was just... gone.

The scar on Kikyo's leg crossed her mind. He'd seen this before and now she understood his fear.

Even a single spark could spell disaster.

Their group proceeded forward covering mile after mile of nothing but gray death. Kiuno still felt burning it was the right decision, but it left an emptiness that tugged at her heart. It was hard to convince herself the animals weren't real when the horse she rode upon acted fearful and skittish. She ran a comforting hand along its neck.

Maybe they'd made a mistake.

Shouting ahead drew her attention, and she exchanged a nervous glance with Elite before kicking her horse into a trot.

A line of grass started where the ashes ended and trees, tall, yet young, guarded the area beyond.

The scene was strange. As if someone had intentionally saved the area from burning.

Silence hovered over the group.

Kiuno jumped from her horse and ash crunched beneath her feet. "What do you make of it?" she asked no one in particular.

K.J. dismounted, but before he could reply Nikita drew everyone's attention. She landed in a crouch and startled the horses. One bucked and a member of their party cursed as he hit the ground. Nikita paid them no attention.

The feline crept forward, her wings folded tight and ears flat against her head. Jim followed on foot, sticking close as he gripped his weapon.

When the young felinian ducked into the trees K.J. instructed Iggy to stay with the troops while Kiuno, Elite, Maltack, and Reece followed.

They paused when Nikita did, her ears twisting this way and that before flattening again as she dashed to another tree and smelled the ground.

Kiuno wondered if they were foolish to follow her into the unknown, but she wasn't about to let Jim go in on his own. She hoped it wasn't the lizard creatures that had Nikita's attention.

Kiuno stepped around a tree and a roar shattered the air. The wind left Kiuno's body as she hit the ground, pinned by a massive paw that made drawing breath difficult. Claws dug into her chest and Kiuno gazed into a pair of emerald eyes.

The creature's maw drew back in a snarl and displayed sharp pointed teeth and a mouth big enough to engulf her head.

Another roar followed as Nikita slammed her body into the larger felinian, allowing Kiuno to take in a breath as she rolled to a seated position.

Nikita paced before Kiuno and expanded her wings to make herself appear larger. Her fur stood on end and a growl ripped from her throat as she dared the beast to attack again.

It was a male, that much was clear from the mane and the set in his jaw. His wings fanned out on either side, one big enough to wrap around Nikita even with hers expanded. He was black as midnight and just as menacing.

Kiuno glanced to Maltack who stood motionless, much like the rest of them. Elite remained still, but his eyes flicked between her and the massive felinian who continued to growl.

"Easy Milo." A woman appeared from his shadow, placing a gentle hand on the felinian's side. It huffed in response, but otherwise remained still, his eyes locked on Nikita.

The woman ducked beneath his wing and smiled when her eyes landed on the smaller felinian. "Well, aren't you a little one?"

Nikita growled, her eyes darting between the woman and the bigger feline. Kiuno remained on her knees, one hand gripping her sword.

"You can relax, he won't attack while I'm here. Unless you're planning your own advance, but I caution against it."

Kiuno returned her sword to its sheath and the felinian's eyes followed her movements.

Nikita shrank back as the male took a few steps toward her. She looked like a kitten encountering a large dog for the first time. He sniffed her and Nikita answered with a fierce snarl. As if mocking her he snorted and circled the woman, his wings tucked close.

"I'll assume you're the ones who tried to burn down our home?"

"You live here?" Kiuno asked.

"Isn't that obvious?" She examined them. "I've lived with these creatures for a while. It was difficult to save this patch of trees and I'll warn you. If you've come to claim it, we'll see you as an enemy."

"We're not here to take your land," K.J. said, stepping forward. "We're simply looking for the portal to the next realm."

The woman laughed. "Why would you want to find that?"

"So we can progress toward the tenth."

Seriousness swept over her features. "I see." She jumped on the back of the large felinian and gestured for them to follow. "I warn you, if you cause any harm to the animals, the pride won't hesitate to kill you."

K.J. nodded. "Understood."

She glanced at them then clicked her tongue and the felinian strode through the trees. They followed and the smell of the blackened forest faded as life took its place.

"What's your name?" Kiuno asked.

The woman cast her a backward glance, her body bobbing with each stride of the felinian she rode upon. "Are names all that important?"

Surprised, Kiuno said, "I suppose not." She glanced at Reece who shrugged, and they continued. Nikita stayed close to Jim, letting out little huffs as she glanced between the thinning branches.

Trees opened to an expanse that caused all to pause.

Wings filled the sky as felinians of all sizes and color hopped between the mountainside plateaus and through the trees that dotted the clearing. Others lounged in the shade, their eyes either closed or watching the younger few wrestle amongst themselves.

The woman smirked at their reaction and continued forward. The youngest couldn't have weighed over ten pounds and the largest were bigger than the fearsome creature their strange escort rode upon.

People walked among them without fear and small houses had been built from the natural structures in the area.

Short ladders led to tree houses, cabins hugged the mountainside, and some even seemed to rest in the crevices between the rocks.

Nikita appeared more curious than fearful as they continued to follow. Some animals lifted their heads and their human counterparts waved. Jim stayed close to Nikita, like a father protecting his child.

Curiosity got the better of Nikita and she crawled toward a group of young felinians. Kiuno looked to the woman who halted their procession, but she only watched with a fond smile.

The little ones froze as they caught Nikita's scent and huddled around one another. One cub, who appeared larger than the rest, took the initiative. They touched noses and it raised a paw to bat at her, but Nikita took a step back and growled.

Before Kiuno could blink a full-grown felinian female flipped Nikita on her back and bared her fangs, Nikita yelped, and Jim drew his weapon and charged.

To Kiuno's surprise the female took a step back, freeing an unharmed Nikita to run behind Jim with her tail tucked between her legs.

"Your friend is brave."

Kiuno's heart pounded as the female took a few steps toward Jim. He lowered his weapon.

"Shouldn't we do something?" Kiuno asked as she watched in helpless anticipation.

"They function as one. If you interfere, the whole pride will turn against you and there'd be nothing I could do."

They remained still as the creature sniffed Jim's hair, examined him, and took a step back. She licked her cub and turned toward the pool of water. The little ones followed.

Jim knelt next to Nikita and she nuzzled him, eyeing the retreating creature and her cubs.

"She acts like she's never seen her own kind," the woman said.

"She hasn't," Jim replied. "At least not since she was younger than that cub. I freed her from a trap, and she's been with me ever since."

The woman's eyes softened. "Her mother was killed then. They're a fiercely protective species and would die before abandoning their young."

The woman turned away from the felinians and once again they followed. Several larger creatures sat on the outskirts of the village and raised their heads as the group passed.

Behind a thick row of trees and beneath heavy brush cold air rushed to meet them from a hidden cavern. Kiuno's hair stood on end.

The woman jumped from her felinian and gestured them inside.

Dim lighting made it difficult to see and Kiuno's foot caught on a rock. Elite's arm gripped her bicep to keep her steady and they continued down the short passage.

Before them stood the swirling vortex, the black center darker than the shadow of the cavern tunnel. The woman walked straight through, disappearing before their eyes. To Kiuno's dismay they followed.

The world spun in a sea of colors and she almost fell upon reaching the other side, but Elite gripped her arm again. His eyes asked if she was all right and she nodded, thankful he didn't draw attention to her issue.

Thick, damp air assaulted her senses and the heat beat down on them as they overlooked a sea of green. Mist hovered between a tall canopy of trees that stood level with the plateau.

Kiuno walked forward but stopped before she reached the edge. The ground stretched far beneath and she'd had enough of cliffs to last a lifetime. Reece tottered on a ledge and whistled. A tremor ran through her body.

Each realm until this point had seemed manageable. They could survive, or at the very least make them livable, but this... this was an endless jungle. The humidity alone threatened to drown her.

Dread washed over Kiuno. Even if they got the civilians through, how would they reach the jungle floor and establish a foothold?

"Magnificent isn't it?" the woman whispered, her gaze seeming to swell with pride. "You won't be able to burn this down."

"I'd expect not." K.J.'s brow furrowed as his gaze swept across the endless green. She wondered how he found his voice and imagined all her worries were going through his head as well.

"Come, let us head back before something catches your scent and decides you'll make a nice lunch."

Kiuno hoped the woman was teasing. It was difficult to tell with her stoic expression.

Kiuno took a deep breath and walked through the portal again, clutching Elite's arm on the other side as she gagged. The woman seemed amused but didn't comment as they waited outside the cavern for her stomach to settle.

"I don't advise lingering, the felinians grow uneasy with strangers. Did you get what you came for?"

"We did, thank you," K.J. said.

She escorted them back through the village and this time Nikita didn't veer from Jim's side.

"Is there a peaceful arrangement we can make that will allow us to bring men through?" K.J. asked.

The woman smiled. "Of course. For the sake of the felinians I think it'll be best if you take the longer path around these trees. They're not territorial of the plateau so you're free to set up there, but they use that realm for hunting, so you'll have to deal with them passing through."

"Their presence won't be a problem. I apologize for the inconvenience we have caused. I didn't realize anyone lived in the forest."

Her face scrunched. "And the animals?"

He paused. "I assumed the creatures were nothing more than pieces of this world. Nothing real."

She set one hand on Milo. "Not real? So, if he killed you that wouldn't be real enough?"

K.J. examined the creature who ruffled his wings. "I suppose it would be. I apologize if I've overstepped."

She huffed. "It's fine, we didn't suffer any loss, but if you plan to bring your people through, I'd like to accompany you and be included in the planning process."

He nodded. "We'll welcome any information about the coming realm."

"You'll need it." She climbed on the felinian's back. He beat his massive wings and sent a wave of dust toward them before taking a running leap into flight.

Kiuno heard the horses yell through the trees and several men cursed. Nikita took off next and pumped her wings to catch up and soar beneath the larger version of herself.

Kiuno took the reins of her horse and watched their graceful flight, but Jim's sad gaze shook her to the core.

"She'd be better off with them."

"She's just curious." Kiuno tried to give him a smile, but Jim's focus never left Nikita. Kiuno had never thought about leaving her friends behind until that moment. When they reached the tenth realm, how many would choose to stay?

RAIN DANCE

REALM: 5

DAY: 279

With the castle walls looming on the horizon K.J. pulled his horse back to ride beside Kiuno. His gaze shifted to the velvet black wings soaring high overhead and the woman who rode upon them.

She'd never given her name and she'd barely spent enough time in their company for Kiuno to make any assumptions.

"What's on your mind?" Kiuno asked.

"How we'll convince her to be an ally. She's only here to ensure the safety of her people."

Kiuno thought the woman probably cared more for the felinians, but she didn't voice her opinion.

The velvet wings dipped toward the ground and swooped back into the air as Milo sped toward the castle walls. He roared in the open sky and Nikita took off after him, leaving Jim behind. Her friend's expression shifted to sadness again.

Kiuno chewed her lip as the black felinian pulled ahead. "The guards won't attack, will they?"

"For our sakes, let's hope not."

They spurred the horses forward eager to catch up before chaos could erupt on the wall.

Milo circled the area a few times before landing by the front gate. The woman sat beside him, leaning her head back with her eyes closed. K.J.'s guards gave him a nervous, yet relieved glance when they caught up.

"It's bigger than I expected." She stood and sauntered toward K.J.

"I'll be sure to find comfortable quarters for you and him." K.J. inclined his head toward Milo.

The woman made a face, reminding Kiuno of a child who'd tasted sour candy. "These walls remind me of a cage."

"Jim," K.J. pointed, "occupies one of the towers. I can ensure the same accommodations if you like."

"Or you could join me." Reece gave her a lazy, seductive smile.

She tilted her head, intrigued yet cautious. "Where exactly?"

"The walls are too cramped for my taste. I have a camp on the outskirts."

"And you're the leader there?"

Reece nodded. "We collaborate with K.J.'s alliance and Kiuno here is a good friend of mine."

The woman ran her gaze up and down Kiuno's form as if studying her, then shifted her gaze to K.J. "I think Milo would like that better. He doesn't do well in small spaces and neither do I." She tilted her head with a mocking smile. "Plus, your guards appear nervous."

"Can you blame them?" Kiuno asked.

The woman glanced at her again, but it wasn't with hostility.

K.J.'s mouth formed a hard line. "If that suits you better."

Kiuno looked between K.J. and Reece. She knew K.J. wanted this woman as an ally and with the felinians she couldn't blame him. But Reece's interest seemed to be centered upon less tactical means.

She needed to intervene.

"Mind if I tag along?" Kiuno asked.

Reece gave K.J. a knowing smirk as he said, "You know you're always welcome."

Reece saw this as a victory, but once his back turned, she locked eyes with K.J. and nodded. She'd get the job done.

K.J. pulled off his gloves and headed through the gatehouse with the others close behind. Jim followed with Nikita on his heels.

Reece swung back into his saddle and gestured for them to follow.

As they rode Kiuno glanced at Elite, but he kept his eyes forward. He hadn't protested, which meant he probably knew what they needed to do.

Only twenty minutes of grassy plains separated Reece and K.J.

Tents stood at various locations and dozens of people surrounded meat roasting over an open flame. Kiuno's mouth watered at the smell that wafted through the air.

Kiuno dropped from her horse and let the animal graze freely.

Her eyes drifted over the clothes lines, the jars of water, and canopies decorated with feathers and shells of all sorts. Their tents were staked into the ground and the grass had worn in notable paths.

"Looks like you've created a permanent residence," Kiuno said.

"Marci suggested it."

At the mention of her name, Marci, Nsane's wife, stood and greeted each with a swift kiss on the cheek. Her plump form didn't fool Kiuno. She knew this woman all but ran the place.

Most stared at Milo with wide eyes, but none recoiled like the guards at the castle had done. If anything, they waited for permission to approach the beautiful creature striding toward their camp.

Marci smiled at their newest member. "Who is this fine young lady?"

The woman covered her mouth and giggled. "I suppose my name is in order. Call me Cybele."

"Like the goddess?" Reece asked.

"Indeed, and don't forget it."

At the touch of Cybele's hand, Milo expanded his massive wings and leapt into the air. He soared overhead for a moment before taking off toward the tree line further south. Nikita often left to hunt so Kiuno assumed Milo was doing the same.

A chilling breeze shifted through the grass and Kiuno glanced up to find dark clouds heading their way.

"Looks like summer rain," Marci said. "Come, dinner is ready." Marci wrapped her arm around Reece's shoulder and whispered something in his ear. She was far shorter and watching Reece bend to Marci's level made Kiuno giggle.

Elite still remained silent.

They sat on logs around the fire and Marci handed them each a bowl full of meat and soup. The wind picked up around the area and tents flapped in the breeze as Reece's people ran to tie down anything that might come loose.

Elite laced his fingers through Kiuno's hand and whispered, "I assume we're here for Cybele?"

"I just need to get a sense for who she is, then we can head back."

"It's probably best if we stay the night. She seems rather guarded."

Kiuno glanced up at the woman when her laugh echoed. Marci sat beside her and fired question after question about the felinians and where she'd come from. But Elite was right. Her answers were precise. Rehearsed.

Another gust of wind blew through the area and thunder cracked overhead. Most swiveled to glance at the clouds and a large drop landed on Kiuno's arm. Another fell in the grass at her feet then more than a dozen followed as the clouds opened to a torrential downpour.

Everyone scattered.

Kiuno grabbed Elite's hand and ran beneath the nearest canopy where Reece, Marci, and Nsane joined them. Water dripped from Kiuno's hair and she wiped the drops from her arms. After a moment they all erupted in a fit of laughter.

Marci threw the towel she'd started wiping down with. "Hiding from a little rain, what have we come to?"

Marci walked into the downpour and threw her head back to relish in the rain. She tilted her head and gave Nsane an inviting smile.

Nsane grinned and joined her. Taking his wife's hand, the two began moving to a rhythm none could hear.

A drum beat in one corner, followed by another across the way. The water fell from their canopy as everyone watched the two lovers circle one another in a premeditated dance.

Two more couples joined, drenching themselves as they followed the steps then shifted partners.

In minutes it seemed the entire camp had jumped in and drums beat from various locations. The people moved in a captivating dance Kiuno had never seen before.

Kiuno tapped her foot and turned to Elite. She tilted her head toward the dancers, but he simply grinned and shook his. She turned back, watching the strangers stamp and twirl then grabbed Reece's hand and pulled him into the rain before he could protest.

They were drenched in seconds. The sound of water added its own rhythm and her heart beat with the drums as she continued to study those in motion and search for the pattern.

Reece took her hands and pointed at their feet. She followed his movements, tripping into him more than once before she found the tempo and stepped in time with the others.

They danced, lost in the rain and drums that radiated freedom and paradise. Reece spun her around and stomped the soaked grass beneath their feet. She spun again. Reece released her hands, and another took his place. Kiuno floated between Nsane, Marci, and Cybele before returning to Reece with more confidence.

Elite caved and joined the fun, twisting her around in steps unknown. She laughed as they fell around the circle of people and the rush flooded her core.

When the rain slowed, Kiuno collapsed on a log and wrung her hair out before removing her shoes and setting them by the fire. Elite sat beside her and she leaned into him, the two soaked from head to toe.

They talked and laughed, telling stories from home until the stars took their seats in the sky.

Though she'd seemed distant at first, Cybele didn't hesitate to join in, telling her own tales and giving Kiuno insight to her character. She wasn't going to be as hard to win over as K.J. had thought.

When conversations dwindled Cybele stood. "I think I'll turn in for the night."

"We have a few tents set up for guests. I can show you if you'd like," Marci offered.

Cybele glanced over the area and pointed to one not far off. "I'll take that one."

Nsane glanced at Reece and back to Cybele. "That's where Reece sleeps."

Cybele ran her gaze up and down his form then cracked a teasing smile. "He's welcome to join me."

Kiuno struggled to swallow her drink and Cybele sauntered off.

Reece stood and stretched. "Can't keep a lady waiting,"

Nsane kicked at him as he strode past and Kiuno watched his silhouette disappear behind the tent flap.

After giving Reece a hard time in his absence, Nsane offered Elite and Kiuno a tent of their own. She gladly accepted.

Kiuno closed their flap, undressed, and fell into the furs that lined the cot. Elite did the same, wrapping warm arms around her waist as she nestled into him. Though happiness had filled their afternoon, night reminded her of the horrors they were about to face.

A jungle. How were they going to get through one of the most dangerous places in the world?

REMINISCENT

REALM: 5

DAY: 280

Sharp hissing woke Kiuno from a pleasant dream. She tried to ignore it, hoping someone had accidentally stubbed their toe, but when it sounded again, she rolled over.

A silhouetted person stood at the entrance of their tent with one hand wrapped around the flap. The individual motioned for her to come outside. She looked at Elite's sleeping form, dressed, then poked her head out.

"Up for a morning hunt?" Reece whispered.

Kiuno rubbed the sleep from her eyes and glanced toward the barely risen sun. She turned to look at Elite who lay undisturbed in a bundle of furs.

"Nsane will let him know where you are."

Kiuno chewed her lip. "I don't have my bow."

"We have plenty."

Kiuno hesitated then ducked inside to grab her shoes before following Reece into the brisk morning air. She tucked a knife by her ankle and another in her belt.

"I should warn you, I'm a bit rusty," she said.

"We'll give you a few practice shots first."

He entered an unoccupied tent and retrieved two bows and quivers. Kiuno followed Reece toward the outskirts of the woods and he positioned her in a patch of worn grass.

She sat the quiver on the ground, withdrew an arrow, and notched it.

Familiar muscles pulled taunt as she drew back and took aim. She tried to remember her lessons and released her breath with the arrow.

The point skimmed the target.

"You won't hit anything aiming like that."

Kiuno pouted. "I told you I'm rusty."

He smirked and pulled an arrow from his quiver before setting it on the ground. Kiuno notched it on her string and Reece shifted her arms and feet as she readied herself to fire again.

Memories of her first weeks with Kikyo tried to resurface, but Reece was different. He didn't flinch away when their skin touched, and he crept closer than she felt necessary. His hot breath sent shivers down her spine.

Kiuno swallowed and focused on the target ahead. *He's just trying to help.*

She pulled the arrow back and Reece raised her elbow slightly before she released. Kiuno smiled. It was off center, but still closer to the mark.

"Not bad at all."

She stepped away when Reece didn't, but the action didn't seem to offend him. He grabbed his bow and started toward two horses she'd noticed earlier. Kiuno had assumed they were for someone else.

"Is it just us?" she asked.

"Is that a problem?"

Kiuno swung up and settled in. "We were attacked last time I was here. Twice."

"And we dealt with it. I go hunting alone all the time." Reece gave her a crooked smile. "Besides, who could stand up to the two of us?"

"I'm sure Marci loves that."

He lowered his voice. "I hide from her most of the time."

Kiuno laughed and the two kicked their horses, racing from the open meadow toward the tree line in the distance. The fresh air whipped her hair back and once again Kiuno found her thoughts floating toward the word freedom.

After staking the horses' leads, Reece indicated for her to keep quiet and Kiuno followed his silent steps through the woods.

After some distance he pointed to a tree and the tiny wooden platform at the top. She questioned whether it'd hold them both.

Reece knelt and helped her to the first branch. Normally, she'd be more concerned about falling, but with Reece there the idea was laughable at best. If he could save her from a cliff, he could save her from anything.

The two crowded in and waited.

Everything was quiet, like the woods held its breath in their presence. She stilled with it, then life slowly crawled from its hiding place.

Birds called overhead. One at first, then another and another until there were more than she could count. Small animals she couldn't spot scurried through the brush below, all oblivious to the two settled amidst the trees.

Reece's eyes shifted from one place to another and Kiuno did her best to be still as they waited.

A rustling to their right drew her attention. Reece moved his eyes but kept his head still as a small doe crept through. Her ears shifted, senses alert.

Kiuno held an arrow in one hand, only moving when the deer looked away. It sniffed the air and circled a tree, giving Kiuno time to position her bow. Inch by inch, the doe stepped closer until she bent her head to nibble at a weed.

Kiuno lifted her arrow and paused again as the deer looked up to examine its surroundings. It chewed, ears pivoting before going back for more. Reece settled behind her, shifting the arrow as she took aim, pulled back, and let it fly.

The arrow struck on point and the deer jumped once before falling.

"Nice shot."

Reece slid down the ladder and she followed. His hands brushed her sides as she jumped the remaining foot.

"Couldn't have done it without you."

He knelt and took out a knife. At one time she might have vomited from the gutting of such a large animal, but this time she watched as Reece did the work.

Once finished, he tied a rope around the rear feet. "Ready to go?"

She nodded.

Kiuno offered to help several times as Reece dragged the creature through the woods, but he laughed, claiming he could more than handle it.

The camp was alive when they returned and Kiuno wondered how long they'd waited in the tree. She worried for Elite but found him laughing at Nsane's side.

"I see you got something good today," Marci said.

Reece handed the animal off to another who drug it across the settlement and beyond her sight. "Actually, Kiuno got this one for us."

Upon hearing their voices Elite turned. He glanced at the deer, then back to her. "Have fun?"

"Always."

Elite pressed a kiss to her brow, then wrapped one arm around her shoulders and led her to a log where they were all seated.

Kiuno leaned her head against Elite's arm and observed the smiling faces. They were family. They had a life here and judging from their conversations it didn't appear they ever planned to leave.

Maybe she could make a life here too. If she were forced. It was a rewarding existence. One where everything you did made a difference to the small community you supported.

K.J.'s group didn't make her feel that way. And home didn't even come close.

"We should head back," Kiuno said.

"Damn, and here I was hoping you'd stay," Reece said. "Visit more often and we'll keep up on your shooting skills."

Kiuno stood. "Blue would tell you I need it."

Kiuno bid them farewell then proceeded toward the castle with Elite's hand clasped in hers. As they walked through the knee-high grass Kiuno thought back to the first time she'd passed over this plain.

She hadn't been sure what to expect back then, but it certainly hadn't been to find K.J. and her husband within a few days.

Cybele would stay with Reece for a while. The woman was curious about them though she seemed as wild as the creatures she lived among.

When they walked through the gate, Kiuno headed straight for K.J.'s office and for once Elite didn't protest. They were both tired, but there were things to be done.

Kiuno opened the double doors after a brief knock and K.J. and a few others turned to her, their previous conversation put on hold.

K.J. rose from his chair. "Didn't expect to see you back so soon."

"I can't goof off forever."

He nodded toward those at the table and they picked up their be-longings and left the room. When the last one closed the door, K.J. took his seat again.

"Discover anything interesting?"

"The woman's name is Cybele. She's about as wild as the felinians, but she's friendlier than she put on."

"Sounds like you made friends."

"Reece did."

K.J.'s brows rose. "Better she went with him then, though you'll be seeing her shortly."

"Why, what's wrong?"

"A meeting has been requested."

"By the alliances?"

K.J. shook his head. "By those who live beyond the forest."

"I didn't think anyone could access the other side," Kiuno said.

"Cybele's group lives within it."

"Good point."

Elite pulled a seat out and sat down. "Does Cybele know about them?"

"I'm not sure. But we might have a problem on our hands if they discover we had anything to do with the fire. Especially if they suffered from it."

"That could mean another enemy," Elite said.

K.J. folded his hands. "We know whoever is there isn't from the alliances. We could be dealing with the creator."

"You think they had something to do with the attack on Silver and Elite?"

K.J. shrugged. "It's possible. It's also possible that the whole thing is a trap which is why I'll be taking our best to ensure everything goes as planned. We'll ask Cybele what she knows. If the two aren't allies, then I imagine she'll want to bring her people up to speed."

TRAITOR

Realm: 5
Day: 275

Lillian handed him a glass of wine then adjusted her gown before sitting across from him in an armchair as fine as the dress she wore. The elegant way the fabric folded around her legs might have been alluring to others, but he wasn't so easily tempted.

Lillian swirled her drink and took a sip. The liquid stained her lips red and he briefly thought of all the blood she'd spilled on this land. She was perfect for his plans.

"Spill it." She crossed her legs and sat back in the cushions. "What do you want?"

A wicked grin spread across his angular face. "My dear, do I have to want something to visit you?"

She huffed. "I don't pretend to seduce you and you don't pretend I'm not part of an elaborate scheme remember?"

His smile widened. "It's time."

Her eyes flashed and she set her glass on the table. "Already? Are you sure?"

"I'm sure and the timing is perfect. With the forest gone, there's nothing to stand in your way."

Lillian sat back again. "What becomes of our relationship," she emphasized the word, "once I've done as you asked?"

"You'll be free to run this world as you please."

"Freedom," Lillian seemed to taste the word before she met his gaze. "Is that something you can promise?"

He gestured with one hand to encompass the extravagant room. "Is all this not up to your standards?"

She tapped her fingers on the glass. "It is, but you don't strike me as someone who leaves loose ends untucked."

He took a sip of wine. "My dear if you pull this off, you'll have this entire world to rule and nothing would make me happier."

"Why go through the trouble at all? What's so important about my conquering it if you could just make your hearts' desire come to be with a flick of your wrist?"

He smirked. "That would ruin the game."

Lillian sighed, but a smile played on her face. "You and your games." She stood, crossed the room, and picked up a pen from her desk. "What would you like me to do?"

His heart sped and he gave her a devious smile. "Only what you do best."

HE STEPPED onto the balcony and the cool night breeze hit his bare chest. The serene night was as elegant as the room he shared with his little pawn. Soon the grounds would be stained red and charred beyond recognition.

Lillian thought she had him in the palm of her hand. She thought she'd finally seduced him with her charisma and wicked ways.

He smirked. Quite the opposite. She was nothing more than a toy he enjoyed winding up. She'd learn the truth soon though she'd never get the chance for answers.

His attention drifted to wild lightning and consuming fire.

Magic would spread over the hills and that woman's heart would darken beyond recognition. Those who claimed to love her might turn away at the sight of such darkness. But he'd bathe in that abyss and push it beyond the point of return.

LAND OF DEATH

REALM: 5

DAY: 291

K iuno coughed and wiped her soot covered hands across her brow. It didn't matter anymore. Everything they touched turned black from the ash-covered land. Breathing. Eating. Sleeping. They did nothing without the Land of Death's involvement.

"Ominous name you've given it," Elite remarked.

"What else would you call it?"

"A new beginning." He knelt and Kiuno crept forward in the dim lighting. "Look." He pushed away a pile of ash to reveal a tiny sprout. "These will grow into more trees and soon the forest will be back to the way it was."

"Let's hope not," K.J. said.

Kiuno crossed her arms. "I'm with him. There weren't exactly friendly things living there."

Elite stood. "No, but those things were placed by the creator. What comes next could be very different."

Kiuno tried to wipe her fingers on her pants, but the black only smeared. "I'll stick to hoping we're out of here before then."

They all turned when Cybele took to the sky on Milo. The burst of his massive wings against the ground sent another wave of ash twirling through the air and Kiuno shielded her face.

"Where's she going?"

K.J. stacked another log on the fire. "We're only a day out from her place and the felinian is growing restless. I told her to go on ahead."

Kiuno envied Cybele's escape, but Elite pulled her around and planted a firm kiss on her lips.

She giggled. "What was that for?"

"To cheer you up. We'll be out of here soon."

She sighed and lay back on the ash-covered ground. None bothered with a blanket anymore. They were covered in soot anyway.

Morning brought on a new level of cheer as the trees surrounding Cybele's home entered their view. The horses trotted toward the green and Kiuno even felt herself moving quicker to escape the void they'd been crossing.

As soon as Kiuno brushed against a tree she tugged at her shoes and relished the feel of sticks and moss beneath her feet. The air smelled fresher beneath the canopy and lifted her spirit as they progressed forward.

When the first felinian roared, chaos erupted.

The horses reared and screamed. One kicked, cracking a hitch and those in charge raced to calm the frantic creatures. One animal bucked his rider and the man's foot lodged in the saddle while it fled for its life.

Cybele, along with several of her human companions, put a stop to the scene and calmed the felinians attempting to protect their home.

With the horses put away and the wagon hidden in thick brush, they entered the clearing they'd visited before.

Once again, Kiuno marveled at the creatures, but her wonderment faded as a growing sense of dread settled in the pit of her stomach.

Kiuno startled when Elite grabbed her hand. "Come on, they said we could clean up over here."

Kiuno glanced at the grayish creature nestled in a tree, then followed Elite.

They walked past several creatures who kept a close eye on their movements. Most moved away if they walked too close and others snapped their jaw in warning. She wondered if they should be heading so far away from the people who cared for them.

Elite led Kiuno around a small pond that rested against the mountainside. The horses had gathered here, but their ears still pivoted, and nostrils flared at every noise. They wouldn't be moving anytime soon.

Elite pulled her around an outcropping of trees, but she paused when he made to enter a crevice in the mountainside.

"Where are we going?"

"Don't trust me?"

A smile crawled to her face. "Of course, I trust you."

He ducked inside the narrow cavern and Kiuno crawled in behind. She crouched to keep from hitting her head on the rock above.

"Are you sure you know where you're going?"

Elite jumped from the cramped tunnel, then turned to help her down. "Yep."

Kiuno jumped into his arms and she gasped at the scene spread out before them.

Water fell from a ten-foot ceiling and several pools lined the inside of the cave. She took a step forward, her bare feet hitting the cool, damp stone in disbelieving steps.

"How did you find this?"

"I asked Cybele if there was a more secluded area and she told me about this."

"Why?"

Elite's fingers untucked her shirt and he pulled it over Kiuno's head. Ash fell to the ground around them, but he didn't appear to notice. Elite's hands wrapped around her waist and he pressed his body closer to hers.

"Because you've looked stressed." He kissed the side of her neck and his hand traced the curve of her spine. His gaze met hers and she playfully shoved him away.

"If you think you're doing anything while we're filthy, you're crazy."

He gave her a devilish grin. "You won't stop me."

She took a step forward. "You're right, but I will do this."

Kiuno shoved him then jumped into the freezing water. Ash and dirt curled along the water's shimmering surface then disappeared along with her worries of anyone catching them.

CLEAN, REFRESHED, and far more relaxed than she'd been the previous evening, Kiuno settled herself into the saddle and gave Elite a sheepish smile.

They exited on the far side of the trees to avoid the felinians and the chaos of calming the horses again. They still snorted in protest, but none reared back until their hooves hit the soot. It returned to every crevice of her skin like a plague.

Once again, they walked across the barren area full of burnt trees and dead life. Maybe Reece should speed things up a bit. She glanced back at him and to her surprise found him staring.

"What?"

"You're awfully cheerful this morning."

"Maybe I had a good night."

Reece's gaze drifted to Elite. "I bet you did."

He glanced back to her and something in his eyes made her think of jealousy, but he smiled and pulled ahead.

The landscape shifted with the afternoon and their horses pulled into a steady trot that none could stop. The men struggling to control the wagons cursed more than once as they crossed the bumpy terrain at an uncomfortable speed.

Grass and uncharred earth. She'd have run toward it too if not for the sharp drop on the far side of the mountain.

Kiuno cringed. Reece dismounted and she followed him toward the edge.

"Looks like a river flows under the mountain."

Cool wind swept up from the depths and she fought against another shiver that snaked down her spine. "Why do there have to be cliffs everywhere we go?"

He glanced back with a smirk on his face. "No need to worry. I'll catch you again."

Kiuno's stomach crawled to her throat as he walked along the edge.

"We should keep moving," K.J. said. "We're close and it's too early to camp."

Kiuno nodded and helped K.J. spread the news. Several horses seemed to protest their continued travel, so the lot of their group contented themselves to move forward on foot.

Her legs and back were sore, but when Elite wrapped his hand in hers, Kiuno couldn't bring herself to wish for different circumstances. He completed her world and it felt as though a light shined deep in her soul with his presence.

Faint smoke rose into the sky and soon after they spotted the small fire on the open plains.

The strangers didn't hide, but their proximity to the cliffside still made Kiuno uneasy. Kiuno released Elite's hand and their squad fell into formation without command. She walked at the front with Maltack and Reece at her sides. K.J. walked directly behind her while Elite and the others covered the rear and sides.

Only three men stood upon their approach. Three. Could one of them be the creator? No, he wouldn't meet them in a place like this. But they had to be magic users if they were willing to come out here alone. And powerful ones at that.

Adrenaline coursed through her veins, but Kiuno kept her outward composure. She didn't need to give them any reason to attack or suspect her as anything more than a bodyguard.

As they neared, the men wrapped their hands around the hilts of their swords and Kiuno paused. Neither spoke for a long time as one group studied the other.

Of the three men, the center one drew Kiuno's attention the most. He was muscular, tan, and carried himself well. If she didn't know better, she might think him the leader of those beyond the forest.

The other two glanced at him and from their straggly appearance it was clear they relied entirely too much upon their magic. Elliott would have enjoyed whipping them into shape.

"We're here as you requested," K.J. said.

The burly man took a step forward. "Are you the leader of those on the other side?"

Might as well be.

K.J. didn't move. "I am."

The man knotted his brows and glanced at their procession. "Our king requests a meeting, but it seems you've come too armed."

"With the forest gone we didn't know what to expect, I'm sure you can appreciate the caution."

He lifted his lip in what looked to be a snarl. "Are you responsible for the forest?"

Silence.

"It was necessary."

"It was stupid. The forest provided food to our people and could have done the same for yours."

Kiuno bit her lip, but K.J. kept his composure. "My apologies, I didn't realize people lived beyond the borders."

The man clicked his tongue. "You can ask for forgiveness after you swear allegiance to our king."

Kiuno glanced back at K.J., then K.J. took a step forward. "I'm sorry. I must have misunderstood."

"We have a way of doing things and our king won't be disobeyed. As a token of good faith, we were told to pass along a gift."

He raised a muscled arm to the sky and a heavy silence fell around them.

Kiuno shifted her feet and pulled the flames to her fingertips. Her skin warmed, the magic buzzing with life as they waited for something to happen. Was someone coming?

Kiuno opened her mouth to speak and a deafening explosion from behind shoved her to her knees. Kiuno clamped her hands over her ears and fought to take a breath as the blast reverberated through her chest.

Rocks and pebbles hit the ground and rolled toward her as dust and particles blocked her field of vision.

Kiuno staggered to her feet and drew her sword. She kept her other hand in front of her and wrapped her body in flames in case of an attack.

She coughed, choking and blinded. Kiuno called Maltack's name, but her voice sounded muffled to her ears.

Maltack shifted the wind and took the dust with it. The area cleared, but her breath caught in her throat at the sight of the crumbling cliff.

A jagged scar had formed where chunks of rock were missing. It continued to crumble, but Kiuno staggered toward it.

Dizziness threatened to topple her over, but a muffled cry drew her attention. Someone was screaming.

She didn't know his name, but he was one of their own. His mouth opened time and time again as he clutched the upper part of his thigh. The lower half of the limb sat in shreds with blood dripping from the end of a dismembered foot.

Kiuno froze and Maltack dropped to the man's side.

She looked across from him to another body. It sat too still for her racing heart to process.

Elite. Where is he?

Another piece of rock crumbled from the edge as she continued stumbling through the chaos. One man wrapped his arm beneath his injured companion and carried him from the edge. Both were covered in dirt, but they were in one piece.

She spun and counted.

Then counted again.

Two were missing.

Kiuno tripped and reality slammed down as her knees hit the shattered rock. Cool mist wafted her in the face as she stared over the edge. She gripped her hair and curled in on herself.

This isn't real. I'm dreaming. Wake up. Wake up.

"There are consequences to disobeying our king," the burly man's voice echoed. "We hope you realize that now. We are favored by the creator and this will be your only warning. Unless you want those behind your walls to suffer, I suggest you comply. I'm certain we can work past the loss of a few men."

A few men?

Kiuno's breath caught in her throat.

A few men?

"We've also received information that indicates the lightning user is among you. Our king would like an audience with this person."

Silence echoed on both sides. Kiuno's heart thundered in her chest and she opened her eyes to stare into the abyss once again. Mist swirled and stretched, reaching its fingers toward her shaking body.

"Well, what's your answer?"

She didn't have the energy, but her body moved anyway and before Kiuno knew it she was on her feet and facing those who'd committed this horrendous act. Maltack focused on the injured and K.J.'s jaw worked.

But the enemy.

They smiled.

Smiled as if they were victorious.

Adrenaline hit her like a raging wave over a rocky beach. Her body didn't want to respond, but it shuddered when she took a breath and she stepped forward.

The scrawny companion cocked his head. *That smile.* "Your magic won't do you any good here."

She took another step, but her friends remained still. K.J. glanced back at her and stepped to the side. His eyes.

No, don't look at me like that.

She didn't want to accept it. She couldn't. She'd wake up soon and this would all be over. Elite would reassure her, and they'd head down to breakfast and—

"Stop there."

No.

She wouldn't.

Flames licked down her arms and spun across her body. The smaller man raised his hands to create a shield.

There was still a chance, right? She'd survived a fall like that. She'd—her vision blurred as she imagined the man's bloody leg—

Her head split and rage tore through her body in a fury of blinding pain. Her soul rent in two as a bolt shattered the ground and collided with the one who'd raised the shield.

He hit the ground and stopped moving.

The burly man and his companion took several steps back.

Magic crackled along her skin in a twisted frenzy of grief and anger. It seared her scars and hummed through the air with her as it's focal.

Another bolt shot from her body, crumpling the nobody that stood beside their commander.

His confidence melted to fear, and he sank to his knees. He pleaded. He promised her riches and power and all manner of things she'd never wanted.

Her arm crackled again as the lightning concentrated itself in her hand. Kiuno wrapped her fingers around his wrist. His nails bit into her flesh as he writhed from the pulse surging through both their bodies.

He fell limp.

The storm raged, fueled by her fear. They were gone, but not an ounce of her feelings had gone with it. She wanted to burn them and keep burning them until the end of time. She wanted their king. She wanted him to know what power really felt like.

The lightning crawled along her skin pulsing in time to her heart.

Kiuno closed her eyes.

It's not too late.

She had to believe that.

The tight coil wrapped around her center and she forced the pulse there as well.

She had to find Elite.

"Reece."

Kiuno headed toward the cliff's edge and Reece's vines wrapped around her body and the two started their descent.

Kiuno's heart raced, but it wasn't from the height or the promise of death. Death had to be easier than the pain threatening her now.

Seconds ticked by as if mocking her and she resisted the urge to spur them on faster. He could be hurt. He could need their help.

But shouldn't he be screaming for it?

Another lump formed in her throat and she couldn't swallow.

The shallow river flowed on as if undisturbed from the rocks that had crossed its path.

Kiuno's eyes scanned the river, then the rocks, and she covered her mouth when an exposed arm lay protruding from a boulder taller than herself.

Her heart jumped and breath faltered. Kiuno's knees collapsed when Reece set her on the ground and ran to aid Maltack in lifting the stone.

Their magic lifted the rock and bile rose in Kiuno's throat when she risked a glance.

Flattened. A smear of blood as if he were nothing more than an insect on a windshield.

Reece called out a name.

But it wasn't Elite.

Kiuno took in shallow breaths. She glanced at the other boulders and piles of rock. Her gaze drifted to the river and then to those who mourned their fallen comrade.

Two dead.

One missing.

A cold, crushing ache seeped into her bones and Kiuno curled in on herself.

Reece knelt at her side, but she refused to look at him.

No, no, no, no, no.

He pulled her into his chest without a word.

She knew what he wouldn't say. They'd overturn another piece of rubble and find Elite just like—

Kiuno shuddered. "Tell them to stop."

"Ki, we should—"

"No, I don't want—" Her voice caught, and the first sob racked her body as if lightning struck her instead.

She couldn't breathe.

She couldn't think.

Kiuno gripped Reece's shirt and he wrapped his arms beneath her legs and carried her away from the voices of sorrow and death.

She didn't want to see Elite like that, but the vision of his blood smeared across the ground wouldn't leave her mind.

Her breath came in rapid gasps and memories tore through her like a sharpened blade. One moment they consumed her. The next they faded.

Consumed.

Faded.

Kiuno cried in an endless cycle as she struggled to breathe and process, but no matter how much she begged, the emptiness throbbing in her heart wouldn't subside.

26

HEARTACHE

REALM: 5

DAY: 294

Despite her request Maltack took it upon himself to search for Elite. His report brought neither comfort nor closure.

Elite's body was nowhere to be found.

The river could have carried him away or some vile creature might be responsible. But whatever the case, it didn't change the likely outcome and Kiuno wasn't sure her heart could take anymore.

Reece held her close and his arms felt like the only thing keeping her stitched together while she grasped at the thin tendril of hope.

He couldn't be gone. He'd promised to never leave her again.

Another image of the man's smeared blood beneath the stone fought to the surface of her memory.

Despite Reece's warmth, an empty coldness echoed from the pit of her stomach. Kiuno watched the smoking coals from the fire for a while, before she moved his arm and made her way to the river.

Kiuno stared at her reflection. Stared at half a woman. Tear-stained

---

cheeks and swollen, empty eyes stared back. The water rippled her image and emptiness ached in her heart. She sat, allowing the steady flow of water to carry her mind to a distant place.

She and Elite had met in high school, inseparable for five short years.

They'd barely scratched the surface of their dreams.

They wanted to travel the world together. Go on long vacations to the beach and hike the beautiful mountains hand in hand. They wanted to tell their friends about their travels together and find places unknown where their dreams could come true.

But now all her pictures would be empty. Future conversations would be barren of the happiness she longed to share with another. Everything would be missing the one person who should be experiencing life at her side.

Kiuno's lip quivered and she bit the inside of her cheek.

No, don't cry anymore. You don't know for sure.

Her heart cracked and splintered.

How could he have survived?

Kiuno left the others lying by the dwindling coals and paced the bank alone. She watched the water flow over the smooth stones and searched for any sign that might rekindle the flame of hope in her chest.

Her heart jolted with every twist and turn. She half expected to see Elite's body lying motionless and face down in the water.

By the time Reece caught up, her hands were shaking.

She walked and walked and walked.

Reece didn't stop her and Kiuno didn't understand why. Anyone else would have convinced her to sit and rest, but Reece just walked and surveyed the bank at her side.

He sent others ahead to search for Elite and she didn't protest. Kiuno only kept walking.

With dusk they slept. Or tried to.

Kiuno stared into the depths of the calm, shallow water. Would they find him here?

With morning, nothing changed, but within a few hours Kiuno's heart thundered as one man ran toward them.

She wavered and Reece grabbed her arm as she stared at Elite's sword. Reece took it and the man excused himself.

Words wouldn't process. If they'd found that, then his body…

Kiuno collapsed and Reece eased her to the ground. She hadn't eaten or slept, but neither helped the pain dissipate. It crashed against her full force and left her incapacitated.

Reece called out instructions, but she couldn't process his words. It didn't matter. Nothing mattered.

Darkness settled around her and Kiuno hid her face in her knees and let the tears flow.

Another player lost. Another grave. Another heartache.

When would it end?

PHOENIX

REALM: 5

DAY: 296

Rock slid down the cliff side and the entire group jumped to their feet. Kiuno's heart jolted, a ray of hope breaking through the fractured pieces, but darkness consumed that hope when a stranger's face appeared.

Greenery held his body against the wall and soot from the blackened forest covered his clothes.

He took a few breaths as if he'd been running. "It's not safe here. Palindrome sent me to bring you back." His gaze floated to Kiuno and for the first time panic took the place of sorrow.

Reece adjusted his wrist band. "Why the hurry?"

"Men are marching on the castle. They were nearly upon it when I left. There's heavy equipment involved, and we have reason to believe they might send units this way.

"Furthermore, I was specifically asked to bring Kiuno. K.J. said you'd know what to do. If you're up for it, they could use you." The man's gaze dropped to her scarred arms.

Reece and Maltack turned to her, each waiting for her decision.

Kiuno closed her eyes and clenched her fists.

The man who'd given the order had threatened the castle. Did that mean they were in pursuit before they'd even met?

Her gaze drifted to the river. They'd found Elite's weapon, but who knew how long it'd take to find—she shook her head.

Maybe she didn't want to find it. Maybe she was better off.

Her gaze returned to the man still hanging on the cliffside.

K.J. needed her to tip the scales.

Heavy equipment.

An army.

With a heavy heart Kiuno marched to the cliffside and jerked her head upward. "Let's go."

No one disagreed or tried to stop her. Reece wrapped his arms around her middle and let the greenery sprout from the ground, tying their bodies together. As they ascended, more vines grew from the mountainside to replace previous plants.

Cybele turned when they emerged from the ravine. "Flying will be faster."

Several large felinians stood at her side.

Kiuno didn't question why Cybele cared. Perhaps K.J. told the woman about Kiuno's abilities. Maybe Cybele thought Kiuno could be captured and used against them. Whatever the reason, her willingness was good enough.

Exhaustion clashed with the waves rolling through Kiuno's core. Her body trembled and heart skipped as she fought against the surges of magic.

Killing three men had done nothing for the rage, but perhaps killing a mass of people would. Maybe it would only make her feel worse. All Kiuno knew was everything she had left of Elite sat within that castle and she wasn't about to let this world have one more piece of him.

Kiuno had watched the felinians soar through the air countless times. She'd watched Nikita play in the wind as she flipped and circled their wagons. But they didn't soar now, they raced. The creature beneath her beat its powerful wings and the wind bit and burned her face.

Reece clung to her from behind as they gripped the saddle together. He'd strapped her legs in without asking and she hadn't stopped him. Her entire body shook with rage and she couldn't look at him or Maltack. Their eyes held pity and she didn't want pity.

The burnt land stretched out below them, passing by as if she were riding in a car. What had taken them days to travel on horseback seemed only minutes in the air.

Kiuno felt like the forest. Her soul smothered beneath the dead clutches of fire and ash. They had stripped her of the most valuable thing in her life. This game had broken her, but she knew powerful things could rise from the ashes. Even if she didn't feel she could stand again, Kiuno knew she would.

The pulse strummed through her veins as another wave crashed over her heart and the castle entered their view. Rocks flew from heavy catapults and over the outside wall, crashing into whatever might be unfortunate enough to be in their path. Magic beat against a shield that domed the wall and spread along the edge like a shimmering sheet of colorful glass.

K.J.'s men stood against the force, keeping behind an invisible line that would ensure the soldiers didn't take friendly fire from their archers. Clashing steel and exploding magic filled her ears.

The felinians dipped, dropping to the ground so fast her stomach clenched. She clung to the leather saddle and Reece tightened his grip on her waist until the felinian opened its wings and carried them into a steady run.

She bent to unlatch her legs and hit the ground sprinting. The coil in her chest tightened as another rock launched from a wooden device and soared to the wall, crashing against a tower. It crumbled, those at the top falling to their death.

Palindrome and K.J. were prepared for this kind of attack. They'd shown her the layout, but were all the civilians safe within the keep? Did they have enough warning?

She knew her task. Distract. Disorganize. Scatter. Use her magic, then join the others. A long path separated her from aid, but judging from the enemy's abilities, those at the back didn't use magic and it would be a weakness she'd enjoy exploiting.

28

K.J.

REALM: 5

DAY: 296

K.J. commanded their second line forward while his generals worked to secure the perimeter.

He spun and his eyes widened as a heavy boulder flew their way. Palindrome shouted commands, but K.J. grabbed her arm and pulled her into a crouch, shielding her head with his body as the rock crashed against the tower to their right.

Screams filled the air as people fell to their death while others were crushed beneath the massive weight of stone.

The two peeked over the wall, their men already moving to help those trapped. Elements mixed and spread out above, fanning along the shield created by those in charge of defense.

Archers continued their fire, but less than half hit their intended targets. The enemy was prepared, like they already knew their battle arrangements.

K.J. had stationed half their ground fighters outside the wall while the other half waited inside and prepared for the breach. It was coming.

Magic users lined the outside curtain wall and most of their defenders stood in the towers, using the height to their advantage.

Palindrome signaled to another of their leads then turned to him. "We can't hold this much longer. We need to take the offensive."

She was right. The enemy would break through the gatehouse soon.

He tilted his head to look at the castle and those still filing into the keep. "They're almost finished securing the civilians."

The timing of it all. Right after their meeting. It seemed this 'king' had planned to attack regardless of their compliance. He craved power and obedience. That much was perfectly clear.

A flash, followed by a thundering crack echoed across the field drawing both his and Palindrome's gazes. Fire burned at their rear. Likely one of the mangonels.

A second flash then the enemy's rear forces turned their attention to the new threat.

"Looks like she's here," Palindrome said. "Should we move to assist her?"

K.J. studied the area to the west, the flashes echoing over and over. Another catapult caught fire. A line of men fell. He knew that rage.

"Best to let her come to us. Get your team ready and meet her at the front. We'll push through once she's at the gate."

Palindrome bolted down the stairs. Her team would give them an advantage and with Kiuno at their side this would all reach an end quickly. Provided the girl didn't exert herself first.

K.J.'s heart grew heavy. Kiuno had never been one to handle loss well. Her heart clung tight to those she treasured. But he also knew rage would be her first instinct and this latest tragedy would be enough to finish this battle.

MEMORIES & MAGIC

REALM: 5

DAY: 296

Memories poured out with the magic, but Kiuno reeled in the lightning. She couldn't let her surging emotions tire out her body before finding K.J. and Palindrome.

Flames burned her enemies to cinders and Elite's memories took over her thoughts. The pain coursing through her body paled in comparison to the ache settling in her heart. She felt robotic, switched to autopilot. A soldier with a job to do, but nothing to call her home.

Maltack's wind slammed into their enemies and expanded to feed the raging inferno. Reece slashed through their foes and his vines twisted through their guts and necks, tearing people apart one by one.

Memories. Memories of him. The first time they met.

Their first kiss.

Kiuno planted her foot, shoved her sword through a man's torso then twisted her blade. His gurgle fell to her right then Reece's vines shot through three men charging her left. The flames took care of the rest.

They'd first met in high school. Back when life was normal. Back before a game forced them to fight for their lives.

Kiuno ducked beneath a sharp blade and brought her own up to pierce her attacker's throat. Reece's arms crawled with vines that carried thorns as long as his hand. Maltack pointed and she continued, a path of destruction left in her wake.

It was a school project and like so many times before the teachers forced her to work with a partner. With Elite. They'd never spoken before then and she loathed relying on others.

Wind pulled tendrils of hair from her braid and they plastered themselves against the sweat rolling down her cheeks. Kiuno clenched her teeth and pulsed the flames outward.

He'd been kinder than she expected, treating her with a respect he'd denied several others. She'd viewed him as arrogant and intolerable, but then he'd told her that those who gave respect earned it. Just as she had.

A booming sound split the air and those maintaining the barrier faltered, several succumbing to the effects of the enemy's magic. The wall shifted and part of it caved from the bottom. Heavy stone crumbled to the ground, and those at the top fell to a rocky death.

Dust rose, blocking her view as the magic users fought to clear the area and assist their comrades. Magic flew from both sides and the enemy poured through the breach.

Kiuno sprinted toward them, hoping they'd gotten the civilians out of harm's way. The enemy continued their assault upon the wall and crumbled the rock bit by bit.

A large stone crushed a man who'd seen it coming and his scream reverberated through her chest. Her mind conjured an image of Elite, but she shook it away.

A section of magic users turned to them and Kiuno's advance halted as wave after wave of magic crashed against her fire. The sheer power hit like a wall and she grit her teeth against the force.

Maltack stepped forward and shrouded them with his shield while

Reece kept the enemy from their rear.

Maltack and Kiuno took a step together. Then another. The wall fought back and more joined from the sides.

Maltack winced.

Kiuno pulled at the deep coil in her chest. Her scars pulsed. She broke from Maltack's shield and let the lightning surge through their enemies, felling those within reach and the magic bearing down upon them ceased.

Kiuno darted through the temporary path with her comrades on her heels. She leapt back as another stone toppled from the wall and zigzagged around the broken bodies and rubble.

The stone cracked again, but the trio raced into friendly territory before it came crashing down. Kiuno kept running until they were beyond the clutches of the enemy's magic and placed her hands on her knees and fought for breath.

Memories assaulted her again.

Elite's proposal behind his parent's house, the full moon as their witness. Their simple wedding with friends and family to celebrate. The promise of a life spent together.

All she had left were the pictures stacked in her closet back home. Friends and family would wear black and offer their condolences, but after they mourned, she'd sit in the living room alone. With no one to quell her fears.

Kiuno clenched her fists, struggling to contain the tears. She'd taken so much for granted. Their simple life, the easy stress of jobs, school, and money. Through all those struggles they were safe.

Screams echoed from within the wall. Enemies slid down on ropes and vines and used their magic and blades to impale the innocent. Fires took over houses one by one and water rained down from above as more magic clashed.

Kiuno ran toward them. They should have cleared the civilians by now. They'd already sealed the inner gate so why—she slid to a halt and her heart constricted.

Liam.

Kiuno clenched her teeth. Why the hell was Liam here?

The young boy held a sword and stood defiant against four men three times his size. Kiuno's breath hitched when one swung his sword. Liam ducked around his enemy, but he pinned his back against a wall in the process.

Kiuno ran toward him but her legs wouldn't move fast enough. Another sword fell toward her young friend. He blocked, but the strength from the blow sent Liam to his knees.

Four tendrils of vines shot past her, all sinking into vital areas of the men threatening her friend. They fell and Liam remained on the ground, his chest heaving.

Kiuno grabbed Liam's wrist and wrenched him toward her. "What are you doing out here?"

He didn't respond, his eyes full of fear. He tilted his head to a shop where someone's head ducked behind a broken wall. Reece opened the door and several people screamed.

Reece spoke softly and coaxed them out. Five children, none older than ten. One girl clung to a sewn doll, tears running down her cheeks.

Kiuno cursed, glanced at their surroundings, then gestured for them to follow. The children gathered at her back, the nearest clutching to the tail end of Kiuno's shirt as she peeked around the corner.

Men. At least twenty and their sole purpose seemed to be burning everything in sight. She glanced at the kids then to Reece. He watched their rear, his eyes darting this way and that as the battle raged around them. She had to get these kids through the inner gate.

A war cry echoed from the opposite corner and friendly forces attacked those setting fires. Kiuno grabbed the child's arm and darted across the street. She only glanced back to be sure the others followed.

A guard gestured for the inner gate to open before they were even upon it. He ushered the children inside the small opening. Liam hesitated, but one look from Kiuno had him following the children without argument. He wasn't built for war. Less than a year ago she might have said the same about herself.

With the children safe, Kiuno glanced toward the wall and the chaos ensuing around it. Fires burned. Men screamed. Steel clashed with steel.

Water particles pulling into a clustered mass drew her attention and Kiuno sprinted toward the nearest tower.

She met opponents in battle. Some with her sword, others with fire. Kiuno didn't pause to ensure their death. Those stationed at the base of the wall would do that. She needed to reach the top.

At the tower's base, Kiuno rushed through the door and began climbing the stairs. Her legs protested as they ran around and around, climbing higher and higher. Her breath came in ragged gasps, as did the others behind her by the time they reached the opening to the tower wall.

Enemies swarmed the exit.

Reece shot his vines around her, some coming so close the leaves grazed her skin. Maltack's fire soon spiraled past and hers joined it, wrapping whoever dared challenge them in its fiery clutches.

Kiuno glanced at Reece then to Maltack. Sweat poured down both their faces, but neither showed any signs of stopping. They were just as determined to ensure the safety of their home.

With a moment of reprieve, Kiuno glanced to either side of the wall. Bodies littered the ground. People trampled their fallen comrades. Thankfully there wasn't as much carnage on the inside, but still. There was enough.

Her gaze lingered on the fallen stones a moment too long and a sword swung too close. Kiuno ducked and drove her blade through her opponent's stomach. He grunted when she twisted and she shoved him to the side, withdrawing the blade without a second glance.

Kiuno reeled in her magic as their comrades came into view. She, Reece, and Maltack threw enemies from the side and broke ladders as they continued to run. Her gaze stayed focused on the water and the familiar way it snaked through the air.

As they drew closer, droplets dampened her skin and hair. She'd seen Scorpios surround himself with magic before, but this far exceeded anything she'd ever witnessed. A serpent coiled itself above and around the area, the body ever expanding.

Kiuno paused at Scorpios's side, struggling to catch her breath. He inclined his head toward her but kept his concentration focused. She glanced up toward the inside of the coil looming at least twenty feet above, then to the width that matched it.

Veins stood out on Scorpio's arms and neck as he continued to build the water around himself. Maltack joined him and their energy permeated the area. Fierce, yet steady. A strange sensation formed in her core and more memories clawed their way to the surface.

Memories of their adventures. Of hiking, camping, and picnics. Memories of their love and laughter as they separated themselves from the world.

Scorpios widened his stance, planted himself, and shifted his hands. Maltack mimicked the action and the massive serpent responded.

It uncoiled and reared its head downward and went soaring from the wall in a beautiful yet deadly display. The water crashed against their enemies and Kiuno tugged at the lightning in her core. It crackled across her skin and she let it melt into the pathways made by Scorpios and Maltack. Maltack would be able to control it long enough to reach their enemies.

The water soaked up her electricity and spread to those still able to stand at the bottom. They wouldn't rise again.

Kiuno's vision blurred, but she fought against the rising fatigue and continued the pulse until she, Scorpios, and Maltack were all left panting in the aftermath.

Even with those enemies down, more surged forward. They were like cockroaches. Kill a few and more took their place.

Kiuno took in a steadying breath. "You guys ready?" They needed to prevent any more enemies from crossing the wall on this side.

Reece's vines wrapped around their bodies and her stomach dropped as he lowered them over the edge and toward the charging enemy below.

When her feet hit the ground, Kiuno charged forward. She struggled to maintain her balance over the fallen bodies. Maltack fanned his flames, Scorpios hardened his water to daggers of ice and Reece's magic erupted on all sides as greenery shot from the ground to fell their foes.

An enemy's blade clashed with her own and Kiuno's forearms threatened to give. She gritted her teeth and shoved. Blinding pain shot through the back of her skull. She fell to the ground with the world spinning.

Footsteps shifted in the shadows of her vision and specks of color flew behind her closed eyes.

Voices rippled. Muffled. She struggled to anchor herself back to the waking world. He stood over her. He raised—

"Get up!"

Sound slammed back as steel clashed against steel. Kiuno wrapped her fingers around the hilt of her blade then placed one heavy foot beneath her body.

Fight. Push until the enemy falls. It wouldn't be long now.

Kiuno tugged at her sluggish magic. She lifted heavy arms and kicked off the ground, slicing through those around her with the flames in her wake.

A roar pierced the air above their heads and Cybele jumped from her felinian's back, spear in hand. Milo snatched the enemy from the ground and tossed him into the air. His companions ripped the man apart and let the pieces fall to the ground.

A thick droplet slid down Kiuno's face and she wiped the red liquid away.

Her body tottered.

Magic swept through the area like a fresh wave of the ocean cleaning away remnants of sand.

Kiuno stumbled back, confused and a hand wrapped around her shoulders. More moved in, their allies she presumed, but Kiuno couldn't convince her body to follow.

"Are you al—"

AFTERMATH

REALM: 5

DAY: 296

Clink, clink, clink.

Kiuno shifted, but her eyes didn't open.

Clink, clink, clink.

She groaned, pressed a hand to her forehead to rub away the throbbing, and cracked one eye open. There were beds on either side of her, some empty, others filled with sleeping persons unknown.

Clink, clink, clink.

Kiuno sat up and blood rushed to her temples. She took a moment to steady herself.

"You're awake."

Kiuno followed the voice and found the source of the annoying noise. "I am now."

"Sorry, I'm mixing a medicine to ease your headache."

Kiuno glanced at his face and her heart skipped. "Vincent?"

He smiled and set his bowl at the foot of her bed. "Glad to see your memories are in working order." His fingers traveled over the tender area on the back of her head. She half expected them to come away bloody, but they didn't. Vincent continued stirring the mixture.

"The woman who brought me here," he paused in thought. "Palindrome? Yes, I think that was it. She set me to look after you and others who are recovering."

He lowered his voice as if just remembering they weren't alone. "She stopped the bleeding, but I'm afraid no one has the energy to spare for taking care of the pain."

"It's all right. What happened?"

"We pushed the enemy back and chased down those who tried to flee. Some managed to escape. There are several injured, not to mention the dead, but we fared pretty well all things considered."

Kiuno shifted so Vincent could sit beside her. "Are the others okay?"

"Your friends you mean? Yes, yes. Maltack?" Vincent said the name as if he wasn't sure and she nodded. "He was persistent in helping Palindrome with the wounded. The others are assisting in other pressing matters."

"When did you get here?"

"Less than a week ago. I assume you found what you were looking for?"

Her heart skipped, and Kiuno averted her gaze as the memories resurfaced and hit her like a punch to the gut.

Kiuno clutched her head. "I—"

What could she tell him? She'd found happiness only to have it stripped away?

Vincent's voice softened. "It seems I'm only meant to find you broken in more ways than one."

He stood and poured the contents from the bowl into a folded paper before handing it to her. "It won't taste good, but it'll ease the pain. I'd advise rest, but I doubt you'll listen so just take it easy for a few days."

Vincent looked as though he wanted to linger, but he moved to another patient, whispering as a courtesy to those still resting.

Broken in more ways than one.

Yes. He'd found her after Kikyo and Elliott's death. She'd been broken then. Kiuno glanced at her fingers. Is that what she was? Broken?

Her fingers trembled and joints ached. Her skin burned, but just as Vincent predicted she couldn't sit around. Kiuno moved her legs to the side of the bed and pulled on her muck covered shoes.

She stood and the world spun, but Kiuno grabbed the post to her right and let her swimming mind steady.

Noise assaulted her as she exited the door. People rushed from one place to another, but one thing was clear. The battle had ended.

Kiuno limped across the field at a slow pace and walked through the inner gatehouse. Several people hammered away on the structure and the resounding noise pulsed within her skull.

Several stones had been shifted and sat at the base of their previous fixtures. The rocks from the catapults were gone, leaving scars in the earth where the heavy stones had skidded across the ground. The bodies were absent, but blood still lingered like a fog in the air.

She'd killed again, but this time she didn't regret. Instead, it felt no different from feeding the animals or moving storage. Just a task that required completion. Did that make her a monster?

Her gaze shifted to the wall as she recalled Scorpios and his magic. He'd never used something so powerful in their sparring matches. The raw force that had crashed over their enemies was relentless. Her lightning added a final touch, expanding his reach to any who contacted the water's surface.

The familiar stench of burning flesh clouded the air and she gagged as she continued toward the crumbling outer gate house.

"Ki?"

She paused and turned to the familiar voice.

"I'm surprised you're up," Reece said. He gently took her by the arm and guided her away from the exit. "Trust me when I say you don't want to go out there."

"What happened?"

"You passed out from that blow to the head. Palindrome and Cybele finished things."

He brushed her hair to the side to examine her wound.

She winced and grabbed his fingers. "Is everyone safe?"

Reece nodded. "Once Palindrome took over, we pulled back." His gaze seemed to search her eyes, but she couldn't hold it. "Most of them are in a meeting." He paused. "If you want to join."

"Why aren't you there?"

He shrugged. "Their inner workings don't require my input."

The pain in her head continued, but it was beginning to dull. At least Vincent's medicine worked.

Reece offered his arm. "I'll walk with you if you want to go."

She nodded and the two made their way back across the castle grounds.

Inside the great hall, someone had shoved the tables and chairs aside to make room for more of their injured. Blankets and cots lined the area with bloody bandages piling up in several corners. She averted her gaze and limped up the stairs. Reece kept one hand on her back to balance her movement.

Noise echoed from K.J.'s office and Reece helped her push the heavy doors open. Several heads spun their way. Kiuno clenched her teeth as more than a few of their gazes shifted to pity.

Dark circles hung under most eyes and everyone slouched in their chairs.

"It's good to see you up and moving," Palindrome said. She rose and pulled out a chair. "Join us."

Though Reece had mentioned not wanting to come, he stayed at Kiuno's side, his hand never leaving her shoulder. She found it comforting. As if he were grounding her to the present.

Palindrome returned to her seat. "As we were saying. I'd venture to agree most of their magic users are gone. They won't be a threat."

"But they could have valuable supplies. K.J. has confirmed the use of gunpowder and if there's more, then I think it's worth getting," Scorpios replied.

"How many retreated?" Kiuno asked.

"Less than a quarter," K.J. answered. "They abandoned their catapults and if we have any luck, there will be more waiting at their castle."

Palindrome folded her hands. "We received a message from Samar this morning. He's willing to help in our recovery. In the meantime, we can focus on getting a unit together to ensure they don't issue another attack."

Samar. She didn't recognize that name.

"Then it's decided. There's work to do." K.J. looked them over. "Silver, Scorpios. I want you two along the wall if you have energy to spare. I'll be there shortly."

Palindrome stood. "Maltack and I will head back to the medical wing."

Those in the room rose to their feet, but Kiuno remained still, keeping her gaze on the spirals in the wooden table. Silver laid a hand on her shoulder in passing and she trembled but bit her lip to hold in the tears. Reece lingered, but when K.J. didn't rise he relented and followed the others out.

The two sat in silence for a long time. She wasn't sure what she needed or why she stayed. Kiuno felt his eyes studying her. He knew her. Surely, he'd tell her how to survive from here on out.

"Do I need to worry about you running off?" *Knew her too well it seemed.*

Kiuno clenched her fists. Sharp pain lanced through her head. Her body trembled from the empty hole at her core and her throat burned from choking back tears. She was in no condition to run off.

"I want to finish what they started."

"We will, but I need time to organize and I can't focus if I have to worry about you. Give me a few days to get things sorted. Can you do that?"

The words caught in her throat, so she just nodded. He stood and the heaviness she'd been trying to avoid clenched her heart like a vise.

K.J. paused at her side. "I'm sorry."

Her shoulders shook after he left the room. She fought, but the tears slid down her face against her will.

When she could breathe again, Kiuno stood and trudged down the spiral staircase. She pressed her forehead against the stone when someone passed in an effort to hide her grief. Thankfully they didn't pause to ask questions.

She walked the long familiar hall until she stood before a door. Their door. Kiuno rested her forehead against it.

This was the first place they'd had a moment alone together. A moment to relish in the fact they were both still alive. It'd been a miracle then.

Kiuno took a breath and pushed it open. The hinges creaked and her breath hitched. A messy bed. Clothes slung across the floor. A cold and empty fireplace.

She took a step in and let the door close. Kiuno stood motionless for a time, then stooped to pick up a shirt. With shaking hands, she buried her face in the material and fell onto their bed.

She cried, her tears coming in wave after wave as she mourned the only person that had ever given her purpose in this world.

BROKEN

REALM: 5

DAY: 299

They knocked and once again Kiuno ignored it, huddling closer to the small pile of clothes that had become the sacred objects of her affection. She'd watched the sun rise three times and the midafternoon sun poured through her small window.

They brought her breakfast every morning and every night they took the uneaten food away without a word. Someone lit the fire at night, but Kiuno didn't bother with stoking it. She preferred curling into the furs that smelled of him, pretending Elite was at her side.

The door opened and she wondered, not for the first time, if she should bar it. If not for the need to drink water, she might have.

Whoever intruded on her now stood in the doorway, footsteps unmoving. "You should eat."

Maltack. Of course, he'd be the one checking on her. His feet shuffled and she tightened her hold on the shirt, cradling it to her chest.

"Is there anything I can get you?"

She lay still for a long time, then shook her head. When the door closed, she looked back and rolled over, her stomach growling at the smell of food.

Kiuno stared at it, debating whether she should give her body nourishment. Or if she wanted to. She sat up, head heavy and eyes swollen.

She looked back at the food and grabbed the plate, setting it on the bed. They wouldn't let her sulk without food much longer. Kiuno choked down a few bites then turned over to let sleep engulf her once more.

Maltack brought dinner, but he didn't disturb her this time. She ate the food when he left then stared at the cold fireplace.

Kiuno thought of everything and nothing all at once. She wondered what normal felt like and how people would act around her now.

Kiuno stood and walked to the window with Elite's shirt still in her grasp. The moon stared back from beneath a clear sky, but it wasn't empty. Hundreds of stars surrounded it, just like her friends still surrounded her. They were waiting, giving her space until she was ready to share the shattered parts of herself.

But would she ever be ready? Kiuno pulled a cloak around her shoulders and exited her room.

No one tried to stop her as she padded down the stone stairs with bare feet. She exited the castle, crossed the field, then left the inner gatehouse, staying on the cobblestone path that would lead her outside.

In three days, they'd settled the base of the wall back into place. Large bricks sat around the area with tools and pulley systems attached to them. During the day, they were manned, and she heard the voices of those working float through her window. But at night they stood still and silent.

She padded toward the stones and ran her hand over their cool surface. The outer gatehouse was locked with more guards than usual stationed above and below. They eyed her, but none moved or spoke. She wondered if it was worth the effort to get through but decided she didn't have the energy.

Kiuno circled the outside wall, walking one step at a time over a battleground. There were still pieces of weapons and splinters of wood hidden in the grass and her bare feet discovered more than their fair share.

"Kiuno?"

She tilted her head and found K.J. standing in the middle of the yard. She hadn't seen him since the meeting. Though she hadn't seen anyone since then. He walked toward her and she fought to keep herself from crumbling.

"Tell me what to do," she pleaded. "You said you'd help me when this was all over, but I don't think I can wait that long."

He didn't speak for several moments. K.J. seated himself in the grass and leaned against a broken stone. She sat across from him, wrapping the cloak around her body as if it were a shield against the outside world.

"You've lost part of your identity. You're lost because the person you planned your entire life with is gone. Grief is part of the process, but you're grieving for more than just the loss of Elite. You're grieving the loss of a life you planned."

Kiuno bristled and clenched her teeth. "What do I do?"

"Find yourself."

"What if I don't want to?"

"You will, eventually. Maybe not tomorrow. Maybe not even a week from now, but you'll start putting pieces of yourself back together."

She wanted to argue and scream. She wanted to reason she'd never move on, but that wasn't the truth. The painful truth rested in the day by day. Minutes and hours would pass whether she wanted them to or not, and she'd be forced to move with the current or drown.

"They're leaving tomorrow," K.J. said. "I'm not telling you revenge will help, but you're not going to get answers by hiding in that room."

She didn't want to admit it, but he was right. All she'd done for the last three days was live in the past. She replayed their life over and over again, drowning herself in every memory she could recall.

"I'll go," she whispered. "Who's leading them?"

"Iggy and we're not short on volunteers."

"What are you doing about the sixth realm?"

K.J. furrowed his brow. "I planned to get a team together after we figured out this mess."

Kiuno remained silent.

"You're not coming back."

It wasn't a question, but she shook her head anyway. How could she come back? K.J. said she needed to find herself, but how could she when everything reminded her of Elite?

"It's all right. I understand. You know this is your home and you can come back when you're ready. I'm giving Reece control over their castle once we've taken it over."

"I want to go with the scouting team."

K.J. fell silent. "I can't argue that your abilities would be welcome. Who do you want to take?"

"Maltack will come and Reece too."

"And the castle?"

"Nsane is more than capable of keeping it together."

K.J. shifted his legs. "I have Scorpios set to leave tomorrow and work on our alliance with Leena. Several of their higher ups are Chinese and with him being fluent I thought it best."

Kiuno adjusted her cloak. "I won't steal him from you. I'm sure he won't be happy with my decision anyway."

Silence fell between them again and the two listened to the sounds of the night. It was enough to be in another's presence as she tried to wrap her mind around forming a new life.

A broken life.

A life without Elite.

TRAITOR

REALM: 5
DAY: 299

She'd barred herself in her room for the last few days, but the high she'd given him was enough to satisfy his need for a while. The way she'd shattered their enemies and forced them to cower.

His gaze traveled over the charred land as he walked among the ripped pieces of flesh. The very air seemed to vibrate with what she'd done to the terrain. As if it responded to her. Or maybe that was just him.

He took a deep breath. Intoxicating. Invigorating. Absolutely primal.

Elite's death hadn't been part of the equation, he'd meant to save that for later, but the power it'd unleashed! He spun in the field with his arms open. It was magnificent.

Now they were planning to attack Lillian's castle and judging from Kiuno's anger he was willing to bet it'd be the show of a lifetime.

Let her soul corrode and twist. Let the tendrils of anger and hatred dig their roots so deep no one would be able to dig them out. Let her become the dark queen none of them knew she could be.

VENGEANCE

REALM: 5

DAY: 300

The following morning Samar's people filed into the castle. She'd finally learned him to be the unnamed alliance leader from the last meeting. They brought supplies and food and part of her felt better knowing someone would be there to guard against another attack.

Kiuno wrapped her hand around the satchel at her side. Elite's shirt rested at the bottom, the only possession she could carry on a journey this long. It hurt to leave their room behind, but Palindrome promised no one would disturb it until her return.

The horse rocked her in a steady back and forth motion as they marched with the army. Reece rode on one side and Maltack rode on the other. K.J.'s general, Iggy, led the troupe with Palindrome's best at his side.

At least half of the enemy's forces had been depleted. K.J. seemed confident it was their stronger half. She was sure he had plans in place if they ran into any trouble.

Kiuno doubted they would need her abilities. She was there for herself anyway. To satisfy something. Or try. Maybe the journey would allow her to figure out what she wanted in life.

Her future was empty. Veiled. She struggled with every eye contact that passed her way. Should she smile? Would they find her heartless if she did?

Day after day passed slowly, as though time mocked her efforts. Kiuno let the sway of the horse carry her thoughts off to happier times and often found herself dreaming of the past. They were pleasant memories. A safe place to hide.

She ate, slept, responded, and rode. A methodical existence.

Days later, Nikita followed Milo through the air to greet the other felinians and their soldiers camped on the outskirts so as not to upset the creatures. It seemed Cybele wouldn't be joining their battle either.

Not battle. Massacre. And for once, she didn't care.

Kiuno turned her horse away from the men and set off on her own. She didn't get far before hearing another at her side.

Reece. He rode but didn't speak. He knew where she was headed.

Dusk settled over the land as Kiuno dismounted and peered over the cliff's edge. It was the same as before, with twisted mist blocking her view from the bottom.

She clenched her teeth as a sob racked her form. Before leaving, K.J. had offered to have his people search for Elite's body. She gave her consent but wasn't hopeful.

Later, when they were free of this place, she'd come back and make all the burial sites of her friends and family beautiful. Maybe she'd move their remains to a central location.

Kiuno recalled their moments in the cavern. They were fond final memories, but then the blast echoed through her mind and her fists curled. She prayed the explosion had killed him. She prayed he hadn't suffered whether from fear or pain.

Kiuno took a step back as grass and bushes sprouted from the ground. Green leaves unfurled and colorful flowers budded then bloomed before her eyes. She turned to find Reece with an arm pointed in her direction.

A young tree broke through the earth and stretched its branches toward the sky. Leaves broke through the bark and small pink flowers budded along the stem. A sweet fragrance washed over her and Kiuno tried to wipe away her tears, but they wouldn't stop.

Reece didn't speak, there weren't any comforting words that would give reassurance, but his actions did more than he knew. It showed her that maybe K.J. was right. Maybe something new could grow from the ashes. Maybe she could find herself in the swirling chaos of her emotions.

Kiuno slept beneath the tree that night listening to the wind howl through the canyon below. Reece stayed at her side without complaint, wide awake as she dozed on and off.

With morning, the troops caught up and she joined the formation at Maltack's side.

The entire army moved with revenge in mind, if their whispers were anything to go by. She knew it wouldn't solve anything. It wouldn't heal her broken heart. It wouldn't bring back the dead, but at the very least they could ensure no one else suffered at the hands of such a vile leader.

Horns blared as the castle came into view and Kiuno's blood rushed through her veins. The enemy's numbers had been depleted, but what other devices did these people have at their disposal?

Kiuno glanced at the faces of her comrades. Anger. Rage. She felt the same, but it wasn't the people she wanted. It was their king.

Kiuno jumped from her horse and Reece followed.

Silence stretched across the field. Armor clanged and swords scraped against their sheaths.

Arrows flew from the castle wall, but the tips sunk into the earth several yards short of their front line. Kiuno wondered if the enemy were trying to scare them or measure the distance.

At the front, men with heavy shields blocked her view of the land.

"They're searching the ground for traps," Reece said.

"How do you know?"

"Because I'm doing it too. The arrows were a taunt. There are spike-filled holes scattered throughout and I'm sure they have other tricks up their sleeves."

"You can feel the holes?"

"I can manipulate the plants so when there's a gap in the ground I feel it. I'm sure they'll be marked before we charge in."

As Reece spoke, plants grew in the open field, sprouting along what she could only assume to be a trap. Iggy drew his blade and let out a war cry and the men surrounding her did the same.

They charged, but she stayed put, the shoulders of several men running into her as they barreled toward the battlefield.

Screams and battle cries filled the air. Black arrows rained down and clashed against her allies' shields. Fire ignited in the grass close to the castle, catching a few of their allies in its grasp, yet those who could manipulate water put a quick end to its devastation.

Their walls weren't as thick or high as K.J.'s. It would fall soon enough.

Kiuno took a step, but a passing solder clipped her arm and she stumbled forward. Reece grasped her elbow and pulled her to her feet.

"You okay?"

She nodded.

"You're planning something."

Had she always been that obvious to read?

"Follow me."

Kiuno ducked between the men, running perpendicular to their ranks in any space she could find. Metal armor clashed so loud she couldn't be certain Reece followed, but when she cleared the ranks, he was right behind.

"What's the plan?"

Kiuno took a moment to catch her breath. "Their king wants the lightning user. I plan to deliver."

"Typical of you to be reckless." She waited for him to tell her they should call for backup, but he only smirked. "What next?"

"You said you can feel out the traps, right?" She pointed to the right side of the castle wall. "How far along the sides do they run?"

Reece knelt and the seconds ticked by until he pointed. "They stop over there."

"Lead the way."

The two ran across the field, leaving the main part of the battle behind. At the wall, Reece wrapped his vines around her waist and carried them both to the top.

Water slammed into her from the left, tossing her body to the ground as if she were nothing more than baggage. Kiuno struggled to catch herself, but Reece's magic reacted faster than her body could. It curled around her torso and Reece turned to their enemy with a murderous gleam in his eyes.

Four men stood ready, but Reece's vines shot through their bodies like butter, silencing them before they could alert their comrades.

He took a breath before turning to her. "Are you all right?"

She nodded, glanced at the men, then surveyed the ground below. It was a ghost town.

Reece lowered them down and they crept passed the empty houses. No resident occupied the area.

Her skin crawled, thought it wasn't from fear.

She wanted this fight.

K.J. wasn't sure if revenge would ease her pain and the logical side of her knew it wouldn't, but with the king so close, Kiuno couldn't help but crave blood.

She wanted to feel his life ebb away in her hands. To watch his eyes alight with fear when he realized everything was over. She wanted this death to be on her hands.

Kiuno glanced at Reece as he peered around another corner. He ushered her forward and the two ran through the castle gate. No one tried to stop them.

She wasn't new to risks. In fact, she'd taken more than her fair share of them. Each time she'd been scolded, called reckless.

But Reece was different. He didn't question her movements. He didn't hold her back. Either that made them both stupid or he had more faith in her abilities than she did.

They snuck through the quiet corridor and paused at a pair of closed doors. She glanced at Reece and he took a step back.

Kiuno took a breath, summoned her fire, and blasted the door open. She tugged the flames tight around her body, anticipating an onslaught, but the hall sat empty.

Kiuno crept forward, eyes scanning the overlook that stood fifteen feet above. It circled the main floor of the hall. Marble columns held up the top floor and she stepped between them, wary of the overlook. An empty chair, or throne as this person would likely call it, stood at the back of the room.

"Who's there?" A woman's voice called from behind the chair. She stepped into the light, tall and elegant, dressed in a dark blue gown that hung to the floor. Embroidery stretched from top to bottom in a floral-like pattern with beads sewn into the fabric. The finest piece of clothing Kiuno had seen since coming here.

Reece chuckled and took a step forward. "I guess having them call you king can have its benefits, but I still have to ask. Why bother?"

Her devious smile caused Kiuno's blood to rage.

"I have my reasons. Are you the one attacking my castle?"

"You attacked first," Kiuno accused. "Twice."

"I commanded nothing of the sort, they acted against my will." She sighed and placed her fingers on her head as if she were tired. "It's so difficult to contain people in this land, don't you agree?"

Reece adjusted his sword. "The cliff wasn't your idea?"

"Goodness no, they informed me after the fact. I couldn't believe what they'd done and then to attack your castle on top of it?" She shook her head. "It seems this world affects everyone differently."

Kiuno's body shook, her fists clenching and unclenching. "The least you could do is have the decency to admit it. Do you think we're stupid enough to believe you lost control of your own men? You wouldn't have survived this long if that were the case."

The woman stood silent then a taunting smile twisted her thin lips. "This is why I prefer dealing with men. They don't ask nearly as many questions."

"Perhaps you've just surrounded yourself with stupid ones."

She wrapped long fingers around a slender sword that rested on the chair. It scraped across the stone floor as she took a few steps forward.

"I suppose that's a possibility, though having a certain charm works with most any man." She took another look at Kiuno, her eyes trailing down her form. "I guess you wouldn't know anything about that seeing as you like to dress like the common dogs."

"Maybe some of us aren't afraid to get our hands dirty."

She laughed, the sound setting Kiuno's teeth on edge. "Oh, getting my hands dirty was never an issue. It's much easier to convince another to handle the heavy lifting."

The woman raised her free hand, the fingers carelessly limp and Kiuno followed it to find archers lining both balconies, their bows pulled tight. "I might consider dropping your weapons."

Kiuno glared at her. "You wanted the lightning user, did you not?"

Curiosity piqued in the woman's gaze and she raised a brow. "Are you that individual?"

"Perhaps."

"Show me."

"Gladly."

Reece took a step back and Kiuno let the sparks dance across her fingertips. The woman commanded the archers to stand down with a flick of her wrist.

She smirked. "I suppose even dogs can be useful."

"I find it amusing that you think I'd do anything for you."

Her smile faded. "I have your life in my hands. I can't imagine you'd be stupid enough not to notice."

Kiuno looked back at Reece who nodded and large trunks sprang from the stone. They intertwined and knotted themselves together rendering the flying arrows harmless as they struck into the thick wood.

Reece held his own against the archers, safely beneath a canopy of his creation. Vines crawled along the trunks like serpents seeking their prey, then flew toward the enemy. Some wound their way around bodies, strangling those in their grasp, while others struck through the gut.

Many flailed, most died, and the rest retreated. Kiuno was certain they'd be pounding on the door soon with swords drawn and magic of their own. Soldiers weren't likely to leave their leader defenseless.

Sparks danced between Kiuno's fingertips. It hummed, a far different sensation than the bolts she'd unleashed during battle. An electrical field seemed to crawl across her body and Kiuno's hair stood on end in response.

The woman snarled like a rabid dog and took a step back. She tightened her grip on the thin blade and drew it close.

If she knew how to use it, then she'd have speed, but judging from the way her eyes darted back and forth...

Kiuno lunged and the woman ducked beneath her blade. She stepped forward in an attempt to drive the thin steel up, but Kiuno spun to the side and the two faced off again, circling one another.

Fear. She reeked of it.

The woman waited for another attack, her eyes assessing Kiuno's every muscle twitch. Kiuno lunged again and just as before the woman ducked. Instead of turning this time, Kiuno shot a jolt of electricity down her sword and the woman recoiled. Kiuno parried the thin blade then brought her own down upon the woman's wrist.

The woman fell to her knees with a blood curdling scream and the severed hand thudded to the floor.

Pain, shock, and disbelief marred her pale, angular features.

Adrenaline coursed through Kiuno's body at the sight. This woman had caused her world to shatter. She'd been the one to take everything. She'd taken her life, her future, her love.

Blood spread along the once beautiful dress as the woman hugged the stub against the fabric. She made a grab for her blade, but Kiuno kicked the sword away and stomped on her remaining hand. The so called 'king' moaned against the floor.

Kiuno bent and the woman looked at her with tear stained cheeks. She pleaded.

Kiuno grasped the woman's intact hand and sent the electrical pulses crawling over her skin and through the woman's body.

She writhed, screamed, begged. Drool seeped from the sides of her mouth. Her eyes rolled back, but right before Kiuno thought she might pass out, she released her hold.

The woman's breath came in ragged gasps and she curled in on herself like an injured spider. A venomous creature that deserved punishment.

REECE BARRED the door and kept one eye on the balcony to ensure no surprises would cause Kiuno harm. He glanced back to the door, but his head jerked around when the woman screamed.

Lightning crawled across Kiuno's skin, giving it a bluish hue. He expected the woman to die in seconds, but to his surprise, Kiuno released her.

Grunts and shouts echoed from beyond the door and he summoned another trunk to reinforce it. The woman screamed again and the sound raced down Reece's spine.

Kiuno released the woman and she crumbled to the floor, her body convulsing.

"What do you want?" She cried. "I'll give you anything, please…"

"I thought I was a dog?" Kiuno stepped over her. "Do you beg to dogs now?"

"I'm sorry, please—"

Kiuno took the woman's wrist again, the lightning crawling along her arm in vengeance. Reece took a few steps forward, struggling to believe his eyes. She was enjoying this. Kiuno was enjoying the torture of another human being.

Kiuno released the woman again.

His mouth went dry.

Kiuno usually turned away from blood and battle. She didn't like gutting a deer, let alone torturing a human. She was kind and caring, almost in a motherly sense. Not this…

Kiuno took the woman's arm again and a smile crept to her face.

He couldn't stand it.

Reece tugged on a vine from the trunk above and shot it straight through the woman's heart. Her body went rigid and Kiuno's anger turned toward him. He braced for her reaction.

Neither moved until the door behind him shattered. Vines and wood caught fire as men burst through the door.

Their eyes fell to the woman lying face down against the stone and several cried out in rage.

Fire raced from Kiuno's hand, forcing Reece to take a step to the side as heat wafted through the room. It engulfed half the men and more screams echoed through the hall. Those second in line barreled through their comrades, and Reece met their swords in a match to the death.

Kiuno hacked through a man who charged him, and he covered her left side post swing. If she were angry with him, they'd sort the details later.

Another burst of flames had those unharmed hesitating and Reece yelled above the clashing steel. "Your leader is dead. Lay down your weapons."

Several paused, while others continued. He drove his sword through another's gut.

"I said lay down your weapons," he urged again.

Kiuno grabbed another man and her lightning crawled through his body. It writhed and he screamed until death silenced him.

Those remaining took a step back. A sword clattered to the floor. Another followed and then another until clanging steel resonated through the hall.

Reece relaxed, but kept focus. "Which of you is the next in command?"

Silence. Then a young man stepped forward. "I am." If Reece could judge age, he seemed about the same as Kiuno's friend Maltack. Eighteen. Nineteen.

The young man knelt in the blood of his fallen companions with clenched fists and kept his gaze on Reece's boots.

Reece took a calming breath. "Understand why we're here. Your leader made a poor decision that resulted in lives lost. I expect no further retribution in her name. I would rather not kill everyone in this castle."

"Speak for yourself," Kiuno said.

Reece glanced at her, wondering if she'd kill this lot just to spite him.

"She was a tyrant," the young man said. "Many of us didn't have a choice in serving her."

"That tyrant is dead and as long as no one acts foolishly, you'll be spared." *Hopefully.* "Take a seat against the wall and keep your hands where I can see them."

They did as instructed. Most slumped against the stone in defeat. Thankfully none looked willing to give their lives for a lost cause.

Reece glanced at them again, then took a few tentative steps toward Kiuno. "I'm sure those outside won't be much longer."

Kiuno looked at the men and Reece still wondered if she would kill them.

Neither moved then Kiuno let out a breath and stormed from the

183

room without a word.

WHAT AM I becoming?

She didn't regret it. Matter of fact, she'd enjoyed it and Kiuno wasn't so sure she wanted to discover who she might be without Elite.

The anger had dissipated, at least for now, but it left her cold and empty, much like the fireplace she'd left behind in their room.

Kiuno stood at the top of the tower, overlooking the battlegrounds. It seemed Iggy had left the wall intact, but he'd blown the gatehouse apart and left its rocks scattered along the inside. Victory fires lined the plains as men celebrated their triumph.

Those who'd yielded sat in a far corner with guards stationed on all sides. She remembered a time when their fates might have concerned her, but those thoughts didn't plague her now. If Iggy killed them, so be it.

The sun set on another day, the orange glow reflecting against white clouds. It left pink streaks across the sky, but she averted her gaze to look at the dull landscape.

Kiuno glanced behind her as the door creaked open. Reece exited and settled himself against the stone, propping his elbows on the hard surface.

He let out a long breath. "What now?"

"I'm going to the sixth realm."

"K.J. told me."

Kiuno clicked her tongue. "Figures he can't keep a secret."

"They're just looking out for you. He didn't want you running off by yourself."

"It wouldn't help anyone if I did. It's not as though I could map the area alone."

"We left a group of men with Cybele for that."

She looked at him, wondering what they'd said in her absence.

"Everything has been arranged. Maltack and I will join you."

She gave him a half hearted smile. "You shouldn't make yourself so predictable. I knew you'd come, but I expected a little resistance."

"You should know better." His face turned serious and she looked away.

"Are you sure Nsane wants the job of running this place?"

"You mean without his overenthusiastic best friend to mess up his organized planning? Yeah, he's good with it."

Kiuno smiled and guilt crashed through her, constricting her lungs. For a few minutes she hadn't thought of Elite or felt the pain of losing him. It was too soon to be forgetting. Too soon to allow herself to smile in his absence.

The two stood on the balcony and eventually moved to sit as they watched the stars come out in the open sky. Kiuno thanked the heavens for Reece's company. He didn't push. He didn't judge and his eyes didn't carry the pity she'd seen in so many others. He was there and tonight his company was all she needed.

REECE

REALM: 5

DAY: 309

The fire crackled at the center of their small gathering and Reece studied Kiuno through the flames. She sat like a statue with one knee drawn to her chest and chin resting upon it.

Cybele had greeted them with open arms that afternoon and got them cleaned up and fed. He was grateful to the woman and even more so that she was willing to help them navigate the sixth realm.

Several faces remained unknown. They'd exchanged greetings at dinner, but Reece hadn't bothered to commit any of their names to memory. He was focused on Kiuno. Distracted some might say.

But she was distracted too and with the coming dangers it would leave her vulnerable. Was this a suicide mission for her? Nothing left to live for so throw yourself to the nearest wolf?

Reece huffed and shifted his attention to those in their circle. Their bracelets glowed a variety of colors in the firelight. K.J.'s scouting team. At least K.J. knew how to pick those capable of handling themselves. They'd traveled unknown terrain before. They knew their mission.

But did Kiuno?

She shifted and their eyes met, but before Reece could speak, she turned away.

Reece scolded himself. Elite was gone. Kiuno was mourning, yet a piece of him wanted her to heal faster for his own selfish desires.

Reece berated himself and leaned against his pack. He stretched his legs out and the action caught her attention. He paused, but she glanced away again, that same sullen expression marring her face.

Jim's voice drew Reece back to the present. "How are you guys getting down the cliff?"

Cybele sat forward and crossed her legs. "The felinians will aid them, but be warned, they are prideful creatures."

Jim continued. "How long will you be gone?"

Reece rubbed the back of his neck. "As long as provisions allow."

Cybele straightened, stretching her back before shifting to a new position. "Water won't be an issue. There's plenty of rain."

"So, we'll be wet and miserable," Reece said.

"And hot," Cybele added.

"Lovely." Reece shifted so he could watch Kiuno without seeming obvious, not that she was paying attention.

A few weeks. Three at most. That's all the time he'd have alone with her. Who knew where she'd want to go after that?

Those surrounding the fire backed away and settled in for the night. Cybele and Jim curled up with their felinians and Kiuno separated herself from the others and used a pack to serve as her pillow.

Her back faced him and Reece's heart ached.

She never slept alone. Even when he'd first met her, Scorpios had always been at her side and when it wasn't him, Maltack took his place.

Reece searched for the kid and found him lying near Jim, his back already to the fire. Perhaps Jim had talked the kid out of hovering over Kiuno.

In the darkness, wild felinians called for their young. Through the shadows, he watched as they wrapped their wings over their cubs before curling up among the pride. A large male stood guard, his keen eyes scanning the trees and mountainside.

Cybele said they were prideful creatures and Reece wondered what that meant for tomorrow.

Reece looked back toward Kiuno and stood. Milo's ears perked, and Nikita watched him as he tiptoed toward Kiuno's shaking shoulders. She was crying. Again.

Reece sighed. He'd be second best for a while, but if his suffering meant her happiness then so be it. He'd be whatever she needed him to be.

Reece lay beside her, careful to keep space between them and placed one hand on her shoulder. She turned, the glistening trail of tears catching in the firelight. He tried to give her a small smile, but she buried her face in his chest. He prayed she couldn't hear his racing heart.

She sobbed, her body rising and falling with each breath, but he offered no words. Instead, Reece wrapped an arm around her and rested his chin in her hair.

Could he have this? When her pain settled and wounds healed, would he be able to call this woman his own?

As her breathing slowed, Reece turned his head to the cloudless sky. Stars flashed across the heavens as if racing one another through the endless night. In his heart, Reece made a promise to the dead. A promise to protect what another couldn't and make her smile again.

REECE SLEPT hard and woke with Kiuno in his arms. He leaned in, pressing his nose to her hair and she stirred.

"Morning."

Red faced and apologetic, Kiuno wriggled away from his grasp.

He smirked. That was more like the Kiuno he knew. Her actions woke the others and she strapped on her pack and sword without passing him another glance.

Cybele gathered supplies and whispered to her own people as their group prepared for the journey ahead. He pulled on his boots and slid his knives into their rightful places. Thankfully everyone in their party appeared just as prepared.

The felinians woke, their yawning roars filling the air as parents followed their eager young to the watering hole. With Cybele at their side, none paid his group much attention. He pitied those on the receiving end of the felinian's fury.

Reece observed Kiuno as they walked. Her face had returned to that distant staring, her gaze unfocused. It seemed after explosive rage, this was her default.

The horses were left behind for Cybele's people to care for and as they walked along the mountainside shards of rock slid down the edge.

Reece inclined his head and noticed three smaller felinians following them with curious eyes. Their claws dug into the rocky surface and their wings spread to keep balance as they tottered along a rocky edge.

The bushes that hid the cavern entered their view and all followed Cybele into the cool darkness of the cave. The portal sat inside.

They entered single file, each person before him disappearing as if they'd been sucked through a vortex and torn apart on the other side. Reece wondered if the portals would have lingering effects on the body once they returned home. Not that he planned to leave.

Reece took a step into the swirling mist and cold washed over him one instant and disappeared the next. Kiuno stood bent over, her hands on her knees. Reece stood at her side while she collected herself and glanced out over the thick jungle canopies.

Unknown animals scurried away through the branches and their calls sent a shiver down his spine. Reece tried to take a breath, but the dense air threatened to suffocate him where he stood.

Last time they'd set foot here, the group had gawked at the scenery, some even displaying awe, but he knew what hid behind this shroud of beauty. Misery and death if they weren't careful.

Reece glanced toward Kiuno, but her gaze remained blank as she took in the vast expanse. He knew she longed to be here with another. To conquer this game with Elite at her side and walk out on top.

Maybe she no longer knew if she had a life on the outside. Maybe he could convince her to stay.

Cybele interrupted his thoughts. "The felinians can fly two at a time. Once we land, we'll be on foot."

Reece focused on the creatures who'd followed them through. There were six massive felinians including Milo. He'd thought Cybele's to be the largest, but the five males before them outsized Milo by at least a foot.

Reece approached one and a deep growl rippled from the creature's throat. Reece bowed his head, remembering Cybele's words from last night. He wasn't about to ruin a free ride by playing the tough guy.

It sniffed his hair and after investigating every inch of his neck with hot breath the beast seemed satisfied and awaited his move.

Reece turned to look at Kiuno and finally found emotion. Fear, or at the very least, apprehension. Her gaze shifted from the felinians to the cliff's edge.

Reece smirked. "What's wrong Ki, scared?"

She should have fired back with a smart comment, but Kiuno stayed silent.

Reece let out a breath, took Kiuno's hand, and pulled her away from the edge. Their felinian perked up and rather than growl, it greeted her, nuzzling her neck as she stroked beneath the massive chin. The edges of her lips lifted, but it was hardly enough to be called a smile.

He'd take the fear of death as a good sign. It meant some part of her still wanted to live and that was light years better than the alternative.

"Here." Reece gave her a boost and strapped her legs to the thin leather saddle. It surprised him the beast tolerated such a thing. There were three buckles on each side. One for around the ankle, one around the calf, and the final strapped around the thigh.

After buckling her in, Reece jumped behind Kiuno and wrapped one arm around her middle. Her warm body pressed against his, but his thoughts quickly turned somber when she trembled beneath his touch.

"Ready?" Cybele called. The woman glanced at Kiuno and Reece then smiled. The action surprised him. After their nights in his tent, he'd figure Cybele to be possessive, but she turned out to be quite the opposite.

The felinian's body shifted beneath him and it unfurled black tipped wings as it walked to the edge. Kiuno clutched his arm and Reece gripped the saddle as the creature leapt from the cliff.

His stomach dropped and breath caught as the ground raced to greet them. The felinian angled its wings and the wind jolted them as it lifted their bodies toward the sky. With a few pumps, the creatures pulled them above the green canopies, and they soared across the tops of trees.

Exhilaration flew through Reece. Riding a horse gave him freedom, but nothing compared to soaring on a predatory creature above the tree-tops.

He watched the canopies fly by like a child who'd just been given a new toy. The felinians soared over the jungle and the high platform they'd jumped from disappeared from their view. Cybele didn't bother to turn around, so he contented himself to relax and enjoy the ride. The less they had to trek through the jungle on foot, the better.

Kiuno's fingers flexed around his arm and he shifted in the saddle to look at her face. She'd clamped her eyes shut and if her white knuckles were anything to go by, he'd start losing circulation soon.

"Relax," he whispered. "I won't let you fall."

Kiuno tried to take a deep breath. "I know." Her fingers relaxed a little.

What else did she know?

It was late afternoon before they started their descent. The dip was sudden, and he gripped Kiuno, determined to keep his promise. She

closed her eyes and he ducked both of their heads low as the felinian ma-
neuvered the branches and softly landed in a small clearing.

"We can rest here for tonight," Cybele said. "There's clean water
nearby and I'm familiar with this area."

Reece helped Kiuno from the saddle. "I wasn't aware we were flying
this far."

Cybele jumped from Milo with the grace of someone who'd done it
a thousand times. "I can map the area up to this point. There's no reason
to waste time with known territory."

Reece stretched his lower back and legs and watched while Cybele
cooed to the felinians as if they were small beings who needed coddled.
Such a strange woman.

"They'll make it back before nightfall without the extra weight dragging them down."

"Is yours staying?" Reece asked.

Cybele patted the side of Milo and smirked. "Of course, I need an
escape route should things go south."

"Not much for valiancy, are you?"

"I don't see any reason in getting myself killed because your lot can't
make a home here."

"You plan on staying?" Kiuno asked.

Cybele cocked her head. "There's nothing for me in the real world. I
have everything I need right here."

They ate the dried meat in their packs and set a schedule for watch.
He would have liked the chance to explore the area, but Reece guessed it
wouldn't be much different from his first few days in realm one. As long
as he didn't have to deal with a pack of rabid animals like that first night.

With the fire lit Reece settled in and watched the map makers unroll
a piece of parchment. Cybele gave them the details on the land. From the
sound of things, the flight had saved them a few days' hike.

Reece looked back to where Kiuno had been moments ago and sat
up straight when he found her missing. His heart jumped to his throat as

he searched the faces in their camp. Milo was missing too. Reece peered through the trees wondering how such a large creature could have snuck off without his notice.

"She's just beyond that tree line." Reece jumped at Cybele's voice. A smirk played on her lips. "Milo is keeping an eye on her."

Reece gave her a puzzled look. "I expected you to be—"

"Jealous?" she finished. "I'm not the type to be held down. I fancied you in bed, but I've fancied a few." She winked and let her gaze rest on something beyond the trees. "The felinians sense her pain. It makes Milo restless."

Reece's eyes adjusted to the dark, and he spotted the large felinian in the brush ahead. "When we retaliated, Kiuno's focus was revenge. She killed their leader, tortured her." Reece shook his head. "I'm not one to hold anyone back, but seeing her like that…"

"It's not the woman you fell for."

"Sorry?"

"A man doesn't hold a woman without some attachment."

"I'm just worried."

"Are you trying to convince me or yourself? I'm a woman, you can't hide those things from us, even though you silly boys try."

A smile tugged at the corner of his lips. "Even if I wanted something more, she's mourning. I can't close the gap in her heart, and I don't want to push her."

"If no one keeps her from falling, she's going to drop into an abyss and never come back."

Cybele left him with that and though he wanted to question her, Reece's attention shifted to the silhouette in the darkness. He wouldn't let Kiuno fall, he'd already promised.

Reece crept through the brush and Kiuno seemed to be studying the water with her arms wrapped around her knees.

He wanted to save her, but how?

"Scorpios would scold you for sitting here alone." Reece leaned against a tree and watched her body shift. She tucked her legs to the side but didn't turn.

"Are you here to take his place?" Cold, emotionless.

"No, just to see what's going through your mind."

Trickling water filled the silence. "Nothing and everything at once. Memories. Things that should have been."

Reece folded his arms. "I could tell you there's plenty to live for, but that probably isn't what you want to hear. I could say time will heal your pain, but that won't help either."

Reece moved from the tree and sat behind her. He wrapped his arms around her neck and tugged her close. Kiuno stiffened.

"The only thing I can do is be here."

"What about Cybele?"

Reece laughed. "She isn't looking for anything serious."

"Are you?" Silence stretched between them as he held her tense body. He knew she struggled with whether to lean in or pull away, but Kiuno did neither.

"Maybe." At that she sighed and leaned forward, but Reece held onto her.

"I can't." Her voice broke and his heart raced.

"I'm not asking anything from you." Reece pulled her back and Kiuno allowed it though her muscles were still rigid beneath his touch. "Just know I'm here, for whatever you need."

Her voice cracked again. "That isn't fair."

"You let me worry about what's fair."

The silence stretched, and Kiuno finally relented and her body collapsed against his.

She was right, it wasn't fair. It wasn't fair for her to suffer. It wasn't fair for her youth to be burdened with so much turmoil and grief, but life wasn't fair and if this world had taught him anything it was that one cruel lesson.

ELITE

Realm: 5
Day: 295

A ir pulled through Elite's lungs like a million shards of glass sawing the tender organs. He coughed and convulsed, pain assaulting his body like a tidal wave. Darkness stretched on all sides save for a small fire flickering to his right. He moved to sit up, but sharp pain lancing through his core shot him back.

"I wouldn't move if I were you."

Elite craned his neck toward the fire. A girl sat on the other side with her back pressed against the wall and legs sprawled. She chewed something, smacking her lips without bothering to look at him.

A woven blanket lay over his chest and his right pant leg had been cut at the knee.

"I set the bone and splinted it. Pretty sure your ribs are broken too, but there's not much I can do about that."

He gasped through the pain, struggling to breathe, but Elite lifted himself to a seated position and leaned against the rocky wall. It took several moments for him to catch his breath. "Who are you?"

She took another bite of the meat, tearing it from a stick as the fire crackled between them. "Vixin."

Elite waited for more, but she didn't elaborate. He licked his cracked lips and winced. "Do you have any water?"

After taking a final bite Vixin set her stick on the cavern floor and slid a flask to him. Her features became visible as she moved in the firelight. Hair as red as flames and eyes just as menacing. Daggers hung at her waist, but she couldn't be much older than his teenage sister.

"Thanks."

Vixin didn't offer any assistance as he struggled to reach the flask. The cool water eased his parched throat. When finished, Elite checked his surroundings and squinted in the dark. Rubble sat piled in what he assumed to be an exit. In the opposite direction lay only darkness.

"What happened?" he asked.

"I was hoping you could tell me. I was fishing when an explosion sent chunks of the cliff barreling toward me. Don't know why, but I grabbed you before the boulder could crush you to death."

"You grabbed me?" He examined her small stature.

Vixin huffed. "I can use earth."

Memories of the meeting rushed back. They wanted to prove a point and had used an explosion as a display of power. Elite rubbed the back of his neck and met tender flesh.

"I guess I have you to thank. How long have I been out?"

"About two days."

Two days? Where was Kiuno and what happened to the others? Elite's gaze drifted back toward the endless dark. "I appreciate you sticking around."

"I didn't at first, but the damn guilt kept nagging me, so I turned around. Figured if you died at least I could say I did my best."

Perhaps empathy wasn't her best quality. Not that he could be picky at the moment. "What about the others?"

Vixin shrugged and rotated two skewers hanging over the fire. "I heard voices outside but couldn't make them out. We're buried too deep for my abilities to be of help."

"We're trapped?"

"No, but it's a long trek and I couldn't drag you."

Elite tried to shift his leg, but blinding pain shot through his body in response. "How far is the exit?"

"For me? About three and a half or four days. For you," she nodded toward his leg. "A lot longer."

Elite groaned. "Where does the exit lead?"

"A few miles from where the forest used to meet the mountain. Want one?" Vixin offered him the small creature and he nodded. At first, he thought she might throw it, but Vixin stood and walked the roasted creature over. She kept well out of his reach.

"I'll warn you now. I might have felt guilty about leaving you before, but if you try anything, I will kill you."

He tried not to scoff. "I don't think I could hurt a fly, let alone an able-bodied person."

"Good, that'll make sleep easier for me."

Once she'd taken her seat across the fire, Elite examined the roasted creature. A large rat stared back at him. At one point he might have turned down such a thing, but now—Elite took a mouthful then shifted his gaze toward the darkness again. It'd take him over a week to get out of here.

"How long have you lived here?" he asked.

Vixin examined the meat, pulled at a bone then tore another piece with her teeth. "Long enough."

She'd heard voices. That meant Kiuno was probably safe, but he still needed to find her. Elite sighed. According to Vixin, he wouldn't be doing that anytime soon.

What had happened in his absence? Were those responsible dead? Was war brewing between the two factions? Would Kiuno fight on the front line without knowing his fate?

Did she—did she think him dead?

Elite shifted and hot pain shot through his leg and torso. He bit the inside of his cheek and a metallic taste filled his mouth. He needed Maltack or Palindrome. Anyone that could heal these wounds.

If Kiuno thought him dead she'd be reckless and out of control. He could send Vixin, but he couldn't survive on his own in this sorry state. And if she did leave there was no telling if she'd ever come back.

Elite leaned his head against the wall. The best he could do now was to earn this young girl's trust. Hopefully it'd lead him out of this cave and to someone who could help.

"How old are you?" Elite asked.

"Sixteen."

"The same age as my sister."

Vixin ignored his comment and took the last bite from her rat before asking, "Where are you from?"

"One of the main castles."

"Oh."

His blood raced at her shifted tone. "Is that bad?"

Vixin rolled the stick between her fingers. "One of them killed my family."

Shit. "I'm sorry to hear it."

She broke the stick in one hand. "He's a murderer." Vixin threw the pieces into their small fire and went silent again.

"So, is it just you down here?"

"Yeah. Been that way for a month. I steal what I need." She smirked. "Those idiots will never figure me out."

Elite tried to calm his racing heart. Since they were beside the mountain it cleared K.J. of any fault. As much as he disliked the guy, Elite couldn't see K.J. slaughtering a family for no reason. That was a plus at least.

"The leader I reside under is stationed across the river."

"I've never been to that side, but I saw the forest burn. Was he responsible?"

"He felt it was the best way through."

"Guess he's an idiot too."

"At the time I might have agreed with you, but after seeing what came out of those trees, I can't say that anymore."

Vixin fiddled with something on the floor, rolling it between her fingers. "Does *he* kill people for no reason?"

"Not that I'm aware."

"Are you a significant person to him?"

Not really.

"I'm present when decisions are made."

"So, it's likely I can get compensated for taking you home?"

Elite chuckled. "And here I thought you'd stayed out of the goodness of your heart."

"No time for that. If this doesn't benefit me, I'm out."

Same age as his sister yes, but this girl had light years more experience.

"I'm certain they'll be willing to give you whatever you want in exchange for my safe return."

Vixin crossed her legs. "Good."

ELITE TRIED to sleep when Vixin did, but the pain radiating from his leg made the task impossible. He pulled himself closer to the fire and lay on his back, struggling to breathe as his ribs protested each rise in his chest. He'd doze, only to have a shock shoot through his body as if the nerves were on fire.

With morning, he took a swig of water and mentally prepared himself for the painful task ahead.

Vixin threw him a large stick that would serve as his cane, lit a torch, and stomped out their fire.

Her intentions were clear. She'd guide him out, but she'd have no part in helping.

Elite shifted so his good leg supported his weight then leaned on the stick. He screamed as he lifted himself from the floor. Elite pressed his head against the cool, damp stone to catch his breath. Every damn muscle contraction seemed to shoot from his leg.

"This'll be fun," Vixin said. She took a few steps then paused to wait for him.

Elite lifted himself from the wall, took a breath, and jumped. The shock of pain that flew through his body almost sent him back to the ground, but he caught himself and summoned the strength to do it again. And again.

Four days, but if he kept this pace it'd be more like eight.

Kiuno. He had to get back to her. God only knew what she might be doing in his absence.

Pain. Abandonment. Sorrow. The drowning sadness that only hit a person when something rooted in their foundation fractured and crumbled away.

He'd felt that when his father passed. But parents weren't supposed to outlive their children. The pain of losing your soulmate was for the old as they reminisced upon a life well lived. Not for someone like her.

Wait for me. I'll always come back for you.

VIXIN SET her pack on the ground and Elite took one last step before collapsing.

"We'll stop here for the night."

Nothing had shifted. Nothing to measure his progress.

Four days.

His body shook, every nerve on fire, yet there was still such a long way to go.

"You need to rest, and I have to find water." Vixin used her torch to start the fire with a pile of wood she must have kept on standby. Once lit, she disappeared into the dark tunnel leaving him in stillness.

He needed to rest. God, he wanted to rest, but the tunnel loomed before him. He sat there for several minutes, catching his breath, then gnashed his teeth together and stood against the wall.

The path was straight, like something cut from the rock ages ago. Vixin could move the fire when she returned, but he needed to make as much progress as possible.

Elite jumped, grinding his teeth from the pain. It was nothing compared to Kiuno's. He jumped again, tears stinging the corners of his eyes. One step at a time. One step closer to her.

JUNGLE

REALM: 6

DAY: 311

*D*arkness. *No matter how much she tried to escape, it was always there, always watching.*

It'd claimed too many and now worked its way to claim her, worming through her heart like a parasite.

Kiuno ran for him as he fell, trying to clutch his sleeve before he slipped into eternal night, but it wasn't Elite. Reece wrapped his vines around her arms and torso, drawing her toward him and they both fell into the abyss together.

Kiuno jolted and took several breaths to calm her racing heart. Reece had talked her back to camp late last night and she'd fallen asleep in his arms again. She looked at his sleeping form then pried herself away.

Kiuno splashed cold water on her face and looked at herself in the small creek's reflection. *I'll be whatever you need.*

Whatever she needed. Did she even know what that was?

Guilt assaulted her as Kiuno thought about him holding her through the night. She rubbed at the raw scars, using the pain to drown the heaviness of her heart. Her hands shook, and she clenched them as she struggled to hold herself together.

Maybe she had to come to terms with losing everything. Maybe the rest of her life would be filled with one painful moment after another. She'd be left alone. For some god-forsaken reason, she'd be the one to survive.

Her raw skin opened and Kiuno let the flowing water carry trickles of blood downstream. Was she left to suffer because she had the strength to survive it? Did her feeling pain mean the others wouldn't have to?

Maltack startled her as he knelt and took her arm. His magic healed her open scars, and this time she let him. Maltack had been silent since they'd left K.J.'s castle. What did he make of her actions?

Maltack stood and held out his hand. Tears stung her eyes as she took it and followed him back to the camp. He wasn't angry—only concerned for her well-being.

Reece and Cybele were packed and ready to go. She'd heard them talking last night. They planned to move deeper inside the jungle and find a suitable place to set up camp. From there, they'd fan along the perimeter and map out the area. If they didn't find anything then they'd move on.

With her boots tightened and heart empty Kiuno followed the others into the thick foliage. Sweat dripped from every pore in her body. Despite being in a braid, her hair glued itself to the back of her neck and she tried to move it every which way for relief.

Bugs crawled over her skin, or so she thought as she swatted at things that weren't there. Irritation picked up among the group and most refused to talk as they trudged through the boiling jungle. Why had she volunteered for this?

Distraction.

Thunder rolled overhead, long and foreboding. Most glanced up, but the thick canopy didn't allow them much insight to what might be above. Cybele had mentioned a lot of rain.

A large drop of water landed on the top of Kiuno's head. She swiped at it and glanced up as another fell at her feet. Thunder rolled again and within minutes rain poured from the green above.

Kiuno leaned her head back and let the droplets hit her face and roll down her cheeks.

The group continued and the rain poured. The felinian shook out his fur several times as they trudged through the jungle. Water soaked through their bags, weapons, and clothes.

When the rain stopped misery took on a new level.

The humidity didn't permit the water to evaporate so not only was she hot, but now she was wet as well. Misery isn't what she'd imagined to be part of the distraction plan.

When those in the front set their packs down to rest, Kiuno hid herself behind a tree and did her best to wring out her shirt. It remained damp and would likely stay that way for the rest of the evening.

Kiuno adjusted her clothes and returned to their camp. Maltack's hands hovered over a sodden log. Small specks of water rose from the wood and into the air. They circled Maltack's hand for a moment then he flicked his fingers to the side and cast them away.

Thunder rolled overhead again, and Reece plopped down on a log at her side.

"If we're staying, then we should set up the tents."

His gaze traveled above and Kiuno followed it. A whole night of rain? Her skin had already started to prune.

"There's no need to set up anything," Cybele said. "Milo found an alternative."

Though her legs ached, Kiuno shoved herself to her feet and away from the tree she'd taken refuge beneath. They tracked over another small incline and through thicker brush than she would have liked but thankfully, the walk wasn't long.

"This should do." Cybele pointed toward a rock outcropping, but it took Kiuno several moments to spot the entrance. Thick foliage surround-

RISE OF THE WOLVES

ed the outside, but once they stepped under the shelf, Kiuno's irritation ebbed.

The cave stretched a good twenty feet across and only narrowed toward the rear. Maltack and the other fire users summoned their flames to cast light upon the area.

Thick moss lined the walls and smaller plants grew in the crevasses, but it was dry and gave them ample space to stretch out.

"Well isn't this gold." Reece threw his wet pack to the ground.

Milo entered and splashed the rest of them as he shook droplets from his fur.

The rain started again outside.

Maltack raised his hand with flames still wrapped around it. "We should see how far back it goes. I'd hate for something to surprise us while we're sleeping."

Kiuno's mind flashed back to the creature who'd chased her and Palindrome. Luckily this cave wasn't tall enough to accommodate such a beast.

Kiuno summoned her magic and spiraled it around her body, then launched it toward the back of the cave. Moss covering the walls fizzled and curled into ash. Her flames found an end and crashed against the wall before dissipating with nothing to keep them alive.

Cybele and Maltack followed her to an edge where the floor dropped in what seemed to be an endless black hole. Kiuno pulled forth her fire again and shot it down. The flames twisted at a bend not far below.

"We'll keep an eye on that," Cybele said.

Vines sprung from the ground and the others took a step back. The greenery shifted and expanded until leaves and branches blocked the entire hole.

"Now we won't have to." Reece removed his shoes and pulled off the damp shirt clinging to his back. He tilted his head and stretched his shoulders. "I could use a drink."

Kiuno watched him for a moment, then averted her gaze. "For once,

I have to agree with you."

"Do you plan on staying in those wet clothes?" Cybele asked. The woman had already removed everything but the wrap covering her breasts and a cloth that barely covered the rest.

Kiuno blushed and glanced at Reece. "Some of us are more modest."

Reece chuckled, and she glared at him, but a smile fought its way through, and she playfully shoved him to the side.

Kiuno unlaced her boots and rubbed at her sore feet.

Reece threw her a tarp and a piece of rope. "It's not much, but at least it'll get you out of those clothes."

Kiuno sighed, took the makeshift dress and hid behind an erected tent. The rain had soaked everything in their packs, but hopefully the fires would take away the dampness by morning.

Kiuno peeled her clothes off one by one and slipped the rough fabric over her head. The bottom stopped just above her knees. She folded the sides and tied a knot at the front. It wasn't fashionable by any means, but she was happy to be dry.

With Cybele flaunting her nakedness, no one turned to look at Kiuno, but she still tucked her legs beneath herself in an attempt at decency.

With several fires going and the map unfolded for all to see, Cybele leaned over and pointed. "We're about here so we'll mark this area as the midpoint and scan the vicinity in the morning."

They made a mark on the parchment, but Kiuno's gaze drifted back to the covered hole. Reece had posted two men to keep watch just in case. She prayed nothing sinister reared its head while they slept.

THRESHOLD

REALM: 6
DAY: 312

Reece and Kiuno crept through the jungle in search of another land-mark to add to their ever-growing map. The rain had ended, but with it the insects feasted on any who dared venture through their territory. Kiuno smacked another mosquito.

"I don't like this place," Reece said.

A shiver ran down Kiuno's spine. She understood what he meant. Something in the shadows seemed to lurk, watching their every move.

Reece used his magic to bend a tree covered in thorns from their path. They moved in silence after that, ducking between trees and brush as they searched. So far all they had were a few waterways and the cavern.

Reece grabbed her arm, pulled her down, and placed a finger over his lips. She waited, surveying the area. Nothing seemed out of place, but her skin crawled, nonetheless.

A branch cracked and Reece pulled her around the trunk. Kiuno's heart raced, but she tried to keep her breathing calm.

Kiuno turned to look at Reece and froze.

The face of a deer, complete with antlers. The fangs of a wolf. Long arms with razor sharp claws that promised a painful death. A predator.

It huffed and Reece slowly turned. The smell of its breath reminded Kiuno of decaying flesh and she struggled not to gag.

A growl rippled from its throat and the upper lip pulled back in a savage snarl.

Vines wrapped around her body and Reece yanked them both back as the creature snapped its jaws where his neck had been moments ago.

"Time to go."

The beast howled in rage when the jungle's vines pulled them high above the ground. Kiuno clutched at the greenery and risked at glance back.

At least a dozen of the beasts gave chase.

"They're gaining," she called.

Reece glanced back and vines grasped her body again, jerking her to the right. Kiuno clenched her teeth, praying Reece could concentrate on the enemy and her at the same time.

"Grab on," he yelled. She grasped the trunk of a wide tree and Reece's magic fell away. Her foot slipped, but she latched onto another branch and used her fire to burn the beast jumping for her leg.

Kiuno searched for Reece amidst the dozen or so flailing bodies that ran between the trees. He used his magic to block, strike, and run again as he fought them off one by one. Three more circled the base of her tree, including the one she thought she'd killed.

Reece's voice echoed through the air and Kiuno's head jerked up. He fell and her heart raced, but another of his vines grabbed him before he hit the jungle floor. Reece skidded across the ground and the creatures circling her charged at the easy prey.

Kiuno scrambled down the trunk and threw her magic when one creature turned around to attack. She ducked around it and ran for Reece. Growling rippled through the area as she used the flames to guard herself.

Why aren't they dying?

Kiuno slid to Reece's side, but he shoved her over and a clawed arm slammed his head against the tree. He slumped to the ground, unmoving, and Kiuno turned to face the snarling creatures.

They pulled their lips over sharp fangs and crazed eyes seemed to mock her. Their numbers hadn't diminished, and cold fear seeped into her bones.

The fire wasn't burning them.

"Wake up Reece." She kicked him with her foot and three creatures launched themselves forward.

Kiuno spiraled the flames around her body and aimed for the creature's eyes. They howled in rage and she drew her sword.

The next reached out with its long claws. She pulled forth more flames, fighting for control as they sought to rage outward and burn anything living.

Kiuno dodged the clawed hand and the flames crawled along her sword as she hacked at the beast's arm. To her dismay, the blade lodged itself in the creature's bone and she lost her grip as it reared back in pain.

She tucked the fire close again and turned to her companion. Reece didn't move.

A clawed arm slammed into her side and pierced flesh as it flung her several feet away. Kiuno cried out as sharp pain radiated up her side. She hit the ground and stood again, fighting to keep her mind focused on the beasts who threatened them.

Half were focused on her, advancing despite the fire flickering around her body. The other half hovered over Reece. Her heart raced and a new wave of panic flew through her core.

Lightning crackled and sparked around her body. The beast holding Reece opened its mouth, but before it could clamp down on his neck her magic soared through the space separating them.

The beast roared in pain as the bolt struck. The others howled in response and took several retreating steps away from her friend. Kiuno shot another bolt to her left then the rest fled, their voices echoing in their wake.

Despite her pain, Kiuno scrambled toward Reece's body. She dropped to his side and pressed her ear against his chest.

His heart was still beating.

But his chest didn't rise.

Kiuno threw her satchel from her shoulder and fought the rising panic as she folded her fingers together and placed them over his solar plexus. His shirt shifted and a mark like the ones that ran along her arms revealed itself on the tip of his chest.

She yanked the shirt down and followed the line.

Kiuno cursed. She cursed her magic. Cursed this wretched world.

She took another breath, folded her hands over Reece's chest again, and began counting.

How many compressions was it again?

Thirty?

Forty?

She did thirty and pressed her mouth against his.

Nothing happened.

Rising panic filled her as she tilted his head back and tried again. This time his chest lifted. She repeated the process and placed her folded hands over his torso again.

Please.

Air filled his lungs, but he didn't stir.

Kiuno compressed his chest again, her movements growing more frantic by the second.

She pressed her lips to his and salty tears ran down her face.

Forty compressions.

Two breaths.

Compressions.

Breaths.

"Reece!" Kiuno slammed her fists on his chest and crumpled over his body.

This isn't happening. This isn't happening. This isn't happening.

Kiuno took a breath, her body shaking beyond control as she wiped her face and continued compressions. She wouldn't give up. She couldn't bear it if—

Reece's eyes flew open and he sputtered and coughed, desperately sucking in oxygen. Kiuno rolled him onto his side, but she couldn't let go. His hand gripped her arm as he took in lungful after lungful of air.

Kiuno clutched him to her chest, listening to each intake of breath as she steadied her own racing heart.

"We have to go," she said. Kiuno took his arm before he could respond and wrapped it around her neck. He tried to help her stand, but the two stumbled back together and a tree caught the pair.

She took a step forward and he followed, leaning almost all his weight against her. Kiuno struggled with step after step under his weight.

"Where?" Reece struggled to say.

"I don't know."

He wheezed and coughed as they pushed forward, both stumbling through the foliage. Blood caked the side of his head. Her own blood covered her shirt, but neither stopped for fear of their pursuers.

The mouth of the cavern brought relief, but only for a moment. A roar echoed from behind that had everyone's eyes darting toward the entrance. "Run," Kiuno yelled.

Maltack appeared, but she slammed into him and grasped his wrist, continuing deeper into the cave. The rest followed. Fire flew behind, but she knew it would only buy them seconds.

Kiuno glanced back. A wall of flames separated them from the creatures. The beasts buried their faces in their packs and ripped through the tents. Kiuno counted heads. Milo growled, his fur raised and Cybele stood at his side with her spear poised.

A long arm burst through the wall of flames, but Maltack shoved the beast back with his wind. The action fanned the fire and expanded its depth.

"What now?" Maltack asked.

"We hope there's another exit," Reece replied.

Two more creatures tried to jump through the flames and the entire group took a few steps back. Kiuno looked at another in the group, glad to see he'd salvaged one of their packs.

Cybele examined the black hole where the cavern dipped into darkness. "Do as you wish, I'm going down."

Cybele jumped on Milo's back and the pair dropped into the unknown. The monsters raged toward them, snarling their frustrations.

"Who else uses earth?" Reece asked.

Two men raised their hands, uncertain.

"Good, come with me."

When they tried to protest, Reece grabbed them by the shirt and threw them into the sloped hole.

"Ready?" Maltack asked her.

"No."

They jumped and hard rock met her bottom as they slid down a steep rocky slope. Screams followed her down the tunnel as the hard surface bit into her skin and clothes. Kiuno tumbled once and came to a slow halt. She clambered to her feet and ran, following the light in Maltack's palm.

With the last man through, Reece used his vines to dig into the wide cavern walls and crumbled the entrance while the rest fled. She took a few steadying breaths and coughed from the dust floating in the air. Silence and darkness surrounded them on all sides.

Kiuno pulled at her magic and flames wrapped around her hand setting a glow to the faces of those still panting. Maltack and two others did the same. She assumed the screaming had come from those unwilling to jump. She'd never learned their names.

Maltack made his way to each of them, checking for serious wounds. The fall had resulted in one broken arm, but Maltack cracked the bone back in place and mended the tissue. He healed the gash in her arm but left the rest of her scrapes for later.

As the group took a moment to collect themselves, Kiuno tried to peer through the darkness. She couldn't tell which way they should go or whether another drop waited for them to stumble to their deaths. Perhaps Milo's sense of smell could lead them in the right direction.

"What are those?"

Kiuno followed the man's gaze toward the ceiling. Small, bluish lights lined the top, swaying back and forth. Kiuno squinted and let her fire fade as she tried to get a better look.

"This is disgusting."

Kiuno turned and Maltack moved to examine the one who'd spoken. A slimy substance dripped from his bicep and he waved his arm back and forth struggling to break free.

"Stop moving," Maltack said.

While Maltack worked to free him, Kiuno's gaze followed the path of sticky goo toward the ceiling. It reached beyond her line of sight. Maltack was just about to touch it when the same man went soaring through the air, a screaming echo left in his wake.

The balls above began to shake and then one fell from the ceiling. Followed by another.

Everyone jumped to their feet.

A slithering noise echoed off the walls and a fat maggot-like creature dropped behind Reece.

Reece ducked as it shot a string of sludge from its mouth, ensnaring another. The man struggled with breath as the creature reeled him in and his head disappeared inside a mouth layered with teeth.

Fire burst from Kiuno, Maltack, and two others. They formed a barrier and revealed hundreds of fat, white bodies slithering in their direction. The creatures retreated from the heat, but their slime shot through the flames and grasped another in their party by the arm. Kiuno grabbed his free hand and planted her feet. She set fire to the substance, burning him in the process, but it broke him free.

"Run," Cybele screamed.

Milo led the way, weaving between strands that shot from the darkness. The balls that seemed to float were the only things that told them how many creatures stood in their way.

Another man screamed, and she turned to be sure it wasn't Reece or Maltack. Someone disappeared, pulled back through the black and a dozen glowing balls congregated to one area, silencing his cries for help.

Kiuno pivoted and turned toward the creatures. She pulled at the white-hot magic in her core and cracks of lightning danced around her body. She surged the energy forward and left a path of oozing bodies wherever it touched.

Maltack grabbed her hand and they ran.

Up ahead, two men with fire crawling along their arms stood at what appeared to be a low crack in the wall. Reece's head poked through and the two men ducked to follow as she and Maltack neared. Reece had already started to collapse it and held the entrance open just enough so they could squeeze through.

Maltack shoved her in first, but a sticky string caught his leg and he tripped, hitting the ground. Kiuno dove for him, using her feet as leverage against the stone. Fear filled his eyes.

Kiuno grit her teeth and pulled at her magic. Her flames lit up the room as she surrounded them both in fire and burst the energy through the hole.

Maltack's leg broke free and Reece collapsed the walls around the tunnel, separating them from the deadly larvae.

Darkness encased their group again and the only sound that could be heard was the steady panting of their breath.

Once again, Maltack used his fire to light up another cavern room. They'd lost two more of their squad in the chaos.

Reece rested his head against the rock. "I really hate this realm."

38

ELITE

REALM: 5

DAY: 303

L ight waited for him at the end of the tunnel. Either he'd died and gone to hell or his escape was imminent. Vixin ran ahead, leaving him to hobble through the last stretch alone.

Time had blurred within the darkness. It taunted him and claimed he'd be lost to its embrace forever.

Elite had been elated to discover Vixin wasn't entirely devoid of sympathy. She'd softened upon seeing his continuous struggle and didn't verbally lash out as much as she'd done the first day.

The two passed the time by talking about his younger sister. Elite shared her likes and dislikes and discovered they vastly differed from Vixin's. His sister enjoyed dressing up, fixing her hair, and her focus for the last few weeks before his disappearance had been a boy in her high school class. Vixin had found that amusing.

She'd grown up with a single father who'd committed every waking moment to teaching the girl how to defend herself.

They hunted, sparred, learned different languages, and Vixin reluctantly home schooled herself. Apparently, algebra and Shakespeare were a colossal waste of time. Not that he could disagree.

Elite reached the exit and shielded his eyes as he gazed through the hole. Vixin waited and to his surprise offered to help him up.

She wrapped her magic around his torso and carefully squeezed him through the tiny opening. His leg hit a rock and Elite hissed in pain, but the sunshine drove away all his fears.

With the hot sun shining upon his face, Elite collapsed against a rock. He soaked in the sun's light and relished in the cool breeze racing through the grass.

Fresh air on his face. Warm rays on his skin. Sounds of life as creatures scurried along the rock. Those things alone were enough to make a person appreciate their freedom.

Plains stretched out in an endless sea of green and tan. Trees dotted the landscape and the mountain side stretched along a curved path riddled with rocks and debris.

Vixin scurried away so Elite settled himself on the ground content to rest after the days he'd spent in agonizing pain.

He'd learned not to question Vixin's whereabouts. She'd thrown a fit the first time and claimed if he was going to be a nag then she'd leave him behind. He wasn't about to test her patience.

Judging from Vixin's descriptions they were on the other side of the river, which meant they'd either be heading to Samar, Leena, or Atilla's domain. He'd prefer the former two. If he had to put money on who might have killed Vixin's family, it would be Atilla.

Vixin returned with four rats and plopped down to skewer them. He imagined his wife would have vomited from seeing how this girl handled the creatures. Then again, maybe not. What had she learned in the time they'd first been apart?

She'd mentioned her teachings with Elliott in the early days, but what about now? Could she survive on her own if forced? Had he been underestimating her all this time?

"How far are we from the nearest castle?" he asked.

Vixin looked up from her task and scanned the horizon. "A few days on horseback, but in your condition?"

Great, yet another long journey riddled with pain and anxiety.

Vixin set their meal over the flames, then stood and wiped her hands on her pants. "We'll move along the mountain's edge. The plains would leave us too exposed at night. Trust me when I say there are things you don't want to encounter after dark."

That would take them to the Chinese. Perhaps Scorpios had already been sent for K.J.'s negotiation plans. That would be the most favorable outcome.

"Are you listening?"

"Yes, I think that's a good plan."

Vixin huffed. "You should respond when people talk. It's rude."

He tried to hide his smile. "Sorry, lost in my thoughts."

"Well, you better get your head out of the clouds. People patrol this area and we'll need to hide if they get too close."

"Wouldn't they be able to help?"

She shrugged. "Maybe you, but they don't show much appreciation to a thief. They've chased me here before, but I know these tunnels better than anyone. Once I'm inside, I'm invisible."

"Where's the camp you steal from?"

"Along the far river. I sneak in from time to time."

She stole from Leena's group then. "Could you take me there?"

Vixin gave him a wary look. "Do you think they'd help? I can't even understand what they're saying."

"From what I understand, our leader is forming an alliance with theirs, so yes, I think they'll help."

"Suit yourself. I'll drop you off, but you'll be on your own from there."

"I thought you wanted compensation?"

"Not at the risk of my own skin."

Elite didn't comment and Vixin returned her attention to their evening meal. If he had to guess, she didn't actually want him to go. She'd been alone for weeks and was probably lonely, but too proud to admit it.

After a time, Vixin handed him a rat and the two settled and watched the sun dip below the horizon.

ELITE WATCHED dawn illuminate the sky. He wanted to wake Vixin, but after all the work she put into caring for him, Elite decided to let her sleep.

His mind traveled back to Kiuno and wondered what she might be doing. Hopefully not crying herself to sleep. His brain ran through all the possible things she might do if he died. What would he do? Elite shook his head. Nothing came to mind that eased his nerves.

When Vixin woke she set off to form Elite a pair of crutches and the two started their long trek along the mountainside.

It was slow, but at least now he had sunlight and knew he wasn't walking in circles.

Vixin often ran ahead and scoped the area for any signs of a patrol. He half wanted to find them and half didn't. Finding them meant leaving her behind. Alone. Sure, she could care for herself, but stealing was a risk that would eventually get her killed.

Elite's arms tingled with numbness when Vixin finally pointed to the area they planned to rest for the evening. He tripped over the rocky landscape and struggled to climb among the uneven stone.

They ducked under a lower overhang and entered a space just tall enough for him to fit in. If he jumped, he'd bash his head into the ceiling. The rear stretched back ten feet and stood wide enough for three people.

Elite didn't care for the small space. Crumbled stone guarded the entrance from prying eyes, but creatures could still pose an issue. Vixin acted as though she'd done this a hundred times. Hopefully that meant the fire would keep whatever stalked the plains at bay.

Vixin stretched out and folded her arms behind her head. "Wake me if anything sneaks in."

She never was one for courtesy. First watch for him, then.

Elite stared into the shadows and threw another log on the fire when the slight noise of sliding gravel caused him pause. He went for the dagger in his boot only to remember Vixin had relieved him of his weapons.

He waited, listening until a rock rolled across the ground and Vixin shot up, drawing her own weapons. She locked eyes with him then crept toward their pack. Without taking her eyes from the den's opening she slid a dagger to him.

The pair waited, neither willing to chalk the noise up to something random. After a few breaths Vixin stalked toward the entrance, her stance low and eyes darting from side to side. Vixin ducked her head out and pulled back fast enough to escape the arms reaching through.

Elite sucked in a breath as Vixin slashed at the man, tearing his forearm open with the tip of her blade. Two men barreled toward her from the other side and slammed her against the wall, knocking the knife from her grasp. She kicked, screamed, and growled like a caged animal. They shoved her to the ground and tied both hands behind her back.

Use your magic.

As soon as the man lifted his weight, Vixin rolled to her feet and dashed for the exit, but another grabbed her arm. She jumped at him, sinking her teeth into his neck. He yelped in pain and his fist collided with the side of her head, knocking the girl unconscious. Blood ran down her captor's neck as he let out a string of curses. His companion tied her legs together.

Seven and she'd barely wounded two. Elite gripped his weapon and their eyes turned to him. Two approached, but Elite remained still. He'd only get one attack with his broken body. His gaze shifted to Vixin. He should have sent her away.

They paused out of reach and one knelt, examining Elite's injury with a practiced eye. He looked to his companion and uttered words Elite couldn't understand before holding out one hand to gesture for the knife.

Elite shifted his gaze to Vixin's motionless form. They'd bound her but done nothing more. Perhaps they knew her as the thief and had other plans. That could buy him some time.

The one before him spoke again and Elite consented. He set the blade on the ground and slid it across the floor. "Don't hurt her."

The man followed his gaze, nodded, then pointed to Elite's leg. Elite used the wall for support as he struggled to his feet. He pointed to the crutches and sympathy flashed across their captor's features. That was promising.

His captor knelt before the injury and Elite hissed when he tugged at the bindings. Words were exchanged with his companions and four disappeared through the dark. The only individual who seemed irritated had a chunk missing from his neck.

The remaining three grabbed their bags and hauled it outside. As he limped toward the entrance, he heard the horses snort. Elite watched with a close eye as they lifted Vixin from the ground, but they didn't handle her with the aggression she'd shown moments ago.

He could get them through this. He'd offer to replace the stolen goods and get her out of this mess. If that wasn't an option, then he'd find another way.

REECE

REALM: 6
DAY: 315

They'd lost most of their food and supplies running from the creatures that plagued this stupid realm. Only one of their surviving companions had managed to grab a pack before they were plunged into this hell.

Reece sighed and his stomach growled as he watched the flickering candle. Cybele and he were the only two who couldn't produce their own light; therefore, they'd split the remaining candles between each other.

They estimated a few days had passed, but with no way to measure, it felt like an eternity. The depth of the cave worried most, but luckily, they had Milo. He'd lead them back to fresher air.

Reece settled on the ground, using his shirt as a pillow. He'd moved himself behind a stone for some space. Every sound echoed and the very breath of his companions had started to get on his nerves.

Reece pulled the knife from his pants and laid it beside his head. They'd discussed whether to recover their materials and decided against it. With the question of how far the tunnels ran, no one wanted to risk staying longer than necessary.

Those in charge of the map marked the area, claiming it could be a good route to explore in the future. Reece disagreed. He didn't feel the giant maggots were worth another run in.

As the light flickered against the darkness his thoughts shifted to Kiuno. His attempts with her were strained at best. Sometimes she'd consent to his touch, but more often than not she pulled away. That was another reason for separating himself. To give her space.

Reece's ears perked when steps filled the silence. He stilled himself, straining to listen as the individual drew closer. He gripped his knife and a face peered over the stone.

Reece let out a breath. "You could announce yourself instead of sneaking around like a criminal," he told Kiuno.

She didn't reply, and her strange gaze caused his hair to stand on end. Reece sat up, but she knelt over him and straddled his body.

Kiuno ran her hands over his chest and leaned forward.

"Ki?"

She silenced him as her sweet lips moved over his mouth. He responded, sitting up to wrap his arms around her back. Her fingers dug into his hair and he traced his hands over her body like he'd imagined doing a hundred times.

Reece tried to pull away, but she deepened their kiss, sliding her tongue into his mouth. He gasped and returned her fervor.

She'd regret. Tomorrow she'd wake an aching mess, wondering what had come over her and how he might react. He should push her away. He should be chivalrous, but he'd never been that sort of man.

Reece lifted her shirt and their lips crashed together again. Tomorrow was another day. If she wanted to change her mind, so be it. Let her regret, but let her regret knowing someone loved her.

She broke away and ran her tongue down his neck, eliciting a moan he was sure the others could hear. She flipped her hair to one side and Reece devoured her beautiful skin, running his hands over her throbbing pulse.

"Reece?" He paused, the woman standing behind the rock causing a jolt of panic to shoot through his core.

THE LITTLE flame danced on Kiuno's palm as she worked to suppress the magic. Maltack slept at her side per her request. She needed to put distance between herself and Reece.

Leading him to believe she had feelings wasn't part of her plan. He'd already established his expectations, but still. Kiuno didn't want to risk hurting him.

Once the group escaped this cave, they would head home and the thought both terrified her and brought joy.

The fire danced and grew three times its size as she fought against her rising emotions.

The truth was, she needed Reece. He kept the darkness at bay. He'd promised to be whatever she needed, but how was that fair? Kiuno had given Elite her entire life, her being. How could she find that part of herself and give it to another? How could she foresee whether she'd even be capable of it?

Kiuno's heart fought between loyalty and fear. She feared never taking a chance, of losing Reece without ever knowing.

Yet she also feared betraying the one she loved most. Was it love she felt or simply the desire to not be alone? It would be cruel to welcome his advances and then change her mind down the road, but would any of them live long enough to regret it?

Kiuno sighed and sat up. Reece had moved away from the group, but she could still see the flickering of his candle. Maybe she should try. She'd been short with him of late, afraid her emotions were too strong, but now guilt riddled her being.

She might not be able to give herself completely, but she could keep their slow pace. She could let him continue as they had been before they'd fallen into this rocky prison.

Kiuno crept between the rocks, keeping her feet soft. Everything echoed, and she was certain her companions would hear, but it didn't matter.

When Kiuno peered around the rock, she froze. A woman with long brown hair moved her hips against Reece's, their lips locked in lustful passion. Reece dug his fingers into the woman's pants and tugged them down an inch. Kiuno's cheeks ignited.

"Reece?"

Reece peered over the woman's naked shoulder with a confused expression. The woman turned and Kiuno's heart flipped as she gaped at a mirror image of herself. Reece's gaze flew between the two and a garbled giggle escaped the woman's throat.

Reece threw her from his lap, and she landed on all fours. An eerie smile spread across her lips. Reece pulled his dagger, but the woman melted before their eyes, disappearing into the rock like liquid.

Kiuno tried to calm her racing heart, but her stomach twisted. What kind of monsters were those? The hollows? Were they in danger?

Reece slid the dagger into his belt and walked over to examine the area where the woman had vanished. His back muscles shifted as he ran his fingers along the surface.

He'd just been—Kiuno's breath hitched when Reece locked eyes with her. He stood, and her one step back equaled his three steps forward.

Reece wrapped his arms around her, burying his face in her hair. He ran his nose up the side of her neck and grazed his lips across her own.

A surge of emotions shot through her core. A wanting to not be alone. A need for something, anything, to fill the void. Kiuno placed one hand on his chest and he allowed her to put an inch of space between them.

"Reece."

"They got it wrong."

"What?"

"The taste of your lips, the way you smell, the smoothness of your skin." He traced a hand down her arm. "They got it all wrong."

Heat flared through her cheeks. "You kissed me to find out what I taste like?"

A devilish grin spread across his lips. "Would you rather me kiss you for other reasons?"

Kiuno stood speechless and his smirk vanished. He traced the side of her face with his fingertips.

"Would you let me?"

Her heart pounded as one hand slid around her neck. Warmth radiated from his palm. A welcome to the aching cold that haunted this waking nightmare.

Kiuno didn't resist when his lips met hers, but this time she reciprocated and the ache in her chest pulsed.

She didn't realize how much she missed this contact with another human being. But it wasn't the passionate love she'd shared with Elite. This was broken hearts and a tearful plea. It was unmeasured grief and unfair promises she wasn't sure she could keep.

Reece pulled back, somehow knowing she'd reached her limit. He drew her into a tight embrace and pressed his lips to her hair.

Hesitantly, she wrapped her arms around him, still wondering if it were fair to hand another the shattered remnants of her heart.

ELITE

REALM: 5

DAY: 306

When the towering, multilevel castle walls entered their view, Elite sighed in relief. If he hadn't been confined to a sled, he might have run through the gates and seemed like the craziest person they'd ever seen.

The sled hit another bump and Elite hissed in pain. They'd strapped him in and were gentle with his care, but they couldn't do anything about the landscape.

Once again, the man who monitored his care offered medicine and not for the first time Elite refused. He wouldn't risk a sedative, not with Vixin confined against her will.

Whenever opportunity presented itself, she kicked, fought, and screamed, but each of her escape attempts only resulted in them binding something else. They'd tried to stuff a rag in her mouth, but she'd almost removed her captors' finger.

She was calm for now, slung over a horse like a corpse with a bag over their head. If his sister had shouted half the profanities Vixin had he'd have washed her mouth with soap.

Vixin shifted as the noise increased and Elite craned his neck to get a better view.

Several sturdy structures sat on the outskirts of the castle walls and lines of people crowded themselves around the stalls that stood in between.

So many people.

Compared to K.J.'s population he'd venture to say double occupied this space. Judging from the castle's size and the width of the curtain wall, they had ample space for housing.

The horse pulling his sled slowed and stopped inside the gate, but Vixin's horse veered to the right.

Elite sat straight. "Where are you taking her?"

At the sound of his distressed tone, Vixin kicked from the saddle, hit the ground, and rolled in the dirt. He didn't know when or how she'd gotten it, but the girl ripped off her blindfold and clutched a knife with her bound hands. The bonds around her feet had been severed.

Elite wrestled with the ropes holding him to the sled as three men circled Vixin. She screamed, cursed, and fought as one disarmed her and another knocked her out again.

"Where are you taking her?" Elite screamed again. He tugged at the restraint, but the one who'd offered him medicine rested a gentle hand on his forearm. Their eyes met, but his weren't full of malice. Elite looked at Vixin again and those hauling her toward the castle. Perhaps they only meant to restrain her.

Wiry hands untied Elite's legs from the sled and helped him to his feet. He wrapped an arm beneath Elite's shoulder and assisted him toward a small cottage lining the stone wall.

They entered and spices of every kind assaulted his senses. Smoke rose from one corner, giving the air a hazy look. Bottles of various shapes and sizes lined the shelves and a woman with graying hair and wrinkled face sat in the back, pouring a mixture into a small paper pouch.

The woman spoke a language he didn't understand, and his escort replied. Her withered face greeted him with a smile, but when her eyes landed on his leg something like sympathy crossed her features.

She pointed behind her counter and Elite hobbled toward a set of cushions that rested on the floor.

After lowering himself, the woman shooed his escort away and her wrinkled hands roamed over his broken leg. She unlaced the makeshift splint they'd provided and Elite hissed when she pressed on his shin.

Her fingers prodded toward his knee and lightning hot pain radiated through the bone. She muttered and a soft glow emitted from her palms. Sore muscles sprang to life beneath her touch, twisting and writhing beneath his skin.

She paused a moment, made eye contact, then something in Elite's leg snapped and he bit down the muffled scream.

The pain dissipated and sweet relief pulsated through his leg. The tight cord in his chest unwound and he relaxed a fraction as she bent his leg and indicated for him to flex. It was as if the bone had never been broken.

She reached for his shirt next and Elite helped her pull the material over his head. Deep bruising ran along the left side of his body, but the light shone in her fingers before he could assess the damage.

Instead of sharp cracks, it felt as if she were stripping away his pain piece by piece. His breathing came easier and the muscles in his back relaxed as those in his chest mended. For the first time in two weeks Elite moved without pain.

Elite clasped the woman's hands in a gesture of thanks, and she smiled before rising to her feet. Her knees cracked and his captor loomed in her shadow with one hand resting on the knife in his belt. Surely, he didn't think Elite would attack the woman who'd just helped him, though he guessed one could never be too careful.

Elite slowly stood and his captor measured his movements with a practiced eye. The woman seated herself and flashed him a smile.

He needed to escape but leaving without Vixin wasn't an option. *Please let Scorpios be here.*

His captor whistled and three men entered the door, one with a rope in his hand. They pointed to Elite's wrists. If there was ever a time he envied those with magic, it was now.

Elite held his wrists forward and they bound his hands to his front.

His escorts guided Elite toward the castle steps and through the thick door that guarded the keep. He listened and inclined his head toward every doorway in search of Vixin.

Elite needed an audience with someone. Anyone who spoke English. If he had any luck, hopefully that's where they were leading him.

Voices filled the next hall, but once again they spoke in a language he couldn't understand. Five men walked into a room, but only one mattered.

Elite planted his feet, twisted from their grip, and dropped his shoulder into another who reached for his arm. Their voices followed him through the echoing hall, but he didn't need long.

"Scorpios," Elite called.

Scorpios turned and froze mid-sentence. His eyes widened and jaw went slack. His expression told Elite his worst fear had been realized. They had thought him dead.

Scorpios clasped Elite on the back and pulled him into a tight embrace. "You're alive." Scorpios pulled back and looked him over. "Though you've looked better."

"Long story."

Scorpios spoke to his captors in what he now presumed to be Chinese and they cut Elite's bonds without protest. Elite rubbed his wrists and Scorpios clasped him on the back again.

"How did you survive the fall? They told me you'd tumbled from a cliff."

"A young woman saved me. She arrived shortly before I did."

"Ah. I know who you mean. I think the whole castle heard her come in."

"Where is she?"

"In a cell below us. She bit a guard and tried to scratch the eyes from another."

Elite winced.

"Follow me."

Scorpios made a quick apology to those in his company and Elite matched his fast pace down another hall. "How's Kiuno?"

Scorpios's pace didn't slow. "A wreck."

"Where is she?"

"Let's get your friend out of trouble before we discuss Kiuno's."

Elite clenched his teeth. Trouble had a whole new meaning where Kiuno was involved.

Scorpios continued, "It seems you've found their aggressive thief and if I understood them correctly, her sentence is to be severe."

The statement brought Elite out of his reverie. "What can I do to clear her?"

"I think I can work something out with Leena."

Metal clashing against metal reverberated off the walls as the two descended three flights of stairs. Obscene screams echoed from below and Elite cringed as the girl threw profanity after profanity at her captors.

Scorpios did most of the talking and a guard led them through an iron door where Vixin screamed at the top of her lungs and beat her shackles against the bars.

She spat on the ground. "Finally find one that speaks English?"

"He's a friend."

She snorted, but Scorpios returned a kind smile. "My name is Scorpios. I apologize if they handled you roughly."

She retreated a few steps at his approach. One guard handed him a key but muttered before walking away.

"Thank you for saving him," Scorpios said as he unlocked the door.

"His wife is a good friend and hasn't been the same without him."

Vixin raised her brows. "You're married?"

Elite smiled. "What do you think pushed me to get out of that cave?"

"I don't know." She shrugged and her eyes flashed toward Scorpios and back to him. "Are you here to get me out?"

"Depends," Scorpios said. "Are you done biting people?"

She lifted her head as if in triumph. "If they're done putting their hands on me."

Scorpios held out his hand and Vixin approached as if she were a cornered animal. Scorpios unlocked the first then the second restraint and she rubbed her bruised wrists.

"Am I free to go?"

"Where to?" Elite asked.

"Well, back home, where else?"

"To keep stealing?"

Vixin paused and looked toward the guards who blocked her exit. "You want me to come with you?"

"I can ensure your debt is paid. If you decide you don't like my home, you'll be free to leave."

Vixin stepped around Scorpios. She studied him, then Elite, and finally the guards. "Do I have your word? That I can leave if I choose?"

"Yes, but you have to at least give it a shot."

Vixin crossed her arms. "Fine. Can we eat now?"

Scorpios chuckled and led the way. Vixin jumped at the guards in passing and they recoiled. She smirked, but Elite didn't reprimand her. They ascended the stairs and Elite wondered if living in the wild had made her feral or if she'd always been this keen on causing trouble.

They followed Scorpios down two main halls and passed several who eyed Vixin with confusion and hostility. She met their gazes with defiance.

Upon entering a simple, yet comfortable room, exhaustion hit Elite like a tidal wave, and he crumbled in a chair. The stress and weight of the last week crashed over his body. Vixin picked at the fruit on a table and demanded a bath.

Elite ran his hand over his face and prepared for the worst. "What's become of my wife?"

Scorpios sighed and sat in the chair across from him. He rested his elbows on his knees and clasped his hands. "She's in the sixth realm."

Adrenaline shot through Elite's body. "Why?" Of all the places she could go.

"Before you panic, know it was an organized plan. She went with the scouts to scope the area."

"But why? Why send her somewhere—"

"Not long after you fell the faction of people responsible attacked our castle. Despite her distraught state, Kiuno acted. We won, but after the battle she locked herself in your room and refused to eat or communicate.

"K.J. approached me about the idea after he found her wandering the courtyard in the middle of the night. He said she needed a distraction."

"Sounds like he pawned her off. You don't send someone unstable on a mission that could get them killed."

Scorpios's eyes flashed. "And you don't keep a ticking bomb near innocent people. I had my doubts just as you, but after considering the options, I agreed. Maltack and Reece accompanied her."

Elite sat back, his heart slowing. "I need to find to her."

"I know, but if I let you go alone and something really does kill you, she'd never forgive me."

"How long do you need?"

"A few days at most. I'll tell them an emergency has come up. Leena will understand once I tell her it's about Kiuno. She's fond of her."

Vixin emitted a loud yawn and crossed the room. "Glad to hear you'll get a fairy tale ending, but when can I take that bath?"

41

LOVE & LOSS

REALM: 6
DAY: 317

Kiuno tilted her head back and let the warm rays of sunlight soak into her skin. They padded up a steep slope, each step shortening the path toward freedom. Milo had found their exit, just as Cybele promised.

Kiuno shook the dampness from her bones. She'd never go underground again. Not if her life depended on it.

After their incident with the Kiuno look alike, she and Reece had alerted the others to the danger. They'd crowded around the fire, hoping the light would ward off anything else lurking in the darkness.

At first, she thought it to be a hollow, but Cybele said she'd never seen the hollows melt into the floor. She'd also never seen one imitate the living, though the dead weren't uncommon.

Great. As if they needed to add zombies to their mixture of problems.

Reece climbed the last few feet then helped Kiuno to the surface. She collapsed on the ground, not caring that rocks and thorns bit into her skin. It was light, warmth, and sunshine. Things she'd missed while trapped in the dark labyrinth.

Kiuno's stomach growled and a dull ache pulsed at the base of her skull. Their food had been lost during their tumble and without light finding anything to consume had been a wasted effort.

Kiuno tilted her head. Milo seemed the happiest of their lot. He rolled in the grass, leapt through the air, and twisted his wings as he danced around Cybele. Once he finished, Cybele climbed on his back and took to the sky.

Kiuno wondered how far they'd wandered from the plateau. Her heart skipped. Without provisions they'd head back to the fifth realm and to everything she'd been trying to run away from.

Thomas, one of their surviving companions, announced his find of water. Kiuno groaned and rolled to her feet. A tiny spring leaked down into the cavernous pit below. She waited her turn and sucked down the liquid before washing the sweat from her arms and face.

Kiuno stood and shook the droplets from her body then Reece circled his arms around her torso from behind. She stiffened and he rested his head on her shoulder.

They were heading home. What would she tell the others about his advances and her reactions to it?

"Reece."

He spun her around and silenced her with a gentle kiss. Kiuno's heart raced as she still fought with whether she wanted him. Maybe it was all wrong, but she longed for the contact and comfort. The only problem was Reece longing for so much more.

"I already told you, I'll be whatever you need. If you need time when we get back to the fifth, I'll back off. If you want to stay while I head back to check on Nsane, then you can stay."

Kiuno sighed and leaned her forehead against his chest. She still had a lot to think about. She'd set out to find herself, but had she started to build that self around another person? Was she incapable of finding her life without another as her guide?

"I still don't think it's fair."

"And I'll still tell you to let me worry about it."

Cybele landed. "Good news. I can see the platform. The tunnels connected us right back to where we started." She pointed up and Kiuno tilted her head to the circling felinians above. "I brought your rides."

The creatures flew in one by one and landed on the ground before Cybele and Milo. They nuzzled Cybele and she greeted them with similar affection.

Kiuno groaned as Reece boosted her up and strapped in one leg. She leaned down to strap in the other, then he joined behind and secured himself.

Lifting from the ground wasn't nearly as smooth as diving from the cliff. The animals required a running start with the weight, and she gripped the saddle as their wings unfurled and pumped vigorously to gain altitude.

Reece wrapped one arm around her middle and it distracted her from the fear. His free hand rested on her thigh and Kiuno's mind floated back to their kiss. It always seemed like he knew when to push. Almost as though he cradled her soul, caring for its every need.

Was he part of her future or was he just a temporary bandage to her damaged heart? Kiuno tried to let the breeze carry her mind away, but Reece shifted his hand and brought her back to the present.

Reece wanted to make a life here. In a world that had taken so much from her, but Kiuno wasn't sure she could do that. There were still four realms to go. Who knew what the future could bring and who might still be alive in the end? She could decide later.

After landing on the platform and unbuckling herself from the saddle, Kiuno passed through the icy portal and entered the fifth realm. Her heart tugged as she followed everyone from the mountainside and into the felinians' domain.

Cybele danced over to them as though she hadn't just gone through a jungle and fought for her life. "Lunch is almost ready. Why don't you join us?"

Kiuno's stomach growled.

Reece reached for her hand, but Kiuno recoiled. She stood beneath the cover of trees and gazed at the people gathered around their cooking fires. They laughed, likely telling stories of days long past. Nikita lay at Jim's side, the two finally comfortable among Cybele's people.

"You should at least eat something," Reece said. He furrowed his brow when she didn't respond.

How could she? She wasn't ready to go back to them yet. Kiuno didn't want to see Blue and Silver's smiling faces as they drank around a table. She didn't want to see Maltack or Liam grimace as they choked down drinks and their friends laughed. She didn't want to see Scorpios smirk from the table right before being pulled into their playful banter. She didn't want to see K.J. and answer questions regarding her wellbeing.

Her breathing hitched.

Reece stepped in front of her line of vision and Kiuno blinked a few times not realizing the tears that had formed.

"You don't have to go back you know."

Her lips parted as she stared into sea green eyes full of concern and—no, not yet. She couldn't recognize that feeling yet.

Reece took her hand. "But you do have to eat."

Reece led her through the crowd of people and took a bowl for each of them before seating himself on the outskirts of the mass.

Some felinians lay beside humans they'd grown close to while the majority went about their day without regard to the people in their midst.

Kiuno finished her meal quickly, then picked up a gray feather from the ground. She twirled it between her fingers.

"I want to go back."

Reece sat his bowl down.

"Only to see if they're all right. After that," she looked at him, "I think I'd like to go with you."

A wide smile spread across Reece's face. "I'd like that." He draped an arm around her shoulder and she leaned against his body. They watched the young felinians play in the clearing.

His breathing. His posture. The way she fit against him. Somehow it all felt wrong.

THEY SLEPT beside a warm fire that night and Cybele offered to fly them to the castle the following morning. None objected.

Just as before, Reece helped strap her in and settled himself behind her. The last time they'd flown to K.J.'s together had been to decimate their enemies. Now she was heading there to say goodbye.

She didn't know how long it'd take or what challenges might arise in their future, but she knew she'd always have an ally in K.J. and that alone comforted her. The others would be okay in his care.

Memories flooded through her as the walls came into view. She glanced toward Maltack and caught him staring. He smiled, probably excited to see Palindrome. If Kiuno returned to the sixth realm, she wouldn't ask Maltack to accompany her again. His place was here.

The felinians roared to announce their arrival and circled above the inner wall before landing beside the castle keep. Those by the stairs scattered toward the buildings. Some grabbed weapons, but when the alarm didn't sound, they kept their distance.

K.J. and Palindrome stood beside the keep talking to Scorpios. Kiuno struggled with the clasps, but once she'd freed herself, she ran to embrace her friend.

Scorpios opened his arms and she circled her hands around his back. "It hasn't been that long, has it?" Scorpios pulled back and looked her over. "I hope everything went well?"

"It was miserable," Reece said from behind.

"I'd like to say he's exaggerating," she added then turned to K.J. "It'll be hard getting everyone through."

K.J. said, "I didn't expect it to be easy, but we'll talk about that in a minute."

She tilted her head. K.J. wasn't normally one to wait for information.

Kiuno looked from one person to another. She spotted Silver with a big grin plastered across his face then turned to Blue who carried a similar expression.

"What?" she asked.

Her friends parted and Kiuno was running before she even registered she'd moved.

A STRANGE feeling rooted itself in Reece's gut as he observed their smiling faces. Many welcomed him back, but Kiuno carried the weight of their stares. She felt it too and appeared wary as she tried to piece together the unknown.

His heart raced. They weren't acting right. They didn't display the sympathetic glances that had seen her off. They didn't step lightly, tiptoeing as if they feared her reactions.

When Kiuno ran, Reece's world split in two.

Kiuno jumped into the man's embrace without a moment's hesitation. She clutched his neck, words flying between them Reece wasn't privy to. They held one another, the world and those in it forgotten. Her friends clapped and cheered, but he stood frozen.

Elite was alive.

Cybele joined him, watching the rendezvous with little interest. "I don't imagine this was in your plan."

No. It wasn't, but in the weeks he'd spent with her, *that* smile had never crossed her face. Not once. He'd managed a few small ones, but what she did now touched her soul. A smile that told him he'd never had a chance from the start.

Reece smirked and dropped his head, trying to steady his racing heart. "As long as she's happy."

I'll be whatever you need. Who knew a promise could be so heavy?

KIUNO PRAYED she wasn't dreaming. She kissed him again, relishing the taste and feel of his familiar lips and touch. Her body molded against his frame, fitting like a perfect glove. She cried and laughed, unable to contain herself as she pressed her forehead against the other piece of her soul.

She'd died. That was the only way to describe planning a life without him. She'd died and tried to live in the echo of pictures floating through a lake of despair.

Elite pulled her into another kiss before they turned to acknowledge the sea of smiling faces.

Kiuno's heart skipped when her eyes locked with Reece's. He wasn't cheering like the others. He wasn't congratulating Elite's return and why would he? Kiuno's heart ached but Reece tilted his head and a lazy smile appeared on his face. He gave her what she needed. Afterall, that's what he'd promised.

Blue hugged them, breaking her eye contact and she returned the gesture. She kept a firm hold on Elite's hand and tried to search for Reece again. His back retreated toward the gate.

Where was he going?

Kiuno planted a kiss on Elite's face and though she hated it, Kiuno forced herself to separate, leaving him to deal with the crowd as she fought her way out.

Kiuno ran for Reece, catching up as he tugged at the latches on a felinian's saddle. "You're leaving already?"

He paused, but resumed pulling, though there wasn't anything to adjust. "I've been away from Nsane too long. It's time to get back."

"You ought to stay and rest, at least for a little while."

Reece let out a long sigh and rested his hands on the animal. "I can't stay and watch you love him." Her heart tightened. "I had a chance. I let myself believe." Reece turned, but instead of looking at her, he looked behind. At Elite and those surrounding him.

"If I stay—" He shook his head.

"I'm sorry." Her voice cracked, and Reece pulled her into his chest.

"Don't do that. Don't cry anymore."

She sniffed and swallowed hard. "I feel like if you leave, I'll never see you again."

Reece pulled back and gave her a crooked grin. "Have a little faith, will ya?"

She choked out a smile and he wiped away the tears. Reece leaned forward and planted a kiss on her forehead, lingering a moment too long. He squeezed her shoulders. "Keep me in the loop of things?"

Kiuno nodded, and he jumped in the saddle. Cybele joined him, and they took flight, catching everyone's attention. Kiuno wiped the tears from her eyes and startled when Elite wrapped an arm over her shoulder.

Kiuno turned into Elite, resting her head on his chest for a moment before meeting his gaze. His brow furrowed and a million questions raced to the forefront of her thoughts.

"What happened to you?" she asked.

"I fell and someone saved me."

"But where did you go?"

His face fell. "I was unconscious for two days. The rocks trapped us under the mountain." Kiuno's gaze trailed up and down his form, but Elite cupped her face. "I'm fine now. I promise I'll tell you everything later."

K.J. pushed through the crowd. "I don't mean to interrupt, but I think we have a few things to go over before you two disappear."

Debriefing. Better to get it out of the way.

Kiuno, Elite, Maltack, and the two remaining survivors in their party followed K.J. and Palindrome up the stairs, down a hall, and through the large double doors that led to K.J.'s office.

Kiuno seated herself at the table and Elite wrapped his hand in hers. She stared at their interlaced fingers and wondered when the dream would end. She imagined herself flung back into the jungle with all the chaos to add to her aching heart. It still throbbed. Even now as Elite sat by her side, Kiuno's heart bled.

Maltack helped unfurl the parchment and set a weight at each corner. Or what was left of the corners. Wet patches had splotched the ink causing it to run along the creases. A large tear ran through the upper middle and the lower left corner had been charred.

"Looks like you had quite the adventure." K.J.'s gaze fell to the chairs that should have been occupied by their fallen comrades. "Tell me what happened."

Kiuno recounted the details but left out anything involving her and Reece. She told them of the creatures in the forest and their immunity to fire. She detailed the white cavern grubs and their loss of good men and finally the woman who'd taken on her identity. Once again Kiuno omitted the part about Reece.

K.J. was silent as he looked over the details on the parchment. "There's still a lot of land to trek through. I think the cave might be a good place to stop along the way, but it sounds like we need to eliminate some threats first." K.J. crossed his arms. "Reece and Cybele seemed to be in a hurry."

"They had to get back to their people."

K.J. eyed her for a moment then continued. "That's fine. I'm happy to say, Scorpios made great progress with Leena and they're on board to help in the coming realms. Reece managing his own castle raised some concern, but that's only due to the belief that he'll be operating under my command. I assured them otherwise."

Kiuno adjusted herself in the chair. "Does Atilla know Reece has his own castle?"

K.J. nodded. "He was furious."

"The meetings are going to be interesting now."

K.J. grimaced. "I'll need your help in ensuring the peace when that happens."

I can't stay and watch you love him.

Kiuno glanced at Elite then back to their hands. What would those meetings be like now?

"Enough already." Palindrome placed her hands on the table and stood. "We can talk about the ins and outs later. Right now, I think a celebration is in order."

K.J. chuckled and leaned back from the table. "And this is why people love her."

BREATHLESS

REALM: 5
DAY: 317

Kiuno padded through the soft grass, her hand clutched in Elite's warm grip as if he were her lifeline. They walked to the far bath-house where Palindrome had commanded a fire be tended.

Kiuno's heart pounded with every step.

Elite knelt and peeled her shoes from blistered feet. He lifted the hem of her shirt and left burning trails wherever his fingertips met her skin. Kiuno's body ached with every movement, but it wasn't the only thing that hurt these days.

She dipped her feet into the water and the heat stung every scratch and scrape as she lowered herself beneath the surface. Elite slid into the hot water beside her and silence settled between them. She grabbed a brush and set to scrubbing her arm.

Kiuno felt numb, like she waded through a dream and all her happiness could crumble with the throw of a stone.

She scrubbed and then scrubbed some more, the skin turning red from both heat and friction. There was so much to wash away, but no matter how clean her skin appeared she couldn't rub away the painful wound gripping her heart.

Elite gently peeled her fingers off the brush and pulled her body against his own. It felt strange somehow. Normal, yet not. She'd rushed into his arms, grateful to see him and all her pent-up emotions had flooded to the surface. Then Reece left and K.J.'s talk had brought reality slamming down.

Kiuno rested against his chest, but it still felt surreal. Like he would disappear any moment and leave her drowning all over again.

Elite ran his fingers through her scalp then traced them over her shoulders. Something in her body responded, a piece of their former life clicked into place. She nestled against him and watched the ripples on the water's surface.

"Something happened between you and Reece." She shuddered at the calmness in his tone. This was it. This is what would tear him away again.

Kiuno fought to keep her breathing even, but her body still trembled. Not again. Her heart couldn't take it. She wouldn't survive a back and forth... but she couldn't lie either.

Trust was their cornerstone. Trust made their marriage strong. It was an equal give and take as one respected the other.

"Yes." It was the only word she could form.

Elite remained silent, but his hand never stopped trailing across her skin. As if he were reassuring her of his presence. She'd been crushed by his absence and Reece had reeled her back from the edge of an abyss so dark she hadn't even recognized herself.

"We kissed."

Elite's fingers paused.

"Reece wanted a future, but I..." She stopped and her heart pounded in her ears. Silence stretched between them so thick Kiuno thought she might choke.

"Do you love him?"

Her heart jolted and she turned to meet beautiful eyes full of sadness and longing. Eyes she thought lost to her. One look and she understood exactly why Reece had run.

Love. Passionate and unbridled.

Kiuno traced Elite's strong jaw, then ran her fingers down his neck, lingering on the throbbing pulse. "I love you."

He grasped her fingertips and kissed them but held her gaze. "That's not what I asked."

Kiuno looked away and their hands fell beneath the water's steamy surface. "I don't know how to answer that."

Elite's jealousy had never been a secret. She'd faced it more than once. With her choice of friends heavy on the male side, it'd led to a quarrel or two. But this. This was different.

Elite tried to tilt her chin, but she resisted.

"I'm angry with myself, not you. But I need to know." She relented and met his gaze. "Do I need to win your heart back or is it still mine?"

Kiuno's eyes misted. "I don't know what I felt. Everything was different. I was different." She took a shaky breath. "A small part of me is grateful to him you know? But love?" She shook away the tears and placed a hand on his face. "You're the one I love and that never changed."

A sad smile tugged at the corner of his lips. Elite grasped her hand and kissed the inside of her wrist. He trailed it down her arm before consuming her mouth in a kiss her soul yearned for.

Elite laced his fingers through her hair. "That's all I need."

FIRES DOTTED the field and the main hall was in full swing by the time they joined the festivities.

Kiuno wanted to run, to disappear in their room and forget the rest of the world existed, but Elite pulled her toward their table. Toward the friends she'd shunned in her grief.

They greeted the couple and Blue slid a drink her way.

They laughed, teasing one another as they always did. Normal. As if the last month hadn't almost killed her. Kiuno studied them, Liam in particular. He'd become stronger, but since coming to the front lines she hadn't made time for him. She hadn't trained him or talked to him and yet he smiled.

She looked to Scorpios, Silver, and Maltack. People who still followed her. She'd rejected them. She'd abandoned them rather than facing her pain. What kind of leader did that?

The activities and conversations moved in slow motion. Like a movie she watched from the outside, desperate to take part, but bound away by some unseen force. She sat frozen as they relished in the warmth of one another's company. They shared stories. They gave sympathies. She gave nothing, unable to pull herself to the present.

"Are you okay?" They repeated the question and it wasn't until the noise at their table paused that Kiuno came to. Each peered at her with worry written across their faces. Elite squeezed her arm.

"Yeah, I'm fine," she lied.

"Exactly what a woman says when she's the opposite," Blue said.

Scorpios set his drink on the table. "Here we are celebrating, and you've barely had time to process. Perhaps you two should retire early."

Kiuno shook her head. Elite wrapped his arm around her shoulders and Silver started conversation again, but each kept eyeing her as if she might shatter at any moment.

And she might.

She might implode never to be found again in the shattered remnants of her heart. The guilt, loss, relief, love, and confusion played tug-of-war in the core of her being.

Elite startled Kiuno by taking her hand and pulling her up. She gave him a confused look until he led her to the dance floor. Every eye burned a hole through her back. This was the last place she wanted to be.

He stepped, forcing her back as she followed the simple movement. It was slow, testing, reminding, but her heart ached too much. They stepped again, the pattern reminiscent from their first lessons.

The next bit required her lead and she answered by stepping forward as if in challenge. A show for the eyes watching. Kiuno took a step to the side, spun, and gave him a pitiful attempt at a smile. He'd know. He'd understand, but as she turned back to the table, Elite tugged her arm and took control again, turning her in a more advanced step.

Another click. A smile.

Kiuno's heart fluttered with each motion and Elite's grin melted the last sliver of ice guarding her heart. He jumped her into a spin and lifted her from the ground before twirling her again. They froze on the dance floor, the noise fading until they were the only two in existence.

Never forget how to dance.

She'd forgotten. She'd forgotten this happiness and the soaring feeling of his love. A smile pulled at the corner of her mouth as he spun her again and their familiar motion reminded Kiuno of promises. Reminded her of him.

Kiuno gripped his hand tighter and moved as she used to. She knew his motions. She knew his love and she'd never let it slip away again.

MALTACK

REALM: 5

DAY: 323

Flames clashed against Maltack's barrier and crawled around the perimeter of Scorpios's body. Scorpios twisted to the side and countered Kiuno's blow. Steam splayed across the area as fire and water collided again and again.

Maltack knew Scorpios could maneuver his way around her attacks without help, but he kept his focus.

One moment of distraction could lead to a scar Scorpios would always possess and regret Kiuno would never forget.

Maltack's gaze roamed from the battle several yards away to Elite who knelt at his side. Elite watched the two with calculated eyes, his hand tearing a blade of grass to pieces.

At one time anxiety would have consumed him, but now Elite's shoulders were relaxed as he studied their movements. Maltack might have even called him curious.

"She's something else huh?" Maltack offered.

Elite grinned and stood, wiping the blades of grass from his hands. His eyes never left Scorpios or Kiuno as the two continued to pit their magic against one another.

Scorpios still outmatched Kiuno and he probably always would. Kiuno struggled to contain her magic, thus expending more energy than necessary. She tired quickly as a result.

Ice crawled along the ground, freezing one blade of grass after another. Kiuno summoned a circular blast of flames to incinerate the danger.

She placed both hands on her knees and took several breaths. "Should we call this a draw?"

Scorpios scoffed and pulled particles of water from the air, surrounding himself with spears of ice. Kiuno huffed, righted herself, and summoned her magic again.

"You never mentioned your wife could use magic."

Maltack turned to find a young, slender woman standing beside Elite. She'd tied her red hair in a tight ponytail and chewed on an apple while observing the two fighters. Daggers hung from each hip.

"You never asked," Elite replied. "Finally decide to join the living?"

She snorted. "A girl has priorities."

Sharp, green eyes met Maltack's gaze and his face heated. He turned back to the battle. Kiuno cursed when a shard of ice plunged into her shoulder and the others exploded in droplets of water that fell harmlessly to the ground.

Scorpios and Elite ran to her side, each assessing the damage.

All eyes turned to Maltack.

His face reddened further, and Elite helped Kiuno from the ground. She winced, grabbing at her shoulder.

Scorpios crossed his arms. "I think Maltack is done for the day."

Elite wrapped an arm around Kiuno's waist and whispered words unknown as they approached him. Maltack cursed himself. He'd gotten distracted.

Kiuno collapsed on the ground and Maltack went to work on the puncture wound in her shoulder.

"Sorry about that."

Maltack's gaze flickered toward the girl again and his heart surged. Green eyes seemed to bore through his being. As if she knew all his secrets.

"H-Hey, I'm Maltack." He inwardly kicked himself for stuttering.

She studied him and took another bite of the apple. "Vixin, and I'm not interested." With that she gave Elite a casual wave and started back to the castle. Maltack stared, feeling as though he'd lost before he even started.

ASSAULT

REALM: 5

DAY: 325

Kiuno sprinted, keeping pace with Scorpios and Elite as they made their third pass around the outside wall. Her legs and lungs screamed for mercy, but she wouldn't stop if they didn't.

They circled the castle gate again, hopefully for the last time that morning, but distant screaming had the trio skidding to a halt. They listened. Waited. Then it sounded again, echoing across the field as four men entered their view.

Kiuno's heart thundered as a group of reptilian-like creatures gave chase. One jumped, its powerful legs carrying it toward its helpless victim. His scream died as blood poured from the tear in his throat.

Kiuno ran toward the men with Scorpios and Elite at her side. Water shot from Scorpios's hand and collided with one of the creatures. The liquid solidified, trapping the reptile in an icy prison.

Kiuno reached for her sword and cursed. She couldn't use her magic without Maltack's help and getting too close to the creatures would only result in—shards of ice flew past her in rapid succession. The beasts shrieked, shriveling in on themselves then collapsed. One attempted to stand, but it fell again, drowning in a puddle of its own blood.

Three men remained, each sucking in air as they stood in the field glancing between her, Scorpios, Elite, and the creatures.

Scorpios knelt. "What happened?"

His voice shook. "The monsters. They just kept coming. We tried."

Scorpios placed a hand on the man's shoulder. "Calm down. Where were you stationed? Where are they coming from?"

His body shook as he pointed. "The portal."

KIUNO PACED outside the medical house waiting for Palindrome's say. The men were fine, but it wasn't their wellbeing that concerned her. It was what they'd said.

The portal. Did he mean the portal to the sixth realm?

The felinians lived there. Jim was there and if monsters were attacking they'd never make it in time.

Palindrome emerged, but Kiuno couldn't read her stoic expression. "Follow me."

Kiuno shot Elite a glance, but neither him nor Scorpios said anything as they followed Palindrome into the castle. She ordered K.J. and a set group of others to join them in the meeting room.

Minutes ticked by as one person entered at a time. Kiuno kept glancing at Palindrome, but the woman seemed determined to keep her lips sealed until everyone arrived.

Finally, K.J. closed the doors. "What's going on?" His eyes darted around the room in search of answers.

"We have a problem. Three men just showed up claiming monsters are emerging from the sixth realm's portal."

He stopped pacing. "Are you sure? They've never been able to transverse the realms before."

Palindrome nodded. "They're sure. Cybele helped them escape to call us for aid. Initially, they flew upon felinians to get here, but they reported being cast off after the creatures heard their brethren's call. From there they ran as fast as they were able."

K.J. cursed and leaned against the table. "We won't make it in time."

Heavy silence settled over the room.

It wasn't just felinians who lived there, but people. People with children. Felinians with their young.

Kiuno's heart ached as she recalled Nikita playing with the cubs. They wouldn't be strong enough to fly away...

Palindrome broke the silence. "Cybele is a strong leader. She'll head this way. The least we can do is meet her in the middle."

K.J. nodded. "Let's go."

REECE

REALM: 5

DAY: 325

Reece and four men heaved another log against the gated door. Their enemy rammed against it, shattering the wood in places that let their weapons slide through. Six bodies lay on the ground already, two groaning for help. The smoke clouded his lungs and Reece traded positions with one of his men.

He jogged toward the castle with the echo of death in his wake.

They were losing ground. Some had already given up, sending prayers to whatever god they worshiped while others worked to keep the wall intact, desperate to fight till their last breath. The lot of them were exhausted from the morning assault and despite their best efforts the creatures had forced them to retreat behind the wall.

Shouts to his right caught Reece's attention. He wiped the sweat from his brow and tugged at energy he didn't have. Vines erupted from the boot trodden earth and wrapped around the crumbling stone. It wove itself between the creases as men leaned boards against the structure.

He bounded up the stairs thereafter and caught his informant by the arm. "Any change?"

The young man shook his head. "They're still crawling from farther than I can see." His voice shook, and his eyes went wide as men hollered from outside and another crash reverberated off the walls.

Reece let the boy go and took a moment to lean against the entryway of the main hall. Dizziness threatened, but he fought against it and righted himself again. Reece entered the castle. Three men stood near a table, worry lines etching dirty faces.

"Have you gotten through?" Reece asked.

"We've lost over a dozen trying. They sense us no matter how we move whether it's above ground or below it."

Reece clenched his teeth. "Help the men keep the barricades up. Hold it for as long as possible."

"Sir, with respect—"

"We're not going down without a fight. We might all die, but I'm taking those bastards with us."

"Yes, sir." The men ran from the hall, drawing their blades and Reece leaned against a pillar in the shadows.

If he could contact Cybele and get reinforcements, they might stand a chance, but without it… Reece shook his head, he finally got a castle of their own and it was going to kill them.

"Seems you're in a bit of trouble."

Reece drew his sword and scanned the shadows. The candle on the table flickered. "Who's there?"

"Someone who can help." The male voice shifted directions and Reece pivoted, holding his blade tight. He didn't have much energy left. "Come now, there's no need for such hostility."

"Considering what's at my front door I'd say hostility is appropriate." Reece sidestepped a pillar, keeping the stone at his back as he peered around another. The stranger was silent for a long time and another crash echoed from outside.

"I can make it all go away."

His hair stood on end. Sweat caked his palms, but Reece kept his voice even. "How?"

A chuckle that didn't suit the situation reverberated from the walls, making it impossible to pinpoint the intruder's location.

Reece spun around again. "What do you want?"

"The same things as anyone else. To be loved, feared, and have control over what pleases me."

"Stop toying with me."

The same sadistic laugh filled the hall again. "Toying is half the fun."

"Well, the game's over."

The laughing continued. "My dear boy, the games have only begun."

"What do you want?" Reece repeated.

"Your cooperation."

"In what?"

"I need you to put the brakes on progress toward future realms."

Reece narrowed his eyes, searching for a shadow, a flicker of movement, anything. He circled another pillar. "What, you want me to fight the alliances?"

"No. I want you to fight our dear, sweet Kiuno."

Cold sweat rolled down his back. "I won't kill her."

He laughed again. The sound grating. "Of course you won't. You love her, though you're one of many. I simply want you to stall. I'm having too much fun for this to end anytime soon."

"You call this fun?"

The voice was silent. "I guess we all have different definitions. But I have a question. If you discovered there wasn't a way out, would it would upset you?"

Another series of screams echoed from outside. "Are you telling me there isn't one?"

"No, I'm merely asking your opinion on the matter. You've stated once that you planned to stay. Has that decision wavered?"

Reece growled. "It's no business of yours."

Stated? Was he listening? Was this the voice of the man who'd put them here?

"Oh, but it is! You see, that makes you one of my favorite players. I need our Kiuno to see things as you do. I need her to consider a different option. I'm certain you can't object to that."

"Why her?"

"Why not her? Who better to test the limits of humanity? That determination and fire, it was too much to pass up."

"So, you premeditated it."

He chuckled. "I've premeditated a lot of things. You'll have to be a bit more specific."

"Kiuno's involvement."

"Is that so surprising? I've included all our friends from Chrono-point, though I lost a few at first so perhaps saying everyone isn't quite accurate."

Reece's skin crawled. "You're pushing her too far. Kiuno isn't strong enough for your games."

He clicked his tongue. "And you underestimate her."

"Underestimate? Have you seen the damage you've caused? The tears she's cried? How can you call that testing determination?"

A shadow pulled from the darkness three pillars down and materialized into human form. "Yet, she stands. You want to talk about damage and pain, then let's talk about how she felt when *you* left the game. You were just one of many who walked away. One of many who stopped writing. I saw it all. I counted every tear you were blind to. Do you have any idea what loneliness does to a person?"

Reece scoffed. "Loneliness? I think you have Kiuno confused with someone else. She was surrounded by people."

A shadowy smile spread across his face. "Those are the worst kind, aren't they? People who claim to be your friends, yet make you feel isolated. They never call upon you unless they need something in return. Tell me, *boy*. What do you know about our dear Kiuno? What do you know about her life? Her real life?"

She was… Kiuno was… Reece bit his tongue.

"Exactly. She's happier here and I want her to see it."

"So, what do you want from me?"

"Lead the monsters to their doorstep and make her question everything."

"You want me to hurt her."

"That seems to be what it takes."

Nsane burst through the door and the clashing of steel and voices followed. "They're breaking through!"

The shadow swirled and faded. "Tick Tock."

Reece looked down the long hall as monsters poured over the wall. His men fell, and fire crawled along the ground.

"Reece, what's the next move?"

Reece looked at the place where the shadow had vanished and closed his eyes in defeat. "I'll do it."

The voice laughed, causing Nsane to spin around in search of its source.

"Hold up your arm."

Reece clenched his teeth. Knowing it would be the biggest mistake of his life, he obeyed and lifted his right arm. Pain shot through his wrist as a green object buried itself in his skin. It twisted to create space and roots shot out surrounding his wrist in black, feather-like marks.

Pain pulsed through his arm and Reece screamed, sinking to the floor. Nsane dropped to his side.

"They're retreating!" Voices rang from outside.

The boy from earlier ran down the tower steps and skidded to a halt before the pair. "The monsters are retreating! The monsters are retreating!"

"I'll be watching." The voice echoed.

Nsane helped Reece from the floor and looked at the jewel embedded in his wrist. "What did you do?"

NSANE PACED the room and Reece took another drink of water. He wiped the sweat from his brow and pulled at the collar of his shirt.

The roots circled his wrist, but the jewel hadn't pulsed since the monsters' retreat.

"I didn't have a choice." Reece said again. He pressed one hand to his burning forehead.

"You just agreed to work with a lunatic."

"That lunatic can hear you. I was out of options. If I didn't agree everyone in this castle would have died."

"So, you're going to attack Ki?"

Reece examined the swollen area around the jewel. The roots wriggled ever so slightly. "I have to do my part."

Nsane gave his friend a sympathetic look. "If you hurt anyone, she'll tear you apart."

"He wants me to play games with her."

"But why?"

"Because they've been part of it all along. He wants to see how far he can push her before she breaks."

MASSACRE

REALM: 5

DAY: 325

Kiuno kicked her horse, striving to keep pace with several teams who raced ahead. Palindrome led their battalion toward the oncoming threat. *Please don't let us be too late.*

Her horse slowed, as did several of the others as dark shadows soared through the sky on the distant horizon.

Kiuno bit her lip and held her breath.

The creatures descended and everyone rushed forward without a moment's hesitation.

Cybele jumped from Milo's back and Kiuno's heart clenched. Milo's right wing dripped with blood and the fur on the back of his neck rose as he roared at those approaching his pride.

His much smaller pride.

What used to be a hundred had dwindled to dozens and they sat on the ground broken in both body and spirit.

Cybele turned to face them and Kiuno's stomach clenched tighter.

The flesh of her cheek hung loose, and blood caked one side of her body. Kiuno couldn't be sure whose blood as Cybele cradled a cub in one arm.

Kiuno's eyes darted from face to face until she found Jim. He crouched and Nikita circled him, pacing back and forth. Her maw was covered in blood.

Cybele ran toward Palindrome and Palindrome's hands glowed. The skin on the cub's back stitched itself together and the small creature cried out.

Palindrome tried to work on Cybele next, but Cybele caught her wrist. "Them first. Heal the felinians first."

Cybele calmed the injured animals beside her and pulled Palindrome toward them. The rest of the healers tried to approach, but dominant males stood guard and growled. The medical team recoiled.

Kiuno grit her teeth and advanced toward one that appeared familiar. His wing was half torn and blood dripped from the wound, staining his gray feathers.

She slowed her movements, but he growled in response, pulling his lip back to reveal long fangs.

"Kiuno," Elite hissed from several paces behind.

She stepped and the beast surged forward, snapped its jaw, and expanded his wings. Kiuno retreated several steps.

This wasn't going to work.

"Cybele," she called.

The woman lifted her head, turning this way and that before she realized the felinians were resisting their medical attention. The woman sprinted to Kiuno, the flesh on her cheek bouncing, and the creature let her run right up to it without so much as flinching.

It stopped growling and Cybele ushered Kiuno forward.

The beast sniffed Kiuno's hair, then Cybele placed her hand on his head. "He's one of the alphas."

Cybele darted to another who had tried and failed to approach the beasts.

Kiuno locked eyes with Elite who stood in the same position. She waved him forward and after an initial growl, the felinian allowed Elite to approach. Kiuno did the same with those who could heal.

Some creatures were burnt, others bloody, and the too few humans who'd accompanied them back helped comfort the injured that wouldn't see tomorrow.

Kiuno's heart stuck in her throat as her eyes scanned past two young that had already fallen still. Other little ones escaped from the healer's grasp and searched for mothers who would never come.

Kiuno glanced at the horizon. They needed to get back to the castle.

Less than twenty minutes later, Cybele grabbed Kiuno's arm. "I need to go back. There are others trapped. You've flown on the felinians before." Sorrow clouded her usually stern features. "Will you help me?"

The flesh of her cheek still hung loose allowing Kiuno to see her teeth. "Shouldn't Palindrome heal that first?"

Her grip tightened. "We don't have time."

Kiuno called for Scorpios and Maltack then turned to Elite. "Help them get back home. We'll be right behind you."

Elite hesitated, worked his jaw, then joined Palindrome. Cybele jumped on the back of Milo and Kiuno hauled herself onto another. Maltack and Scorpios did the same.

Kiuno worried for his stamina, but strong muscles beneath her told Kiuno he possessed enough strength.

Kiuno clutched his fur and they were flying in seconds. She squeezed her legs into the animal's side and ducked her head low. The passing air ripped her hair from its braid and the tendrils slashed at her eyes.

Without a saddle there wasn't much to hold onto, but she'd swallow her fear if it meant saving lives.

His mighty wings pumped the air past as they soared over what used to be a black landscape. A sea of monsters had taken its place. Hundreds. Thousands.

Her mouth fell open and the monsters' roar for blood filled her ears in a wicked song that raised the hairs on the back of her neck. She clenched her teeth and scanned the area.

Chirping, roaring, gnashing of teeth. It all sounded like a chorus of death. The chirping creatures from the third realm circled among the throng, their half heads snapping toward her feet as they flew passed. The reptilian creatures that could bend shadows waved their long claws and the antlered, fire-resistant creatures from the sixth realm roared at their side.

Then there were the hollows. Their eerie smiles following their flight path in a promise of pain.

Could the felinians have hid from this?

Kiuno glanced at the setting sun. In and out. They had to be quick.

The felinians snarled and their fur rippled beneath her fingertips as Cybele pointed to a den. The creatures surrounding it didn't seem to be paying attention to the location. Either that meant the small felinians were safe or the beasts had already devoured them.

The felinians roared and swooped toward the ground. Kiuno's stomach dropped and she clenched every muscle in her body.

Cybele hit the ground first, followed closely by Maltack and Scorpios. The two fanned their magic in a circle that disrupted the monsters' ranks. Kiuno's felinian landed in the clearing. She dismounted, drew her blade and plunged it through a hollow before letting her magic spread like wildfire.

Cybele chopped at the ranks and shoved toward the den. The rest covered her rear.

Maltack shifted the flames around the small burrow and directed the frenzy of magic where he deemed fit.

Cybele ducked in, then emerged seconds later carrying three young in her arms. An older felinian trotted at her side and it too carried a cub in its mouth.

Cybele strapped the young to a saddle and commanded the large felinian to take flight.

In her distraction a burst of magic sent Kiuno backpedaling. She hit the ground hard, elbows scraping against sticks and debris. Monsters swarmed, but Scorpios jumped to her aid. He sliced through a hollow's arm then sent spears of ice flying in all directions.

She turned.

Six men stood to their front.

No, not men. Hollows. Hollows that possessed magic.

Flames spiraled down Kiuno's arms and she took a step back. A gust of wind knocked her off balance again and she used the hilt of her sword to block claws from piercing her throat.

Kiuno struggled to her feet, only to be shoved aside by Scorpios's body. He lifted in the air and she reached for him, but missed his hand.

Her adrenaline spiked, the hollow smiled, and she called for Maltack's aid too late. Scorpios fell and hit the ground with a sickening thud.

Lightning pulsed from her body and Kiuno shot it straight toward their assailants, exploding the ground they stood upon.

The bolt created the distraction needed for the felinians to drop again. Maltack ran to her side and Kiuno swallowed the magic that fought against her control like a rabid animal.

They each wrapped an arm around Scorpios and ran his limp form toward the felinians. Cybele tied Scorpios on then Maltack jumped in behind, his hands already working on the blood pouring from Scorpios's head.

They took flight and Cybele called for Kiuno; her arm outstretched. Their hands clasped and the felinian took flight before Kiuno could settle in. She slipped and the monsters converged, reaching their talons and claws toward escaping prey. The felinian tilted and Kiuno climbed up and gripped Cybele's waist.

Her heart thundered as she tried to see Scorpios and Maltack ahead, but the wind dried out her eyes and forced her to look away.

What seemed a short flight on the way there felt like an eternity on the way back. The sun descended. Maltack's hands glowed. Scorpios remained still.

They landed and a frenzy launched as Maltack called for a team of their best medics. They lifted Scorpios's unconscious body from the felinian and carried him inside. Palindrome joined them, but they pushed Kiuno away. The door shut, leaving her on the outside.

Blood covered her shaking hands. All the power in the world and she couldn't help.

Kiuno slouched against the wall and eventually Liam wrapped his hand in hers and led her outside. She took a deep breath and repeated a mantra in her head. *He's still breathing. He's still breathing. He's still breathing.*

DECISIONS

REALM: 5
DAY: 325

Kiuno rested her head against Elite's shoulder. Liam had led her from the medical building, and she'd found Elite trotting toward her on the way toward the castle. She'd run to him as if he'd be the one to fix all their problems. If only one person had that kind of power.

Scorpios. He was her friend, mentor, the one who helped rationalize her emotional decisions. And he'd gotten hurt trying to protect her.

Kiuno clenched her fists. Why did they all do that? Why couldn't they place their lives above her own?

Maltack exited the building and Kiuno jumped to her feet.

He sighed and crumpled against the wall. "Palindrome will be out in a minute."

His blood-stained hands shook and Kiuno bit her tongue. How much burden had they placed on him lately? Maltack always ran to their aid and more often than not their lives rested in his hands.

Time ticked by. Taunting.

Palindrome walked out cleaning her hands with a soiled rag. "He's alive."

"But?"

"There's brain swelling. It's difficult to keep him stable. The impact should have killed him."

Kiuno chewed her lip and shifted her weight. "So, what happens now?"

"As it stands, we're in for a rough night, but I'll do my best."

Palindrome wiped her brow and went back inside. Kiuno exchanged a glance with Elite then followed. Blood and sweat met her nose, but she refused to recoil. Moans of pain sent a spike of energy racing through her heart, but Kiuno reminded herself that Scorpios was still unconscious.

Palindrome disappeared in a side room and Kiuno peered inside. Three people hovered around Scorpios's head, their hands glowing and eyes closed in concentration.

Elite placed a hand on her shoulder. They watched for a moment, then he guided her out.

"Will you stay with him?" she asked.

"Where are you going?"

"I just need some air."

Elite brushed a strand of loose hair behind her ear and kissed her forehead. "Don't go far."

Kiuno nodded and left him at the medical house. She marched toward the main gate and turned her head from the felinians who whimpered in their sleep.

If she'd had the strength, she might have run, but Kiuno felt like the weight of a thousand lifetimes had sapped her energy.

Outside the gate, Kiuno stopped before the only tree that stood near the castle. Its trunk had split in half and it leaned in a way that should have killed it, but small branches shot from the base.

If a tree could survive a war, then Scorpios could do the same. He'd battled through too much to quit now.

Kiuno collapsed on the ground and picked at the dead bark. She'd gotten a second chance with Elite, but she still wondered if she was cursed to lose them all.

She scanned the horizon. Another war was coming.

Reece. Had part of the enemy's force marched upon her friend? Was he even aware of the danger lurking on his doorstep?

The soft clinking of metal caused Kiuno to turn. K.J. strode through the field, his gaze locked on the ground. She shifted and he sat beside her, the two watching the stars.

"How are you holding up?"

"I'm tired of losing people."

"No one is lost yet."

"He protected me."

K.J. shifted his legs. "People sacrifice themselves for what they believe in."

"I wish it wasn't me."

"I imagine anyone in your position would feel the same. Your power and the decisions you make with it has saved far more lives than it's taken. Rest assured in that at least."

She sighed. "So, what's the plan?"

"I've gotten reports. They're lining up."

"Will someone help?"

K.J. shook his head. "Our closest ally, Samar, is south right now with part of his forces."

"What about the other one? Atilla?"

K.J. scoffed. "He's more likely to take my head than help me keep it. We'll set up barricades and traps to diminish their numbers. This time we'll be ready." He paused. "Are you up for doing your part?"

"Doesn't seem like we have much choice."

A question sat on the tip of her tongue, but she couldn't ask. Palindrome was the only one skilled enough to keep Scorpios steady, but they would need her in the coming battle. K.J. always focused on what benefited the greater good, not individuals.

"Palindrome says the worst should be over tonight and if Scorpios survives, she has three people who can tend to him during the fight."

Kiuno hated how transparent her worries always seemed to be. "Thank you."

"We estimate they'll be here in two days. I want you to rest as much as possible before then."

"I'll be ready."

K.J. left and she waited another twenty minutes before creeping toward the felinians. She hated to lie, but she wasn't taking any chances. The castle wall had already fallen once.

She snuck between the sleeping creatures, avoiding those injured and found Cybele stroking Milo's neck. Two young cubs sat nestled in her lap and she scratched behind one's ear. It stretched out, but the other didn't seem to notice.

Cybele placed a finger to her lips when Kiuno approached.

"I need to borrow a felinian," she whispered.

Cybele tilted her head and her stitched cheek stretched in response. "Plans in the middle of the night?"

"Plans to ensure we don't have as many casualties when this nightmare hits us."

Cybele's eyes fell to the little one as she stroked down its neck. "What are they?"

"We need allies and since K.J. doesn't seem as willing to get them, I'm going to."

"So, you're going against another's better judgement?"

Her countenance fell. "After what I saw out there, I'm not sure we can win on our own."

Cybele continued petting the creature in her lap. "Take Asher. He's the one you rode earlier, and he'll be our fastest flyer." Cybele pointed. "Be careful."

Kiuno nodded and crept through the sleeping giants. She spotted a sleeping Jim, but walked several yards around to avoid waking him. Heads rose as she passed, and a few warning growls echoed behind her.

Upon reaching the large male, Kiuno paused. He raised his head, but his expression remained neutral as he crawled forward.

Without a saddle, Kiuno climbed onto the creature's back and he took off into the night air. Powerful muscles beat beneath Kiuno's body and she hunkered low.

Atilla might not care for K.J., but he'd shown an interest in her. Perhaps she could use that to their advantage even if she had to sacrifice her freedom to do it. Atilla craved power and control. She was the lightning user. She wasn't about to let her friends die no matter what deal had to be made.

Time flew with the wind and Kiuno prayed she'd make it back before sunrise. If not, she'd have some explaining to do.

When the castle entered her view, Kiuno straightened and steered the felinian toward the tallest tower. Men pulled their weapons and called for backup when she landed.

"Who are you?" one demanded.

Asher snarled at him, causing the guard to take a few retreating steps.

"Tell Atilla Kiuno needs to see him and it's urgent."

One man fled into the castle, seeming glad for the task when faced with such a powerful creature. Kiuno doubted any of them would stand a chance if the beast wanted to tear them apart.

She swung her leg over and slid from its back, her legs throbbing and back painful. So much had happened in one day.

Kiuno glanced at the men, their pikes all positioned toward her and Asher. The felinian sat and folded its wings. She patted his side. The nervous way his eyes flitted this way and that told her he wouldn't stay away from Cybele long.

Kiuno had often wondered what kind of connection Cybele shared with the creatures. Perhaps it went further than anything she could imagine.

Kiuno walked to the edge and placed her hand over the wall. One guard stepped forward, but a rippling snarl from Asher had him backpedaling.

"Don't do anything stupid," he said.

She bit back the retort for him to do the same.

Kiuno tapped her foot and shifted across the space again before someone emerged from the tower stairwell.

"He'll see you."

Kiuno filed past the guards and turned before she went inside. "Don't threaten him. I won't be held responsible if you do."

When she turned back, the man before her held out his hand. "Your weapons."

She grimaced, untied her belt, and pulled the daggers from her boot.

The guard led her down a series of maze-like halls. Shadows danced off the stone from the fires contained in braziers, but otherwise the castle was quiet.

When they neared a room, two men stood at attention, their hands resting on weapons.

"Tell him she's here."

The guard looked her over, snickered, and announced her arrival. He stepped aside, and she walked through alone.

Candles of every shape and size lit the inside of an orderly room. Papers were stacked perfectly, and several rugs covered the cold floor. Trophies from a good hunt.

Atilla stood with his back to the door and Kiuno walked through uncertain. The guards exited and closed the door, leaving the two of them alone.

Atilla turned with a glass in each hand. He pointed to a chair with a soft cushion resting on it, then sat behind a desk.

"I have to say; this is an unexpected visit." He slid the glass to her side of the table.

She took it but didn't drink. "But I hope not unwelcome."

Atilla chuckled. "The hour isn't ideal, but I've been hoping you might come."

"Sorry to disappoint, but that's not why I'm here." She remembered his offer back at their first meeting and prayed he wouldn't ask for her service as payment.

"Shame." He sat back in the chair and sipped his drink. She eyed hers but didn't touch it. "What can I do for you then?"

"I'm sure you've heard about the recent attack?"

"I did. I also heard you retaliated and took control of another castle." His face scrunched at the thought. Kiuno reminded herself of Atilla's conflict with Reece.

"Monsters are pouring from the sixth realm and headed our way."

"And you want my help." Kiuno nodded and Atilla swirled his drink. "What did Samar say?"

"He's still south. With Grayson."

That piqued his interest. "I didn't realize the two were meeting."

"Neither did I." It was an honest response, though she didn't really care what one alliance leader did with the other.

Atilla rubbed at the stubble on his face. "Interesting. Aren't you one of K.J.'s advisors?"

Kiuno didn't think Atilla was the sort of man to understand friendship so she nodded. "We met the monsters on their turf a few days ago and one of my friends was critically injured. I'm not asking you to send your entire force. Just enough people to prevent a breach in the wall."

"Does K.J. know you're here?"

She averted her gaze. "No."

His eyes seemed to flicker, but he regained his composure and set his empty glass on the table. "We've had our differences, but with innocent lives at stake I won't be the first to deny an ally's call for aid." He poured himself another drink. "I'll assume there are traps around the area?"

She nodded. "But if you go around the back, you'll avoid them.

K.J. is stationing us outside the castle for the fight. I hope your army isn't needed, but if they break through…"

"We'll be there. Do you fight at the front?"

"Yes, with many of the magic users." She paused as he took a swig of wine. "Thank you for doing this." Kiuno stood.

"You're leaving?"

"I have to get back before they notice I'm gone."

"I see." He sat forward. "Just remember, I'm doing this for you. I know you have friends in that castle, and I'll do what I can to protect them. In return I hope you take my proposal seriously."

"Thank you, I will." Kiuno dismissed herself and the guards opened the door. She tried to match the steps of her escort. Atilla would expect a return on his favor, of that she was certain.

Kiuno relaxed as she stepped into the open air and saw Asher safe and sound. She mounted and took off without looking back. She had no intention of joining Atilla, but if he ever found out she was the lightning user then K.J. might very well have another fight on his doorstep.

ASHER SOARED slower than she would have liked, using the wind to carry them home. She might have pushed him to go faster if not for all the trauma he'd suffered.

Elite paced inside the front gate when she landed. Kiuno took the time to say her goodbyes to the felinian before turning to her anxious husband.

"Cybele told me where you've been."

Kiuno pressed a kiss to his lips and whispered, "Not here." She took his hand and led him through the castle.

With most asleep, the couple passed through the halls unnoticed and crept to their room. Kiuno locked the door, let her weapons fall to the floor, and kicked off her shoes. She knelt at the fireplace and heated the logs.

"Are you going to tell me what's going on?" Elite crossed his arms.

"I sent for reinforcements."

"From who?"

"Atilla."

Elite sat on the edge of the bed. "I didn't think him and K.J. were on good terms."

"He's not, but I am. Or seem to be. The nearest castle can't help, and the other two alliances are too far to make it in time." She sighed. "You weren't here, but the wall fell during our last fight and with Scorpios hurt, I just couldn't risk not having backup."

Elite ran his hands up and down her arms. "Why do you always feel the need to do things on your own?"

"Flying is faster with one person."

"But you never tell me anything."

"Because you wouldn't have let me go."

He sighed, wrapped one arm around her back, and pressed his forehead to hers. "How many times are you going to put yourself in danger?"

"As many times as it takes to get us home."

BETRAYAL

REALM: 5
DAY: 327

Kiuno stood at the front of their waiting army with Palindrome on one side and Maltack on the other. Most sat in the grass at this point, anxiously awaiting the coming battle as the sun peeked over the horizon.

The morning air filled her lungs, but it did nothing for her nerves as she switched between sitting and pacing back and forth.

Her body trembled as she recalled the sea of monstrous faces. They had an insatiable lust for blood. Teeth, claws, and smiles. Not a human in sight.

Kiuno sat again, this time facing the castle. The sun gleamed from the stone bringing back images of fire and near failure. She prayed it wouldn't fall this time.

She glanced at the men. Some whispered to their comrades while others meditated upon the coming battle. The sound of sharpening weapons and shifting steel made Kiuno grit her teeth.

Their forces were lined along the curtain wall's front and fanned to either side in a strategic line. Archers stood ready and magic users, like herself, had been stationed at the front.

The civilians were hidden. The supplies ready.

She took another breath and stood. Silver and Elite were stationed in the second line of defense. He still didn't like her in the front guard, but she'd agreed to join them upon exhausting her capabilities.

If their tactic even worked.

Humans naturally feared for their lives and upon seeing her magic, they scattered. But did monsters feel the same? Would they converge upon the magic users without regard to their safety?

A blaring horn echoed across the field and Kiuno's heart raced in the passing silence. The horn sounded again. A long, deep bellow.

Metal clanked against metal and shouts rose above the noise as leaders gave their orders and boosted morale.

Kiuno wrapped shaking fingers around her sword.

Maltack stood at her side, his gaze sweeping across the green landscape that would soon be red with blood and bodies. She hated the smell and the way it crawled to her tongue, tasting of copper.

Shadows rose against the horizon.

Once the traps triggered and the enemy closed in past the archers' range, she'd make her move. Maltack and his subordinates would ensure her safe return.

Those who could see her face would know the lightning user after today, but the news was spreading, and it seemed likely that many knew her identity already. Kiuno hoped that brought them peace.

The shadows grew closer, their numbers as great as she remembered on the rescue mission for the young felinians. K.J. didn't have a way to contact Reece. She worried for him. He didn't have the manpower they did, nor the magic users to defend himself.

Screams echoed from behind and Kiuno whipped her head around. An army, smaller than Kiuno would have liked, marched from the backside of the castle. Their flags were black and white, crossed over one another in a diamond-shaped pattern. The colors Atilla had chosen to represent himself.

"Why is he here?" Palindrome asked.

Kiuno didn't have a chance to respond as magic engulfed the rear part of K.J.'s army. Flames rose high, screams followed, and Kiuno's heart thundered at the carnage invisible to her eyes.

Palindrome darted through the crowd without a second thought and commanded part of her regiment to follow.

The monsters cried out and growled, sending a shiver down Kiuno's spine. They were closing in from the front, barreling toward them like the crazed creatures she knew them to be.

Long claws promised death. Sharp teeth promised pain.

She knew the traps wouldn't hold them long.

Murmurs echoed among the lines of men as their eyes followed Palindrome and then darted toward the creatures closing in.

Kiuno clenched her fists. A traitor. K.J. was right. Atilla would rather see K.J.'s head on a spike than help. She'd brought death to their door on both sides.

Fire exploded a mangonel and part of their rear ranks scattered as half went to aid their comrades and the other half filled the line.

She needed to help but—growling screams echoed as the first line of creatures fell into long spike-filled trenches. Kiuno's head whipped around, hoping the traps might buy them some time.

The beasts surged forward, trampling their fallen brethren without a passing glance.

Palindrome was supposed to lead this line. The men responded to her, but judging from the chaos still unfolding, it didn't appear she'd be back in time.

Kiuno glanced at Maltack. He was a young man ready to take on the world, yet he seemed bewildered at the events unfolding.

The line faltered. Men took a step back. If they ran, the monsters would overtake their ranks and it'd all be over.

"Stand firm," she shouted. Kiuno stepped out, all eyes following. "Those assigned to Palindrome, secure the back. The rest of you, trust your comrades and focus on the enemy before you. Remember your formations and stand your ground!"

Kiuno hoped she sounded more confident than she felt. Maltack raised one hand. The archers shuffled, notching their arrows as monsters fell into the wide ditch they'd hidden beneath ground. The archers fired, and Kiuno charged, screaming with her allies at her back.

The enemy met a wall of fire and shards of ice flew in every direction. Wind fed the flames into a roar and Kiuno ran ahead, letting the lightning wrap her body and crack across the ground.

She let another bolt fly and sparks echoed to her right where Maltack altered their route and sent them back toward their enemy. The more monsters they took out, the better their chances of survival.

The original plan was to conserve energy, but that plan needed some adjustment. Kiuno let the lightning loose upon their enemies time and time again. She stayed close to Maltack as she danced between the carnage.

The lizard beasts trapped her comrades in shadow, but earth users wrapped their bodies in vines, strangling the creatures to death. Mangy dogs with long fangs lunged at several throats, but near invisible shards of glassy ice met them in the air and they dropped one by one.

Kiuno burned through the hollows, the most difficult of their enemies. Even with half a body, they would put a blade through your leg with a smile on their face.

One creature fled, followed by another, but Kiuno pressed forward, urging her group to do the same. She killed the hollows who refused to retreat, then let herself melt into the passing crowd.

Maltack paused as men gave chase to the fleeing creatures. "You all right?"

She nodded, struggling to catch her breath. "Go on ahead."

He looked her over once then took off. Kiuno turned her attention to the rear. The damage frightened her. She prayed Elite hadn't been caught in the frenzy.

Kiuno raced through the crowd, pushing past her comrades. Upon reaching the fight she twisted her blade in any who carried Atilla's colors. Men lay scattered on the ground, several crying out for aid, but she didn't pause. Couldn't afford to.

Atilla's forces blocked their way into the castle. Those on the curtain wall rained down rocks and arrows while those at the bottom hit the wall with their magic. Green crawled through the rocks, but she wouldn't let it fall again.

Lightning crackled around her body as Kiuno surged forward. Her comrades scattered and Kiuno let her magic incinerate all in her path.

Their forces dispersed, fought for a moment, then called for retreat. She chased them down and her allies followed.

Fatigue chipped away at her body, but Kiuno let a final bolt fly through their retreating forces before she paused to catch her breath. She wished Atilla had the nerve to show his face. She spat on the ground. He'd pay for what he'd done.

The monsters had circled around their army. Almost as though they planned to join with Atilla's forces. Palindrome was there. As was K.J. and the battle still raged.

She took a shaky step forward, but Maltack grabbed her arm.

"I need your help."

She looked from him to the magic still flying across the field. "It's not over."

"Let them handle it. I need you here." He pointed to the injured. "Line the worst by the gate, separate the dead, and tell anyone uninjured to do the same."

Kiuno spotted Elite and Silver carrying a man with no leg, his blood painting the ground, and she scanned the mass of bodies sprawled across the earth.

She relented and knelt to wrap an arm beneath the nearest man pleading for help. Next to him, another struggled for breath. The two at either side didn't move.

Medics ran between the chaos, but too many were dying.

Kiuno shifted the man's weight for a better grip, but his body fell limp and they both collided with the ground.

She glanced up. Arms reached toward the heavens and healers. The smell of burning flesh permeated the air. Death cries echoed in her ears and the disgusting taste of copper filled her mouth.

Kiuno shifted her shaking body to a kneeling position and checked the pulse of the man she'd been carrying.

He was gone.

Kiuno sat back on her knees and glanced over the carnage again. *What have I done?*

DRIED BLOOD caked her arms as Kiuno continued to move bodies, both dead and alive. They piled the enemy's dead and lined up their own.

Maltack flitted from one person to the next. He directed those arriving and aided the critical. Despite his age, he commanded the medical unit better than she ever could. He knew the stakes and he knew his job.

She sighed and laid another body next to his comrade before folding his arms over his chest. Many wouldn't live to see tomorrow no matter what they did.

Kiuno leaned against the castle wall to catch her breath. Sweat poured from her brow and her body trembled from the exertion of the day. She prayed the healers had more energy because their work was far from over.

A small crowd pulled her attention as they lifted someone from the ground and carried them into the castle. She watched for a few moments and then saw K.J. trotting after them. Her heart spiked and she made to move, but another grabbed her arm.

"Can you help me move someone?"

Kiuno met the eyes of a young woman and nodded, following her through the crowd, but Kiuno glanced back at her friend and where he'd disappeared through the castle gates.

Kiuno lifted a man and shifted his position, then did the same with another. She followed the healer from body to body, shifting, wrapping, and doing anything asked of her.

They declared another dead then assigned Kiuno to move the body. She took the opportunity to escape.

She placed the man with so many others, then darted toward the gate, ignoring any who tried to stop her. Her body cried for rest, but she ignored it.

Kiuno trotted toward the medical house, sure there wasn't anywhere else they could have taken someone injured. *Unless they were dead.*

Kiuno reached for the handle, but a man leaning in the shadows of the wall drew her attention.

K.J. stood with his arms outstretched and hands pressed flat against the stone. His head hung low. The stillness disturbed her, but he shifted slightly at her approach.

"K.J.?" He didn't move, his body as still as the wall he leaned upon.

"Betrayal is in man's nature." His voice was hoarse. "Because of this, I've kept my eye on most in the event they waver. I expect it."

He shifted and clenched his fists. "But I didn't expect this. Out of everyone, I never imagined betrayal to come from you."

Kiuno's entire being shifted as his words echoed through her chest. Her heart fluttered. She'd been the one to go to Atilla, but—

"I didn't betray you."

Cold silence floated between them but he remained pressed against the stone. How could she explain?

"If you want it done, then get on with it."

"What are you talking about?"

"Wipe out the generals and cut the lead. That was the plan wasn't it?" He snickered. "It's brilliant. There'd be no one left to oppose you."

"K.J. listen, it's not what you think."

His voice hardened. "I know you went to Atilla."

"I went there for help. I thought we needed it."

"And you conveniently told him where my generals were stationed?"

"No…" She hadn't. How could Atilla have known? She'd mentioned some of the layout, but she hadn't gone into detail.

"That's what I thought. Are you going to finish the job, or do you lack the ability to do it yourself?"

Kiuno's heart pulled and a wave of emotions crashed through her core. "Do you really believe I'd betray you?" He couldn't possibly. Not after how long they'd known one another. Not after all they've been through.

Silence stretched between them.

"I don't know what to believe." K.J. threaded his hands through his hair and tugged on the ends. "You should have listened to me."

"I didn't mean for any of this to happen."

"Regardless of what you meant Iggy and Blade are dead and Palin-drome…" His shoulders shook, and he slammed his fist against the wall. "They aren't sure she'll make it."

Iggy and Blade? Palindrome? She glanced to the building. That's who they carried in? Kiuno opened her mouth, but K.J. spoke first.

"Leave."

Tears formed and fell as her heart rent in two. It was her fault. Because she hadn't trusted him. Because she'd questioned someone ranked above her.

"K.J. please."

"I said leave!" His harsh tone froze her body, but the coldness in his eyes had her backpedaling. The hatred, the confusion, the grief. People he loved had died because of her naivety.

RISE OF THE WOLVES

Kiuno dropped her gaze and turned, each step like a stake driving through her heart.

She took off running and found Maltack among the healers. "You need to find Palindrome."

"I'm sure she's outside, why—"

Kiuno gripped his shoulders. "She's dying." His eyes widened and Maltack took off without another word. She looked over the chaos. Took in the damage she'd caused, then walked through the gate, knowing it would be for the last time.

49

REECE

REALM: 5

DAY: 331

Reece stared at the black feather-like roots. Three tendrils had pulled away from the thick band circling his wrist and crawled up his forearm day by day. They wriggled beneath the skin and pulsed with his heartbeat.

He sighed and rested his head in the palm of his hands. He'd been the one to lead the attack on K.J.'s castle. Reece remembered Nsane questioning his actions. He remembered marching and how the monsters had answered his call. Yet he couldn't remember what drove him to do it.

He'd watched as his body rode on horseback with hordes of monsters in his wake. The horse had bucked, frightened of the creatures and they'd eventually devoured it, leaving him to march on foot.

As a result, Reece was behind when the first wave of creatures attacked, and it seemed like a good thing too. K.J. had set traps to kill the first of his line, clustering them within a deep ditch as arrows rained from above. The beasts didn't see fit to help their allies. Instead, they'd walked over them, charging headfirst into battle.

It wasn't until he'd seen her face that Reece regained control over his body. With the attack on the rear underway he'd called for retreat and the monsters obeyed.

The scaled creatures that bent shadows reeled in their darkness. The chirping humanoids shrieked and fled in a cluster toward his keep. And the worms, who he knew tunneled beneath the ground, buried themselves deeper.

Those events were strange enough, but when the hollows twisted around, his skin crawled. They reminded him of a doll. A being with no emotion that smiled at the pain they inflicted. Their name suited them.

The mysterious man, whom he'd named the creator, wanted the alliance's progress slowed. He wanted the games to continue, not end. He wanted entertainment. If Reece provided that, he wouldn't be violating their agreement, even with the retreat.

His mind blanking out would be a problem. He'd have to find a way to communicate the incident with Nsane without their watchdog knowing.

The roots writhed and tugged beneath his skin causing Reece to gag and clutch the area. His mind tottered as he fought for control, a welcoming darkness pulling him from reality. He fought, gripping the table, but the tendrils wrapped him in their sweet embrace and he collapsed into shadow.

50

PALINDROME

REALM: 5

DAY: 330

Palindrome woke in her room alone. She blinked away the dizziness and shifted, placing her feet on the cool floor. Maltack had healed her broken leg and ribs though the puncturing of a lung had certainly given him trouble.

"What are you doing?" K.J. carried a steaming bowl of broth and the aroma caused her mouth to water. K.J. pushed her back into the furs with a gentle hand.

"I don't need bedsores to accompany my already aching body."

The enemy had thrown and stabbed her more times than she could count. Her blood had been everywhere and the struggle to breathe left a pain in her chest she couldn't block from memory.

Palindrome closed her eyes. It'd been days of recovery even with Maltack's help.

"You're such a stubborn woman."

"And you're an insufferable man."

He sat on the bed and she sighed, pressing her forehead against his. "I'm sorry, I didn't mean that. Walk with me?"

K.J. helped her stand, but Palindrome's legs trembled, and she leaned on him more than she would have liked. K.J. held her arm around his neck and helped her ascend a flight of stairs that led to a tower.

She leaned on the railing and glanced out over the field. The grass had blackened from fire and magic, leaving an acrid stench in the air.

Palindrome glanced toward Atilla's castle. "Have you figured out what made them retreat?" K.J. shook his head. "Could it have been because of Kiuno?"

"I'm not sure." He didn't meet her gaze, but his jaw locked at the sound of Kiuno's name.

Their castle hadn't taken damage this time, but their army certainly had. At least a quarter of their forces were down. Some injured and others dead. Iggy's and Blade's loss weighed on their hearts, but K.J. also suffered due to Kiuno's betrayal.

Palindrome folded her hands. It didn't make sense. The lightning had spread at both the front and the rear. Kiuno ran to aid them. If she'd wanted the castle, she wouldn't have attacked Atilla's group.

"Do you really think she did it?" Palindrome asked.

He kept silent, scanning the area, no doubt running the scenario through his head again. "I don't know."

"You know what you see. We're alive, the castle's still in our care. She didn't kill you, yet you say she had the chance. Isn't that enough to convince you?"

"Why would she go to him?"

"Maybe because of Scorpios. Maybe she was afraid."

K.J. sighed and ran a hand through his hair. "She asked if I'd go to him. I declined."

"Kiuno had no desire to turn you over to a man she hardly knows. She's smarter than that. I'd expect her to take matters into her own hands if she wanted to do something so drastic."

"That's my point. She is smart. Smart enough to pit two opposing castles against one another. Smart enough to know Atilla's group couldn't possibly take us on. She saw an opportunity and took it. It would have given her two castles instead of one."

"Except she doesn't have two castles. What if she hoped to bring two unfriendly alliances together? Make the bond stronger in the face of their enemies?"

His jaw worked, but K.J. remained silent.

"Ask yourself this. If she planned to betray you, why didn't she kill you when she had the chance?"

"I don't know."

CONQUEROR

REALM: 5
DAY: 332

The late morning breeze caressed Kiuno's loose strands of hair as she stood upon the hill. Contempt and malice filled her gaze and lightning buzzed beneath her skin as she stared at Atilla's distant castle.

He'd offered aid. He'd pretended to care. And now because of him she'd been exiled like a traitor.

K.J.'s cold eyes flashed in her memory. She focused on the black and white flags billowing in the distance and prayed Maltack could save Palindrome. If he couldn't, then she'd never be able to face K.J. again.

"What's the plan?" Blue asked.

Kiuno glanced at her friends. Years of forming bonds led them to follow her even now. None believed her a traitor and none believed she couldn't lead them to victory.

Elite and Silver stood with their sword hilts gleaming in the morning sun. Blue and Liam gazed out over the castle grounds and the army that stood waiting outside the gates. Vixin, to whom Kiuno owed a debt she'd never be able to repay, crossed her arms and seemed to welcome their challenge.

"I'm going in alone."

Silence.

They didn't protest. They knew her sins and knew Atilla as a liar. He was more likely to kill her friends than keep any promise of safety. And without Maltack to reel in her lightning they'd only be a liability.

Lines of soldiers stood outside the castle gate, all armed to the teeth. Perhaps Atilla expected a counterattack. Maybe he thought the other leaders would rise to claim his seat on the throne. It didn't matter. They wouldn't get the chance.

Blue shifted his feet, then knelt to pick at a blade of grass. "Are you sure?"

"I can't concentrate if I have to worry about all of you. He wants me to join him. I can get close enough."

Elite kept silent. He had tried to convince her it wasn't her fault, but the truth was a harder pill to swallow. She should have known. Atilla had tried to kill Reece. He'd offered K.J.'s men as a sacrifice to the forest. And K.J. had warned her.

Kiuno took a step, but Elite grabbed her wrist and pulled her back against his chest. They stood still for several moments then he kissed the back of her head. "Be careful."

She nodded and stalked toward the castle.

For once, no one tried to stop her. For once, they knew she could handle the fight. Rage boiled beneath the surface of her skin as she pictured Atilla's face. She wondered about his plans. About what he expected to gain. Her fear?

Several men shifted their weapons at her approach. Bows drew back, and wind tore at her clothes in warning. Kiuno let the flames wrap around her body. The lightning clawed for release, raging like a current blocked by rock. It chipped away at her self-restraint, but Kiuno ground her teeth and held back.

The arrows pulled back further and other magic cracked through the air. She faltered. Perhaps she'd made a mistake. Maybe Atilla had betrayed both her and K.J.

Kiuno let rage drown her fear and continued her march forward. The arrows didn't fire and the front line parted.

Men stepped aside as she strode past, but Kiuno kept the blaze swirling around her body. She needed to let some steam out, otherwise she'd implode the minute she saw Atilla's wicked grin.

A guide waited by the gate and positioned himself to her front. Six others fanned out on either side. None bothered to speak, but their sidelong glances spoke of their fear. *Good.*

The fire encircling her body simmered and faded as they led Kiuno through the castle and to a familiar room. Atilla waited with a smile on his face. She clenched her teeth.

"You took longer to get here than I expected."

Her stomach twisted and Kiuno fought to keep her breathing even. "Why?" Her voice shook, and he smiled again. Knowing the kind of man Atilla was, Kiuno imagined he thought her fearful.

Atilla flicked his hand as if stating the obvious. "K.J. was becoming a threat. I had to level the playing field. You had concerns about leaving his side, so I made things easier for you."

Kiuno all but growled. "I had concerns because of my loyalty to him. Now he believes me a traitor."

Atilla clicked his tongue and poured himself a drink. "He's still alive then. That's a shame. No matter, if he thinks you a traitor that's enough reason for you to stay. We'll crush what's left of him with your lightning abilities."

Kiuno clenched her fists but remained silent.

Atilla raised his brows. "Didn't think I knew? You covered your scars at our first meeting, yet you failed to do so a few nights ago. It wasn't hard to piece together." He set a glass on the table. "We can work together. You and me. We can rule this entire realm."

"You've already betrayed me once."

"You're upset." He rubbed his brow in agitation. "It was strategy, nothing personal. Defeat an enemy while they're distracted."

"And how do I know you won't hurt those I care about?"

"Is that why you left them outside? I haven't done anything yet, have I?"

Kiuno's jaw ticked.

"Pledge your allegiance to me and I'll ensure it stays that way."

She glanced at each man in the room. They tightened their hold on their weapons, colorful stones displayed openly. Even Atilla's blood red one stood out against his thick wrist.

Her blood pulsed in her ears, but Kiuno fought the adrenaline coursing through her body. She drew her sword slowly and his men did the same. Atilla raised a hand to still them. She placed the tip of the blade in her palm and dropped to one knee.

"I didn't expect such formality from you, but I can't say I mind it." Atilla set down his drink and crossed the room until he stood before her. "Does K.J.—"

She lunged, sinking the blade through his gut all the way to the hilt. Blood poured over her fingers as she jerked up and twisted.

"Do not say his name."

Atilla's features contorted in pain and his flames rose, but they were nothing compared to the lightning surging through her body.

For a split second no one moved, then angry shouts echoed off the walls and his guards charged.

The static crackling snaked through the air and collided with any close enough to meet its deadly voltage. Cries of pain, then writhing bodies, then silence. Kiuno stood over them and her gaze met those left standing.

The clattering of a sword hit the floor. Followed by another. Kiuno took a step forward and most took several steps back.

The stone had been charred in places, painting the walls in a similar pattern to the scars on her skin. She hadn't meant for the blast to hit as many as it had.

The smell of burnt flesh filled the room and people clung to their seared arms and legs. They cowered in corners, but she couldn't afford to let them see her sympathy yet.

"Anyone else?" she challenged.

None moved.

Kiuno let the hum around her body fade then glanced at Atilla's body. "Is there anyone left who can answer my questions?"

They kept still, but a few quick glances pointed to one man along the wall.

He stepped forward of his own accord. "What can I assist you with my lady?" His hands were clenched, but his voice remained even.

"Atilla claimed he knew where my friends are. I want them brought to me. Safe. Otherwise," she glanced at those on the ground, "After that, bring the soldiers inside and close the gates."

"If I may, they were stationed in case of a counterattack."

"That's irrelevant now." She hoped. If K.J. chose to retaliate, he'd expect to see Atilla, but if he saw her… Her mind floated back to his face. To the anger. Perhaps he'd attack anyway. Everything still rested on whether Palindrome survived.

"Should I bring them here?"

"Yes, and I expect it to happen without incident. Is that understood?"

He nodded, and she raised her voice so all could hear. "Let it be known this castle is under new leadership. If someone attacks my people, you'll all pay the consequences." Her body still shook from the adrenaline, but she grimaced as the man turned away. Fear wasn't the way she ruled, but she'd have to make do for now.

Muffled cries of pain had Kiuno turning toward those who still hunkered in the corners. "I assume you have healers?" Another nodded. "Take the injured to the infirmary. The rest of you can wait until my group arrives."

Kiuno tapped her foot and paced the floor. Those in the corners hunkered as her shadow fell over them and a part of her heart tugged. She hated this. Hated using the same tactics as the man now lying face down in his blood.

She didn't turn away from the carnage. He'd deserved it. Kiuno paced the length of the floor again and her heart nearly jumped out of her chest when familiar voices echoed down the hall. She kept her air of composure, folded her hands behind her back, and waited.

Elite and Silver walked through first, their eyes scanning the vicinity until finally landing on her. Blue whistled when he saw the carnage and a smirk crossed Vixin's face. Liam stood there motionless, his eyes scanning the victims of her wrath.

Those seated whispered amongst themselves, but Kiuno didn't silence them. She'd have to gain their trust eventually. It would be hard earned. To them she was nothing more than another tyrant who'd barged in and taken over.

"Guess the cat's out of the bag about your abilities," Blue said as he gazed around the room.

"Atilla already knew. I sent the injured to the infirmary."

Kiuno approached the man who'd escorted her friends. His eyes met hers in quiet defiance.

"If anyone has an issue with my leadership, it's best you speak up now. I'll allow you to leave in exile. You won't be harmed."

"Why not?" The one before her asked. He drew his shoulders back. Proud. Determined. She glanced around the room. Every eye watched them. Some pleading for him to stand down. Others determined to fight should she choose to act against him.

Kiuno met his gaze again. "I don't enjoy senseless violence. Atilla attacked and killed several people. He paid the price for it."

"Atilla was a joke. His people are starving and most in this room sought to overthrow his rule."

"So, you're the leader of a potential coup d'état?"

He smirked. "Something like that."

She definitely needed his support.

"What would you say to following me in his stead?"

He crossed his arms. "Depends on your aim in all this."

Kiuno's gaze softened. "Home. To prevent more people from dying than necessary. To convince the alliances to work together."

His smirk faded. "That's all any of us have ever wanted." He turned to look at those still seated and Kiuno noted the bit of confidence they seemed to have gained. "You'll have my allegiance for now."

She nodded. For now would have to do. "Good. I need someone familiar with the people to help organize."

"Before you do that, might I suggest feeding the people?" He inclined his head. "Those within these walls ate fairly well, but the ones outside. Well, let's just say it's a problem."

"Wouldn't he let you hunt?" Kiuno asked.

"No, he wanted the people dependent."

Kiuno's lips parted. "What kind of leader refuses to feed his own people?"

"A bad one."

She cringed and the earlier rage bubbled to the surface. She'd known Atilla wasn't the most pleasant of people, but starvation?

She took a breath then held out her hand. "I'm Kiuno."

He eyed it, tracing her scars all the way up to her shoulder before taking it in a firm hold. "Daren."

"Well Daren, care to show me around?"

He inclined his head again. "What are you going to do with them?"

She followed his gaze to those seated. "Nothing yet. I promise nothing will happen to them in your absence."

"Unless they're stupid," Vixin said.

Kiuno and Daren both eyed her, then Daren turned and proceeded down the steps. Elite and Vixin followed.

J.E. REED

Now that some of her rage had quelled, Kiuno took the time to observe her surroundings.

Run down houses. Muddy streets. And the smell. Kiuno fought the urge to cover her nose. Sweat and feces floated through the air like a rotting perfume.

As they passed, many people ducked into their houses or shops. Planks had been nailed over broken windows and doors hung on the edge of their hinges.

A woman scooped a child from the street and ushered it inside. A far too skinny child.

Starving.

Why would someone willingly cause this kind of devastation?

"Let go of me!"

Kiuno's head whipped toward the voice. Several soldiers—judging from their uniforms—shoved a teenage girl against the side of a crumbling building. None stopped to intervene, and bile rose in Kiuno's throat as they tugged at her clothes.

Daren drew his blade, but Kiuno stalked toward them first.

Her anger flared, stirring the magic that ran through her veins. "What do you think you're doing?"

Lustful gazes shifted to her. "The girl was stealing and Atilla has strict orders to punish thieves."

"She wouldn't steal if she weren't starving."

He shoved the girl to his partner, then ran his gaze up and down Kiuno's form. "Pretty little thing like you all dressed up for war. You must be part of that resistance group." He let out a mocking laugh. "What do you think you can accomplish?"

"Atilla's death."

He let out a roar of laughter and his friends echoed it. He twisted a blade in one hand and took several steps forward. "You better watch your mouth."

"And you ought to shut yours."

His face scrunched and he gripped the blade. Kiuno drew her dagger in challenge. The two stared at one another for a moment then he lunged. His arm barely raised before Kiuno sank her blade into the pit of his arm.

Daren and Elite dispatched his friends while Kiuno planted her foot in the back of their leader's knee. He howled in pain and fell forward.

Kiuno twisted his arm back and whispered in his ear, "How does it feel to be helpless?" She cut his throat and let the body fall to the ground.

Magic pounded in her veins and Kiuno met Elite's gaze. She couldn't decipher what she saw there. Shock?

"You're all right now," Daren said.

The girl cried and Daren escorted her to a small group of women waiting further down the alley. They seemed to thank him as they cradled the shaken girl.

Vixin laughed, drawing them all from the moment. She pointed to Kiuno. "You know, I wasn't sure I liked you all that much." Vixin tilted her head toward the body. "But I think you've changed my mind."

KIUNO PAUSED at the gate, staring at the pitiful livestock that looked just as starved as the citizens. The crops were worse, if they could be called crops at all. Strangled plants struggling for life was more like it.

"How many men can you gather?"

"For what?" Daren asked.

"To hunt."

"I have enough. We can head out anytime."

"Please see to it."

"How do you know I'll come back?"

Kiuno looked out over the crops again. "I saw how much you cared about the people when you helped that girl. They look up to you and you don't seem like the type who'd abandon them."

Kiuno left Daren outside and returned to Atilla's chambers where she'd left Silver in charge. They had removed the dead bodies, but those alive still sat against the wall.

All heads turned to her as she entered the room.

One man stood. "What have you done with Daren?"

"I sent him hunting. We need food if anyone plans to survive."

He opened his mouth to speak, shut it, then opened it again. "And what do you plan to do with us?"

"I need to get this place back in working order. The livestock need tending. As do the crops. And I need people who will bring arising problems to my attention."

Whispers spread around the hall, but no one stood.

"I don't want to see anyone else go hungry, but I need your help to do it."

An older man rose on shaky legs. "I can help with the animals."

Kiuno nodded. "See to it. Fix the pens, separate the sick, do whatever is needed."

After a moment another stood. "My father was a farmer. I grew up working the land with him."

She gave a nod of approval. "Take whoever you need."

NIGHT FELL and Kiuno collapsed on the furs laid across their bed. She needed to bathe, but with tensions high she didn't dare make herself any more vulnerable than necessary.

Elite slid their thick lock into place, but when he didn't join her in bed, Kiuno glanced up.

He stared at her; his eyes confused.

"What?"

"You killed that man today."

She shifted to sit up on the bed. "And you killed his friend."

"But you enjoyed it."

She opened her mouth to deny it, but the words didn't follow. So what if she'd enjoyed it? He'd deserved what came to him.

"And?"

Elite sighed and ran one hand through his hair. "I know we have to do unspeakable things to survive, but don't let this world change you."

His soft eyes sent a pang of guilt crashing through her gut. It wasn't the first time she'd enjoyed a kill. At one point Kiuno had made a promise to herself. That no matter what she wouldn't let this world change her.

But it already had.

A NEW FUTURE

REALM: 5

DAY: 334

Two days later, in the early light of dawn, Daren delivered. Kiuno watched from a window as he sprinted ahead of his convoy and greeted the villagers. They eagerly obeyed his every word. If she weren't here, he'd be the new lead, of that she was certain.

Kiuno sent a messenger to inform those in the kitchens to prepare for a feast. She needed to mingle, let herself be known and with time, gain the trust of these damaged people.

The sun faded fast and it seemed as if the halls were cleaned and fires lit before she had a chance to ask. Many acted as though they'd never set foot in the castle and eyed the place with wary glances. Those still manning the kitchens even erected tables outside for the people unable to squeeze within.

She walked among the pillars, keeping to the outskirts. Some saw her and pointed, whispering of the woman who'd slaughtered Atilla in one fell swoop. Others had no idea who she was, but it didn't stop them from staring.

The kitchen hands who'd taken charge ran from table to table with plates of food while others kept mugs full.

She hated Atilla for this. She hated him for concealing food in the basement while it rotted, and the people starved.

She took a breath and focused on the laughter in the hall. They were starting to believe a better future could exist.

Kiuno met Elite's gaze from across the room. He kept a sharp eye out, but Kiuno watched Daren. Most trusted him and he seemed okay with her role for the moment, but that didn't mean others felt the same. She had to tread carefully, gain his trust.

Silver and Blue's voices echoed over the crowd as the two indulged in a drinking contest. Maybe she could learn a thing or two about their ability to socialize. Several men had joined them, and she couldn't help but laugh. They'd be at it for the rest of the night, though she'd ensure they were safely tucked in bed before she retired.

Kiuno led Elite to the front table, and a hush fell over the masses when all heads turned in her direction. She placed her fingers on the smooth wooden surface then looked over the sea of questioning faces. Her stomach fluttered, and mouth went dry.

She wasn't a leader, or at least she'd convinced herself she wasn't, yet her friends would say differently. Scorpios would say differently; he'd done so several times. And these people. How did they view her?

Her eyes scanned their faces, some still dirty, others washed and clean as they picked at plates of warm food. Their stomachs were probably fuller than they'd been in months. They waited for her. They waited for the person who'd delivered their freedom to speak.

She wasn't Palindrome or K.J. and even Scorpios would have known how to better handle the situation. She wasn't clever or good with words. She didn't know how to encourage them and the longer she stood with their expectant eyes lingering, the more she felt she couldn't do this at all.

Blue stood. Then Silver. Liam did the same and a man in the back clapped his hands. Others joined, the sound echoing through the halls. One man yelled, and another slammed his mug on the table.

Then it hit her. She didn't need words. Words were nothing more than empty promises and they'd heard their fair share of those. The actions of the last few days spoke far louder. They were freer now than they'd been since entering this realm.

Blue stumbled up and handed her a mug, almost tripping as he righted himself much to everyone's amusement. She lifted it and many around the room did the same.

"To a new future."

"To a new future," they echoed.

53

QUEEN

REALM: 5
DAY: 335

The sun illuminated their room too early for Kiuno's liking. She pulled the blanket over her head, hoping the simple cloth might hide her from the responsibilities she'd soon face.

She remained still and listened to Elite's deep breathing. Sleep hadn't come easily and even now her heart quickened and thoughts raced.

Kiuno sat up, but kept the warm furs wrapped around her body. This room was far larger than her last. And far too extravagant. A fireplace rested in the far corner, but it'd long since died out, leaving a chill to the air.

She placed her feet over the bed and her toes ran through the soft fur rug lining the center of the room. A waste. Especially when she knew others were suffering.

Dark curtains hung over the window, but they'd been pulled open when she viewed the moon last night. This castle was a breeding ground for the wicked. So many had taken advantage of the weak and her first move as leader was to rectify the situation.

Kiuno sighed. Those still loyal to Atilla were likely planning her demise. Somewhere, someone still suffered at their hands and it was her job to stop them. She had to prevent them from infiltrating her upper ranks. She wondered how much Daren knew. Perhaps he could help her weed out most of the riff raff.

Elite shifted and gave her a puzzled look. "Awake already?"

"Unfortunately."

He rubbed at tired eyes and the pair dressed without speaking. It'd be a long day and likely a long week ahead.

After dressing and cramming a chunk of bread down her throat, Kiuno headed down the stairs and into the main hall.

Blue stopped her on the last step. "Do you want an update now or later?"

"You're up early," she said.

"Actually, I haven't slept yet."

Kiuno noted the bags beneath his eyes. "Update me, then go rest. I can't have you collapsing on your first day."

"Daren left this morning to go on another hunt. The sick animals have been removed from the herd and those healthy have been shifted to the other side of the castle. I have a small group of people tilling the ground to start new crops. They said the ones left weren't worth saving."

Kiuno bit the inside of her cheek. That meant meat would be their primary source of food for winter. It'd be challenging, but if they put enough work into preparation now, they might be able to pull it off.

"Thank you."

"Anytime. I'm here to help, but I think I'll take you up on the offer to sleep. Good luck."

Blue trudged up the stairs then Kiuno exited the main hall and entered bustling streets. It'd transformed from the pitiful place she'd seen yesterday.

Men hauled wood from outside the gate and worked on patching the holes in their roofs and doors. Buckets of water splashed along the street to wash away months of muck. Old dirty rags were stacked in wagons, either to be cleaned or burned Kiuno didn't know.

They didn't run, but many still ducked their heads as she passed. It'd take time for their fear to subside. She couldn't imagine the punishment these people had been forced to endure.

Kiuno kept walking and she took special note of those carrying buckets of water. Then she realized what was missing.

No one used magic.

She did a small circle, paying close attention to those building, but no vines extended from the earth. A gentle breeze didn't ruffle anyone's clothes.

"You see it too?" Elite asked.

"Why isn't anyone using their magic?"

A WEEK filled with questions, fear, and uncertainty crawled by at a snail's pace. Kiuno had ruled out the possibility of K.J.'s retaliation and set her focus on those adopting a routine. It was only now that she understood the true challenges of leadership.

Kiuno sat at the head of a table with Blue on one side and Liam on the other. Blue took notes and Liam observed, though the boy often gave insight of his own.

"Next," Blue called.

The doors opened and a young man walked toward the table. He limped on his right leg.

"What can I do for you?" Kiuno asked for the twentieth time that morning.

The man's eyes darted to Blue and then to Liam. "You put someone named Matthew in charge of building. He's ignoring my section. I want permission to work there."

Kiuno glanced at Blue who shuffled his papers and searched for a name. "I have it set that he's working on the west side of the keep. Where are your quarters?"

"The east side."

Kiuno folded her hands. "It's likely he hasn't made it there yet. We're still working out the details. If you'd like to organize your own set of builders that can be arranged."

He nodded. "I'd like that. My craftsmanship outclasses his anyway."

Kiuno resisted the urge to roll her eyes. "We'll note it and assess your work upon completion. What's your name?"

"Paton."

Blue scribbled it down.

"Begin construction as soon as you'd like."

"Thank you."

He exited and Kiuno leaned back in her chair. "We need to start a training regimen. Maybe that will take the tension down a few notches. Are Elite and Silver still helping build on the west end?"

Blue nodded.

Kiuno weighed her options. "I'm pulling them from the assignment. He's the third one today who mentioned an issue with a rival for their craft."

"So, your solution is to let them beat it out of one another?"

"Do you have a better idea? They're pitting themselves against one another because they've been oppressed for so long. I need to see how they work together and if they've had any sort of training."

Blue set his quill down. "Daren might have an idea. I doubt he'd stage a coup without some formalized training."

Kiuno stood. "Then he can help Elite and Silver."

The door squeaked on its hinges and Kiuno rubbed her temples. She didn't have the patience to deal with any more trivial matters.

"You look far too stressed for someone who's recently taken over."

Kiuno's head shot up at the familiar voice and a large smile spread over Maltack's dark face.

She trotted from behind the desk and wrapped him in a warm embrace. "When did you get here?"

"Just now."

She pulled back and glanced him over. Dirt covered his clothing and he appeared tired, but otherwise unscathed.

"How are things?" she asked.

"Palindrome's alive."

Kiuno let out a breath and sent up a silent prayer. "And Scorpios?"

"He's stabilized, but his condition hasn't changed. We've been keeping a healer on him around the clock. As far as the ranks go, we lost more than I would have liked, but Palindrome is getting everything back in order."

"I didn't think you'd come."

Maltack tilted his head. "Of course I came. Palindrome is a great mentor, but as Scorpios would say, you're still my queen."

She smiled but a dark cloud smothered the endearment. "Have you talked to K.J.?"

Maltack shook his head. "I haven't seen much of him."

"He thinks I betrayed him."

"Palindrome told me."

"What does she think?"

"That he's hurt and needs time to sort through it on his own."

Kiuno guessed that was better than nothing. "It's good to have you back. If you need anything, just let me know."

"Shouldn't that be my line?" The two turned toward the castle door. "So tell me, what's happened in my absence."

"We're covering the bases. Food, water, and better shelters."

"How are you doing with the magic users?"

Kiuno sighed. "Honestly, I haven't seen one person using any. It's like—"

"They're hiding."

Kiuno paused. "But why?" Before the question left her lips, she understood. They'd hid themselves from Atilla to avoid giving him more power. And now they were hiding from her.

"With the way Atilla ruled, wouldn't you?"

Kiuno recalled hiding her stone all those months ago. "Yes. I would." Kiuno caught sight of Daren riding through the front gate. "Why don't you go get cleaned up and rest. After that, you can check out the medical wing. It's all yours."

"Will do."

Kiuno jogged away from Maltack and drew Daren's attention, but he turned away when a younger male tapped him on the shoulder. Upon seeing everyone's stares, Kiuno slowed to a walk.

She glanced at the wrists of those working. Most were covered and Kiuno couldn't help but wonder if the non-magic users protected those gifted with abilities.

Daren directed a few men and women and Kiuno patiently waited for him to complete his tasks. Everyone still watched him, looked up to him. She might be the one who'd allowed their freedom, but Daren was the face they saw providing.

He wiped his hands and turned to her. "Need something?"

Those within earshot cast them both glances. She wondered if they still saw her as a threat to Daren's life.

Kiuno's eyes traveled to his wrist, but a leather gauntlet hid his stone from view. "What can you tell me about Atilla's war strategy?"

"Other than him being a power-hungry maniac?"

"So there's a system?"

Daren picked up a rope and started winding it around his elbow. "Yeah, but there weren't many willing to take part in it. Not that they had much choice."

"It looks like they might for you."

He grinned and continued winding. "They might."

Kiuno followed him into a barn as he hung the rope on a nail. "I need to know what you've decided about me."

He raised a brow. "If I can be honest?"

"Please."

He glanced out toward the people. "Things are running smoothly, but only because that tyrannical asshole finally met his match. You took away the obstacle, but the people know what to do."

Kiuno leaned against a post to listen.

"But you're also kind and that has shown through not only to me, but to many who are still watching. They see your desire, but they also question whether it will last."

Daren pushed off from the wall. "If you keep the power from going to your head then I'll trust you. But these people won't stand for another egotistical maniac in charge."

"I've been accused of many things, but egotistical isn't one."

"So, maniac is?"

She smiled and watched those passing by. "I think you have to be a little crazy to step up and lead this many people."

"So, what do you want from me?"

"I need to find the magic users."

He leaned one shoulder against the barn entrance. "Atilla never had many."

Kiuno peered down at his hidden wrist, then watched the sweat roll down his arm. "I have a feeling there's a lot more of you than he knew about." Daren followed her gaze. "What do you use?"

He smirked. "Water."

"Do you think you can help convince others to come forward?"

"I'll give it a shot, but I think it's you who should be convincing them."

Daren pushed himself up and unbuckled his bracers. He sat them on the ground then pulled at particles from the air before marching through the street. He bent the water to his will, clearing the filth from the road.

He'd spread the word, but Daren was right. As their leader, the responsibility ultimately fell to her.

MALTACK'S GAZE swept through the crowd gathered before the castle steps. Kiuno wanted to find the magic users but judging from their wary expressions it would be a hard group to convince.

He glanced at their wrapped wrists. It seemed as if everyone had a secret to hide.

Those volunteering their help stood behind Daren, as if the man would protect them should things go awry. Maltack imagined most of them to be part of the coup Kiuno had told him about.

If luck prevailed, they might be able to form a team like Palindrome had done.

Kiuno trotted to the top step, turned to face the crowd, and a hushed silence fell over the masses. She took a few steadying breaths. "Thank you for coming. I know things in the past have been difficult, but if we don't come together, they'll only get worse.

"Days before I came to you, monsters poured from the sixth realm's portal and attacked another castle." Panicked whispers flew through the crowd and Kiuno raised her arms to quiet them.

"I know you're scared, and I know Atilla was a horrible man, but I'm not him. I won't ask you to die for me and I won't make you do anything against your beliefs. But if we're to survive, I need you to work together. Learn from your superiors and friends. We were all brought here for reasons we still don't understand, but if you'll trust me, I promise to do everything in my power to get us home."

"And what gives you the right to call yourself our leader?" a man called. Several voices echoed similar concerns.

Kiuno gazed at the crowd then she tugged at the strings on her bracers and let the leather fall to the ground. Maltack grinned.

Kiuno descended the steps and several people stepped back. She pulled the cloth from her wrist and tucked it in her pocket.

After visiting the infirmary, Maltack had seen the wounded and heard how Kiuno marched in and shattered the very stone. Those who carried scars like his questioned him over and over, asking why he'd follow someone so dangerous.

All this time she'd kept it hidden. She'd been afraid. But she wasn't helpless anymore.

Kiuno padded across the field, separating herself from the people. Murmurs followed.

Kiuno pivoted and raised her voice. "You want someone who will fight with you. Fight for you."

Static surged around her body and gasps echoed from the crowd.

"I will not hide behind these walls." It cracked and hissed as a bolt shot toward the sky. "If you will fight for me, then I will fight for you."

Mixed reactions flew through the crowd at first. Some faces filled with awe while others backed away in fear.

Then the cheering started.

One by one the men shouted their approval until the whole castle front sounded like a raving band of monsters themselves. Maltack joined as they chanted her name.

This was Kiuno. This is what they'd always known she had the potential to be and what others feared she might one day become.

MALTACK

Realm: 5
Day: 344

Maltack grouped the magic users by type and ability. Kiuno urged him to move fast, but—

He pulled at the fire in his veins hoping his students would do the same. They tried and some failed. He fought against the rising frustration. Newbies to work with, yet again.

"Okay, let's try something different. Sit."

They obeyed, each glancing at one another as if this was the stupidest thing they'd ever done. All were older than him, but Maltack shoved his feelings of inadequacy aside and focused on the task at hand. Kiuno was counting on him.

"Okay. This is a focusing exercise." He turned his palm out. "Find the center point of the flame. It'll rest somewhere in your gut and feel like a burning cinder. Close your eyes."

One raised his brow and when Maltack nodded toward him, the gray-haired gentleman rolled his eyes. Maltack tried not to envision how

Kiuno would react to teaching. He doubted she'd have the patience.

"When you find the cinder, feed it. Breathe it to life and turn it into a flame in your mind's eye."

Maltack cracked one eye open to find most concentrating, their previous doubt vanishing by the second.

"Now imagine your arm has a direct path, like a vein if you will, and expand that small flame toward your hand. Focus on warming the skin."

A tingling sensation that'd become all too familiar crawled across his arm and hovered in his palm. It'd become second nature. A companion. His sword.

He'd been put to the ground enough times to prove he was far better with magic than weapons.

Maltack continued. "Okay. Now burst it from your palm and hold the flame that emerges."

All at once fire surrounded their small circle and gasps flew from one person to the next. One burst so well that his neighbors stood and backed away.

"Good, now control. Bring it down to a smaller flame and hold it steady."

Smiles spread from one face to the next. Even the one who'd rolled his eyes grinned from ear to ear.

"Spend a few days working this exercise. Let the flames die and then feed it to your other hand. Then your feet. Do this until you're comfortable enough to summon it in seconds."

Maltack stood, wiped the dirt from his pants and left them to their own devices.

Maltack's gaze drifted to the water users. They bent and swept the liquid through the air. Another group focused on pulling particles. It seemed he wouldn't be needed in that area for a while at least.

Maltack paced across the grass toward swirling vines and caught sight of Vixin. Her red hair bounced as she sauntered back and forth like a predator examining its prey. A lump formed in his throat. Maybe he should go back and deal with the men instead.

He steeled himself.

Vixin sighed and pressed the heel of her hand against her head. "No, no, no. You're never going to get it if you keep doing that."

"Doing what?" a man shouted.

Maltack couldn't place his face yet.

"Acting like it's some delicate flower. Pull like you mean it. Like it's a weed that needs ripped from the ground."

He clicked his tongue. "Maybe I need a real teacher instead of a little girl."

Maltack groaned. *Here we go.*

She flashed him a glare and vines shot from the ground, wrapping the man in a vise so tight, his breath caught in his throat. She lifted him up and blood trickled from his arms where thorns bit into his skin.

"Vixin," Maltack shouted.

She turned to him and tilted her head.

"You can't kill your students."

She turned back to the man and gave him a wicked smile. "Looks like the *little boy* is here to save you. Are you okay with that or would you prefer someone older?"

He mumbled, but Maltack couldn't make out what he said. Vixin squeezed tighter.

"Vixin, that's enough."

She sighed and let her vines loosen. The man dropped to his knees and grabbed his throat, coughing and sputtering.

"Find a new teacher. I'm done with you."

She stormed off and after briefly checking to ensure Vixin hadn't crushed the man's windpipe, Maltack ran after her.

"Hey, we need to talk."

She made a sound of disapproval. "I'm too busy to talk."

Maltack planted himself to her front and she stopped short. Vixin examined his form. If her recent activities were anything to go by, she was likely contemplating the best way to strangle him.

"Listen. I know I asked you to help teach, but you can't go around half killing our men. We need their morale lifted not crushed."

"He's weak anyway."

"That's not the point." Maltack rubbed his temple.

Vixin held up her hand before he could continue. "I know what you're going to say. We need to make them stronger and the only way we can do that is blah, blah, blah." She pointed a finger at him. "People die. That's just how it is. What's the point of putting effort into the weak?"

"Because that effort could be the reason they live. Didn't someone teach you?"

Vixin faltered. "It doesn't matter." She started to walk away.

"What if I put you with the more advanced? Would that work better?"

"You mean you're not going to be some love-struck boy coddling me and protecting me from danger?"

"After seeing what you did with him, I don't think that's necessary."

She cocked her head. "So, you're not like Kiuno after all."

"What do you mean?"

"With her and Elite. She treats him like he's glass and it's infuriating."

Maltack couldn't hide his smile. "So, you'll listen to me if I don't treat you like glass?"

Vixin uncrossed her arms. "I wouldn't go that far." She cocked her head again. "We'll see what happens if you can beat me."

"What—" Before he could react a vine snaked its way around his leg and threw him into the air. It released him thirty feet up. His stomach dropped and Maltack called upon his own magic to encase his body and ease his fall. The vines slowly lowered him to the ground as he pulsed magic through their stems.

She turned to leave, but Maltack trapped her foot. Vixin stumbled, righted herself, and turned to face him. "All right lover boy, let's see what you got."

REECE

REALM: 5
DAY: 345

Reece took another step, his vision blurred, and blinding pain shot through his wrist. He collapsed against the hard wall. Reece clenched the area with his free hand and cursed the jewel's existence.

"Reece?"

He peered at Nsane through hazed vision. His best friend stared back with cautious eyes. He was ready to retreat. To run.

Reece clenched his jaw and leaned his head against the stone. He'd never intended for this to happen.

He took several breaths. "I'm all right."

Reece used the wall to stumble to his feet and he pressed a palm to his forehead. The blackouts were more frequent now. He'd killed during the last one and woke to find himself straddling Nsane with a blade held against his friend's neck.

It was always like watching a movie. Or inhabiting another's body. He knew what had happened, but Reece had no control.

Whatever evil consumed him during those periods raged against him now. It rattled the mental cage around his conscious mind.

Reece glanced down at the black tendrils living in his veins. The roots were growing again, inching up his forearm in an ominous shadow. They'd already twisted over his hand, their spiraling roots covering one another beneath raised skin. Their movement still made his stomach turn, but he'd managed to stop gagging.

"Do you need anything?" Nsane asked.

Darkness crept in, further hazing his vision. Seething. Raging. "Get everyone out of the castle. Lock me in the hall till morning."

Nsane nodded and a sympathetic glance crossed his features. He took a step back before turning and marching down the hall. The retreat of his echoing footsteps helped the coil unwind from Reece's chest.

Isolation would prevent him from harming anyone else, but how long could they keep that up?

Reece collapsed against the wall again. Sweat trickled down the sides of his face, his lungs constricted, and a chill shot down his spine.

"Enjoying my present?"

Reece glared at the man who appeared from around a pillar, seeming to have materialized from thin air.

The creator's mouth twisted into a smile. "If you'd surrender it wouldn't hurt so much."

"I'd rather not beat my friends to death."

He scoffed. "If your friends learned obedience, there wouldn't be consequences."

Reece laughed. "Forgive them if they don't want to let the monsters roam within the castle walls. I can't say I disagree."

He glanced at his nails. "You'll falter soon, but since you're so keen on keeping a grip on your pathetic reality, I'll give you an update."

"Do you enjoy hearing yourself boast?"

He clicked his tongue. "For all her talk of good friends Kiuno sure picked some rude ones." He circled the area and knelt before Reece, just out of arm's reach. He seemed to examine the roots from the jewel.

"I liked your choice of withdrawing from the battle. It put Kiuno in a position of power and removed another player I didn't care for. However, things have gotten quiet."

"And you want me to stir it up."

"Of course, but don't ruin my fun. I want to meet her face to face."

Reece clenched his jaw and pushed to sit up. "Not a chance."

His face fell and he tilted his head to the side as if confused. "And why not?"

"I won't bring Kiuno to the likes of you."

The creator stood, and Reece cried out, clutching his arm as blinding pain shot from his wrist to elbow. The tendrils shifted like sandpaper grating against exposed nerves.

"I shouldn't need to remind you who's in control or why you're in this position. If you remember, you agreed to this to help the poor saps cowering in this pathetic place."

Reece growled. "None of them are worth her."

The creator sighed. "So difficult. I guess you'll have to explain to Nsane why you tortured his wife then. That alter ego of yours really is ruthless." His head leaned to one side. "Of course, there's always that Maltack kid. Kiuno seems very fond of him. I wonder what she'd do if you killed him?"

Reece clutched his wrist again and his body trembled from both pain and anger. "Why do you want to talk to her?"

"Why? Because she's my favorite player! I need to meet the celebrity of this world and what better time than now when she's sitting at the top?"

Reece smirked. "She'll kill you. You don't have a chance in hell of Kiuno listening to anything you have to say. Not after what you've put her through."

"Oh, she'll listen. That's why I have this." He pulled a small orb from his pocket. The glass-like surface shimmered in the dim lighting and several colors swirled within.

"Like the item in your arm, this is a relic. It suppresses any magic around the carrier, including hers. You will plan another assault on the castle, and she'll come running and disappear in the chaos. It's as simple as that."

Reece dropped his head. "Don't kill her."

"I wouldn't dream of it." He pocketed the item, turned to leave, and paused. "Oh, and Reece? If you ever stand up to me again, I'll rip Marci's head off myself."

56

PREPARATION

REALM: 5

DAY: 350

"Kiuno, he's back. We found him at the inn." Daren stood in the doorway with a sword in his belt and two men at his side.

"Bring him here. Discreetly."

K.J. was known for his ability to infiltrate almost any encampment and insert his spies. He liked to stay ahead of the game, but last week Daren had identified the man and reported his findings.

Kiuno dropped her head in her hands. She'd still not heard anything from K.J. Not that she'd expected much else, but—

"I haven't done anything," a male voice protested. His voice echoed off the walls as Daren escorted him into the room.

"I never said you did. Guilty conscience?"

"Then why are you dragging me here?"

"Because someone wants to talk to you." Daren shoved him through the door, and he tripped, falling at her feet. Kiuno gave him a look, but Daren snorted. He wasn't one to tolerate injustice.

"You can go," Kiuno said.

"You sure?"

She eyed the stranger's wrist, the light gray stone showing in the firelight. "I can handle it."

Daren looked down on him as one might glare at an insect. "I'll be down the hall." She appreciated his loyalty and how quickly it'd taken root.

The man stood and wiped the dirt from his pants. He glanced at the door and then to her. "I'm sorry miss, but I think you've mistaken me for someone else."

"I hope not. Have a seat." She pointed to the chair and poured them both a drink before sitting across from him. He eyed the mug, swirled its contents, then set it on a nearby table.

Kiuno ran her finger over the rim of her cup. "You're a spy for K.J."

His eyes widened and his gaze flickered toward the exit. "You have the—"

"Are they all right?"

He looked her over, confusion crossing his features.

Kiuno sat on the edge of her chair. "Palindrome, K.J. and the others. Are they okay?"

He examined her face, his breathing still rapid. "Miss Palindrome is healing. K.J. is alive."

Kiuno let out a breath. Maltack had given her good news about Palindrome, but she needed to be sure. "Don't worry. I won't hurt you. I'm not K.J.'s enemy."

He bit his lip. "I'm afraid he doesn't feel the same."

Still? What kind of crazy plan had he concocted in his brain? "Has he said much about it?"

"I'm not at liberty to speak about his actions." Her face fell and his eyes softened. "He's angry."

Kiuno remained still. "I want you to know you're welcome here. I don't have anything to hide from him. I apologize for the way Daren treated you, but don't be afraid to come to me for anything you need."

He stood slowly, his movements still unsure and Kiuno turned toward her desk. She clenched her hands to prevent them from shaking.

"I've heard Palindrome trying to convince him of your innocence."

She didn't turn as he exited and Kiuno kept her gaze fixated on the flames in the fireplace. If he hadn't figured it out by now, then he never would. She'd have to visit him and face his anger head on.

As the spy's footsteps receded, heavier ones took their place and Daren stood in the doorway again, this time alone.

"I didn't realize you and K.J. were so close. I knew you worked for him, but I didn't imagine you as friends."

"We knew one another before the game, but after what I did…"

"Even leaders make mistakes." Daren handed her another drink, and the two stared at the flickering fire.

"Have you ever betrayed anyone? Even if you didn't mean to?"

He laughed. More to himself than at her. "I fell in love with my best friend's girl."

"What did you do?"

"I left. Abandoned them both rather than face the pain of losing one or discovering happiness at the expense of the other."

"Which do you regret more?"

"Still trying to figure that out."

KIUNO TRIED to busy herself with overdue tasks, but later that afternoon Daren burst through her door again. This time one of their scouts stood at his side, struggling to catch his breath.

"They're amassing at the border again."

Kiuno stood. "Who are?"

"The monsters, they're lining up at the forest edge and it looks as if they'll hit K.J.'s castle again." The scout paused, looking from Daren's face then back to hers. "You wanted me to inform you of something like this, right?"

"Yes, I just didn't expect them so soon." She turned to Daren. "Get Elite, Silver, and Maltack in here."

Kiuno strode into a room she'd hoped never to use. She unfolded a map and used candle holders to weigh the edges. K.J. was their leader. He initiated most of their ideas and held the strongest military force. He also stood at the monsters' front door. Samar was the closest after that.

Her friends filed in one by one, but she kept her gaze on the little drawn castle that marked K.J.'s territory. He was at the center of everything.

With everyone seated, Kiuno began. "The monsters are gathering at the forest border again."

"Are they headed this way?" Elite asked.

Kiuno shook her head. "They'll go for K.J.'s territory first, but the scout said it looks as though they're fanning out. It's likely they'll try to circle in from behind and hit all sides."

"What are we going to do?" Silver asked.

"March to Samar's castle and force him to join the fight. He's sat on the sidelines long enough. With three armies, we'll be able to handle and hopefully eliminate them for good."

"Not to be the negative one," Daren said, "But what do we owe these groups?"

Kiuno looked at each of them in turn. "Personal feeling aside, if K.J. falls what do you think that means?"

"Fewer men."

"Exactly. They'll go after Samar next, then us, then Grayson. They'll pick us off one by one. It's better if we stick together."

Daren leaned on the table and nodded his approval. "Are we sure this Samar will fight?"

Kiuno stared at the map, then met his gaze. "I'll ensure he does."

THEY MARCHED over open fields, and Kiuno gazed upon Samar's castle long before they arrived. His scouts would see them soon and raise the alarm.

Kiuno wasn't sure if Samar knew about Atilla's betrayal or whether he cared. It wasn't until now that she admitted her level of ignorance concerning the alliance's inner workings.

She swallowed hard. Calling upon Samar's aid like this was a gamble, though most things were these days. But they didn't have time to come up with a better plan.

As they drew closer, a dozen men left the castle gate on horseback. Kiuno exchanged glances with Elite and Daren, then spurred her horse forward with them at her sides.

Kiuno pulled her horse to a halt several yards from the men and their eyes scanned her face.

"What's the meaning of this?" one demanded.

"I'm a friend. I need to speak with Samar. It's urgent."

He exchanged a glance with his comrade. "Only you?"

"And one other. To be sure I return." Truthfully, she didn't need protection, but Elite had already let her go into one castle alone. She wouldn't push her luck with a second.

His horse turned and the man tugged at the reins. His gaze danced from her to the army behind her. "Come with us."

Daren pulled back while Kiuno and Elite followed their escort.

Worried glances met them at the gate. People rushed through the streets, gathering supplies and locking gates. Their citizens lined themselves before an underground cellar, filling down the stairs one by one.

Kiuno and Elite followed two men into the keep, down a long hall, and up another flight of stairs.

She'd never seen someone so relieved when their escort announced her arrival.

"Kiuno?" Samar slumped back in his chair. "Good lord, couldn't you have sent a messenger?"

"I could have, but I had hoped you were already preparing. You know there are monsters pouring from the sixth realm's portal, right?"

"I've been informed."

Heavy silence filled the room.

"I'm riding out to meet them."

"I thought you and K.J. weren't…" He trailed off.

"What happened between K.J. and I is a misunderstanding. I tried to fix a situation that would have been better left alone. But we don't need to be on speaking terms for me to help."

"So, you're asking me to risk my mens' lives for the sake of another?"

"You realize if K.J. falls, you're the next nearest target."

He didn't speak as he seemed to think the scenario through. "You didn't intend to betray him, did you?"

"No."

Samar pinched the bridge of his nose. "Give me till morning and I'll march with you."

Kiuno shifted and glanced at Elite. "Just like that?"

"Just like that."

KIUNO SAT with Elite at her back, his arms draped over her shoulders in an embrace she'd sorely missed. Fires dotted the landscape and her heart quickened as the uncertainty of battle loomed ahead.

When she'd lost him, she'd lost herself and that pain wasn't something she could survive again. If it were up to her, Elite would have stayed at the castle, in fact, she'd tried to convince him of it, but naturally he'd refused.

Elite buried his face in her hair. "I hate waiting while you're first on the field."

She clutched his hand. "I hate seeing you there at all. At least I have a way to defend myself."

"One that hurts you." His fingers traced the floral-like patterns on her skin. The scars lit up and burned whenever Kiuno released the lightning, but no new marks had appeared. It solidified Palindrome's theory that outside influences had caused her injuries. As long as another storm didn't blow through, she'd be fine.

"I knew it." The two turned to Daren's voice as he sat across from them. Neither Elite nor Kiuno moved. "Some bodyguard."

"Keep it to yourself."

He squinted in confusion. "Why?"

"Because I don't want certain people to use him against me."

Daren looked Elite up and down. "Man looks capable of defending himself."

"He doesn't have magic."

Daren chuckled. "Neither does half the army, but it doesn't stop them."

KIUNO STOOD before her army and watched as Samar's forces filed from the castle gate. They assembled themselves over the field in a separate regimen. It was better that way. To prevent confusion and friendly fire.

Samar was wary and he'd agreed far too easily to bring her any comfort. She doubted he'd turn against her as Atilla had done, but Kiuno wondered if word about Atilla's demise had reached his ears.

Samar tightened the reins on his horse and Kiuno rode up behind him. "Since we're working together, I thought you should know I'm the lightning user." He didn't look surprised, so she continued. "It's been my tactic to head in first, disorient the enemy, and then allow the rest of the forces to take over. I need space to ensure no one is caught in the cross-fire."

Samar's eyes shifted down her arm, tracing the scars she let sit visible for all to see. "I knew K.J. was hiding you."

"It wasn't his secret to tell. I'll expect the same discretion from you."

Samar clicked his tongue. "You want me to keep something like this from the other leaders?"

She nodded. "I'll tell them, but in my time, no one else's."

"It's not right to withhold information like this."

"Whether it's right is irrelevant. If you want, we can discuss it later." Kiuno glanced at the men awaiting their orders. "We have more pressing concerns."

Samar followed her gaze. "Later then. Shall we?"

Both armies moved north, marching side by side, two leaders making a pact that wouldn't end in betrayal or bloodshed. At least that's what she hoped. Samar didn't have a reason to betray her and he wasn't the type to act for personal gain. Not at the risk of losing a powerful ally.

Kiuno imagined K.J.'s castle in the distance. He might not want her help, but she'd be there anyway. She'd never abandon her friends and she would prove herself no matter how long it took.

TAKEN

REALM: 5

DAY: 355

Chaos, blood, and burning flesh permeated the air and clashed against her senses. Copper filtered through her nose, and raging magic pulsed beneath her fingertips. Kiuno ducked and slid her sword through another's ribs, though whether they were human or hollow she could no longer be sure.

Elite's words returned to her.

Don't let this world change you.

But it had changed her. The question remained if it were for the better or worse.

Kiuno's magic surged and blasted another hole through their enemy's forces. Their flesh burned and the creatures fell, but once again another swarm took their place. They moved without fear or hesitation.

Hollows twisted their magic toward Maltack's ever reacting barriers. Shadows raced across the ground and tripped her comrades. Those without magic plunged their swords into beast after beast. A mace shattered a skull to her left, then fire engulfed the body.

Kiuno swung her sword and collided with bone. She let the magic overwhelm her enemy and dislodged the blade before turning to face another.

A familiar chirping set her teeth on edge.

Kiuno's gaze lifted toward the humanoid creatures crawling across the ground in a swarming herd. The first lunged and Kiuno cut straight through the individual's spilt skull and let her flames catch its companions in the crossfire. She took a few steps back as they converged and repeated the same never-ending dance of death.

Thrust, shift, fire, block, pivot. She knew the steps. Her friends had taught her well. They'd prepared her for moments like this. Back then, she remembered holding a blade and how ill fitted it had seemed in her hand. She remembered how the thought of killing someone had made her feel. How she'd sworn she wouldn't let this game change her. Yet here she was, part of the madness anyway.

Screaming drew her attention and greenery shot from a crowd, felling several of their comrades. Kiuno darted toward the shift. Daren, Vixin, and Maltack followed as best they could.

Kiuno fought her way through the monsters, her legs spurring her forward. She recognized those movements.

Green eyes shifted from enemy to enemy and his vines responded.

Her heart jolted. Kiuno ducked beneath another blade and dispatched the creature, then returned her gaze to the way he danced through his enemies.

The man who'd claimed to love her. The man who'd made an impossible promise.

Reece met her gaze, but his movements didn't cease as he felled enemy after enemy.

Not her enemies, she realized.

His.

In her momentary distraction, monsters assaulted her again and

Daren cut the arm from one closing the distance.

Kiuno ran toward Reece.

His vines pulled from her comrade's corpse and plunged through another. Kiuno's heart surged as he held one down, trapping her limbs and a scaled lizard-like creature tore a chunk from her shoulder.

Reece ripped his vines from the woman and sprinted in Kiuno's direction. His plants shot through those who tried to block his path and Kiuno paused.

Was this Reece or another carbon copy like the one from the cave? Was he a hollow? Had Reece been—

Their blades clashed and Kiuno's hands stung from the impact. His magic shot toward her surrounding allies and Reece smirked. A sickening expression that punched straight through her gut. "Seems we're on opposing sides this time Ki."

"What are you doing?"

He replied by twisting his blade and kicking her to the ground. Vines wrapped around her wrist and torso, but she summoned the flames and burnt through his restraints. A nameless comrade charged from behind, but Reece parried their blade and cut their throat.

"Stop it!"

He turned back and the monsters separated, leaving the two in a small circle amidst the fight. She staggered to her feet.

"Did you think everything would be okay after what you did?" He slammed his blade into hers again. The monsters kept their distance, ignoring the pair's quarrel, almost as if—as if they'd been commanded to.

Kiuno shoved back. "What the hell are you talking about?"

The ground beneath their feet shook. Kiuno pivoted to run, but the earth split, and an upward force sent her airborne. Maltack's vines wrapped her body and Daren launched spears of ice toward Reece.

A familiar worm-like creature rose from the depths, but the large plate on its head differed it from the ones she'd faced before. Longer fangs flexed from its mouth as it let out an ear-splitting shriek.

Kiuno hit the ground and launched her flames toward the beast. It dived and the earth split again.

"Move!"

Green shot through her shoulder and Kiuno cried out as pain lanced down her arm. Her gaze followed another vine racing toward Maltack, but he rendered it useless.

Daren's gasp turned Kiuno's blood to ice.

Kiuno glanced to her left, knowing exactly what she'd see, yet praying it impossible.

Daren stood in wide-eyed shock with five vines puncturing his torso. Reece smiled at the other end. His vines slackened, then his gaze shifted to Maltack.

Kiuno pushed to her feet, but the earth opened once again, and a large mouth closed in around her. Maltack's magic grabbed her wrist and pulled her away before the beast could snap its massive jaws shut.

Maltack's vines slackened and gravity took over. Kiuno tumbled down the creature's body. She reached for anything to stop the fall, but her hands couldn't grip the hard skin.

A familiar voice called, and a sense of déjà vu engulfed her as Reece's vines wrapped around her middle and pulled her to his chest.

Kiuno slammed her fist on his collar bone, then the beast shifted. Reece's vines snapped and gravity took her again.

Kiuno twisted to watch her descent and a large spine at the base of the beast's tail caught her leg. The cracking of bone echoed from the wall followed by her scream.

She fell through never ending black, but vines wrapped around her body again. Kiuno pushed against them, but the pain in her shoulder ignited.

"Stop struggling," Reece yelled from somewhere in the darkness.

Kiuno hit the ground hard and burning pain lanced through her leg in violent waves. Flickering light drew her attention to a tunnel at her front. A tunnel with torches. Stone crumbled from the walls and she peered into the gaping black hole to her rear where the creature had made a turn underground.

Reece ran toward her and Kiuno tried to use her one good arm to crawl away. His hands went to her leg and every confused emotion surged to the surface.

"Get away from me."

He ignored her protest. "It looks broken." His gaze shifted upward. "I can get us back to the surface and find—"

"I said get away," she screamed. Flames surrounded her body in a protective embrace and Reece backpedaled.

He grimaced and gripped his wrist. "I have to get you back to the surface. Now."

Tears flooded her vision. "You killed him."

His sad expression seemed to beg for her understanding. "I didn't have a choice."

Her anger flared. "Bullshit."

Reece clicked his tongue and… groaned? She wasn't sure. "I can't explain right now. Let me help you."

Her leg twitched and she gripped the area above it, rocking as she fought through the sharp pain radiating through her limb.

Green life sprouted from the rocky ground and Kiuno's heart raced. It paused and in a split second anyone else might have missed, Kiuno watched his face shift from concern to a wicked grin.

Reece turned from her and the sprouting plants wrapped around his body and carried him from the dark hole, leaving her alone in the darkness.

Kiuno's eyes followed him until he disappeared at the surface. She couldn't hear what happened after that.

Kiuno tried moving her body, but pain raced through her limb again. She needed Maltack, but Maltack wouldn't hear her cries for help. She clenched her teeth.

Kiuno glanced at the large hole and then to the smaller tunnel with flickering light. If another of those creatures came through, it'd crush her. She didn't have time to waste.

Kiuno grimaced as she tried to scoot her body toward the smaller tunnel, but garbled noises echoed from the very place she was trying to reach. Kiuno sat motionless as shadows passed through the dancing light.

A throaty language met her ears and Kiuno's skin crawled when the lizard beasts with scaly skin and sharp fangs entered her view.

They walked upright and carried weapons on pelted belts. She pulled at her magic only to have cold fear blossom through her core.

She couldn't reach it.

The warmth that promised protection and had saved her from so many encounters had vanished. As if she'd never had it to begin with.

Kiuno tried to scamper back, but a thick hand with long claws wrapped around her wrist and began dragging her down the tunnel. Her leg shifted, excruciating pain shot through the limb, and Kiuno's world faded.

IT COULD have been seconds, minutes, or even hours, but Kiuno woke to a continued dragging down the passage. Her side had been rubbed raw from the rocky floor grating against her skin. She twisted, resting her bad leg on the good one. The creature dragging her didn't seem to mind as he continued his long strides through the tunnel.

It was still gone, her magic, and she couldn't wrap her mind around why. Kiuno looked at her captor and its companion. She could handle two without it.

In an act of desperation, Kiuno yanked herself up and sank her teeth into the creature's scaly skin. It gurgled what might have been a curse and released its hold. Kiuno pulled a dagger from her boot and stabbed it through the other's foot. The creatures screamed but the first recovered and slammed its clawed foot down on her broken leg.

Something else snapped and Kiuno cried out in pain again. Tears rolled down her cheek, but clawed footsteps returned her attention to the hall. Several more scaled creatures marched toward her.

She watched through teary vision, but wherever they were taking her, gentleness didn't seem to be on their list of priorities.

TORTURE

REALM: 5

DAY: 355

Chains rattled in the darkness as Kiuno tried to piece together the remnants of her journey, but all she could recall were the violent cold fingers grasping her wrists and the even colder shackles they'd clasped around them.

Chills ran down her arms as Kiuno tried to wiggle stiff, numb fingers. Her vision blurred, or was that the lighting in the room? She clenched her eyes and fought against dizziness and confusion.

Kiuno flexed her foot half expecting a shock of pain to rattle her body, but oddly enough, nothing happened. She placed an unharmed leg to the floor and lifted herself to a standing position. Blood rushed back to her cold digits and the fog in her mind cleared as she peered around the dim room.

A single candle flickered in the far corner. It'd almost burnt to the quick and barely cast enough light for her to see the table it sat upon.

Kiuno glanced at the chains binding her wrists to the ceiling above.

She tugged, but the rock didn't budge.

A flicker of light drew Kiuno's attention. It came from her left, bouncing from a small hall she'd not been able to see before. The opening was squared off with wooden support. Dismay filled her core as Kiuno realized she was still underground.

Her gaze fell to the dwindling candle again.

How long had she been here?

Kiuno's heart thundered as she waited for the mystery person to walk down the hall, but a young woman emerged instead of the lizard-like creatures that had dragged her here.

Kiuno let out a small breath of relief and watched the teenage girl place the candle on the table.

Their eyes met. Pity filling one. Confusion in the other. The girl averted her gaze and moved to a small fireplace. More like a hole.

Fire meant a chute. A chute meant escape. They couldn't be that far underground.

As more light filled the space, Kiuno observed the small circular room. There weren't any defining marks, but a second hallway rested to her right. Perhaps it led outside.

Once she was finished the woman stood and started back down the hall she'd come from.

"Water." Kiuno's throat burned, but whether it came from dehydration or her earlier screaming she couldn't be sure.

The young woman paused, but she remained still for several moments before bending to a ceramic jug beneath the table. She wouldn't meet Kiuno's gaze as she raised the jug to her parched lips.

It tasted of bitter stagnation, but it relieved the dry patches all the same.

"Who are you?" Kiuno asked.

She didn't respond and instead took off down the tunnel.

Time ticked by and Kiuno hung there in silence. Her body trembled, both cold and exhausted. Kiuno glanced at her shackles again and took a breath before tugging on her magic.

It didn't respond.

She furrowed her brow. Had she exhausted herself? She didn't think so.

Kiuno tugged on the flames again, harder this time. She pulled and pulled before finally giving up.

Nothing.

What could possibly—

Kiuno glanced back to the candle and then to the fireplace.

It'd already died down since the girl left, but something beside it caught her attention.

An orb.

It sat on a wooden pedestal about a foot from the floor. The fire flickered across its smooth surface and cast a variety of colors against the wall.

She thought back to the library with Maltack. The relics. He'd mentioned an orb with the ability to suppress magic. Could that be it?

Her mind raced with relics, Reece, the creator, and magic. Whoever had ordered her capture wanted her alive yet controlled. Could the creator be responsible? Were they finally going to show themselves? She couldn't think of anyone else able to control the monsters of this wicked world.

Kiuno glanced up at the domed ceiling. Was the battle over? Were Maltack and the others safe? How many people had Reece injured?

She had so many questions, yet she wouldn't get any answers trapped in this dirt prison.

Kiuno planted her feet and tugged at the chains again, using all her remaining strength to pull against them. Metal bit into the flesh on her wrist and she winced before giving up.

Another glow flickered from the same hall. Perhaps the girl was returning.

She waited, her heart racing as the figure emerged from the shadows. But it wasn't the girl.

Green eyes met hers and fire flashed through them from the surrounding light.

Kiuno's mouth went dry. "Reece."

He'd attacked her. He'd killed Daren.

I didn't have a choice.

What had he meant by that?

Something had shifted when he'd abandoned her in the tunnel. Something in his eyes. As if he no longer recognized her. Or didn't care.

"Being tied up looks good on you."

Anger and sadness surged as she tugged against the restraints. "What's going on?"

He smirked and leaned against the wall. Reece folded his arms and ran his gaze up and down her frame. At one time she might have blushed. Now his actions only served to infuriate her further.

"Now you want to listen?"

"It's not as if I'm going anywhere."

"I brought you here."

"I figured out that much. Are the chains necessary?"

"For what I have planned, yes." He lifted from the wall to circle her. "You see, the creator wanted me to bring you to him." He leaned forward, whispering into her ear from behind. "But I'd rather keep you all to myself."

Kiuno pulled away as much as the chains would allow and he continued circling until he was back in her line of sight.

"What did he do to you?" she asked.

Reece sauntered toward the fire and lifted the metal fire poker from against the wall. "Freed me. Honestly, I should be thanking him, but delivering you is too steep a price. He'll have to do better than my freedom for that."

"So why am I here?"

He hit the rod on the ground and the metal sang against the walls. Reece swiveled to face her. "I was willing to give you everything. You took one look at him. One look, and everything we shared was gone. Not forgotten, not stored away in some remote region of your heart. Gone."

He pushed the rod against her chest, right over her racing heart. "I would have given you the world Ki. Laid it at your feet like the queen you are." He stepped forward and the fingers of his free hand traced along her cheek. She turned away.

Her mind floated back to the day she'd discovered Elite alive. She remembered Reece's sad expression, but a fond smile had followed. "I needed you to be my friend. I still need that from you."

His laugh penetrated her heart and her stomach sank to the guild-ridden hell she'd created. "I don't think friendship was on your mind in the cave."

"That was different," she said.

"Because Elite was dead?"

"Because I was shattered. My world gone. How could you expect anything from that?"

"I expected you to remember." He was in her face now, eyes wild. "I expected you to look at me and feel confusion, pain, longing, something. I expected more than—" He cut himself short and turned back to the fireplace in silence, shoving the metal into the embers.

"I didn't mean to hurt you. I'd never dream of hurting you." She took a breath. "I meant what I did. I don't regret it, but things are different now."

Reece was silent for a time. "So, you'd consider those feelings again? If he were gone?"

A chill lanced through her core and Daren flashed through her mind. "Not after this."

Reece stood still for a long time before shifting to the side. He pulled the hot metal from the fire and examined it.

"The creator wants to break you. Or push you to your limits. It's hard to tell with him. But I think he believes it's an impossibility."

Cold sweat rolled down the back of her neck as she watched him tilt the hot tip back and forth. "So, what, you plan to prove him wrong?"

"If I have to. I'd rather you join me; reclaim those feelings you've hidden from yourself."

"You're going to torture me into loving you?"

He smirked. "No. I want your admittance. I want you to admit it's not gone and that you'd rather spend your life here with me than go back to the pitiful one with Elite in the real world."

Kiuno struggled against her confines as he turned the hot iron toward her. She pulled, pushing her legs back as he stalked forward. Kiuno wrapped her hands around the chains and kicked off the ground, slamming both feet into his chest. Reece fell, the hot poker rolling from his hand and Kiuno regained her footing.

He coughed, clutching his chest. "See, this is what I like about you. You fight, never willing to accept your fate even when it's inevitable."

Reece picked up the metal rod and she pushed herself back again. This time when she kicked off, he sidestepped, and the rod slipped through her gut like a knife through butter.

She screamed, a burning sensation plunging through her core, searing parts of her body she didn't know could hurt. Kiuno fought for breath as he pulled the rod out and she violently tugged at her chains as tears raced down her cheeks.

Kiuno slumped, trying to curl her body in on itself as he returned to the fire. Every breath sent a fresh wave of pain coursing through her midsection.

"You're not Reece." She bit off every word.

"That would make this easier wouldn't it? To pretend I'm a fashioned creature from this world just like the reptilians who brought you here."

Tears of pain ran down her cheeks. "Reece wouldn't do this."

He sat the rod against the wall and turned to face her. "How do you know what Reece would or wouldn't do?"

"Because I know."

Callused fingers gripped her chin and tilted her head back forcing

Kiuno to look into those strangely distant eyes. "You remember what I said about the touch," his fingers turned soft, running along her cheek, "smell," his lips pressed against hers, and he gripped her chin harder when she tried to pull away.

The feel of his lips brought back memories from the cavern. He was gentle rain cradling a broken soul. Soothing a fire that sought to devour. Her mind returned to the present and Kiuno sank her teeth into his lip until she tasted blood.

He yelped, ripped himself away, and backhanded her across the face. "That fight is alluring even if it does cause a cut or two." He wiped the blood from his mouth. "You remember, and now I see the hurt and questions racing through that beautiful head of yours."

Her heart ached. "Why?"

He unlaced his gauntlet and rolled up a sleeve, exposing it to the firelight. Her eyes slid down his arm and rested on the black feather-like roots stretching towards his elbow. They wrapped his wrist, seeming to stem from a green jewel seated just within the skin.

"Like it? It was a gift from the creator himself. Freed me from all those silly emotions that tie one down. Honestly, I wish he'd given it to me sooner." Reece pulled his sleeve down and picked up the rod again.

The jewel. One of the relics. Her gaze shifted to the orb. Two in one place. It seemed too coincidental, but Reece's actions made sense now.

Maltack had warned her of the jewel's danger. It gave the user power over the monsters in the realms, but it also stripped away one's humanity and would eventually result in their death.

"It'll kill you."

His gaze followed hers, landing on his wrist, but he shrugged. "We all die eventually, what better way to go than having everything I want?" He twirled the rod in his hand, the red tip drawing her attention again.

"This isn't you. Please."

He smirked and her heart faltered as he took another step and drew back. Tears sprang to her eyes and she screamed again as the rod slipped through her midsection.

"Reece." It was a whisper, a plea. He paused and their eyes met. Hers weary, his flickering with regret.

The metal tore from her body and hit the floor. His breathing accelerated and he fell to his knees, moaning in pain as he clutched his wrist.

For a split moment, hope blossomed in her chest, but when he looked up again that cold expression had returned, and her hope crashed like a wave against the sand.

"Seems these pesky feelings just keep trying to pop up." He examined her and sighed as if bored. "Shame, if I continue you'll pass out and that won't be any fun." He stood. "If you try anything, I'll kill the girl."

Reece left her hanging bloody, but hopeful.

He was in there.

The Reece she knew was in there drowning in the evil magic the creator had forced upon him. If she played her cards right, she might be able to reach him.

The same girl from earlier trotted in, her gaze sorrowful as she looked at Kiuno's bloody shirt. With trembling hands, she grasped the tiny orb and moved it down the hall.

The familiar heat of magic blossomed in Kiuno's chest, but the young woman's fear-filled eyes prevented her from using it.

She took cautious steps. Light emitted from her palms and relief flooded Kiuno's body, though it did little for her pounding head.

"I can get us out of here," Kiuno whispered.

The girl's lower lip trembled. "I can't. He has my sister."

Kiuno clenched her teeth. "Can you get to her?"

She shook her head. "She's at the castle." A tear ran down her face. "He's already killed so many."

Kiuno's heart ached as the two sat in silence. The magic swept through the inner recesses of her body like cool water filling a volcanic void. Breathing became easier, but no amount of magic could reach the pain in her heart.

When the girl pulled back, pain still radiated from a deep part in Kiuno's body, but she didn't complain. She knew magic had limits. Who knew what else Reece had put her through?

The girl replaced the orb and trotted down the hall, likely to inform her captor that she'd successfully completed her task.

The blood covering Kiuno's shirt turned cold in the fading firelight. It caked to her skin, causing it to itch and another shiver ran through her body. She never remembered being so cold.

And tired. God was she tired, but she needed to come up with a plan. Something that would bring the real Reece out long enough for him to free her. If she could just get away from the orb, she could summon her magic, escape this place, and hopefully save her friend in the process.

REMEMBER

REALM: 5

DAY: 355

Kiuno faded in and out of consciousness as the fire turned to embers. With no sunlight it was impossible to tell how long she hung there, her body numbing by the second. She'd sleep for what felt like minutes only to jolt awake from the aching in her arms.

"I hope you're feeling better."

She hadn't heard him walk in and though her body was heavy, Kiuno pulled her feet beneath her and stood on shaky legs.

The same smirk. The same darkness. The Reece without morals or a conscience.

Could the relic make everyone like this? Would she be capable of similar evils if their roles were switched?

Metal scraped against the floor and her vision shot down to the poker in his hand, the tip red. How long had he been there?

Kiuno took a breath, keeping her voice calm. "I'll admit it."

He scoffed. "Because of the pain? You'll have to do better than that."

A chill ran from the base of her spine and up through her scalp. If he kept going, he'd kill her, and she didn't know if enough of her old friend resided in that darkness to prevent him from doing it. He'd come back after the fact, of that she was certain, but then it'd be too late.

Kiuno met his dark gaze and fought to see the man she'd once imagined a future with. She dug past her feeling of Elite, past her loyalty and what she might have to face later. She put herself back in those moments of pain and shattering heartbreak. She recalled the relief Reece's presence had brought to her life.

Kiuno had told Elite she didn't know what she felt and that was the truth, but if she didn't convince Reece right here and now of her feelings for him, she'd never see Elite again.

"I loved you."

He paused, which she expected, but she didn't expect the truth to come crashing down on her at the same time.

She wouldn't allow it and if not for this moment she never would have admitted it to herself.

She'd loved again. Been able to love after the person she'd cherished most had vanished from the world.

Guilt tugged at her like she'd never experienced, ripping a hole through her chest as she fought to register the initial reason for her confession.

Reece took a few steps forward and the rod fell from his grasp and clattered to the floor. He pressed his forehead to hers and gentle hands cupped the sides of her face.

He kissed her.

It wasn't desire. It wasn't need. It was an apology and she accepted.

Their eyes met. The beautiful eyes of the man she knew as her friend.

"Kill me when you get the chance." He slid his fingers up her arm and unclasped the shackle from her raw wrist. He supported her body as it fell. When had it become so heavy?

Reece grunted under her weight. "Come on Ki, you can't pass out now."

Kiuno leaned against him, struggling to collect herself as he unclasped the left.

They collapsed to the floor and he held her. Kiuno fought to stay conscious. Reece pushed her back and clutched his wrist.

He scrambled to his feet, grabbed the orb, and hurled it down the hall to her right.

He crumpled to the floor. "Don't hesitate. Do it before my magic comes back."

Kiuno struggled to her feet and the familiar warmth of fire flooded her core. It circled around her wrist beneath the skin, but she couldn't convince herself to pull it forth.

Tears stung her eyes. "I can't."

"Damn it Ki, I'll kill you." He ground his teeth. "I made my choice. Just do it."

She shook her head. "I'll find a way. Whatever you need, remember?"

His lips parted and then the Reece she knew vanished. Darkness entered his eyes like a parasite latched to his soul.

Her magic flickered in her chest and she steadied herself, preparing for the evil to come.

Reece stood, his smile sickening. "Will you now? I look forward to seeing you try."

She clenched her fists as his vines shot through the floor and danced around him as if in mockery to her promise. She would find a way. Reece had saved her, and she'd be damned if she didn't return the favor.

Voices echoed down the hall. The same hall Reece had hurled the orb down.

Another voice, then footsteps, and that sickening smirk on Reece's face grew.

"This is going to be fun."

Her stomach dropped as Elite emerged with Silver and Maltack at his side.

Elite's wild eyes dropped to the blood caked against her shirt, then roamed to the chains that hung from the ceiling, and finally to the sneer on Reece's face.

"I'm fine," she said before Elite could ask.

Reece was too close and the way he tilted his head to look at her had every hair standing on end.

Reece lifted his arm and the vines shot straight for Elite. Kiuno took a step too late.

She cried out and drowning fear overwhelmed rational thought, but Reece's magic fell limp before it could strike a fatal blow.

Reece's brow furrowed and Kiuno thought her heart might explode from her chest. She glanced down to Elite's palm and the orb he clutched in one hand.

He hadn't even flinched.

Elite placed the orb in his pocket and drew his sword.

Fire reflected the murder in his eyes and Kiuno pleaded. "Don't kill him."

ELITE

REALM: 5

DAY: 355

E very cell in Elite's body flickered with rage. *Don't kill him?* He tight-ened the grip on his sword and stared at the smirk playing on Reece's face. Blood caked Kiuno's shirt. She could barely stand and judging from the evidence, Reece was the one responsible. Yet still.

Don't kill him.

He'd led an army against theirs. He'd killed their comrades. Men Elite had fought beside since the first realm. Reece had kissed his wife, tried to claim her after his supposed death, but still. *Don't kill him.*

Elite huffed. Fine, there were more satisfying ways to exact his revenge.

Elite rushed Reece at the same time Maltack raced toward Kiuno. Even if she were hurt, Maltack couldn't do anything with the orb so close.

Maltack had known what the sphere was as soon as he'd laid eyes on it. Elite eyed Kiuno. Judging from the amount of blood on her shirt, he'd have to end this quickly.

Their swords clashed and Elite shoved Reece off balance then brought his blade up and clipped Reece's arm. Reece snarled and grabbed the injury.

This man had hurt his wife and Elite would ensure he suffered for it.

Reece rushed him again, but Elite shot through his guard and planted the hilt of his sword in Reece's solar plexus.

Reece wretched and doubled over, fighting for breath, but Elite didn't give him time to catch it. He could kill him, he had the chance to plunge his sword straight through Reece's gut, but Kiuno was watching. Even without taking his eyes from his opponent, Elite could feel her gaze burning into the back of his head, willing him not to do what he knew he should.

Elite cursed and brought his fist up under Reece's chin. Elite kicked the man's sword away and flipped Reece onto his back, pinning his arm with one knee.

A glint in the firelight caught his attention and Elite pulled at the sleeve of his opponent. His reflection stared back from the surface of a jade jewel.

It all made sense now. The dark relic.

Thick roots twisted from the tainted magic and interlaced themselves beneath the raised flesh. Elite cringed.

Reece bucked his hips just enough to throw Elite off balance and scrambled toward his weapon. Elite stood, a renewed sense of understanding at their predicament. Kiuno wanted to save Reece, but she'd be putting herself in danger. Like she always did.

He let out a slow breath. If he ended it here, then she wouldn't have to.

Reece adjusted the grip on his sword. "You should have taken the shot when you had the chance. You won't get another."

"I think you've been relying on that magic too much."

A growl echoed from Reece and Elite positioned himself.

That's right, get angry, rush in, and this will all be over.

"He plans to kill me you know," Reece said louder, his target clearly Kiuno. "I can see it in his eyes. He's decided I'm not worth saving."

Elite didn't turn. He didn't have to. He knew her mind churned between the possibility of Reece being right or having enough faith to trust in her husband.

Elite cursed. He couldn't. Not after everything she'd already been through. He wouldn't let this world take the integrity he'd worked so hard to build.

Reece smirked. "She always was too soft, though when you died," he whistled, "She really went off the deep end. Cold-blooded murder. That's what I'd love to see in her eyes again. The moment she smiles as she tortures another human being."

Rage boiled in him as he fought to keep calm. "Shut your mouth."

"Ooh, so she hasn't told you? Should make for an interesting conversation. Has she told you about our kiss, or the way I held her and ran my hands over her body?" Reece licked his lips. "How about how much she liked it?"

"I said shut up!" Elite charged. He knew Reece was baiting him, but fury tore through his body at the thought of Kiuno in another man's arms.

Kiuno wanted to save Reece, but had she also developed more feelings than she let on?

Elite parried another blow and avoided the fatal shot meant for his throat. Reece was good, but there were countless moments where he could have ended this fight. Perhaps he could remove an arm. He could cut off the one with the jewel.

Elite raised his sword again, but Reece's lowered, and the man's eyes darted toward Kiuno. A man shouldn't let himself become distracted during a fight, nor was he supposed to let his enemy escape, but when Reece ran from the hall Elite did nothing to stop him.

REECE

REALM: 5

DAY: 355

I loved you. Her words echoed like a mantra in Reece's head. He repeated them. Over and over and over.

I loved you.

Maybe she did. Maybe she didn't, but the power of those three words enabled Reece to pull himself together and flee from the underground torture chamber.

His body screamed in crippling agony. His wrist pulsated and the roots gripped the muscles in his forearms, but he didn't give in. He wouldn't. Not until he separated himself from her.

With distance from the orb, Reece's magic returned. He could reach out to the seedlings in the dirt and force their growth.

Green burst from the ground and wrapped itself around his body. His stomach plummeted as he lifted himself from the hole and back into the sunlight. Reece squinted, trying to see what enemies might come for him.

Those standing around the hole cried out and moved from his path as he hit the ground then sprinted as fast as his legs would carry him.

He kept his head down, his eyes still adjusting. Lifeless bodies left from the battle passed by as he ran.

The clashing of steel grew louder, but his vines whipped out before him to create a path. He couldn't fight. All he could do was run through the raging battle. Monsters and people. Magic and steel.

None of it compared to the nightmare in his head. The constant sharp prick against his mind urging him to yield.

He dodged swords, shields, magic. His name might have been called once, but he didn't pause.

Reece tripped and choked as his vision faded, but he yanked back, playing tug-of-war with the unseen force.

Kiuno. Focus on Kiuno.

She'd brought him back.

He gritted his teeth at the memories and took off running again.

Reece had done the unthinkable. He'd tried to kill her and the longer this thing grew beneath his skin the less control he'd have. What would happen next time?

Would he vanish from existence or forever be condemned to a prison? Would he watch as his own hands killed those he cared about?

A pulse ran through his arm, echoing over his body and Reece hit the ground. The surrounding creatures paid him no mind, their sole purpose to obey and kill.

The roots wriggled and Reece clawed at the skin as they rose toward his elbow.

He took several long breathes and stared at them. They'd kill him. He'd already come to terms with that, but it still left him with a choice. Either watch those he cared for die or end things while he still had a shred of control.

Reece bit his lip and drew his knife. He yanked the fabric back and plunged the blade straight through his wrist. Blinding pain shot from the jewel and the roots gripped his muscles in a vise.

He withdrew the blade and plunged it into the other side, but his world went dark and he floated back into the recesses of his subconscious.

Back to his prison.

And for the first time in his life, there was nothing he could do to escape.

SHADOW OF DEATH

Realm: 5
Day: 355

Silver grasped Kiuno's arm and helped her to her feet. He wrapped an arm around her back and draped hers over his shoulder. Maltack lit the way.

Bodies of reptilians, as Reece had called them, lined the tunnel's floor. Some were charred beyond recognition while others had been punctured or had their heads removed.

She shivered and Silver tightened his grip on her wrist. Kiuno glanced at her friends, observing the scrapes along their bodies and the blood on their blades. After everything they'd been through, she prayed they wouldn't encounter another obstacle on their way out.

Reece.

Why was this happening to him? How did the creator convince him to use something so dangerous?

Would others want to kill him after what he'd done?

Kiuno tripped, but Silver maintained his hold and shifted his hand to support her further.

Her midsection burned. God did it burn. It seemed every part of her body had either been ignited or frozen. Like different parts rested on two planes of existence.

The evening sunlight entered their view and it did nothing for her pounding head.

Plants unfurled from the ground and Maltack wrapped his magic around their bodies. One vine pressed painfully around her stomach and she winced when they lifted from the ground.

At the top, a small group of people guarded the hole. The battle had moved far enough away to be little more than an echo.

She took in a breath, but even that came in a sluggish muddle. Like her body no longer knew how to care for itself.

Reece. K.J.

She had to fix it. With both of them.

Kiuno's body trembled and she fell to her knees when Silver released her. She needed rest, but there wasn't time. She needed to warn the others. Tell them—what exactly? What could she do except beg for Reece to be spared? He was dangerous now. Uncontrollable. Just like her magic. But they'd found a way with that.

Her arms shook and Maltack tilted her head back to look at him. "What's wrong?"

What wasn't wrong?

Her world tilted again, and a black haze hovered over her vision. Maltack ran his fingers along her abdomen. "She's bleeding."

"So fix it," Elite said.

Kiuno tilted her head and watched as the red and black banners of K.J.'s army floated in the breeze. The corner of her mouth lifted. He'd come.

"I need Palindrome's help. Something's not right."

Elite cursed and took off, leaving her alone with Maltack.

"Hey, I need you to stay awake."

"I'm awake," she assured him. Though she didn't quite know how. She was helpless as they lifted her onto a cot and trotted toward a castle she thought she'd left for good.

KIUNO GROANED as they dropped her outside the gate and Maltack ran toward the guards. She didn't have much strength, but Kiuno rotated her head to watch the exchange. Maltack waved his arms in a frantic fury until they agreed to let him through. After that, he disappeared.

How ironic. Her life depended on the person K.J. had thought she'd killed. Would they even permit her inside? Knowing Palindrome, K.J. wouldn't have a choice in the matter, but if Palindrome blamed her too…

If Kiuno hadn't been so cold she might have been more afraid, but her body welcomed rest. She closed her eyes, promising herself it would only be for a moment. Her consciousness floated, but a rough hand shook her shoulders.

"Stay awake." Elite's hand ran down her arm and wrapped around her fingers. She tried to smile.

"Bring her in," Maltack's voice called.

Kiuno's heart jolted slightly, woken only a little from its need to slumber. The looming gates passed by as she stared at the clouds above, but Kiuno closed her eyes as they ran through the crowds.

She knew they watched. Whispered. Pointed. Maybe they knew her as a traitor. Maybe they had no idea.

The castle walls blotted out the sun and her vision dimmed as they entered the keep. The jostling ride kept her awake. Maybe they should run all dying people up a few flights of stairs. No one could die during that ride.

They set the cot on a bed and Maltack knelt at her side. Elite and Silver stood over her like guardians. The cracks in the ceiling drew her attention.

Kiuno wondered if they'd formed during a battle or if the creator had paid attention to the smallest of details and included them in the design.

Gruff voices echoed down the hall. Someone sat beside Maltack and a new wave of magic washed over her body.

It twisted the burning sensation and sent pain coursing through her abdomen. Kiuno yelped and tried to curl in on herself, but Maltack grabbed her shoulder and held her flat.

She wanted to fight, half torn between pain and exhaustion.

Then she turned to the woman.

Palindrome.

Their eyes locked and Kiuno's heart beat faster as she looked at the man in the hall. He leaned against the stone wall, arms crossed, but Kiuno couldn't tell who his concern rested with.

"She's good now, but she should eat something before she rests."

"Palindrome?"

The woman gave her a sweet smile. "You'll be all right now."

With that, she stood and left, and K.J. followed.

HOPE

REALM: 5
DAY: 356

After eating a few pieces of bread and devouring a bowl of soup, all at Elite's command, Kiuno fell into a deep sleep. She didn't dream, but upon waking every surface of her body ached. They'd piled furs on her so thick she wasn't sure anyone would know a person lay beneath.

Kiuno moved to sit up, but Elite pushed her back.

"You need rest."

"We have to leave. We're not welcome here."

"Palindrome said you could stay. Until you recovered."

Kiuno pushed his hand away and swung her legs to the side of the bed. Dizziness threatened to throw her back, so she tucked her head down and sat still for several moments.

"I'm awake, that's good enough." She studied the stone floor. "Reece is being controlled by the jeweled relic."

Elite sighed and sat back. "I know, I saw it." He pulled the orb from his pocket. "And Maltack found this."

She took the round sphere and rotated it in her palm. The colors shifted as light passed through.

Kiuno handed it back. "What are we going to do now?"

"I don't know. Silver went to speak with Samar. He isn't happy about Reece's involvement and from what I understand K.J. isn't either. Reece is the one who led the attack."

Tears stung her eyes. "We have to help him."

Silence settled in the room. Elite sat forward and took her hand. "We can try, but we don't know anything about the relics. With what he did. He might be a lost cause."

She tightened her grip on Elite's hands. No. He wasn't. Her friend was still in there. All she had to do was draw him out.

"In the meantime, I have something that might take your mind off it."

Kiuno glanced at him.

"Scorpios is awake."

EXCITEMENT. DREAD. Excitement. Dread.

If she went an entire year without either, Kiuno's heart would thank her for it.

She was excited. No. Ecstatic. To see Scorpios up and well. But the thought of running into K.J. in the hall sent her stomach twisting in knots.

No battle had ever given her so much to fear. She'd rush in, damn whatever might happen to her physically, but when it came to her heart? Those were the battles she'd never be ready to face. To have her soul torn in two as someone she loved looked at her as if she were a person they no longer recognized. That was hell.

Neither Elite nor Maltack wanted her to walk, but she didn't want to be bound to a cot either. Kiuno had settled upon allowing Elite to guide her toward Scorpios's room.

Her vision swirled as they walked, but she kept her focus on the ground. Kiuno avoided peering into the corners, afraid her former friend might be watching.

She knew K.J.'s mind was churning, thinking of all the ways she might get around what she'd done. What advantage it might have given her and why he was still alive. Maybe he thought her incapable of completing the plan. That's sure what he had implied when he'd banished her.

She limped around another corner and her thoughts drifted to Reece. He'd wanted her to kill him, yet if their positions were reversed, she knew it wouldn't be an option. Reece would tear down entire alliances for her, and she planned to do the same.

Kiuno's heart skipped when they stopped before a door and Maltack emerged.

"How is he?" she asked.

"He's weak, as expected, but otherwise good. He's been asking for you. It seems everyone has been cryptic with him to avoid unnecessary stress."

"Scorpios not knowing what's going on *is* stress."

Maltack cracked a smile. "I know, but I thought you should be the one to explain."

Scorpios gave her an expectant expression when she entered the room. "I was wondering how long it'd take you to visit me."

Kiuno left Elite's arms and all but ran to Scorpios. His clothes seemed too baggy on his frame, but the smile on his face eased her fears.

Scorpios laughed and patted her head like a child, but for once she didn't care. Kiuno pulled back and seated herself on the edge of his bed. Elite stood at the end.

"All right, who's going to explain?" He glanced between her and Elite. "I have all my limbs, I know how I received my injury, and all my friends are alive. So, why is everyone keeping secrets?"

She tilted her head. "Driving you crazy?"

"Kiuno."

She took a deep breath. "I've been banished."

His brow furrowed. "Why?"

"It's a long story."

He glanced around the room. "I'm not going anywhere."

She sighed. "Where to start?"

Kiuno gave Scorpios a detailed account of her meeting with Atilla and how he'd betrayed them instead of helping which resulted in K.J.'s accusation. She reiterated her guilt for the entire mess and how she had plans to fix it, though didn't know how to just yet.

He nodded, but stayed quiet as she recounted her kidnapping by Reece and the torture session he'd put her through. Kiuno then told him about the relic and her not so detailed plan to set that right too.

Scorpios shook his head. "How long have I been out again?"

"Too long."

He shifted and winced. "Have you spoken to K.J. yet?"

Kiuno shook her head, recalling him in the doorway. "I don't think he wants to see me."

"So, you're sure he's made up his mind? You're here aren't you?"

"I am, but I think he needs time. It's not as though we can blame him. I know what it looked like."

"Appearances are deceiving, and assumptions are worse. One shouldn't cloud their mind with such things. He should trust his instincts. Even I know what they're telling him."

"He trusts facts and rationality."

"Then he should know it's impossible for you to do what he thinks you did."

Kiuno lowered her gaze. "Maybe."

They were silent for a short moment. "Maltack mentioned you were here to take me with you?"

"Only if you feel up to it."

Scorpios smiled. "I think it's you we should be concerned about.

You're white as a ghost." He shifted again. "Maybe some fresh air will do us both good. Besides, Palindrome will keep me cooped up for the rest of my life if she has her way."

"At least half your life."

The two laughed and Elite helped Kiuno move as they allowed Scorpios to shift his legs to the bed's edge.

Maltack entered and draped Scorpios's arm around his shoulders and the four hobbled from the room. Kiuno imagined Palindrome throwing a fit at the entire scene.

Outside the castle, a wagon waited. Kiuno didn't have the nerve to ask if Maltack had sent for it or if Palindrome had provided it.

Scorpios let out a breath as he sat in the far corner. "I don't remember ever feeling this weak."

Kiuno groaned, pulling herself up beside him. "Blue couldn't protest at your unfairness now."

Scorpios chuckled. "That he couldn't, but I doubt I could stand straight let alone get a good hit in."

"Do you need anything before we go?"

"I think my current company is good enough."

Elite jumped in the front with Maltack at his side and the two ushered the horses forward. The gathered crowd dispersed and Kiuno settled in for the long journey home. She'd likely sleep most of the way.

The gate slammed shut after they rode through and the guards took their rightful positions.

She looked at the large doors and a small shred of hope blossomed in her chest. He'd allowed her help. He might have even come to check on her. Perhaps those gates wouldn't always be closed.

Kiuno glanced to the top of the wall and her heart clenched. K.J. didn't move. He didn't wave but stood as a statue guarding his people.

His cold expression told her his feelings hadn't changed and she was still an enemy in unwanted territory. But his actions. His actions told her all hope wasn't lost.

64

REECE

REALM: 5

DAY: 370

Reece slammed back to reality and then into the nearest wall. Breath left his lungs as he slumped forward and a fist hit his jaw followed by another to the gut.

The footsteps retreated thereafter and stopped once the creator reached the balcony. "I gave you a simple command."

Reece spit blood on the stone. "Maybe you should take it up with the crazy thing you put inside me."

"You still don't get it. I didn't put anything inside you. I released you. I gave you freedom from the oppression you suffer from due to your morals and emotions. You are still you."

"That's horse shit." Reece staggered to his feet and leaned against the stone. "I would never hurt Kiuno."

At that he turned, his eyes glaring. "Hurt her, hurt her how?"

"You mean with your all-seeing abilities you don't know?"

The man stalked forward and swung, but Reece ducked and

RISE OF THE WOLVES

slammed his shoulder into the man's back. Reece lunged toward his neck, but the creator blinked out of existence only to reappear behind Reece where he kicked Reece to the ground again.

"I wasn't watching. I was waiting and you never showed. I assumed Kiuno had given you a run for your money."

"How could she with the orb?"

"I know firsthand how well she can fight, and I don't expect you'd be able to stand long against her."

"Well, I did, and I captured her and I…" The words fell from Reece's lips like a stone sinking into a pond.

"You what?" He demanded. His nostrils flared.

"I tortured her, that's what. Because of you, I tortured Kiuno."

"And now she hates you."

I loved you.

Reece stayed silent as the creator paced back and forth along the balcony. "Animosity was expected, but torture? Perhaps the jewel *has* altered your mind. No matter. If she hates you that means the game can continue."

"I'm sick of your games and I won't go after her again."

"No." He rubbed his chin. "No, I won't need you to. K.J. is planning to leave his castle and she'll follow." He turned back to Reece. "It's brilliant. You'll meet them in the sixth realm, and it'll open a rift sparking a whole new chapter I never planned."

His smile caused bile to rise in Reece's throat.

"Now, what shall we do for your punishment?"

SURPRISES

REALM: 5

DAY: 371

Question after question after question. Weekly food stores, criminal activity, accidents, expanding the living quarters, feeding the animals. The list went on and on and on.

Everyday a small crowd of people followed her, seeking her approval and every day she answered. They were a plague and no matter where she hid, they always seemed to follow.

Kiuno fumbled with papers and nodded in agreement to issues that could have been solved without her input. She oversaw task management, but it seemed the smallest of details still required her immediate attention. Always immediate. Always an emergency.

She sighed when the next emergency involved solving a conflict over housing. Honestly, they just fought through a war together. One would think their bitter quarreling would have ended there.

Kiuno ascended the castle stairs and glanced out a window. Silver and Elite worked on the battle arrangements and training. Further out,

Maltack aided those still struggling with their magic.

Voices sounded from below the stairs and Kiuno bounded the remaining few and ran behind a pillar to avoid another messenger. She'd already been to a dozen places and it was barely noon.

When the hall cleared, Kiuno ran toward another staircase, darted up the few flights and slammed the wooden door to her office. She shifted the lock in place and leaned against it, sinking to the floor. Kiuno sighed and closed her eyes for a moment of reprieve.

Sleep deprivation had worn her down and despite Elite's warnings, she couldn't say no as often as she would have liked. K.J.'s constant tired state suddenly made sense.

"I'll go out on a limb and say this is a bad time."

Kiuno cracked one eye open to find K.J.'s spy, Xander, seated in a chair. He appeared half ready to stand as he studied her on the floor.

"I guess I've been caught already."

"I can go."

She waved him down. "Don't worry about it." Kiuno rose to her feet. "If you're here, then it's important."

Silence filled the room while Kiuno crossed it and sank into the chair across from him. Xander's loyalties still lie with K.J. and speaking to him required carefully chosen words.

"K.J. is marching toward the sixth realm. I thought you should know."

She rubbed her temple. "What about the monsters?"

"The reports have been silent. Cybele moved back home and K.J. is taking the second route to avoid the jungle."

That stopped her. "What second route?"

"Oh, right. There was a meeting with the other leaders recently. A second portal was found that leads to the sixth realm."

"I thought only one portal connected each realm."

"You and everyone else."

Kiuno rubbed her temple. "Where's this portal?"

"Further down the burnt forest's border. It opens away from the jungle and appears safer. At least that's what they're hoping."

"Trust me when I say there's nothing safe about that realm." Kiuno sat back. "I'll assume he's prepared should the monsters attack again?" She couldn't bring herself to mention Reece.

He shrugged. "I'll assume so. We were the first to move from the fourth realm. The other leaders weren't inclined to follow until K.J. assured them the area was safe."

Kiuno folded her hands. "Please tell me he's not going to the sixth realm alone."

Xander bit his lip. "I wasn't informed otherwise."

Alone. In that realm? It was suicide. How many men had K.J. taken? Palindrome would go with him, but they'd also have to leave enough people behind to guard the castle. What if Reece attacked in their absence?

"Are you telling me this because you're worried?" Kiuno asked.

Xander glanced to the fireplace, its embers cold. "I saw what came from that realm. Without your and Samar's forces I don't think we would have survived."

Kiuno rubbed a hand across her face. The leaders had let him go alone before. Who was to say they wouldn't do so again? K.J. was a man about furthering their progress. He wasn't afraid to take a risk if it meant putting them on top. With the enemy's forces depleted, now was the perfect time to move.

Kiuno stood. "I know you normally run errands for K.J., but would you make an exception?"

"What do you have in mind?"

"Ride to Samar's. Tell him I want a meeting and it's not a request."

COWARDS

REALM: 5

DAY: 373

Disdain covered several faces as Kiuno marched into the square room. The long wooden table and chairs surrounding it were the only things that seemed to greet her.

Two sets were empty. K.J's and Atilla's.

Kiuno had made them wait, hoping to make an impression. She no longer cared if it was good or bad. She just wanted them to pay attention.

Elite and Maltack followed and stood behind Kiuno as she took her place in Atilla's seat.

Grayson grunted. "Can we start now? Why are we here?"

Kiuno said, "Because I was absent from the last meeting."

"Murderers aren't welcome," Grayson spat.

She folded her hands on the table. "So, you've heard about Atilla."

"And K.J."

"One side of the story."

"Your claim of innocence you mean? Seems a bit too convenient for my taste."

Samar interrupted. "Are we going to listen to you two bicker or get on with it?"

Kiuno pulled her gaze away from Grayson and addressed the group. "I want to know if any of you are planning to march to the sixth realm."

"No," Grayson said. "And if that's all you wanted, I think a messenger would have sufficed. We aren't marching on another realm on a whim. K.J. made his decision the first time and he's made it now. He can reap the benefits or suffer the consequences on his own."

Kiuno glared at him. "But if he reaps the benefits, so do you." She glanced at them all. "All of us do. Can't you see this is the perfect time to move? The enemy is weak. We can band together—"

Grayson interrupted this time. "We'll band together when everyone agrees to do so. If you and K.J. are so determined to rush to your death, then don't let us stop you."

Kiuno spread her fingers over the table to prevent balling them into fists. "I'm certain you know about the last fight. How Samar, K.J., and I worked together to drive the monsters back. If we hadn't done that then there would be fewer people alive today. If we tackle the worst battles together, then we'll all come out on top."

"You're asking us to move hundreds of people without the hope of a home," Grayson said.

"No, I'm asking you to move a portion of your military."

Samar spoke next. His words careful. "Kiuno. I know you're worried about your friend and you want to right whatever wrong you committed, but we can't be held accountable for your actions or his."

"You think this is personal?"

He took a breath. "Understand. We are responsible for those around us, just as you are responsible for the people around you."

This time she clenched her fists. "I understand just fine. I've been listening. I've been patient. I've kept track of the exchanges between alliance leaders and who's been willing and reluctant. I've paid attention as you and the others have avoided confrontation at any expense."

She pointed her gaze at Samar. "Why do you think I showed up at your gate with an army? You question everything. You're reluctant and talk in circles when you should be acting." She took a breath. "I know things have gotten comfortable, but you can't live like this. You can't let yourselves settle for this place."

"And why can't we?" Grayson asked.

Her brow furrowed. "Because this isn't home."

"That depends upon who you ask."

She leaned back in her chair, examining each face. "So that's it? You just give up?"

Silence echoed and Samar and Grayson averted their gazes. Leena held hers. Waiting. Watching.

Samar leaned forward and cleared his throat. "We'll see how far K.J. gets and decide from there."

"Do you hear yourselves? You're willing to sacrifice another to see if advancing is even possible?"

Grayson said, "Sometimes sacrifice is necessary."

"Now you sound like Atilla. The sacrifice of people is never necessary," Kiuno said.

Samar tapped his fingers on the table. "Survival is the focus. As we've said, we'll wait and see what happens."

Silence echoed and each shifted as if they were ready to leave. Ready to let K.J. take the fall. If they were safe, no one else mattered.

"You're all cowards."

Grayson stood. "I beg your pardon?"

Kiuno stood with him. "If you're comfortable with this life, then you're a coward."

Grayson's face purpled, but Samar spoke first. "We're not cowards for wanting to protect our people."

"You're cowards for letting others do your dirty work."

"We have no obligation to anyone," Grayson spat.

"You're a leader, you have every obligation." She pointed to the door. "What would happen if I walked outside and told your men you had no intention of escaping? What do you think they'd do?"

Grayson's fists curled. "You have no right. This meeting is over, you've wasted our time, and should you need an ally in the future I suggest you look elsewhere."

Kiuno slammed her hand on the wooden table, sparks flying as it splintered down the center. Everyone shot from their chairs and backed against the wall. Guards drew their swords and stared her down.

Each seemed at a loss for words, eyes darting this way and that. Their hands shook and mouths parted as if they wanted to protest but didn't dare.

"I knew he was lying," Grayson said. "I knew K.J. was lying about the lightning user."

Kiuno glanced at Samar whose eyes were just as wide as the others. All except Leena.

"It wasn't his secret to tell. I didn't want to open myself to those who might try to use me as their pawn. I made my own decisions and K.J. allowed me to do that."

"But you'll use us?"

Kiuno took a breath but didn't respond.

Samar took a tentative step forward. "We can't Kiuno. Go to K.J., convince him to come back and we'll regroup for a later time."

"It's too late for that. I'm going. I'll stand by K.J.'s side. Who knows, maybe I'll die. Maybe this entire world will crumble if I do. But I promise you this. If I lose any of my friends because you were too cowardly to show your faces, then I'll hold you responsible."

Grayson snorted. "You can't threaten us."

"Can't I? When you don't show, I'll come back and then throw you to the men you claim to lead. I'll tell them of your faults and tear everything away from you piece by piece. I'll control your army and when we find a way out, I'll ensure you don't come with us."

Kiuno stormed around the table and those in her way cleared a path. She paused at the doorway. "You know where the portal is. I'll be expecting you."

She gave them a final look and only Leena was smiling.

PLANS

REALM: 5
DAY: 375

Anger burned through Kiuno's core as she swung from her horse and marched up the castle stairs to a room filled with maps and documents. She sent Elite and Maltack to gather everyone then sat in the room in brooding silence.

She needed a plan in their absence. Should something go wrong, the alliances wouldn't aid the castle's defense. Thankfully two castles separated them from the monster's line of attack. K.J. had the hard part.

Kiuno glanced at the map and ran her finger around the perimeter. She could set the same traps K.J. had. Perhaps they should begin construction on an underground bunker should things fall through.

After what seemed too long a time, Blue, Liam, and Scorpios filed in. Her racing heart steadied at the sight of Scorpios. He was recovering. He could walk on his own now and part of his frame had started to fill in.

Scorpios seated himself. "Judging from the expression on your face the meeting didn't go well."

Kiuno resisted the urge to curse. "There's a chance we might be on our own."

"Aside from Leena," he corrected.

She smiled. "Yes, aside from Leena. She seemed happy with the outcome."

Kiuno glanced at the map laid out before them. "I don't believe the alliances will risk attacking so the most we'd have to worry about is renegade groups and possibly a small legion of monsters."

"Traps will deter most things," Blue said.

Kiuno nodded. "That's what I was thinking. Scorpios. Blue. Liam. I'll be leaving you here to run the place. Elite, Silver, and Maltack will be coming with me and I'll send a messenger to Cybele to inform her of the situation."

"Has K.J. already left?" Scorpios asked.

"He has."

"Time is of the essence then."

"I'll start collecting our supplies." Maltack stood and the others stood with him. She nodded to each as they left the room. Scorpios remained.

Kiuno sighed and placed her head in her hands. She was tired. More than tired. It seemed battle after battle followed without a moment of peace. Every moment they wasted was another they might not make it in time. What if she found K.J. dead without ever having fixed her mistake? What if Reece followed them to the sixth realm?

"Are you up for this?" Scorpios asked.

She peeked at him from beneath her fingers. "I can't just sit by. I'd never forgive myself if something happened to him."

"I mean are you ready to play the politics. Leena will join you, she likes the fight, but you might have made enemies with the other two." He leaned forward, folding his hands on the table. "I know you don't want to hear it, but you'll also need to decide what to do about Reece."

"One thing at a time. Right now, I need to get our army to K.J. as fast as possible."

"And what will you do if Reece is there?"

Her heart clenched. That's what she feared. She feared Reece making an appearance and causing more damage than she could undo.

"I'll fight him, subdue him, and use the orb to keep him in check until Maltack figures out a way to remove the jewel."

"You sound confident."

"Isn't that how a leader is supposed to sound?"

"A good leader admits when they need help."

Kiuno rubbed her hand across her face. "Do you think what I'm doing is wrong?"

"No, you gave them the hard truth. Becoming sedentary as a leader is unacceptable. I just hope they're able to take your advice rather than become angered by it."

"I guess time will tell." She rose.

"Be safe Kiuno."

REINFORCEMENT

Realm: 5
Day: 383

Kiuno drained the last of her water as they marched past the border of the burned forest.

Life had taken root again. Young saplings fought through the ash and plants grew through the burnt soil. She couldn't help but wonder if Reece would ambush them along the way.

Scorpios's words bothered her. Would Reece meet them in the sixth realm? Would she have to fight him again?

Kiuno glanced toward the overcast sky. Sweat rolled down her neck. They'd trudged on for days. Through storms, mud, and heat, but the end loomed before them. The same purple, spiraling mist she'd grown to loath.

Kiuno positioned herself beside the portal while the first of their magic users ran through. If one ran back, then she'd dart in and ensure their safe retreat. Or as safe as they could get. The monsters could traverse the realms now.

Their guard returned. "All clear."

Kiuno breathed a sigh of relief and raised one arm. The first regiment lined up. She exchanged a water skin with those in charge of refilling then trotted back to Elite and Silver.

The vortex shifted the wagons before their eyes. The material shrank, twisted, and somehow emerged on the other side in one piece. It unnerved her how the human body did the same and she wondered if there were ever a risk for never escaping that swirling void. Perhaps those experimented on were stuck there, screaming for help that would never arrive.

With half their forces in the sixth realm, Kiuno passed through. The colors stretched and pressed into her body before spitting her out on the other side.

The desert heat hit her full force. Several people had already sprouted trees for shade and others tugged at underground water sources to quench their thirst.

Kiuno glanced up into the glaring sun and shielded her eyes. Her exposed skin warmed.

"The heat complicates things," Silver said. He took a swig from his water pouch.

Elite wiped sweat dotting his brow. "We'll need to keep an eye on the animals. They weren't made for this kind of environment."

The last of their men filed into the sixth realm, night descended, and Kiuno collapsed by a fire. Daytime had brought with it insufferable heat, but without the sun a chill swept over the sand and Kiuno shivered.

Tomorrow she'd find K.J. and while Palindrome hadn't seemed to blame her, he still might. Perhaps with Palindrome's help Kiuno could convince K.J. of the truth.

Elite sat beside her, tugging at his gloves. "The scouts are ready to leave with first light."

"Good." Kiuno watched the flames dance then Elite pulled her to lie back with him.

"Stop worrying."

"I can't. What if we don't find them alive?"

"K.J. knows what's out there and you got here as fast as you could."

Kiuno fell silent and curled into Elite. She played with the string on his shirt. "What happens if we encounter Reece?"

Elite stiffened beside her and Kiuno closed her mouth. They hadn't discussed anything Reece mentioned from the torture chamber. She wondered if the thought of her murdering another bothered Elite, but if she had to guess, her make-out session bothered him more.

"Then you'll use your best judgement to do what's right. If you think we can save him, then I'll help you try, but you need to prepare for the alternative."

She knew that, but when it came time to swing her blade, Kiuno wasn't sure she'd have the strength.

KIUNO WOKE with dawn and paced the camp while they waited for news. She glanced over the horizon and her heart skipped at the sign of smoke.

Their scout arrived soon after.

"We found them." The man dropped from his horse and unwound the cloth from his face. "They're a short ride through the sand, but I think they're under siege. I don't know how many."

Kiuno's head shot toward the area with smoke rising fast.

She took off at a run and grabbed Elite's arm in passing. "Get the men ready."

He clutched her forearm and spun her back. "Where are you going?"

"K.J." She pointed.

Elite pulled her in, kissed her lips, then whispered, "Be careful."

He released his hold and Kiuno ran for her sword. She fastened it to her belt, swung into a horse's saddle, and kicked it hard.

The animal spurred forward and she gripped the reins as it weaved around the men and obstacles in their camp.

The heat of the day rose fast. Kiuno's heart thundered with the horse's hooves and she spurred it on.

Her skin bristled as she neared.

A mass of bodies poured from the jungle's trees and men huddled behind trenches while magic sparked and flew in all directions.

She jumped from the horse and the creature took off in the opposite direction. Men shouted orders over the roar of clashing steel and growling beasts. Kiuno disappeared in their line of troops, unnoticed by those struggling to contain the ambush.

She shoved her way toward the front, pumping her legs as hard as they would go. Kiuno crashed into an individual, muttered an apology, and kept running.

He'd brought more people than she'd realized, and Kiuno prayed it would be enough to hold until the others arrived.

If they arrived.

The shields sparked and wavered. Droplets of water ran down the dome and glistened in the sunlight. Those with offensive abilities launched their counterstrikes. Spearmen sank the tips of their weapons into any foe able to penetrate the magic users' attacks.

Kiuno didn't pause. She jumped the trench, spiraled flames around her body, and burst through the first line of enemies. Kiuno tugged at the flames again and used their force to knock the creatures off balance.

She summoned the lightning. The barriers would protect her allies.

Men and women alike screamed for her to return to safety, but she ignored them and let lightning rip from her core.

The screams faded as roars of pain filled her ears. Seared flesh burned her nose, but just like their last fight, the monsters didn't cower.

Kiuno steeled herself and tugged at another bolt and sent it ripping through their enemy. She only needed to keep it up long enough for K.J.'s forces to get themselves in order. Elite and the others would arrive soon.

Those with advanced abilities joined her, protecting one another in waves of magic that rivaled her own. Kiuno let the bolts shift to flame, but it raged beneath her control.

A rough hand grabbed her wrist and she allowed the individual to pull her away from the main part of the battle. They weren't willing to sacrifice anyone. That was Palindrome's teaching.

Kiuno collapsed, struggling to catch her breath as a healer looked her over and stitched a wound on her arm she hadn't realized was there.

"Take a breath, we got it." The woman jumped past her and Kiuno followed with her eyes. A shimmering bubble of magic ricocheted their enemy's attack. They had it for now, but for how long? Leena would come, but Kiuno had no way of knowing when.

"Kiuno?"

Her head snapped around at K.J's voice.

REECE

REALM: 6

DAY: 384

Reece hated this. Hated every minute of control the creator poured into him. He longed for his freedom, but that seemed to rest on someone else. Perhaps Kiuno, if she could forgive him after this. If she could find it within herself to help dig this jewel out of his arm despite the pain he'd caused.

Reece prayed she wouldn't come, but as the hordes assaulted K.J.'s army, he saw hers on the horizon. He had to fight. As himself no less. It would be easier to blame the jewel, but the creator had done something to suppress it.

He wanted to teach Reece a lesson. He wanted Reece to feel the guilt of his actions so that he'd never want to show his face again. So he'd relent.

Reece clenched his jaw. He didn't have a choice. Marci's life was on the line and he wouldn't put Nsane through that loss. Not after seeing his face when she'd been threatened.

Reece took a breath and descended, running among the monsters as their leader and as much a vile creature himself.

FRIENDS

REALM: 6

DAY: 384

K.J.'s gaze shifted from her to the field. "What are you doing here?" Kiuno stood. "Hoping to right wrongs." Calls of warning echoed from the rear and they both turned. "They're with me."

Silence echoed between them as the sounds of battle raged.

She took a step forward. "I swear I'm here to help."

He smirked. "Save your apologies for later. This is going to be one hell of a ride."

The line broke. Shouts of warning followed. Those manning the front sank their spear tips into thick hide and magic converged in flashing sparks.

Kiuno drew her sword and glanced at K.J. He unsheathed two blades then darted toward the fray. She followed. Kiuno's battle cry echoed in her ears as she brought her blade down upon a hollow's arm. Fire flew toward her face and she raised one hand to block it.

Kiuno pivoted when an axe flew toward her shoulder and shoved her weapon through her attacker's gut. Crazed eyes locked with hers and it smiled. Kiuno pulled a dagger from her belt and planted it in the hollow's throat. It gurgled and fell.

The enemies converged and K.J. grabbed her wrist, pulling Kiuno toward him. His blade sank into an enemy at her rear. Kiuno planted her feet and returned the favor as the fangs of a reptilian threatened to sink into his shoulder.

Kiuno didn't know why K.J. had changed his mind and truthfully, it didn't matter in the present moment. Perhaps Palindrome had gotten through or maybe her being here was enough to prove her innocence. Whatever it was, she was glad to have him guarding her back.

A roar echoed overhead and Kiuno followed the multicolored wings as they swooped down on their enemies. The felinians landed and sank their teeth into monsters that had broken through their defenses.

Good, Cybele had gotten the message.

Maltack and Cybele jumped from Milo's back. Cybele swung her spear and the wild woman joined the fray with her creature at her side. The two tore through their enemies like wildfire in an open plain.

Kiuno glanced toward their rear. Now if only the others followed. She bit her lip. Perhaps she'd made a mistake. Maybe she should have taken command of their armies and led them herself. Afterall, cowards remained cowards. She prayed they proved her wrong.

A hand wrapped around her ankle and Kiuno planted her free foot beneath a jaw. The hollow's half body rolled across the ground and stopped on its back. Blood poured from the missing waist and pieces of flesh dragged as the creature rotated itself and crawled toward her again.

A shiver ran down her spine. Chirping sounded to her right and Kiuno pivoted, yanking her sword around. She wrapped the blade in flames and sliced at the creature's torso. It screeched and recoiled.

K.J's body slammed into hers and Kiuno hit the ground. Monsters swarmed, but she summoned the flames and burst them in a tight ball to knock the creatures back.

Her eyes locked on K.J. then her blood shifted to ice.

Blood dripped from a puncture wound in his side. Kiuno traced the green vine with her eyes to find Reece on the other end.

Fear raced through her blood and Kiuno scrambled to her feet and charged Reece. She wanted to save him, but Kiuno wasn't about to let him kill anyone else.

Her flames collided with a barrier and their swords clashed. Reece's step faltered. Kiuno grit her teeth and shoved. The flames wrapped around them both and the surrounding creatures shrieked, but the fire didn't touch Reece.

Reece didn't smile, nor did he mock her efforts. If anything, he looked normal.

"Reece?"

He grimaced. "I'm sorry Ki."

Reece shoved her to the side and made another pass at K.J. She grabbed his shoulder and slammed her elbow into his back knocking them both off balance.

Kiuno struggled for dominance. "Sorry? That's all you have to say?"

He planted his fist in her solar plexus, locked one leg around her own and pivoted to pin her body beneath his. "I don't have a choice."

Her hands heated and Kiuno tightened her grip on his wrists. He winced and tried to pull away.

"You always have a choice." She kneed him in the groin and sent him rolling.

Reece struggled for breath. "You're right and someone else's life is on the line."

His gaze flicked toward K.J. again and hers followed. K.J. struggled against a hollow and reptilian, keeping his distance from one while striking the other.

Kiuno stumbled to her feet. "You can't kill one person to save another."

He rose and stared at her with weary eyes. Plants grew at his feet, then shot past her body. Kiuno's heart burst with fear and lightning cracked from her center. It raced toward Reece before she could reel it back.

Reece hit the ground and tears stung her eyes. She tried to run after him, but creatures swarmed his body before she could assess the damage.

Kiuno's gaze swiveled back to K.J. The blood from his wound dripped down his shirt, but he didn't stop fighting.

Kiuno lifted her sword to block another hollow then closed the distance between her and K.J. The two backed themselves toward a group of magic users and retreated into their circle to catch their breaths.

Another scream.

Another break in their defense.

Kiuno grit her teeth as she used everything Scorpios, Elliott, and Kikyo had taught her to keep herself alive. Slash, break, plunge, repeat.

Another deep gash in K.J.'s arm had her cursing.

Kiuno grabbed a magic user and shoved him toward K.J.

"Shield."

He obeyed without hesitation and Kiuno let the flames take over. They crawled across the ground like serpents and consumed the enemies who'd penetrated their line.

The magic users regained the upper hand and Kiuno turned to find Maltack working on K.J.'s injuries.

She dropped to one knee beside them.

"This is bad."

K.J. struggled, pulling at breath as though he were suffocating.

The battle echoed and Kiuno's gaze darted between the injured and those still fighting. They couldn't hold this much longer. Where was Leena?

"I need Palindrome." Maltack moved his hand away and looked out across the battlefield.

Kiuno's heart jolted. "What does that mean?"

Maltack went back to work on K.J, but Kiuno focused on K.J.'s breathing and the sweat pouring from his brow.

"Maltack what does that mean?"

"I can't fix this."

Kiuno's heart skipped and she surveyed the field then dropped to K.J.'s level. "Where's Palin?"

He took a few shaky breaths. "Center. Healers."

"Keep them off us, Mal." Kiuno wrapped K.J.'s arm around her shoulder and pulled him up.

"I was an idiot," he said. "I should have known you wouldn't—"

She took an unsteady step. "I thought you said to save the apologies. You're not dying, you have a game to beat remember?"

He chuckled then his body went limp. "K.J.?" His deadweight pulled her to the ground. Heart pounding and frantic, Kiuno searched the sea of faces.

"I see her," Maltack yelled.

"Go!"

Kiuno tore at K.J.'s leather armor and her hand came away bloody. She shook him and called his name, but K.J. didn't respond.

Palindrome, covered in dirt and blood, skidded to her knees and shoved Kiuno to the side. She repeated K.J.'s name and went to work, pointing for Maltack to position himself across from her.

Kiuno stared for several long moments, willing some kindness in this universe to spare her the death of another.

Their hands glowed.

He took a breath.

Then another and the knot in her chest unraveled.

A horn echoed in the distance.

Kiuno stood.

It echoed again and she followed the sound to the rear.

They came. Someone else came.

With a final glance at K.J. Kiuno sent up a prayer and raced through the men. She screamed in passing, telling whoever would listen to prepare for an offensive attack.

Kiuno saw Leena's face first.

The woman's eyes fell to the blood on Kiuno's shirt. "I hope we aren't too late."

Kiuno shook her head. "Might be cutting it close though."

Leena dismounted and Kiuno's gaze floated past the woman and men lining up at their rear.

More than just Leena's group.

"Everyone came?" Kiuno asked.

"Let's just say your speech was inspiring." Her gaze hardened. "Where do you need us?"

"The front defense is about to break. We should secure that first."

A leader knows when to ask for help.

"Line the rest of the magic users behind them. I'll meet everyone there."

Yes. A leader did. It was never meant to be a one man show.

Leena turned to shout commands and Kiuno stormed back toward the front.

She possessed power, but it didn't matter. One would always falter. One always had a weakness.

It was the masses that would ensure their victory. And she'd lead them to it.

WITH K.J. safely tucked inside one of their medical tents, Maltack sprinted toward the gathering line of magic users.

His body trembled, but despite the pain hope blossomed in his chest.

They came.

They all came.

He ran toward the line and placed himself at Kiuno's side.

Those worn and weary broke from the front and retreated, allowing their group to function as replacements.

Men and women filed past, but it wasn't defeat that covered their faces.

His blood pounded as a static charge of electricity surged through Kiuno's body. He could redirect it. Prevent friendly fire.

Maltack shifted the sparks and cradled them forward in a funnel that surrounded her body.

Kiuno took several steps to separate herself from the crowd and he followed.

Currents of hot air swirled the ground before them, creating a whirlwind of biting sand. It tugged at the flames and pulled them into the circling air to create a vortex like he'd never seen. It stretched and expanded, until the sun blotted out the top.

The ground shifted beneath their feet, magic crawling to swallow their enemies in its deadly vise. Shards of glass formed and suspended themselves in the air.

The air hummed as destruction sat on the verge of release.

The enemy growled and snarled, baring fangs while others brandished swords.

Kiuno stepped forward and shifted to a trot.

The five alliances watched her every move.

They watched the leader who had finally taken charge of this world.

Maltack twisted the static in the air and ran at her side.

Let them watch.

Let them awe.

Let them follow.

71

APOLOGIES

REALM: 6

DAY: 384

Kiuno fell back as the battle wound down. The enemy retreated to the safety of the jungle's trees and her allies pursued. Every scar on her body burned with the magic still crawling beneath her skin.

Maltack knelt at her side with his magic ready, but she ushered him away. They were both spent.

Kiuno stood and stumbled, but another caught her arm.

"Looks like you're a bit woozy," Palindrome said.

"How's K.J.?"

"He'll pull through." Palindrome ran her hand down Kiuno's arm.

Kiuno tugged her hand away. "You should save your energy for someone who needs it."

"All right, but K.J. is asking for you."

Kiuno bit her lip, but she followed Palindrome toward the rear part of the field. They stepped over countless dead bodies and the scent of burning flesh filled the air.

Several people carried the injured and Kiuno's heart tugged when she saw how many wouldn't see tomorrow.

The pair paused at the end of the first row and Kiuno waited outside while Palindrome went in.

Her heart pounded at their hushed whispers. She averted her gaze from the tent and viewed those lying in the sand. Trees and waterways formed before her eyes, weaving their way between the injured. She didn't want to imagine what this scene might look like without magic.

Palindrome exited, gave Kiuno a warm smile, then marched off to tend to the wounded.

Kiuno took a step forward then paused. She wondered what kind of scheme he might have concocted about her supposed betrayal. Perhaps he needed time to evaluate her recent actions.

"You can come in."

Kiuno's heart skipped and she entered the stuffy tent. Why in the world would Palindrome keep it closed in this heat?

Apologies can come later.

Had those words been true or just a play on her emotions to ensure his men's survival?

She bit her tongue. No, K.J. wasn't like that.

Kiuno avoided his gaze, studying the floor as if something of interest could tear down the wall of awkward silence.

"How do you feel?" she asked.

"Shitty is an understatement."

She grimaced. "Do you want me to get someone?"

K.J. repositioned himself and shook his head. "They have enough to worry about. I've had worse."

"I doubt that."

He chuckled. "So, how did you do it?"

"Do what?"

"Convince the alliances to come."

She shrugged. "They know what I'm capable of."

He raised a brow. "Kiuno turning to threats as a negotiation tactic? I must have missed a lot."

"My friend was running to his death. I was desperate."

"Tell me."

She folded her arms. "I threatened to take away everything they built and expose them for the cowards they were."

He chuckled. "Yeah, I've definitely missed a lot."

Heavy silence settled over the tent again and Kiuno shifted her feet. "I'm sorry."

He sighed. "I'm the one who should apologize. The idea of you betraying anyone is laughable at best."

Her voice cracked. "People died because of my stupidity."

"People died because of an ally's betrayal. That ally wasn't you. I should have known you needed more reassurance."

"You have too many people to worry about as it is."

"My officers are the ones I concern myself with. That's how leadership works. Knowing you as well as I do the fault goes to me for neglecting your tactical opinion."

Kiuno let herself collapse to the ground and took a relaxing breath. "So, where do we go from here?"

"Before the ambush, I was informed of a cavern not too far away. It should be able to house the lot of us. At least for now. Our biggest challenge will be establishing order with the leaders in such a tight space."

"From battle to politics."

"Honestly, I'd take the battle any day."

COMPLICATIONS

Realm: 6

Day: 386

Kiuno sighed, tugged the braid from her hair, and fell face down onto the fur blanket lining their space in the cavern. She buried her face in the fibers and let out a long exhale.

"I don't get it. Why can't they just shut up and come to a reasonable agreement?"

Elite unbuckled his sword and leaned it against the wall before lowering himself to her side. "They don't trust one another. What did you expect?"

She huffed. "They didn't have a problem with it a week ago." Kiuno propped herself on her elbow. "They're leaders. They should know how this works and it'd go a lot smoother if they just picked a job and stuck with it."

"You're expecting people to work together who never have."

"Yeah I know." Kiuno threw up her arms. "I'm surprised they haven't argued which hand is better to wipe their own asses."

He leaned toward her. "The left."

Kiuno shoved him over, but he wrapped his arms around her middle and planted a playful kiss on her neck. The two lay in one another's arms and Kiuno remained quiet as she listened to the sound of Elite's heartbeat.

"Think of it this way. Each of them is a dictator who's been forced to receive permission from a council."

"Councils have their advantages."

"Councils also eliminate individualism."

Kiuno huffed again. "Well, if the majority agrees upon a decision then those noncompliant should conform."

"Like you did when the others suggested letting K.J. fight his own war?"

"That was different."

"But you see what I mean?" Elite moved her hair aside and kissed her neck again. He trailed tender kisses to the edge of her jaw, and she couldn't help the smile that tugged at the corners of her lips. "You need sleep. The worries of tomorrow will still be there when you wake up."

"And more worries on top of it." Kiuno closed her burning eyes. Sleep sounded nice. Peaceful.

After the battle it'd been nothing but decisions and politics.

Kiuno winced when she turned over. Her scars burned, but it was minimal compared to past times.

Elite's slow rhythmic breathing soothed her body and her bound muscles relaxed as he rubbed her shoulders. Kiuno let the luxury lull her back to a time when her only concern had been to find Elite safe and lie like this every night for the rest of their lives.

THE CREATOR

REALM: 6
DAY: 387

Kiuno rubbed sleep from her eyes as she trudged through the cavern. The damp musky smell of moss assaulted her waking senses, but it served as an improvement to the dry desert air.

Others, some appearing more tired than she felt, muddled along to complete their assigned tasks. There'd been no end to them in the last few days.

K.J. stood beside their meeting area and gazed out over the sea of faces with glassy eyes. Always the first to arrive.

Kiuno yawned. "I miss coffee."

"You and me both."

"Do you think we'll be here much longer?"

"I—" K.J. cut himself short as the world shifted. Colors merged into one another and swirled through a whirlwind that moved faster and faster until everything blended into a cloud of gray.

Kiuno clenched her eyes and fought the sinking feeling in her gut as the room spun out of control. She reached for something. Anything to steady her spinning head.

Her feet hit solid ground and Kiuno tried to focus on her surroundings. Nausea tugged at her empty stomach, but she bit back the rising bile.

K.J. took her arm and steadied her.

Once Kiuno had gathered her bearings, she glanced at the people around them.

Thousands.

No, more than that. Far more.

Kiuno met the confused faces of Scorpios, Blue, and Liam.

But they were in the fifth realm. Right?

She took a step back and tried to absorb the scene.

Was this… everyone?

Kiuno shook her head and examined the room. The ceiling, floor, and walls all seemed to stretch forever in each direction. An endless sea of pure white.

"Thank you so much for coming." A booming male voice echoed around the room. Several, including herself, took a step back as an apparition materialized above their heads.

She drew her weapon, as did many others, but the man only smiled as his body slowly descended.

"To make our lives easier, I thought I'd bring everyone in the game, those still alive at least, to this holding place." He held up a finger. "But don't worry, as soon as we're done, I'll return each and every one of you to the exact location you came from."

His gaze searched the sea of faces and stopped when their eyes met. A slow smile spread across his face and she could have sworn she recognized it.

He clapped his hands together. "Now, I'm sure you've all been dying to know where you are and how you got here. As a reward for passing into the seventh realm, I'll give you some answers."

Seventh realm?

He paused and Kiuno's stomach sank when he pointed at her. "Will you come forward my dear?"

Those around her tightened their circle and the man clicked his tongue. "Come now, I won't bite."

Kiuno gave each a quick look then took a few steps forward. She kept her hands firmly clenched around the hilt of her sword.

Hundreds of screens flashed into existence, each double sided and suspended overhead.

"I was surprised when you revealed yourself as the lightning user. Mind you, it's made this even more fun. But for those who still don't know," He raised his voice, "This is Kiuno. My special player." He tucked a hand behind his mouth as if to whisper, but his voice still echoed. "And my favorite as well."

More whispers started behind her. The man continued staring as if she were a toy he'd longed after for years. "I'm sorry, this is just so exciting. I've dreamed of meeting you for so long my sweet Kiuno."

He stretched his arms wide and floated closer. "I'm happy to finally tell you I created this entire world just for you."

A chill ran down her spine. "What does that even mean?"

"Exactly as it sounds." He lowered his hands. "I've watched you for a long time. I saw how sad you were, how often you cried. It hurt and the solution was so simple. All you've ever wanted was to be needed."

He spread his arms wide again. "So, I made this extraordinary world just for you."

Watching her? Creating a world for her?

"Who are you?" K.J. demanded.

He sighed and lifted his gaze from Kiuno. "Ah, the one that bites. Well, since you asked, I used to be a good friend, at least until someone threw me away as another failed alliance leader. That hurt, you know, but I'm capable of forgiveness."

Failed alliance leader? From the game? Then this man also played

Chronopoint, but there were hundreds of failed alliances. That was just part of Chronopoint's structure. His entire motive couldn't be centered around an injustice as insignificant as that. It was easy to start over in a game.

The man's feet touched the white floor and he clasped his hands behind his back. "I'll admit. At first, this was all an act for revenge. I wanted to create a purgatory where I could watch each of you suffer. Your lives were boring anyway."

His gaze fell back to Kiuno. "But then I saw you. It stirred something in me. Being thrown away wasn't your fault. It resulted from the pain inflicted by others. I knew I had to do something."

He spun around and looked over the crowd. "You see, all your lives were dull at best. The modern world has made us lazy and resentful. We bicker about the stupidest things instead of appreciating the gift of life." His head tilted back to her. "But here, you've learned to appreciate every breath. Every moment."

Kiuno's body trembled and her hands curled into fists. "It's your fault. You're the one who killed them."

He placed a hand over his chest and looked appalled. "My dear, I haven't killed anyone. If we're going to point out who has blood on their hands…" he raised a brow and looked pointedly at her.

"I created this world, yes, but I don't control it nearly as much as I'd like. In fact, I seem to lose more control day by day. It's a dilemma I didn't foresee."

K.J. took a step forward. "You don't have control? What would have happen if Kiuno died? Since she's your key player."

The creator roared and his laughter echoed through the crowd. "Kiuno? Die? Please tell me you're joking. This *is* Kiuno we're talking about. She can't die."

Did he honestly believe that?

"You're insane," Kiuno said.

He tilted his head. "The same could be said of many who revolutionized the world."

"So, what, you just watch us on your little camera and enjoy the show?" she said.

"I used to, but that got boring, thus I inserted myself into the game." He took a few steps toward her. "A long time ago, I might add. I'm surprised you haven't figured it out." His gaze drifted behind her and his familiar smirk shifted into place.

"You never suspected." Two voices echoed. "Not once." One painfully familiar. He walked through the crowd and those gathered in the vicinity stepped as far away as possible. "I've had so much fun watching you from this angle," Liam said.

Kiuno stared and cold rage spread through her veins. She remembered all the times Liam had been by her side. A silent shadow.

He'd been there the night Kikyo died. He'd been there when she thought she'd lost Elite and Scorpios. He'd listened to all her doubts and fears as if he were her friend. All this time—

The man before her stood as an older version of the kid she'd have given her life to protect. She'd spilled blood to defend him. Blood that could have been avoided.

Kiuno's eyes ran down the older Liam's arm and rested on the scar where her fire had burned him.

That meant he could be hurt.

Kiuno turned back to the younger version and her eyes widened as Liam's small form smiled one last time before melting into the floor. Kiuno turned back to the creator. Back to the real Liam.

Lightning sparked around Kiuno's body against her control. Several yelped and shoved through the crowd to separate themselves from her magic. It flowed like lava in her veins and melted the final strands of control she had in place.

He knew all her promises. All their plans.

He watched. He blended, and the most sickening part was how well he'd done it.

Kiuno charged and swung her blade in a wide arch over his head. It collided with an invisible shield that even her lightning couldn't penetrate. She screamed in rage and pressed her sword against it, hoping to crack his defense through sheer force of will.

"So, the little wolf bites too." He clicked his tongue. "You're angry with me? Do you know how long I've waited for this moment?"

Kiuno clenched her teeth. "Because of you thousands of people are dead!"

He tilted his head. "I'll admit the experiments were harsh." His eyes hardened. "But let me make one thing perfectly clear. Without me, you'd be nothing." His hands opened to encompass the crowd. "These people you call friends would have drifted away and in a few short years they wouldn't even remember your name."

"At least they'd be alive."

"True. Just like you to sacrifice your happiness in order to prevent another's pain."

"Go to hell."

"I've been there and so have you."

He pointed up and a rift in the seam of their reality ripped open behind him. Sun shone through and a grassy meadow filled the space on the other side.

"If you wanted to see them again. All you had to do was ask."

Shadows stepped forward. Shadows she recognized and Kiuno's heart shattered all over again.

Kikyo.

Elliott.

"I can give you anything your heart desires. All you have to do is stay here with me."

A dry patch formed in the back of her throat. "You think a fake reality would satisfy me?"

"Hasn't it thus far?"

Her entire body trembled and Kiuno's vision dropped to the scar on

Liam's arm. "I'll stay, but only until the day you're vulnerable enough for me to run my blade through your heart."

His jaw twitched. "Such unappreciation." Liam's gaze lifted past her. "Honestly Elite, how do you do it?"

"Leave him out of this."

"You think I'd kill him? I already told you, I don't kill people. At least not on purpose." He tapped the side of his face. "But that doesn't stop me from enjoying a few games."

Liam lifted his arms and a portal opened beneath Maltack's and K.J's feet. The two disappeared in seconds, their voices the only thing left in their wake. People around them screamed in horror.

Her frantic gaze shifted back to Liam. "Leave them alone," she yelled.

"Relax, they're still alive. I'm adding a twist."

Two portals appeared on either side of her. Both swirled a familiar purple mist and the cold air tore at her clothes.

"I've placed both in a predicament of sorts." He pointed to the portal on her right. "Maltack is in the first realm, though the beast that lives there might not welcome his company."

Liam pointed to the portal on her left. "K.J. is in the eighth. A terrible area you have yet to discover. Rest assured, the terrain is far worse than the creatures who occupy it."

He pointed up and a set of numbers appeared above their heads. "You have twenty seconds to decide who you will save. Of course, there's also Reece to consider and the people you've chosen to lead."

Her heart skipped. Reece was alive?

Liam tilted his head and gave her a crooked smile. "So, tell me. Who will you choose?"

The number above flipped. Then flipped again. And again.

16

15

She had to choose? Maltack, K.J. or Reece? She had to choose one of her friends?

13

Her heart and mind raced. One warring against the other.

The people could care for themselves. They had leaders like Palindrome, Leena, and Scorpios. They would thrive in her absence just as they'd done before she arrived.

10

Kiuno turned to Palindrome. "Don't kill Reece."

8

Palindrome nodded even as her feet tried to carry her forward. She'd never make it in time.

Kiuno spun on her heel as the numbers continued to tick down.

5

Kiuno took a final look at Elite. He called for her, running, begging, but she didn't have a choice. Once again, they'd be parted despite their promise to never separate again.

2

Kiuno stepped through the swirling vortex and all colors twisted to gray as the whirlwind yanked her body back to where everything started.

K.J. was strong. He could survive on his own. Even if she took months to get there, he'd live. Out of everyone Liam could have threatened, K.J. was the least of her worries.

But Maltack. He was still a kid with a kind heart and someone who needed protection.

Kiuno landed on the soft forest floor and the portal behind her closed. She could only hope Liam would live up to his word and return everyone from where they'd come.

A deep roar echoed through the trees and Kiuno's legs pounded against the earth as she bounded toward the noise.

Ironic.

After crossing so much terrain. After so much heartache and drive to reach the front line, here she was. Back where it all began.

Back to realm one.

ACKNOWLEDGMENTS

Kyle – Thank you for always listening to my crazy ideas. You're the only one who gets to see into the depths of my imagination. I hope it's not too scary there haha.

Catherine with Quill Pen Editorial – I can't thank you enough for the work you do. The way you edit and look into characters is like magic.

Kirk with Dog Earned Design – You captured my story in the artwork for this book cover. Thank you so much!

Readers and Fans – This story wouldn't be worth writing without someone in the world to share it with. Thank you for your continued support and I hoped you enjoyed *Rise of the Wolves*.

ABOUT THE AUTHOR

J.E. Reed lives in Cincinnati, Ohio with her husband and two cats. She's always had an interest in writing but didn't explore that talent fully until 2015. During the day, Reed works as a Licensed Massage Therapist in the quiet town of Anderson. She graduated massage school in 2009 and has spent the last five years building her small business as well as developing her writing craft. She enjoys swimming, yoga, and the occasional mud run with friends.

Visit her webpage at jereedbooks.com

CPSIA information can be obtained
at www.ICGtesting.com
Printed in the USA
FFHW022332260919
55231705-60984FF